PENGUIN

Forgotten Child

Katie Flynn is the pen name of the much-loved writer Judy Turner, who published over ninety novels in her lifetime. Judy's unique stories were inspired by hearing family recollections of life in Liverpool during the early twentieth century, and her books went on to sell more than eight million copies. Judy passed away in January 2019, aged eighty-two.

The legacy of Katie Flynn lives on through her daughter, Holly Flynn, who continues to write under the Katie Flynn name. Holly worked as an assistant to her mother for many years and together they co-authored a number of Katie Flynn novels.

Holly lives in the north east of Wales with her husband Simon and their two children. When she's not writing she enjoys walking her dog Tara in the surrounding countryside, and cooking forbidden foods such as pies, cakes and puddings! She looks forward to sharing many more Katie Flynn stories, which she and her mother devised together, with readers in the years to come.

Keep up to date with all her latest news on Facebook: Katie Flynn Author

Also by Katie Flynn

A Liverpool Lass
The Girl from Penny Lane
Liverpool Taffy
The Mersey Girls
Strawberry Fields
Rainbow's End
Rose of Tralee
No Silver Spoon
Polly's Angel
The Girl from Seaforth Sands
The Liverpool Rose
Poor Little Rich Girl
The Bad Penny
Down Daisy Street
A Kiss and a Promise
Two Penn'orth of Sky
A Long and Lonely Road
The Cuckoo Child
Darkest Before Dawn
Orphans of the Storm
Little Girl Lost
Beyond the Blue Hills
Forgotten Dreams
Sunshine and Shadows
Such Sweet Sorrow
A Mother's Hope
In Time for Christmas

Heading Home
A Mistletoe Kiss
The Lost Days of Summer
Christmas Wishes
The Runaway
A Sixpenny Christmas
The Forget-Me-Not Summer
A Christmas to Remember
Time to Say Goodbye
A Family Christmas
A Summer Promise
When Christmas Bells Ring
An Orphan's Christmas
A Christmas Candle
Christmas at Tuppenny Corner
A Mother's Love
A Christmas Gift
Liverpool Daughter
Under the Mistletoe
Over the Rainbow
White Christmas
The Rose Queen
The Winter Rose
A Rose and a Promise
Winter's Orphan
A Mother's Secret
The Winter Runaway

Available by Katie Flynn writing as Judith Saxton

You Are My Sunshine
First Love, Last Love
Someone Special
Still Waters
A Family Affair
Jenny Alone
Chasing Rainbows
All My Fortunes

Sophie
We'll Meet Again
Harbour Hill
The Arcade
The Pride
The Glory
The Splendour
Full Circle

Katie Flynn

Forgotten Child

PENGUIN BOOKS

PENGUIN BOOKS

UK | USA | Canada | Ireland | Australia
India | New Zealand | South Africa

Penguin Books is part of the Penguin Random House group of companies
whose addresses can be found at global.penguinrandomhouse.com

Penguin Random House UK,
One Embassy Gardens, 8 Viaduct Gardens, London SW11 7BW

penguin.co.uk

Penguin
Random House
UK

First published by Century 2025
Published in Penguin Books 2025
001

Typeset in 11.18/14.19pt Palatino LT Pro by Jouve(UK), Milton Keynes
Printed and bound in Great Britain by Clays Ltd, Elcograf S.p.A.

The authorised representative in the EEA is Penguin Random House Ireland,
Morrison Chambers, 32 Nassau Street, Dublin D02 YH68

A CIP catalogue record for this book is available from the British Library

ISBN: 978–1–804–94249–9

MIX
Paper | Supporting
responsible forestry
FSC
www.fsc.org
FSC® C018179

Penguin Random House is committed to a sustainable
future for our business, our readers and our planet.
This book is made from Forest Stewardship
Council® certified paper.

*Everybody should have an Yvonne Wilson
in their lives – she truly is an angel without wings!*

Prologue

Isla desperately tried to break free from her father's iron grip as he dragged her down the street by her wrist. 'Please don't do this, Daddy,' she begged. 'We can manage, I know we can, you just need to give it a bit more time!'

Deaf to his daughter's pleas, her father, Patrick, hurried on without so much as breaking his stride. 'We've been through this already, Isla, and I've tried, you know I have.'

'No you haven't! You'd rather run away and to hell with everyone else!' cried Isla.

His lids fluttered briefly as if trying to block out the truth of her words. 'It's not like that, you know it's not. Ever since . . .' He sighed heavily. Unable to complete the sentence, he continued wearily, 'I wish I were a better man, but I cannae do this, Isla. Not on my own I can't.'

Still trying to wrench herself free from his grip,

1

Isla insisted, 'Only you're not on your own! You've got me!'

He looked to the storm clouds which were gathering above, a manifestation of his current situation. 'It's not the same, Isla, and you know it's not.'

Isla desperately searched for another tack. She'd tried begging and pleading, so she could see only one viable option left to her: emotional blackmail. 'Mammy would've moved heaven and earth to prevent this from happenin', you know she would.' She hoped her words might make him crumble, turn back even, but instead, he agreed with her.

'Aye, but your mammy knew what she was doin'; I, on the other hand, don't know where to begin!'

'Then I'll look after us,' replied Isla promptly. 'I can cook and clean, as well as find another job.'

But he was shaking his head dolefully. 'I'm sorry, luv, truly I am, but you're too young to be bearin' that kind of responsibility.'

'Codswallop! You love my egg and bacon sarnies, and I've been doin' the housework as well as holdin' down a full-time job since the doctor confined Mammy to her bed!'

'But only for a short while,' said her father. 'And besides, there's more to it than that.'

As they approached the poorhouse, Isla pointed a trembling finger at the forbidding building 'You cannae make me go in there because I shall refuse, and what will you do then?'

He spoke in grim, sympathetic tones. 'I have no

choice, Isla; my ship leaves tonight and I have to be on it – I'm sorry.'

Tears welled in her eyes. 'So that's it?' she choked. 'I'm condemned to hell with no chance of parole?'

'It's not for ever,' Patrick assured her, 'just a couple of months, until I get myself sorted. After that everythin' will be back to normal – whatever that is.'

'I could be dead before then,' said Isla, the tears now blanketing her cheeks. 'We've all heard the rumours . . .'

He faltered mid-step. 'You shouldn't listen to rumours.'

'Why not, especially when we know them to be true? Mammy used to call it God's waitin' room. She'd turn in her grave . . .'

It seemed that this last comment was one step too far. 'That's enough!' roared Patrick, his usually warm and smiling eyes blazing angrily. He tightened his grip on her wrist as he strode towards the front door of the poorhouse while speaking through gritted teeth. 'I will *not* have you bring your mammy into this!'

'Only because you know that I'm right!' sobbed Isla. 'Bringin' me here is as good as signin' my death warrant, you *know* it is!'

Mounting the shallow steps, he banged his fist against the soulless door. 'Stop bein' so bloody dramatic,' he hissed angrily. 'I'm sure they wouldn't allow them to operate if that were the case!'

As he finished speaking the door was thrust open and a sharp-looking woman with horn-rimmed spectacles peered down her long nose at them. 'I'll thank you to stop hammerin' on my door before you take it off its hinges!' she snapped waspishly.

Isla stared imploringly at her father. Surely the woman's curt attitude would get him to change his mind. 'Please, Dad?'

His jaw flinching, he cleared his throat before speaking in leaden tones. 'This is my daughter, Isla Donahue. I believe you're expecting her?'

The woman held out her hand towards Patrick, her dark and beady eyes surveying Isla from her head to her toes in a critical manner. 'Where are her papers? I told you earlier, she cannae come in without them, it's the rules.'

He pulled an envelope from his inside jacket pocket and thrust it into her hands. 'Everything you asked for is in there.'

She peered into the envelope and slowly walked her fingers over the contents. Only when she was fully satisfied did she put it in her pocket. Standing to one side, she jerked her head in a backward motion, gesturing for Isla to enter whilst giving a single instruction. 'In.'

Instead of doing as the woman had commanded, Isla pleaded with her father one last time. 'It's not too late to change your mind . . .'

Unable to look into the green eyes which were the image of her mother's, he averted his gaze. 'It's only for a couple of months.'

The woman tutted sarcastically, mumbling, 'Of course it is,' beneath her breath.

Ignoring her, Patrick looked back to Isla, and the tears trickling down her cheeks. 'A couple of months, I swear it. Make sure you're good for Miss . . . ?' He glanced briefly at the woman.

'Harman.'

'Miss Harman,' he finished. His voice obstructed with raw emotion, he tried to embrace his daughter, but she held her hands out to prevent him from doing so, mumbling 'Don't'.

Taking a step back, he looked at her through glassy eyes. 'I'm so sorry.'

Isla's voice was barely above a whisper. 'I wish Mammy was here.'

'So do I,' murmured Patrick. Casting her one final look of longing, he spoke quietly. 'Love you to the moon and back.'

Unable to bear the aching of her heart for a second longer, she murmured 'You too' before quickly stepping inside. Hearing the lock click in the door behind her, she had to fight the urge to rip the keys from the woman's grip and unlock it again, but she knew that to do so would only make matters worse. So instead she followed Miss Harman who was striding away, her salt and pepper bun bouncing with every step as she barked 'Come with me' over her shoulder.

On the other side of the door, Isla's father had raised his fist to knock again before changing his mind. Turning on his heel, he lifted his collar as the first drops of rain began to fall. *I'll come back for her when I'm able to look after her properly*, he told himself as he strode towards the docks. *I'm no use to man nor beast at the moment, and Isla deserves better than that.* Hearing a rumble of thunder, he glanced to the clouds that had gathered above. *I've done the best I could by her, Agnes, but you were the glue that held our family together, and without you I'm nothin'.* An image of his wife formed in his mind's eye. She was smiling at him in sympathy, but even so, she kept glancing towards the poorhouse. *I know what you thought of Coxhill, but I swear I won't let that happen to Isla,* Patrick told her. *I'll be back for her just as soon as I'm able to give her the home she deserves, and not some kind of half-life.*

Chapter One

Fluffing up the pillows behind her mother, Isla guided Agnes into a more comfortable position as the late summer sunshine filtered through the window.

'I'm sure it wouldn't do any harm for me to get out of bed just to eat my breakfast,' objected Agnes as she picked up the plate of toast her daughter had brought through for her. 'And it would certainly be a lot easier.'

Isla's sea-green eyes – which she'd inherited from her mother – sparkled kindly as she wagged a reproving finger. 'Bein' as I'm only sixteen I know nothin' of babies and the like, but I do know that you should listen to your doctor when he says you're to be confined to your bed until the baby arrives.'

Speaking thickly through her mouthful of toast, Agnes grumbled, 'That's all well and good for him to say, but doin' nothin' all day is drivin' me loopy!' She smoothed her free hand over her bulbous stomach. 'I shall be jolly glad when this little one decides to put in an appearance – and I did think that siren might have set me off last night. The damn thing near give me a heart attack. I'm sure the warden only sets it off cos he's bored, cos we've not had a sniff of an air raid since the war began.'

'And thank the Lord for that,' Isla said, hastily drawing the sign of the cross over her breast. 'I was talkin' to some of the lasses in work about that, and they reckon the wardens like to keep us on our toes in case we have to do it for real.' Sitting on the end of her mother's bed, her eyes rested over the unborn child as she pinned her auburn curls away from her face. 'Were you overdue when you were havin' me?'

'Nope. You were early, but only by a week.'

Isla appeared to be in deep thought as she spoke in slow and deliberate tones. 'Do you think it has anythin' to do with the age gap? Only . . .' She fell quiet, not certain how best to voice her thoughts without causing her mother offence.

Agnes chuckled beneath her breath. 'That I'm past it, you mean?' Seeing her daughter's cheeks warm, she continued before Isla had a chance to reply, 'I'm only teasin', hen, although I wouldn't blame you if you did. After all, sixteen years is a big gap, and I am pushin' forty.'

Always determined to see the brighter side of life, Isla looked to the positive. 'Thinkin' about it now, Mrs McGrath had a baby and she was *much* older than you,' she said loyally. 'But all that aside, just what did make you and Daddy decide to have another baby after all this time?'

'I don't think much decision came into it,' said

Agnes, who was doing her best to swallow her smile. 'I blame your father – he never did have a good sense of rhythm!'

Looking puzzled, Isla was wondering what dancing had to do with having babies when her mother cut across her thoughts. 'On a serious note, I'm sure the baby will be here soon. I'm nigh on two weeks overdue as it is – not that it seems to fuss the midwife any. She's like a stuck record is that one, sayin' the same old thing over and over again.'

Isla smiled sympathetically as she and her mother reiterated the midwife's words. 'Baby will come when baby is ready.'

Hearing the sound of approaching footsteps they both turned as Isla's father entered the room, his white teeth shining brightly against the darkness of his beard. 'And she's right,' he said as he strode towards them. 'So no housework whilst I'm at work, Agnes Donahue, and that's an order!' Smiling, he gently laid his hand on his wife's belly, his smile broadening as the baby kicked out. 'I reckon this 'un could give Stanley Matthews a run for his money.'

Agnes chuckled softly. 'Presumin' it's a boy, of course . . .'

'Why does it have to be a boy?' said Isla indignantly. 'Women can play football too!'

'Aye, they can that,' agreed her mother, 'but the devil will be wearin' woolly knickers before we get the same recognition as the men, on or off the pitch.'

Leaning forward to kiss first his wife, then his daughter, Patrick winked at Isla as he drew back.

'Not if our Isla has anythin' to do with it. She won't stand for no man tellin' her she's not good enough just cos she's a woman, will you, lass?'

'No fear!' said Isla stoutly. 'We've come a long way since the eighteen hundreds – thank goodness – but we've still a fair way to go.'

'Spoken like a true Donahue,' her father agreed proudly. 'Just don't go throwin' yourself under any horses!'

Agnes winced as she tried for a more comfortable position. 'Don't you go puttin' ideas into her head, Patrick Donahue!'

Isla gave her mother a reassuring smile. 'I'm no Emily Davison, but neither am I a pushover.'

'Quite right too!' said Patrick. He glanced to the alarm clock which sat on top of the chest of drawers. 'I'd best shake a leg.' Pausing briefly before leaving the room, he called out the traditional family farewell: 'Love you to the moon and back.' Both women responded 'You too' as he left the room.

'I'd best be makin' a move too,' said Isla, as the bedroom door closed behind her father. 'Old Branning can be a right stickler for the rules when it suits him.' Kissing her mother goodbye, she spoke thoughtfully as she leaned back. 'Only, what will happen if the baby does decide to put in an appearance when you're here on your own?'

'Don't you worry your head none,' said Agnes. 'Bridget will be poppin' by every so often to see how I'm doin', and Mrs Carson's only in the room upstairs, so all I have to do is holler and she'll come runnin'.'

'That's all very well,' said Isla uncertainly, 'but nei- ther of them are family, and I think you should have either me or Dad . . .'

Agnes shook her head, sending the auburn locks, so like her daughter's, dancing around her shoul- ders. 'Your father won't be settin' foot in this room until I'm presentable. You neither, come to that.'

'We don't care what you look like!' cried Isla, but her mother was adamant.

'Maybe not, but I do, and havin' a baby is a private matter. The last thing I need is an audience.'

'Well just you make sure you call for help should you need to,' directed Isla. 'I know how stubborn you can be when it comes to your independence.'

Agnes smiled. 'So now you know where you get it from.'

Raising her brow fleetingly, Isla collected the empty plate. 'You and Dad. So you've only yourselves to blame.'

'And we wouldn't have you any other way,' Agnes assured her. 'Now get you gone, else you'll be late.'

Isla pulled off a mock salute. 'Cheerio, Mammy. I'll pop in to see you at lunchtime. Will cheese and onion sarnies do you?'

'They will indeed,' said Agnes, adding, 'Love you to the moon and back.'

'You too!' Isla called back before hurrying out of the room.

Isla had spent most of the morning clock-watching, something that hadn't gone unnoticed by Mr Branning, her ill-tempered employer. 'You're behind in your work,' he snapped as he stopped to examine her stitching. 'This lot's no good. You're to unpick it and start again!'

'Sorry, Mr Brannin', but I cannae stop thinkin' about my mammy . . .' Isla began, but it seemed the cantankerous old man wasn't in the mood for excuses.

'I couldn't give a rat's behind about your private life; you're here to work. If you cannae do that you may as well go home, and not bother comin' back, cos there's plenty linin' up to take your job.'

Mumbling another apology Isla inspected the stitching to which he'd referred. *There's nothin' bloomin' well wrong with it*, she thought as she ran her eye along the line, *he's just bein' a bad-tempered old so 'n so, same as he always is. No wonder he's not got a family to call his own. You'd have to be desperate to marry someone like him.*

Returning to her work, she was making doubly sure that each stitch was perfectly aligned when one of the delivery boys came over to her bench.

'What is it?' hissed Isla, while keeping a keen eye out for Branning, who would undoubtedly have something to say if he saw them talking.

'I don't want to alarm you, cos I know your mammy's expectin', but I've just seen an ambulance outside your flat.'

Isla's heart bombed. She didn't know much about the birthing process, but she was pretty certain it didn't involve ambulances unless things had gone dreadfully wrong. Hoping against hope that he had made a mistake, she spoke in lowered tones whilst continuing to keep an eye on the door to Branning's office. 'There's a lot of people livin' in them flats . . .'

'Aye, but it very much looked to me as though Mrs Carson was showing them into yours.'

'Oh, no!' gasped Isla.

Mr Branning appeared in the doorway to his office, a scowl etched upon his face. 'Do I have to tell you again, Miss Donahue?'

'Sorry, Mr Branning, but it looks as though they've had to call an ambulance for my mammy,' Isla said, getting to her feet. 'So I'll be takin' my lunch a bit early if that's all right with you.'

Shaking his head angrily, he folded his arms in a defiant manner. 'You will do no such thing!'

She eyed him incredulously. 'I cannae leave her on her own! And it's not as if I won't make the time up—'

Cutting her off mid-sentence, he was unapologetic as he handed her an all too familiar ultimatum. 'If I've told you once, I've told you a thousand times, there's plenty—'

'Of people willing to take my place,' snapped Isla, slipping her tabard over her head. 'Well they can have it!'

He stared open-mouthed as Isla thrust the tabard against his chest. 'Don't think you can come crawlin' back,' he barked after her retreating figure. 'Cos you've well and truly burned your bridges this time!'

'Don't you worry!' yelled Isla over her shoulder, her pale complexion burning with anger. 'I wouldn't *dream* of it!'

*

Running along the pavement, it didn't take Isla long to reach the flat, and she was about to go inside when Mrs Carson appeared.

'Isla!' gasped the older woman. 'What on earth are you doin' here?'

Isla looked to the ambulance as she quickly explained her conversation with the delivery boy, ending with, 'Was he right? Is the ambulance for Mammy?'

Mrs Carson was wringing her hands. 'There's been . . .' she paused briefly, '. . . complications,' she finished lamely.

'What sort of complications?' squeaked Isla.

Before Mrs Carson could answer, Isla's father exited the flat, at a run. Seeing his daughter, his face fell. 'What the hell are you doin' here? I didn't expect you home for hours yet . . .'

'I could say the same about you,' said Isla, 'and don't try to fob me off by sayin' there's been complications! That's obvious by the ambulance.'

He glanced fretfully at Mrs Carson before looking back to Isla. 'Mammy's got to go to hospital, but only as a precaution,' he said, but the beads of sweat on his forehead told Isla that this was far from cautionary. She twisted her auburn curls around her finger.

'If it's only a precaution why are you lookin' so worried? And why . . .' She stopped short as their attention was drawn to Agnes, who was being brought out on a stretcher. Desperate to see Agnes, Isla ran forwards, only to have Patrick catch hold of her by the elbow and bring her to an abrupt halt.

14

'Not now, Isla,' he warned. 'They need to get your mammy to hospital.'

Her eyes filling with tears, she tried to shake him off. 'But I want to see her!'

'I know, love, but the sooner we get her to hospital . . .'

Isla gaped at him. She was right: this wasn't anything precautionary. Something had gone wrong, and badly at that. Tearing herself free from his grip, she ran to her mother's side. 'Mammy!'

Agnes turned to face her daughter, her face and hair drenched with sweat, but she managed a feeble smile as she held up her hand. 'Isla, sweetheart.'

Gripping her mother's hand, Isla felt the tears cascade down her cheeks. 'I knew I shouldn't have left you . . .'

Agnes brushed her lips over Isla's knuckles. 'This isn't your fault!'

The ambulance man cast Isla a grim yet sympathetic smile as he pushed the stretcher into the back of the van. 'Sorry, lass, but we have to close the doors.'

'Can't I go with her?' Isla pleaded, but the ambulance man was shaking his head.

'Sorry, only one person allowed.'

Already jumping into the back of the ambulance, Patrick held Agnes's hand in his as he looked back to Isla, his face a mask of grim concern. 'Try not to worry; we'll be back before you know it.'

Standing to one side, Isla yelled, 'Love you to the moon and back!' as the ambulance man closed one of the doors.

'You too,' Agnes mumbled weakly, just before the other door was closed. She watched as the ambulance pulled away, tears streaking her cheeks as she fervently wished she'd never left her mother alone that morning.

SEPTEMBER 1940

Now, as Isla crossed the herringbone floor to the room marked 'Office', she watched in a trance-like state as Miss Harman unlocked the door. *I don't know which is worse*, she thought, *me not wantin' to be here, or her not wantin' me here, cos judgin' by the look on her face I'm hardly welcome.* This gave her an idea. 'Since it's plain that I'm clearly not welcome, coupled with the fact that I'm more than happy to walk away, why don't I do us both a favour and just leave?' she said. 'It's not as if anyone would care, or even know for that matter.'

Miss Harman laughed in a patronising fashion. 'If only! But no can do, I'm afraid. You see, your father handed you over into my charge, so I'm now responsible for your welfare whether you like it or not.'

'But nobody knows,' Isla implored, 'and it's not as if either of us have signed anythin', so no one will be any the wiser!'

'You seem to forget your father,' Miss Harman pointed out. 'He'd know eventually, and what do you think his reaction would be if he found out that I'd let you walk out of here?'

Isla shrugged. 'Does it matter, considerin' you don't think he's comin' back for me?'

'You're right, I don't,' Miss Harman said bluntly.

16

'But there's always a chance that he could be the first, and I'm not willin' to take the risk, knowin' the repercussions.'

With Miss Harman making it clear that she wouldn't be allowed to leave, Isla glanced around the office, and its barred windows. *They certainly don't want people gettin' out, but there's bound to be the odd occasion when the door's left open, and as soon as it is I'm out of here, because there's no way I'm goin to be one of their statistics*, she promised herself.

She looked to Miss Harman who was peering at the contents of the envelope which Isla's father had given her. Taking the documents from within, she walked over to a filing cabinet which sat in the far corner of her office and placed them inside, but rather than throw the envelope away she folded it in half and tucked it back into the folds of her pocket. *Money*, thought Isla. *I'd bet a pound to a penny that my father gave Coxhill a donation, but if I'm correct then surely she should put the money somewhere safe?*

Unaware that Isla had guessed what was still in the envelope, Miss Harman began listing the rules and regulations which Isla was to obey. 'You are to refer to me as Miss Harman, and you will address all members of staff as either sir or ma'am. You will only speak when spoken to, and you will not fraternise with the other inmates. Anyone caught forming a group will be met with the strictest punishment possible, and the same applies to anyone trying to escape,' she said, following Isla's line of sight to the barred windows. 'Is that clear?'

'Yes, Miss Harman,' said Isla dully, while thinking:

in which case I shall make sure I don't get caught, cos there's no way I'm stoppin' in this hellhole a minute longer than necessary.

Miss Harman's eyes travelled the length of Isla before settling on her bag. She snapped her fingers impatiently. 'Hand it over!'

'But they're my things,' said Isla, clutching the bag to her chest. 'Surely I'm goin' to need them?'

'Personal possessions aren't allowed. Now do as I ask.'

Isla reluctantly handed the bag over, although for the life of her she couldn't see why it was necessary to do so. Not bothering to look at the contents, Miss Harman slung it down on her desk with one hand whilst picking up a grey and shabby piece of material with the other. Holding it out, she ordered Isla to strip.

Thinking she must have misheard, Isla gave the despicable woman a look of uncomprehending. 'I beg your pardon?'

Miss Harman rolled her eyes impatiently. 'You heard me. Now strip!'

Isla eyed the dirty-looking smock with distaste. 'Why can't I wear my own clothes?'

Miss Harman placed a hand to her forehead in the style of someone who could sense a headache coming on. 'As I've already stated, personal possessions are not allowed and I shall *not* be telling you again, so for goodness sake do as you are told!'

Tears trickled down Isla's cheeks as she began to remove her clothes. Embarrassed and ashamed, she held her hand out for the grubby cloth, which she assumed was to serve as her clothing, but Miss Harman was shaking her head. 'Take that off,' she said, pointing to the locket which hung round Isla's neck.

Isla clenched her fists defiantly. 'I know you have your rules, but this is the only thing I have left of my mammy's, so—'

Reaching forward, Miss Harman ripped the necklace from Isla's neck. Horrified, Isla gasped, 'Give it back!' but Miss Harman had already locked the necklace in the drawer of her desk.

'You should've done as I asked,' she snapped irritably. 'Now get dressed and wait here until I return.'

Isla quickly threw the smock over her head as Miss Harman left the room. Searching for something to prise the drawer open she kept an ear out for the woman's return. *I am not goin' to let her take the only thing of my mammy's I have left*, she thought as she began to yank the drawer handle in desperation. *I don't care what sort of punishment she has in mind because it cannae be worse than losin' Mammy's necklace.* With the drawer refusing to budge she continued to look for something with which she could force it open. Her eyes flickered over the wall-mounted certificates, all of which proclaimed the poorhouse to be of exemplary standard. *Whoever handed them certificates out obviously doesn't know what high standards are*, Isla told herself, *cos this smock must be donkey's years old.* She glanced down at the garment with a disgusted look on her face.

Was that faded blood that ran round the neckline? It certainly looked like it. She turned her head as the aroma of the smock reached her nostrils. *I've been here less than five minutes and yet look at the state of me already*, she thought bitterly. *I wish I could show my daddy how quickly things have deteriorated cos I'd wager he'd soon change his mind if he could see me now.* She paused; what *would* her father do if he could see her now? She hoped that he would be outraged by his daughter's appearance, but there again, everyone knew what the poorhouse was like even before going in, so would he really be surprised? Probably not. Her thoughts were interrupted by the sound of approaching footsteps. Abandoning her attempts to break the drawer open, she hurried back round to where she'd been standing prior to Miss Harman's leaving the room.

Perhaps guessing that Isla might have tried to retrieve her necklace, Miss Harman glanced to the desk drawer whilst jerking her thumb to a frail young woman with mousy, shoulder-length lank hair and dull blue eyes who had entered the room behind her. 'This is Sophie.'

Isla smiled briefly at the newcomer but the smile wasn't returned. Miss Harman peered at her over her spectacles. 'Don't think about pallin' up with anyone, cos that's not how it works here.'

Isla felt her heart drop. Being in this horrible place was bad enough, but on your own? She glanced back to Sophie, who was dressed in an identical smock to hers, but whereas Isla's ample figure filled hers out, Sophie's looked as though it were on a clothes hanger.

Holding the door open, Miss Harman spoke directly to Sophie. 'Show her round, but be brief, and don't forget, I've eyes in the back of my head when it comes to you lot.'

Wanting the awful woman to know that she had her number, Isla looked pointedly at the pocket which held the suspected donation. 'Don't you think you ought to put my father's contribution somewhere safe? Only you wouldn't want it to end up in the wrong hands,' she finished testily.

Miss Harman's jaw tightened but she failed to respond, instead locking eyes with Sophie and speaking in a meaningful manner. 'While you're showin' Isla around, I think it would be wise to teach her how to keep her head above water, and I mean that in the literal sense.'

Sophie's complexion paled – something which Isla wouldn't have thought possible considering the grime that covered her face. She jerked her head at Isla before turning on her heel. 'Follow me.'

As Isla walked out of the office behind Sophie, she stopped momentarily to glance longingly at the front door, and had to jog in order to catch up to Sophie who was striding ahead of her down the long corridor. Falling into step with the other girl, she asked the question uppermost in her thoughts. 'Does she ever leave the front door unlocked?'

'No, because she's not stupid,' said Sophie. 'Something which you'll do well to remember.'

'What do you mean by that?'

'She knows what you're thinkin' before you've thought it,' said Sophie, 'mainly because *everyone* here has thought about breakin' out at some stage or other. Oh, and whilst I'm about it, you know the list of rules she gave you?'

'Aye.'

'I'd obey them if I were you, cos punishment in Coxhill isn't supervised.'

Isla frowned. 'How do you mean?'

'Unlike schools and what not, Harman can dish out punishment as she sees fit, with no holds barred.'

'But that's ridiculous!' Remembering the chain of command in her former place of employment, she pressed on. 'Surely there's someone higher up the line to keep her in check, and make sure that she's runnin' the place properly?' She mentioned the certificates.

'And you think they honestly give her those things without knowin' what she's like?' asked Sophie in scathing tones as they continued to walk down the drab and dreary corridor with its wood-panelled walls and herringbone floors. 'Of course not! They turn a blind eye because they know they'd be hard pushed to find any other mug to run the place.'

'So she can do what she likes with no fear of the consequences?' asked Isla, aghast.

'That about sums it up,' said Sophie, adding, 'And that bit about keepin' your head above water in the literal sense?'

'Aye, what about it?'

'There's more than one person disappeared from

Coxhill without explanation and we're all certain we know where they went – not that we'd ever let on to her, of course, we're not that daft – but she knows that we know, which is why she made the threat.'

Isla thought of the river that ran along the banks of the poorhouse. 'You think she *drowned* . . .'

'Aye,' hissed Sophie. Gripping Isla's wrist in a bid to silence her, she continued in hushed tones, 'An' about havin' eyes in the back of her head?'

'Aye?'

'She's referrin' to her spies, Mary and Gordon,' said Sophie. 'But there's always others waitin' to tattle-tale if they think it'll buy them favours.'

'How do you know this Mary and Gordon are spyin' for her?'

'Because their clothes are in better nick than ours, and their boots haven't got more holes in than stitches,' said Sophie simply. 'But as a general rule of thumb you'll do well to always mind what you say cos you never know who's on the look-out for an extra slice of bread with their dinner.'

'Thanks for the heads-up,' said Isla, who was casting furtive looks into the various rooms they passed, although they were walking too swiftly for her to actually see anything inside them. 'I'll bear it in mind.'

Sophie shot her a sidelong glance. 'Did she take your things?'

'She did, aye. And whilst I'm not bothered about the clothes, I am about my necklace. It's the last thing I have of my mammy's.'

'I'm afraid you'll not see that again,' said Sophie matter-of-factly.

'Oh yes I will, cos—' Isla began to protest, but Sophie was speaking over her.

'Only you won't, cos she has it now,' said Sophie. 'And besides, who's goin' to object, apart from you of course?'

'My father,' said Isla. 'He won't let her get away with it.'

Sophie eyed her cynically. '*If* he ever comes back.'

Isla swallowed. 'He will. He's a man of his word. He said he'd be back in two months, and I know he won't let me down.'

Sophie smiled kindly. 'People are full of good intentions, but sometimes life just doesn't work out that way.'

'Even if you don't believe that my father will come for me, surely to goodness some people must get out of here?'

'In a pine box, maybe,' said Sophie, 'but not otherwise.'

Isla eyed her incredulously. 'Not even one?'

Sophie shook her head. 'You'd be the first.'

Unable to believe what she was hearing, Isla spoke softly. 'Doesn't anyone care?'

'They care that there would be hundreds of homeless roamin' the streets if Coxhill wasn't here to house them—'

Isla interrupted without apology. '*Hundreds?*'

'Aye – although it's hard to be accurate what with people comin' and goin' on a weekly basis.'

'When you say goin' . . . you mean, in a box?'

'Or down the river,' said Sophie.

Isla was shaking her head slowly. 'I dare say you've heard it all before, but first opportunity I get I'm out of here, and I'm takin' my necklace with me. Harman's bound to slip up sooner or later and I'll be gone the moment she does.'

Sophie eyed her speculatively. 'And just how do you intend to look after yourself with no money or documents?'

'I'll manage.'

'How, though? You'll need your papers in order to find employment and accommodation, and you can hardly ask for them before you leave.'

'I'll tell the polis that Miss Harman's keeping them from me.'

Reminding herself that all newcomers were as naïve as Isla, regardless of age or sex, Sophie spoke in a deliberate fashion. 'They'd bring you straight back to Coxhill, and tell Harman to keep a closer eye on you in future, and you're livin' in fantasy land if you think otherwise. As for gettin' your necklace back, you'd best hope you get to it before the pawnbrokers sell it on, cos she'll have pawned it before the day is through.'

Isla's face paled. 'She wouldn't – would she?'

Sophie cast her a sympathetic glance. 'She'd do anythin' for a few extra bob.'

'Why does she insist on keepin' us here, when it's clear we're not wanted?' said Isla, who was struggling to understand Miss Harman's motives for staying in a job she clearly detested.

'Like it or not, there's money to be made from the poorhouse,' said Sophie simply.

'I highly doubt that,' Isla said sceptically.

'My father used to be an accountant,' Sophie told her, 'and he always used to say that where there's muck there's money. And believe you me, there's plenty of muck to be had in Coxhill.' Seeing the look of disbelief on Isla's face, Sophie elaborated. 'Where do you think she gets the money to feed and clothe everyone?' With Isla shrugging her shoulders in a hopeless manner, Sophie provided the answer. 'The government, that's who. They pay Harman something for every poor soul that enters Coxhill. Add to that the contribution the families give her for takin' their loved ones in, as well as the money she makes from us doin' laundry for the hotels and whatnot, and she's on to a nice little earner.'

'If we're so profitable, then why does she act like she hates us?' asked Isla, who was finding it hard to believe that running a poorhouse was profitable, given the state of their clothing, and the apparent undernourishment of Sophie.

'Because she does! She might like the money we bring in, but that's where it ends.' Sophie was beginning to sound exasperated.

Realising that she had exhausted the topic, Isla moved on. 'How long have you been in Coxhill?'

'Fifteen years.'

Isla's eyes nearly left her skull. *'Fifteen!'*

'Aye. My daddy died of septicaemia when I was

a wee lass, and Mammy died of tuberculosis when I was just fourteen.'

Isla quickly closed her mouth after realising that she was gaping. 'But that means you're . . .'

'Twenty-nine,' supplied Sophie, shaking her head sadly. 'I can hardly believe it myself sometimes. With no access to the outside world you find that time stands still, with one day melting into the next; before you know it, a decade has gone past, yet nothin's changed, or not for you at any rate.'

'If one day is pretty much like the next, how can you be sure you've been in here so long?' asked Isla reasonably.

'Because of the war,' said Sophie. 'Not that we get any information about what's goin' on or anythin' like that, but Harman had to tell us about the war because of the air raids – well, the false alarms at any rate.'

'And that's all you know about the war?' cried Isla in disbelief.

'Aye,' said Sophie with a resigned sigh. She eyed Isla curiously. 'For all we know it could be over by now. Is it?'

Isla stared at her in disbelief. 'Good God no! Do you not realise the scale of the thing?'

Sophie shrugged. 'We know that we're at war with Germany again, but I cannae imagine it will go on for too long – certainly nothin' like the last lot.'

Isla swallowed. 'It's really bad, Sophie, and it's exactly like the last lot, if not worse! London has been bombed really badly, and the Krauts have taken over France, as well as a few other countries.'

Sophie's jaw dropped, her eyes rounding in horror. 'Are you pullin' my leg?'

'I wish I was, but no.'

Sophie glanced at a young boy who was dragging a large sack down the corridor behind him. He gave them a shy but swift smile as he passed them by. 'Don't tell the bairns. You'll give them bleedin' nightmares, on top of the ones they already have,' said Sophie softly.

'Shouldn't they be in the orphanage?' asked Isla as they rounded the corner into yet another corridor, which was just as dark and gloomy as the one they'd turned off.

'Not when they're born here,' said Sophie.

Isla felt her stomach jolt in an unpleasant manner. Being in the poorhouse was bad enough, but giving birth in here? She said as much to Sophie, before going on to explain the circumstances behind her own arrival at Coxhill. 'Mammy died givin' birth to my little brother, who also died, and my daddy . . .' She paused as an image of her father standing on the steps to the poorhouse entered her mind. 'A big part of him died too.'

Sophie pulled a sympathetic face; sadly Isla's story was all too familiar. 'Couldn't cope, eh? Where is he now?'

'Joined the merchant navy. He said he'll come back for me once he gets himself sorted in a couple of months' time, and I believe him.'

Sophie grimaced. She'd lost count of the times she'd heard newcomers say that their loved ones would be coming back for them as soon as they'd got themselves back on their feet. 'Don't think too badly of him if he doesn't,' she said kindly. 'Sometimes life just doesn't go the way you want it to, you know?'

'I do, which is why I'm goin' to bust myself out of here.'

'If you can find a way of gettin' out without gettin' caught, you can take me with you,' said Sophie. She had said it in a tongue-in-cheek fashion, because no one ever got out of Coxhill alive, but Isla had taken her comment seriously.

'Don't worry, I will!'

Rather than douse Isla's optimism, Sophie opened the door to a large dormitory. 'In the meantime, this is home.' Isla's heart sank as she looked around the room, which was bare of anything but the bunk beds which flanked the mould-speckled walls. Sophie pointed to a pair near one of the few windows. 'Mine's the bottom one, but I don't mind sleepin' on top if you'd prefer?'

Isla shrugged her shoulders to indicate that she was easy either way. 'It must get bright awfully early,' she said, indicating the small curtainless window, the glass of which was cracked.

'Which is why they don't have curtains,' said Sophie. 'Harman wants us up and at 'em, cos there's no profit to her from our lyin' in bed.'

'She's got a cheek,' snorted Isla. 'Treatin' us like vermin whilst she reaps the rewards for our hard work!'

Sophie hastily hushed her. 'Keep your voice down. You never know who's listenin'.'

'But there's no one but us in here!' Isla pointed out.

'Aye, but it's best if you get into the habit,' said Sophie.

'So what am I meant to do? Act as if I'm on cloud nine?'

'Yes, because doin' otherwise just ain't worth the aggravation. No matter what Harman says or does to annoy you, turn the other cheek. Always be polite, and never draw her attention. Do that, and your life will be just about bearable. In short, if Harman's happy, then so are you.'

Isla eyed her curiously. 'How on earth have you survived in here for as long as you have?'

'By bein' fortunate enough to befriend a smashin' girl by the name of Kayleigh when I first arrived. She was top notch when it came to knowin' the ins and outs of Coxhill.'

Isla spoke slowly, in the hope she'd misheard. 'You said "was"?'

Sophie lowered her gaze. 'Aye. Unfortunately she didn't always follow her own advice.'

'Which was?'

'Same advice as what I've just given you. Turn the other cheek no matter what.'

'You make it sound as though someone did somethin' to her,' said Isla in stilted tones.

Sophie shot her a dark look. 'If you were to believe Harman, then Kayleigh slipped whilst doin' the laundry and banged her head on one of the drums. They reckon she was dead before she hit the floor.'

Isla spoke thickly through the fingers which covered

30

her open mouth. 'That's dreadful! But why do you say *if* you believe Harman?'

'Cos nobody saw the accident occur, and I know for a fact that Kayleigh had got on the wrong side of Harman just a few days before.'

Isla's face fell in an instant. 'You think *she* . . .' her voice trailed off as though she couldn't believe what she was about to say, '. . . killed Kayleigh,' she finished, her voice barely above a whisper.

'Kayleigh had found somethin' out about Harman. I don't know what exactly, because she refused to go into detail, but it was obvious it was somethin' big and I don't think it's a coincidence that she died just a few days later,' said Sophie, stony-faced.

Isla stared at her aghast. 'But if you're right then that's as good as murder!'

'Where's the proof?'

Isla's eyes widened. Sophie might be right when it came to the matter of evidence, but even so . . . 'How can you be so calm?'

'Because I have no choice. If I create a fuss I might end up the same way as Kayleigh, and what good will that do? Harman knows what she's doin'. I don't think there's a single inmate that doesn't march to the beat of her drum – staff too, come to that.'

'Well I ain't waitin' to be clobbered over the head because I've said summat that she doesn't like the sound of,' said Isla, 'cos if that's the case, I won't last more than five minutes!'

'I cannae stop you from tryin', but I can tell you this: you're better off waitin' for your dad to come

back if you want to make it out of here in one piece!'
Hoping she had brought the conversation to an end,
Sophie jerked her head in the direction of the corridor. 'Come on, I'd best show you where you'll be
workin'.'

'How big is this place,' asked Isla as they passed door
after door, 'and what are all these rooms for?'

'No idea. I only know the rooms I need to know,
because it pays not to ask questions!'

Isla followed Sophie through a maze of corridors
before they eventually arrived at the laundry. Sophie
opened the door, and they both stepped inside the
hot and steamy room, which was filled with bubbling
cauldrons and piles of washing. The women, all of
whom were dressed identically to Sophie and Isla,
were busy working.

'This is the laundry, and that . . .' here Sophie
pointed to an off-set room, 'is the dryin' room.'

Isla looked to the windows, all of which were shut
tight, much to her disappointment. 'Why on earth
don't they open the windows? It's like a furnace in
here!'

'And risk someone escapin'?' Sophie hissed from
the corner of her mouth. 'I don't think so!'

Isla jerked her head in the direction of an elderly
lady who was struggling with the heavy load of laundry she was attempting to carry to the drying room.
'Why don't the others help her?'

'Nana Mulville?'

'If that's her name, then yes.'

'Because if word gets back to Harman that she cannae cope she'll not be of any use, and if she cannae pull her weight, what's the point in feedin' her? So believe you me, even though we'd like to help, Nana Mulville wouldn't thank us for it,' said Sophie, so matter-of-factly Isla was shocked.

'So what are you sayin'? That Harman would let her starve to death?'

Leading the way back into the corridor, Sophie continued to speak over her shoulder. 'Yes. Everyone has to earn their keep if they want to keep a roof over their head, it's as simple as that. Age and sex don't come into it.'

'Well, I think it's a disgrace,' said Isla as she followed Sophie down the corridor to another room.

'Don't we all,' said Sophie, opening the door to the kitchen. 'But it's best not to say anythin', cos you'll either get punished or worse.'

Suddenly, Isla emitted a high-pitched squeal as her eyes were drawn to a family of rats scurrying behind an enormous range.

'Ah, tomorrow's lunch!' said Sophie. 'You cannae complain it's not fresh.'

Isla was waving her hands in front of her, while backing into the corridor. 'No! I am *not* . . .'

But Sophie was chuckling. 'Relax, I'm only kiddin' – or at least I hope I am. We only get meat when there's a special inspection due, which won't be for another year or so yet.'

Isla stared in disgust at the thick grease and the food remains which lined the stove as well as the walls and floor. 'I bet she doesn't bring the inspectors in here!'

'You'd think not, but she does.'

Isla stared at her open-mouthed. 'How can they possibly turn a blind eye to that?'

'Your guess is as good as mine,' said Sophie, leading the way around the serving counter into the dining hall.

Isla looked at the rows of tables and benches. 'You say there's hundreds of people livin' here – not that I've seen many of them – but surely if that's the case, there must be a lot of sickness and disease, with rats sharin' the same food as yourselves?'

'Of course there is. Why do you ask?'

Isla glanced to where the rats had run. 'Isn't there some sort of sickbay where the ill are looked after?'

'Of sorts, but I don't think the staff are real nurses, and the doctors don't come here unless it's an emergency. As far as they're concerned you're bound to get a lot of illness with so many people livin' under the same roof, regardless of hygiene.'

Isla stared at her in disbelief. 'But that's ridiculous. It's glaringly obvious the place isn't fit to serve food.'

'Agreed, but that's what they say.'

'Surely there must be someone . . .' Isla began, but Sophie was shaking her head.

'Not even God.'

'Sorry?'

'Coxhill has its own church,' Sophie explained. 'First time I ever went in, I confided in the priest, hopin' that he would help.'

'What did he say?'

'He said that God works in mysterious ways and has a greater plan for us all. Oh, he also said that I should be grateful for what I had.'

'He didn't!'

'He did,' said Sophie grimly. And for the first time, Isla saw a glint deep within her new friend's eye. 'It was all I could do to stop myself punchin' him through the wooden lattice.'

'What stopped you?'

'I figured my life was bad enough without gettin' on the wrong side of God, and even though I think the priest is a pillock and the existence of God is questionable, I don't want to take any unnecessary risks.'

'He should be ashamed of himself,' said Isla. 'I certainly won't be rushin' to see him any time soon.'

'Well, I'm afraid you have to see him on Sundays because Harman insists that everyone attend.'

'Perhaps she thinks that if she fills a church, God will forgive her sins.'

'I very much doubt she believes in God,' said Sophie. 'Maybe she's hedgin' her bets.'

Isla started as a loud bell rang out. 'What the . . . ?'

'The dinner bell,' Sophie explained, as people began to stream into the dining hall.

Joining Sophie in the queue which was already beginning to form, Isla tried to work out what it was that was so unusual about the people swarming into the hall. Was it the way they were dressed? No, that wasn't it. Isla continued to watch as the queue in front of them swiftly shortened. It was only hearing someone cough that brought it home. *They're not talkin' to each other*, she thought. Seeing two people exchange 'Excuse me's as they accidentally walked across each other, she added, *not conversationally, at any rate*. She whispered as much to Sophie.

'Didn't you hear Harman when she told you about no pallin' up with anybody?' Sophie whispered back.

'Aye, but I didn't think she meant it,' said Isla. A frown forming, she posed the other question which had been bothering her somewhat. 'We've just been in the kitchen, and there wasn't anyone in there apart from the rats, so how can we possibly be havin' dinner?'

'Sarnies,' said Sophie, before correcting herself: 'or rather bread and butter; you don't need a cook to prepare that.'

As they moved towards the front of the queue Isla saw two women ahead of them, one cutting the bread, the other passing a sparsely buttered knife over each slice before handing it over to the hungry recipient. *No wonder they're all so skinny*, she thought as she cast an eye around her. *I should imagine the rats get more to eat than us.*

Sophie cut across her thoughts with a barely audible whisper. 'No matter how vile the food, never give it back or pass comment, because if Harman gets to hear about it you'll be on bread and butter for the foreseeable.'

'So no one complains because they'll be punished if they do,' said Isla. 'The woman's a flamin' dictator.'

'Got it in one,' agreed Sophie. 'She gives us bread

and butter once a week to serve as a reminder of what life would be like should any of us step out of line.'

'She's the female version of Hitler,' said Isla, before being hastily hushed by Sophie.

'Just remember, walls have ears!'

Isla eyed her incredulously. 'Why on earth would anyone tattle-tale when they're bein' just as badly treated?'

'Only they're not, are they?' Sophie said in exasperated tones. 'She gives special favours to those willin' to turn on the rest of us.'

'Spies,' muttered Isla. 'Which ones are Mary and Gordon?' Her eyes settled on a girl with shoulder-length brown hair and suspicious brown eyes, a smock which looked relatively new and boots which appeared to be of good quality.

'The girl you're lookin' at is Mary, and I'd stop starin' if I were you.'

Isla hastily averted her gaze. 'At least you can see who they are.'

'Not always,' warned Sophie. 'Harman has her up and comin' favourites too.'

'How does that work?'

'Those that tattle-tale the most get the most favours,' said Sophie, 'so every one of them is willin' to snitch on the others, if it makes them top dog.'

'I see! So am I to take it that Mary and Gordon are the present top dogs?'

'You are indeed.'

Having reached the top of the queue, Isla took a mug of water then grimaced as she took the slice of buttered bread. Completely forgetting Sophie's advice, she started to pick bits off. 'This is mouldy,' she began, but hearing a gasp from the cook she quickly corrected herself. 'Nothin' wrong with a bit of mould, mind you.'

'That's better,' said Sophie, adding for the benefit of the cook, 'Meg, this is Isla.'

Isla guessed Meg to be around the same age as herself. She had frizzy ginger hair, brown eyes, and a face full of freckles, and she gave Isla a ghost of a smile, revealing a gap between her front teeth. 'Hello, Isla . . .' she glanced towards the door and lowered her head, hissing, 'Watch out.'

Isla followed her line of sight to Miss Harman, who was walking towards them.

Sophie tugged at Isla's sleeve, murmuring 'C'mon' over her shoulder. Selecting a bench at the far side of the hall, the girls watched Miss Harman supervising Meg and the other cook as they sliced and buttered the bread. *She probably wants to make sure they're not slicin' it too thick or puttin' too much butter on it*, thought Isla. *She's even worse than I thought.* Seemingly content with what she had seen, Harman cast an accusing eye around the diners before leaving the hall.

'You can almost feel the room exhale,' Isla said to Sophie as she continued to pick the bits of mould off her bread.

'She probably wanted to make sure that you were toein' the line,' said Sophie. 'She likes to nip trouble-makers in the bud.'

Isla washed down the last bit of bread with a swig of water. 'Is that how she sees me, then?'

'That's how she views anyone who questions her, and you did that from the get-go, so I'd say so, yes.'

'My keepin' my mouth shut or toein' the line will never work,' said Isla decidedly. 'Do you know of anyone who's tried to escape? Only it would be handy to know where they went wrong.'

'If they have, then we don't know about it.'

'So some of the ones who've disappeared without trace might actually have made it out?'

'I suppose it's always possible,' said Sophie as they left the hall, 'but if she's discovered their route of escape she'll have made sure it's no longer viable.'

'So what happens now? I'm assumin' it's early to bed?'

'When there's work to be done?' scoffed Sophie, holding the door to the laundry room open behind her. 'I should cocoa. It's back to work. Bedtime's nine p.m. sharp.'

Isla followed Sophie to one of the cauldrons. 'What's the routine? I'm assumin' there must be one.'

'Bells,' said Sophie simply. 'You have a bell to wake you up, another to let you know when it's time for breakfast, another for work, another for lunch, and so on.'

'So there's a bell for bed?'

'Spot on!' said Sophie. Plunging a sheet into the hot water, she eyed Isla sympathetically. 'You're one strong young lady, Isla, I'll give you that.'

Isla followed suit with another sheet. 'What makes you say that?'

'You've lost the whole of your family within less than a month, yet here you are plannin' your escape. Have you always been a fighter?'

Isla told Sophie how she'd jacked her job in on the day of her mother's passing.

'At least you got to see her,' said Sophie.

'Fleetingly,' said Isla. 'I just wish I could've gone with her to the hospital.'

Sophie began to scrub her sheet with a large bar of yellow soap. 'For all the people that pass through these doors sayin' that they're goin' to run away, I reckon you're the only one that might actually do it.'

Isla brightened. 'Really?'

'Given the way you stood up to your boss? Yes.'

'And you'd come with me?'

Sophie pushed the sheet over a scrubbing board. 'If you can honestly and truly find a way without gettin' caught then yes, I would – but you have to be certain cos I don't fancy a one-way trip to the bottom of the Clyde!'

Isla beamed. 'I'll find a way, I promise.'

Many hours later, when the bedtime bell rang, Isla looked at Sophie in surprise as her friend slipped between the sheets on the bottom bunk without removing her clothes. 'Aren't you goin' to get changed for bed?'

'Oh aye. Just fetch me nightie, would you?' cackled Sophie, before hastily apologising. 'Sorry, Isla, but you cannae seriously think they'd give you night-wear? You'll be askin' for fluffy slippers next!'

'It's ridiculous when I've a perfectly good nightie sittin' in Harman's office,' remarked Isla as she kicked off her plimsolls. Climbing on to the top bunk, she tried her best to snuggle beneath the thin sheet which was the only form of covering provided.

'Just a tip, but no talkin' after lights out, cos that's when Mary's ears are waggin' like an elephant's!' Sophie whispered.

'That Meg seemed pretty trustworthy, wouldn't you say?'

There was a brief silence while Sophie mulled this over. 'She did, but she's new, and even the nicest of people can change in order to survive in this hellhole.'

'You trust me, though?'

'Aye, but you're different; you wear your heart on your sleeve.' As the words left her lips the dorm fell into darkness. 'Goodnight, Isla.'

Isla settled down to try to get some sleep, but all she could think of was her necklace, which lay locked in Harman's desk drawer. *I'm goin' to get that necklace back if it's the last thing I do. Harman might think she's won the battle, but she's not goin' to win this war!*

It was Isla's first morning in Coxhill, and due to a restless night she was up and ready for breakfast long before the bell rang. 'How'd you sleep?' yawned Sophie as she walked alongside her to the dining hall.

'I didn't hardly,' said Isla, 'but on the other hand,

41

neither did I cry myself to sleep – somethin' I've been doin' since losin' Mammy.'

'Is that better? Not sleepin', I mean?' Sophie asked uncertainly.

'Much. Cos plannin' our escape proved to be a good distraction, and if it helps us get out of here, a useful one to boot.'

'I've been thinkin' about that too,' confessed Sophie, 'but even if we do get out, Harman will have the polis on our tail as soon as she's discovered we're missin'.'

Isla nudged Sophie to bring her attention to Meg, who was being marched out of the dining hall, tears lining her cheeks. She looked briefly at the two girls before glancing pointedly at the girl holding her arm, who was grinning spitefully as she escorted Meg towards Harman's office. 'What d'you reckon's gone on there?' Isla hissed as they joined the back of the queue.

'No idea, but I'm guessin' it must be bad if the grin on Mary's face is anythin' to go by.'

'Aye, she certainly looked pleased with herself – the evil cow,' murmured Isla. 'What I wouldn't give to wipe that smile off her face.'

'You and me both,' said Sophie. 'Maybe one day, eh?'

Falling into silence as they neared the front of the queue, they each took a meagre bowl of gruel from the hands of the cook who had taken Meg's place. Settling on to a bench far from everyone else, Isla was the first to break into speech. 'You'd think they'd give us more than this,' she said as she dipped her spoon into the bowl. 'Goodness only knows, we never had much money, but Mammy always put decent grub on the table, and plenty of it too.'

Having finished the few spoonfuls of gruel in her bowl, Sophie drained her water mug. 'What do you think your mammy would have made of you bein' here?'

Isla hungrily scraped the remainder of the gruel from her bowl. 'It would've broken her heart, plain and simple.' She got to her feet. 'And she'd have fought like a lion to keep us together. It's funny how you instinctively think men to be stronger than women because they've got bigger muscles, but when it comes to emotions women are far tougher, or at least they are in my experience.'

The two girls walked their dishes over to the counter before leaving the hall and making their way to the laundry. 'I kind of feel sorry for your dad, though,' said Sophie as soon as she was happy they couldn't be over-heard. 'I bet he feels dreadful for doin' what he did.'

Isla gave a disbelieving harrumph as they passed through the laundry door. 'Then why isn't he here, arrangin' for my release? It's not as though Harman could refuse to hand me over!'

Sophie headed for the nearest cauldron and picked up a pillowcase belonging to one of the city's hotels. 'Didn't you say his ship sailed last night?'

Isla wore a frown. 'He did, aye.'

'Then he could hardly come back for you if they were already out to sea,' Sophie pointed out as she pushed the pillowcase beneath the water.

Isla stared at her open-mouthed, before shaking her

head. 'You're right. And if he were goin' to change his mind he'd have done so within seconds of Harman closin' the door.'

'Do you worry about him bein' at sea?' asked Sophie as she rinsed the pillowcase. 'What with the war and everythin'?'

'Not with Mammy watchin' over him,' said Isla resolutely. 'Same as she won't let any harm come to me.'

Sophie was looking hopeful. 'Do you think she'll help us get out?'

'No two ways about it,' said Isla. 'With my mammy lookin' out for us everything's goin' to be just fine and dandy!'

Chapter Two

A few days had passed since Isla's arrival at Coxhill, and neither she nor Sophie had set eyes on Meg since the day she'd been taken away from the dining hall.

'Do you think Harman's got rid of Meg the same way she did Kayleigh?' Isla whispered to Sophie as they joined the back of the lunch queue.

'I really hope not,' said Sophie in lowered tones. 'I cannae see Meg sayin' anythin' out of turn.'

'Then where is she? And more to the point, just what sort of innocent remark could have caused her to be hauled away?'

'I don't know,' said Sophie ruefully, 'but I wish I did, because I've no desire to make the same mistake!'

More determined than ever that they should escape, Isla whispered a confession. 'I must've tried every door and window this place has to offer, but I reckon it would be easier to break out of the Tower of London!'

The cook handed over two plates of the meatless gunk which passed for stew, and they made their way to their usual seat at the far end of the dining hall. Isla lifted her spoon up, allowing the mixture to plop back on to her plate, and said, 'On the bright side, if we're fed this stuff for much longer we should be thin enough to slip between the window bars.'

Listening with half an ear, Sophie glanced in the direction of a smart-looking man with neatly cut dark hair, a pencil moustache and cunning brown eyes who had entered the dining hall. 'I see Madson's here again.'

Isla followed her gaze. 'Is he not one of the staff?'

Sophie shook her head fervently. 'You'd think so, but no. He's one of the inspectors.'

Isla gaped at her. 'Should we say somethin' to him? Perhaps point out—'

Sophie made a strangled noise in the back of her throat. 'No we should not!'

'But if he's an inspector—' Isla began, only to have Sophie cut across her once more.

'Have you not seen the way he looks at Harman? If he was a dog he'd wag his tail whenever she walked into a room! With that bein' the case, he's hardly goin' to welcome any criticism we have of her – an' besides, he's here often enough to know what this place is really like.'

Isla pulled a disgusted face. 'Do you reckon he's got the hots for her? It doesn't seem likely, given he must be half her age, but I've heard tell that some fellers find older women attractive – although I find it hard to believe *anyone* would fancy someone as cold and stony-faced as her.'

'Maybe it's not her he's after but her money.'

Isla inhaled sharply, which caused her to cough. 'She'd have to be filthy rich,' she managed, after regaining her composure.

'I know she makes money off our backs,' said Sophie, 'but I wouldn't think it enough to make her any kind of rich, never mind filthy.'

Isla wrinkled her nose. 'Surely you don't think he actually finds her physically attractive?'

Sophie scratched her head. 'They do say it takes all sorts.'

'Aye, but he's not exactly ugly. Some might say he's good-lookin', if you go for that sort of thing.'

Sophie considered Mr Madson, who she guessed could be around the same age as herself, if not a little younger. 'I suppose I can see what you mean. He's clean, well dressed, nice teeth – just shifty-lookin'.'

'It's his eyes,' agreed Isla. 'They seem to be permanently narrowed, as if he's weighin' everythin' up, or is hidin' some deep dark secret from the rest of us.'

Sophie clicked her fingers as a thought sprang to mind. 'I've always suspected that Harman was payin' someone off to keep quiet about the state of this place. Perhaps it's him?'

'Could be,' said Isla. 'From what you've told me, Harman's got a few sidelines on the go—' she stopped speaking suddenly as an epiphany came to her. 'Surely not.'

Sophie swallowed. 'Do you think she's payin' him . . . er, in kind?'

Isla pulled a disgusted face. 'Good God, I hope not!'

'Then what?'

Isla spoke in hollow tones, as though she couldn't quite believe what she was about to say, although she had to admit it wasn't as bad as Sophie's theory. 'If she's payin' him to keep shtum, it means he knows what it's like here, and given he's here quite often it's highly likely he's guessed she's makin' money on the side—'

'Which is why she's payin' him to keep quiet,' interrupted Sophie, but Isla disagreed.

'Unless he's in on her money-makin' schemes. I'm guessin' that could be more lucrative than takin' backhanders.'

Sophie stared at her open-mouthed. 'Good God.'

'The only bit that doesn't make sense is why he's here as much as he is, cos his presence doesn't make much difference to the work we do,' said Isla thoughtfully.

'Unless he doesn't trust her to be honest about the amount of money she's makin',' said Sophie, 'whereas if he's here he can keep an eye on what's goin' on.'

'We need to tell someone.'

'Who, though? Cos I can guarantee no one would believe us over him, especially when we've no proof.'

'So that's it? They take the very food from our mouths, and there's nothin' we can do to stop them?'

Sophie hastily brought Isla's attention to Miss Harman, who was standing in the doorway of the hall waiting for Mr Madson to join her. 'Look sharp, the old—' She broke off, staring at Isla. 'What was that you said about takin' the food from our mouths?'

'I don't mean literally,' said Isla, 'I meant the money

she makes from the laundry could be spent on us . . .' Seeing Sophie staring off into space, she waved a hand in front of her friend's face, bringing her out of a trance-like state. 'Are you listenin'?'

'Yes, but you've got me wonderin' just how much the government pay Harman to feed us,' said Sophie, examining the unappetising slop in her bowl.

'Not much if this lot's anythin' to go by, although I hardly see what that has to do with Madson and Harman.'

Sophie scraped the last of the stew from her plate while speaking slowly. 'It would if they were creamin' money off the top.'

Isla looked blank. 'How'd you mean?'

'The government give Harman a certain amount to look after us, but what if instead of spendin' all of the money on us she keeps some back for herself and Madson?'

'If that's true, then she's even more devious, selfish and wicked than I thought,' said Isla bitterly.

'I've told you about my daddy bein' an accountant before he passed?' Sophie waited for Isla to nod before continuing. 'Well, he once told me about how there are two types of accountants in this world, the honest and the dishonest. The dishonest ones make an absolute fortune, hiding the profits of some of the big companies by running two sets of books, one for the tax man and one that shows their real earnings. When you think about it, Coxhill is a business, just like one of the big companies, and as we're guessin' she's not tellin' anyone else about her sidelines I'd be very surprised if she *wasn't* runnin' two sets of books.'

Isla used her thin slice of stale bread to mop up what was left of the barely palatable gravy. 'And there you were sayin' we had no proof! Imagine the power we'd have if we got our mitts on those books. I reckon they'd agree to just about anythin' to stop the truth from comin' out.'

'Blackmail?' hissed Sophie.

'Sounds good to me,' said a voice from behind them, 'especially if it means we get out of here.'

Practically jumping out of her skin, Isla spun round to see Meg smiling at her.

'Meg! We thought . . .' Isla stopped speaking as Sophie shot her a warning glance.

'That I was toes-up?' said Meg. 'Not this time, but I reckon I came pretty close, so if you've got a hold on Harman I want in.'

'It's all purely hypothetical,' said Sophie. 'Please don't tell.'

Meg glanced around before pulling up her sleeve, revealing two large welts. 'You seriously think that I'd grass on the two of you when she done this to me? No chance!'

Isla stared in horror at the open sores. 'Harman did that to you?'

'She did, aye.'

Sophie gulped. 'But why?'

'All I did was ask one of the others whether they knew if Madson was workin' at Coxhill, what with him spendin' so much time here of late, but they hadn't the foggiest,' said Meg, as she pulled her sleeves back down. 'I thought no more about it until Harman came and got me from the dining hall. She went bleedin' mental once she got me back to the office! Screamin' at me for pokin' me nose in where it's not wanted and sayin' she'd teach me to mind my own business.' She glanced meaningfully at her arms. 'She did these with the poker.'

Isla's hand flew to her mouth. 'She – she burned you?'

'Aye, she did that. After which she chucked me into a room with nothin' in it bar a guzunder, sayin' that I could come out when she was satisfied I'd learned my lesson.' Meg sighed. 'I didn't know that Mary was listenin' when I'd been askin' about Madson, but she must've been, cos Harman gave her a bag of sweets as a reward for keeping her ear to the ground.'

'She needs to be stopped!' snapped Isla. 'And seein' as we cannae report her to anyone, I think we should consider our only alternative.'

'You cannae be suggestin' we try and blackmail her?' said Sophie, her eyes widening. 'Just look at what she did to Meg for askin' a simple question, and then imagine what she'd do to us for blackmail when we haven't even got any proof.'

'We cannae just sit back and let her get away with it!' protested Isla. 'Surely there's got to be someone we could turn to?'

'No one will listen to us without proof, and before you say anythin' we don't even know for certain that she *has* two sets of books!'

Meg sat down next to Isla. 'So how do we find out?'

Sophie looked pointedly at Meg's arms. 'We don't, because it's just not worth the risk.'

'And what about this lot?' said Isla, indicating the rest of the diners with a sweep of her arm.

Sophie followed her gaze. 'What about them?'

'They're all half-starved, livin' in atrocious circumstances just so those two have a few extra quid in their pockets.'

'Which is dreadful, but we just *can't*—' Sophie began, only to be cut off.

'I can.' Isla looked to Meg. 'And I reckon Meg would stand with me.'

Meg nodded fervently. 'Too bloomin' right I would.'

Sophie stared at them aghast. 'This isn't a game.'

'I know it's not!' hissed Isla, as quietly as she could. 'But if you think I can sit idly by, while others are still sufferin' at the hands of Harman, then you don't know me at all!'

Sophie drew a deep breath before letting it out in staggered gusts. 'If we get caught . . .'

Isla beamed. 'So you're in?'

'Not that I'm sayin' it's a good idea, but at least I'll be able to keep an eye on the pair of you and stop you from goin' off half-cocked.'

Meg emitted a small, practically inaudible squeal of excitement. 'So where do we start?'

'I haven't the foggiest,' said Sophie, 'but we need to think long and hard about this, because we need not just one plan but two.'

'You mean have a back-up plan?'

Sophie gave a short, mirthless laugh. 'If the first one

didn't work, we wouldn't be around to execute the second. No. I'm talkin' about the three of us blowin' this joint.'

Meg's mouth hung open, her large brown eyes growing wide. 'You mean escape?' she hissed.

Isla provided the answer. 'Me and Soph are determined to leave this dump,' she said, 'and I cannae think of anythin' sweeter than sendin' Harman on her way before we do.'

Meg glanced to the barred windows which lined the high walls of the dining hall. 'How are you plannin' on gettin' out?'

'No idea as yet, but we've got a lot to think through, cos things will be a lot tougher on the outside than they are in here at first, what with us not havin' any money, or food, or somewhere to lay our heads.'

'Well, I for one would rather take my chances on the outside than I would in here,' said Meg, 'cos at least out there folk don't burn you with a red-hot poker just for askin' an innocent question.'

'Which brings me to another matter,' said Sophie. 'We all know to be careful what we say and do around Harman, but we're goin' to have to be as silent as the grave from here on in, because if she should get so much as a whiff that we're on to her she'll have us down the river before you can say knife.'

'Agreed, but at the same time we need to keep a close eye on her,' said Isla, 'which'll be far easier with three of us.'

For the first time, Meg was looking dubious. 'Is it

really goin' to be necessary? Only I don't imagine she'll take kindly to bein' spied on if she were to catch us in the act.'

'Which is why we'll have to be careful,' said Isla. 'We cannae prove she's up to no good if we don't have a clue what she's up to, and in order to do that we'll have to keep an eye on her in the hope that her routine will give the game away somehow!'

'So, see what she does and when she does it type of thing?' supposed Sophie.

'Aye. Anythin' untoward should stand out like a sore thumb, but we'll have to be super careful if we're to pull this off.' She looked to Meg. 'Now that you know the full score, are you in?'

Meg didn't hesitate. 'Too right!'

'Me too,' confirmed Sophie.

Isla smiled. 'All for one?'

'And one for all!' grinned her friends, albeit with an air of trepidation.

NOVEMBER 1940

A couple of months had passed since the conversation in the dining hall, but despite their efforts to find out what Harman and Madson were up to the girls were still no closer to uncovering the truth.

Now, as they made their way to have their bi-weekly bath, Isla turned to her pals. 'I wonder what the staff make of Madson's weekly visits?'

Sophie pulled a downward smile. 'From what I've seen they don't seem to be in the least bit bothered.'

'I dunno so much,' said Meg. 'I have caught that new chap . . . what's his name again?'

'Mr Ellis,' said Isla.

'Aye, that's right. Well, I've seen that Mr Ellis watchin' them a few times,' said Meg. 'But there again, I suppose he might just be gettin' the lay of the land, as it were, cos he doesn't look suspicious, just curious.'

'Well I hope he doesn't rock the boat, cos he's the only decent one amongst the whole staff,' said Isla. 'I was there when he came into the dining hall for the first time, and the look on his face said it all.'

Meg arched a single eyebrow. 'Which was?'

'Disgusted,' said Isla simply.

'He was the same when he came into the laundry – almost as though he felt sorry for us,' remarked Sophie.

'It's a pity he's not the one in charge instead of Harman,' said Meg. 'The place would be a lot better with someone like him at the helm.'

Being the last to arrive, the girls entered the room which housed the single tin bath and peered at the scummy surface of the water in disgust.

'How can bathin' in that get us clean?' Isla asked, her nose wrinkling with distaste.

'It can't. If anythin' we'd be dirtier comin' out than we were goin' in,' tutted Meg. 'Quite frankly I dread to think what sort of diseases are floatin' round in there.'

Sophie picked up one of the jugs which had been used to fill the tub. 'We're not bathin' in that. Grab a jug each and come with me.'

'Where are we goin'?' asked Isla, picking up two jugs.

'The water in the laundry is cleaner than it is here, and it'll be a good deal warmer too,' Sophie explained as they left the room.

Meg's face fell. 'I thought we were meant to be stayin' on Harman's good side? If one of her cronies were to see us . . .'

'Ah, but her favourites are always the first to bathe, so they'll be in bed by now,' said Sophie over her shoulder as she led the way to the laundry.

'And we know that Harman's not around because she always retires to her room at seven o'clock on the dot,' said Isla happily.

When they reached the laundry there were still wisps of steam emanating from the cauldrons. 'The ones at the back are always the last to be lit, so they should still be nice and warm,' said Sophie, bypassing the ones nearest the door.

Isla tentatively placed her elbow in the cauldron she'd been working at earlier that day and smiled. 'Ooh. This one's perfect!' Quickly filling their jugs with water, the girls followed her back to the bathroom, taking care not to spill a drop on the way. 'It's goin' to be more like a shower than a bath, but maybe that's for the better.'

They watched the filthy water disappear down the plughole, Meg wrinkling her nose in disgust as she held up one of the towels which the others had used to dry themselves. 'If you thought the bathwater was bad just take a look at these! I ain't gettin' nice and clean just to dry meself on that!'

'Where are you goin'?' asked Isla as the other girl headed for the door.

Meg grinned. 'Sophie isn't the only one to have bright ideas. Shan't be a mo!'

Sophie beckoned to Isla. 'You go first.'

Quickly slipping her smock over her head, Isla timidly stepped into the bath, holding one of the large bars of yellow soap they used to do the laundry in her hand. Smiling as Sophie – now standing on a chair – slowly tipped the jug over her head and shoulders, she revelled in the warmth as she lathered herself in soap. 'Heaven!' she said, rubbing her hands through her hair. Giving Sophie the thumbs-up to indicate she was ready for rinsing, she watched the last of the bubbles disappear down the plughole just as Meg re-entered the room holding three clean towels.

'I swiped these from the drying room,' Meg said, passing one of the towels to Isla as she stepped out of the bath. 'Nobody'll notice if we put them under the pile that's waitin' for the wash, and even if they do, there's no proof of how they got there.'

Isla thanked Meg for the towel, which was deliciously warm. 'They say it's the simple things in life that please us the most, and boy are they right. I feel like a human being again – something which I haven't felt since arriving in Coxhill.'

'We'll have to do this every bath night,' said Sophie, as she beckoned for Meg to get into the tub.

'Still, I cannae wait until we break out of here,' said Isla. Pulling her smock down over her head, she continued thickly, 'But the more I watch Harman the

57

more I wonder just how we're goin' to lay our hands on those two ledgers.'

'She certainly never leaves the office door unlocked, not even for a second,' Sophie agreed as she took her turn in the bath.

'Never mind all that! Just how are we meant to get our hands on somethin' we've never even seen!' cried Meg. 'Cos let's face it, we don't even know for certain that they exist!'

'They simply must,' said Sophie decidedly. 'Keepin' an eye on Harman might not have brought us any closer to findin' the ledgers, but there's no doubt in my mind that her and Madson are screwin' this place over.'

With all three girls dried and dressed, they headed for bed.

'We'll catch them in the act sooner or later,' said Isla. 'We just have to bide our time!' As the words left her lips, the girls heard the air-raid siren wail its ominous warning, and she looked from Meg to Sophie, her jaw dropping. 'What do we do?'

Jerking her head in the direction of the corridor which they'd just passed, Sophie said, 'Follow me.'

Hurrying along, they were soon joined by a mixture of staff and most if not all of Coxhill's inhabitants.

'For anyone thinking of leaving the premises, I'd like to remind them that they do so at their own peril,' Miss Harman called out to the crowd in general.

Isla scowled at the back of Miss Harman's tightly wound bun. 'She's only sayin' that to scare them,' she hissed to Sophie and Meg. 'We're too far north for the Luftwaffe.'

'How can you be sure?' Sophie hissed back.

'They're targetin' London and the south, cos they're the biggest threat to Hitler,' Isla said confidently. 'They wouldn't waste their fuel or bombs comin' all the way up here.'

'If that's the case, then why don't we leg it whilst we've the opportunity?' suggested Meg.

'Cos I'm not leavin' here until we've come up with a plan to get shot of Harman,' Isla reminded her. 'I couldn't live with myself knowin' I'd left that wicked witch in charge.'

Meg nodded ruefully. 'I forgot about her. But you're right, we cannae leave until we've sorted things here first.'

They headed into the dank and dreary cellars along with the rest of Coxhill. Shuffling to the back, Isla pointed to Mr Ellis, who had rushed forward to save Nana Mulville from being pushed over by the people crowding their way in. 'A prince amongst men is that one,' she said, before indicating Miss Harman, who was glaring at him disapprovingly. 'How can she object to him stoppin' Nana Mulville from gettin' trodden underfoot? Surely she should be thankin' him for savin' one of her workers.'

'I don't think she likes him, because he's nice,' said Meg, 'and he shows her up for bein' the cruel beggar she is.'

'I feel sorry for him workin' in a place like this,' said Sophie. 'It must be soul-destroyin' seein' what it's like, but not bein' able to do a darned thing about it.'

'Who knows?' said Isla idly. 'Maybe he'll say somethin' to the authorities.'

Sophie wrinkled her nose. 'It doesn't matter how nice a person is, everyone needs money in their pocket and a roof over their head.'

Isla looked to Mr Ellis with his kind, amber eyes and ash-brown hair. 'Perhaps she fancies him, but knows he's too good for her?'

'Could be,' supposed Sophie, 'he certainly gives Madson a run for his money in the looks department, as well as personality.'

Meg grinned at Sophie. 'Do you fancy him? Ellis, I mean?'

Sophie blushed. 'Don't be daft!'

'Why is she bein' daft?' said Isla. 'He's around abouts your age, as well as good-lookin'.'

'And you are single,' Meg pointed out.

'And an inmate in a poorhouse,' said Sophie resignedly. 'He can do way better than the likes of me.'

'Stuff and non—' Isla began before being cut off by the siren sounding the all-clear. 'Blimey! That was quick!'

DECEMBER 1940

Sophie came rushing into the laundry and did her best to hide amongst the cauldrons.

'What the . . . ?' Isla was beginning, when all became clear. Miss Harman was peering through the laundry windows as though on the hunt for someone. Guessing that the someone must be Sophie, Isla deftly stepped

60

in front of her friend's hiding place, totally obscuring her from view. Picking up a few dirty sheets, she piled them on top of Sophie whilst taking care to not look in Harman's direction. Keeping her back to the older woman, she exaggeratedly billowed one of the sheets whilst speaking. 'What on earth's goin' on, and why is Harman starin' through the window?'

'She caught me watchin' her,' hissed Sophie, adding hastily, 'Has she gone?'

Isla's heart sank. Getting caught spying on Miss Harman was something they had all feared, but they had been lucky – until now. 'Keep your head down while I take a look.' Turning to plunge the sheet she was holding into the cauldron, Isla watched peripherally as Mary scurried up to the older woman. After a brief conversation, Miss Harman moved on at a brisk pace, but to Isla's dismay Mary decided to enter the laundry.

Her heart in her mouth, Isla rubbed her arm over her forehead in the pretence of wiping away sweat whilst bringing Sophie up to speed, finishing with, 'Whatever you do, don't move or speak until I tell you it's safe to do so.'

'Gotcha!' came Sophie's muffled response.

Hoping that Mary wouldn't come over, Isla busied herself with the laundry. *I hate to think what she'd do if she were to find Sophie hidin' amongst the sheets, but I dare say it wouldn't be anythin' pleasant*, she thought as she vigorously pumped the sheet she was washing against the scrubbing board.

Not bothering to search the rest of the laundry first,

Mary walked steadily in Isla's direction. Barely glancing at the other women as she passed them by, she eyed Isla coolly. 'Where's your little pal?'

Isla did her best to appear nonplussed. 'We're not allowed pals in here, Mary. You know that.'

Ignoring Isla's reply, Mary continued curtly, 'There's only one person Sophie would run to for help.'

'Not me,' said Isla. Making it clear that their conversation was at an end, she continued to scrub the sheet with such enthusiasm that water slopped over the sides of the cauldron, half-soaking Mary's smock. Leaping to one side in an effort to avoid further splashing, Mary scowled.

'You stupid bitch! Mind what you're doin'!'

Isla shrugged as if to say it was Mary's fault for standing there in the first place. 'I've got work to do, so unless you want to help . . . ?'

Being one of Harman's favourites Mary had never done a real day's work in her life, and with no intention of starting any time soon she was about to turn away when her eye fell on the heap of laundry under which Sophie was hiding. A sly smile curling her lips, she pushed Isla out of the way and lifted her leg up high before stamping down hard on the pile of sheets. Disappointed that she hadn't connected with flesh and bone, she began stamping randomly before jumping right into the middle and continuing to stamp up and down.

Pretending to feign disinterest in Mary's behaviour, Isla could only wait with bated breath for cries of alarm from Sophie or of triumph from Mary, but neither came. Her face set in a scowl, Mary began pulling the laundry to one side.

'What the hell are you playin' at?' cried Isla as they both heard one of the sheets rip. 'You need your bleedin' head examinin'!'

Angry and frustrated that she had made herself look a complete fool, Mary gave the pile of sheets one final kick and yelped with pain as her foot connected with something solid, nearly pushing Isla against the cauldron as she hopped up and down on her uninjured foot whilst clutching the toes of the other.

'What did you expect?' said Isla tartly.

Tears pricking her eyes, Mary limped painfully away. 'You cannae just leave!' Isla called after her. 'Who's goin' to take the blame for this sheet?' Yelling a couple of profanities over her shoulder, Mary hobbled out of the room.

Bending down to scoop the laundry back into a pile, Isla hissed: 'She's gone. Are you all right?'

Tears streaming down her cheeks, Sophie drew the sheets back from her face, revealing the blood which was seeping from her nose.

'Oh, Sophie! Did she kick in you in the face?'

'No. She kicked the foot of the mangle,' said Sophie, somewhat thickly. 'I'm surprised it moved, what with the weight of the thing.'

'Is that what hit your poor nose?'

Sophie shook her head. 'Luckily for me it was a bucket next to the mangle. It still hurts, though.'

'At least she didn't find you,' said Isla. She dipped a piece of cloth into the warm water and handed it to her friend. 'Here, you can use this to mop up the blood.'

'Thanks,' murmured Sophie. Gingerly dabbing the cloth against her nose, she added, 'This is a nightmare.'

'So what exactly happened?'

'You know how Harman always goes to her office around this time of day?'

'Aye?'

'Well, today she headed to her private quarters instead, which is pretty unusual to say the least, so I decided to follow her.' Seeing the look on Isla's face, she quickly added, 'I know I shouldn't, but I really thought I could be on to something, so I followed her up the stairs hopin' to see what she was up to, only she must've forgotten somethin' because she come back out of her room while I was still halfway up the stairs.' She rolled her eyes. 'She went ballistic. She was that angry I couldn't even make out half of what she was sayin'. I know I should have come up with an excuse for bein' there, but my feet took over and the next I knew I was in here with you.'

'Oh, Soph . . .'

'I should never have followed her,' said Sophie miserably. 'What the hell am I goin' to do when she catches up with me?'

'Tell her you wanted to have a word but bottled it at the last minute?'

'But what could I possibly have to say to her that would warrant me followin' her to her room, rather than approachin' her outright?'

Isla fell into silent contemplation. There wasn't a doubt in her mind that Harman would punish Sophie severely for following her, so there was only one option. 'Tell her you've heard a rumour that I've been stealin' food from the stores.'

Sophie stared at her aghast. 'I'm not doin' that!'

Isla swallowed. 'You have to, because we both know that without some kind of explanation Harman will do to you what she did to Meg – if not to Kayleigh.'

Sophie was shaking her head fervently. 'I'd rather that than throw you under the bus. This is my mess, not yours.'

'I'll tell her that you've got it wrong! That way the most she can do is punish me for suspected stealin', which will be nothin' in comparison to what she'd do to you for spyin' on her.'

'That's if she even asks for an explanation, cos she didn't with Meg.'

'Then you must explain whether she asks you to or not, and in the meantime you must do your best to keep out of her way. She'll catch up with you eventually, of course, but hopefully she'll have calmed down by then.'

'Avoidin' Harman will be a piece of cake, cos I know her routine. Mary on the other hand will be a different kettle of fish.'

Isla wiped the steam from her forehead with the back of her hand. 'Not to worry. We'll find you somewhere to lay low for a few days.'

Sophie smiled. 'Thanks, Isla. You're a real pal.'

'You'd do the same for me, as would Meg.'

'Talkin' of Meg, where is she?'

'Gone to the lavvy, so she should be back in a jiffy.' As she spoke, Meg walked back into the room. Her face a mask of concern, she headed straight for Isla, who was the only one clearly visible.

'I've just seen Harman and she was furious. She asked me if I'd seen Sophie, and demanded I tell her as soon as I do. I didn't ask what she wanted her for, but I think we'd best find her and tell her to make herself scarce.'

Carefully, Isla glanced over her shoulder, indicating Sophie who was still half hidden beneath the washing but peered out at Meg and gave her a small wave as she passed Isla the piece of cloth she'd been using to stem the flow of blood.

'Oh boy!' breathed Meg. 'Why don't I like the look of this?'

Isla quietly explained Sophie's current situation, ending with: '. . . so that's why Harman's on the warpath.'

Meg swallowed. 'What do we do now?'

'Sophie and I have a plan for if the worst should happen, but we're hopin' Harman will've calmed down before then. It does prove one thing, though.'

'What's that?' said Sophie, settling herself into a more comfortable position.

'You only think you're bein' followed or spied upon if you've got summat to hide,' said Isla, 'the same as it's only people who know they've summat to feel guilty about who act as if they're guilty. And judgin' by the way she reacted I'd say that's Harman to a tee.'

'Without doubt,' agreed Meg. 'I'd love to know what she'd gone to her room for.'

'Thinkin' about it now, I did notice she was decidedly twitchy this mornin' when I left the dinin' hall,' said Isla as she plunged the sheet she was holding back into the water. 'Bit like a cat on a hot tin roof.'

'If she's runnin' two sets of books, I highly doubt she keeps them in the same room,' Sophie said thoughtfully. 'If I were her I'd keep the one for the tax man in her office and the other . . .'

'. . . in her private quarters,' said Isla.

Sophie checked her nose for blood. 'So now we know where they are, all we have to do is work out a way of gettin' our hands on them!'

It was much later that same day and, having successfully hidden Sophie in a disused broom cupboard, Meg and Isla had made it their business to keep their ears to the ground in the hopes that they would learn what Harman and Mary were up to.

'Mary's broken her toe,' said Meg, trying to swallow her grin. 'Which just about serves her right.'

'And as far as I know Harman's retired to her room for the evening,' said Isla.

'So what do we do about Sophie? Cos she's not eaten since breakfast.'

'She's got to have somethin' to eat, but as we cannae smuggle food out to her I reckon we've got no choice but to take her into the dining hall,' said Isla. 'We know Mary won't be on the prowl on account of bein' laid up, and Gordon will have eaten already – as will all the favourites who always get first dibs – so I reckon we're safe enough as long as we wait until the last minute before goin' in. That way we can be in and out in the blink of an eye.'

Agreeing that this was the best course of action, the girls fetched Sophie from her hiding place.

'Are you positive Harman's not around?' Sophie asked as they entered the dining hall.

'I've already checked and Harman's retired to her room the same as she does every evenin'.' Isla stopped talking as they approached the cook, who dutifully dolloped food on to three plates. Taking them to the far end of the room, the girls sat with their backs to the dining room doors so that their faces were shielded from view.

Isla scooped stew on to her spoon while gazing thoughtfully at the barred windows. 'We've just got to find a way of breakin' into her room—'

Nearly choking on her mouthful of stew, Sophie stared at her aghast. 'You must be off your rocker if you think I'm goin' anywhere near her room again!'

'I wouldn't dream of askin' you to go back, but I'm game – if we can find a way in, of course.'

Sophie had just opened her mouth to say she thought the idea very unwise when she caught the reflection of Miss Harman in one of the windows. 'Hide me!'

Isla and Meg instinctively drew together, blocking Sophie from sight. 'Can you still see her?' asked Isla, on the assumption that if Sophie could see Harman the same would be true vice-versa.

'No, but I'd bet a pound to a penny that she's lookin' for me. Why else would she be here?' Sophie froze as Miss Harman's voice came across the room, her tone sharp.

'You, girl!'

Wondering how on earth the older woman had seen her through Isla and Meg, Sophie looked wildly round and caught her own reflection in another of the windows. Her eyes glassy with the tears which had already started to form, she whispered, 'Please don't leave me.'

'Don't you worry. We'll be with you every step of the way,' Isla assured her.

'And if she tries to take you away we'll all make a break for it,' confirmed Meg, although if questioned she'd have to admit she didn't know how they'd do that exactly.

'Come here,' Harman barked, pointing at the floor before her feet.

The silence of the few diners who remained was deafening as Sophie walked towards her, only coming to a halt just before she judged she would step within arm's reach. Feeling everyone's eyes on her, she prayed for it to be over, whatever "it" was, so that she could put the events of the day behind her. *I don't care what she does to me*, Sophie thought now, *as long as she doesn't ask me to explain myself in front of everyone. I cannae bear the thought of them thinkin' I'd willingly snitch on me pals.*

'This,' Miss Harman cried to the room in general, 'is what we do to nasty little busybodies!' Lunging forward, she grabbed Sophie by the wrist and dragged her to the range, which was still lit. Terrified of what she feared the older woman was about to do, Sophie tried to dig her heels in, but it was no good. Grasping Sophie's hands in both of hers, the warden attempted to hold Sophie's bare hand above the brightly burning flame.

Knocking the saucepans over as they rushed forward to save their friend, Isla and Meg were stopped in their tracks as a male voice called out from behind them. It was Mr Ellis.

Chapter Three

'There you are, Sophie. I've been looking everywhere for you!'

Sophie looked at Miss Harman, who was staring at Mr Ellis open-mouthed as he made his way towards them. Seemingly unaware of what had been about to take place, he turned his attention to Miss Harman.

'I can see that you're busy, but would you mind awfully if I stole Sophie from you for half an hour or so? Only I've been wantin' to speak to her since this morning!'

Annoyed that she had been interrupted mid-punishment, Miss Harman eyed him suspiciously. 'And just what, exactly, do you want her for?'

He held her gaze, a smile forming on his lips. 'To see if she'd had a chance to ask you about the play we've been discussing.' He glanced briefly at Sophie's hand, which was no longer above the naked flame, but still in Miss Harman's grasp. 'Am I to take it you don't approve of the idea?' he finished with a hint of sarcasm.

Miss Harman shot him a withering look. She knew

when someone was lying to her, and she'd bet a pound to a penny that he was doing just that. 'Poppycock!'

He blinked. 'I *beg* your pardon?'

'You heard me!' She rolled her eyes. 'Play, indeed.'

'It's true,' said Sophie timidly, her heart hammering in her chest like a bird trapped in a cage. She could only pray that Mr Ellis had something in mind as she continued, 'That's what I wanted to ask you earlier.'

'Is it really?' Her voice dripping with sarcasm, she eyed Mr Ellis in a cynical fashion. 'And what play would this be?'

'*Macbeth*,' he said before Sophie could respond. 'I've already run it past Mr Armitage, and he thinks it a splendid idea.'

Miss Harman's cheeks paled as she released her grip on Sophie. 'How dare you talk to him before coming to me first!' she hissed angrily, the colour returning to her cheeks faster than a river in full flow.

'I didn't mean to tread on anyone's toes,' Mr Ellis assured her. 'I only mentioned it in passin', but he thought it was a brilliant suggestion.'

Her jaw flinched. 'Well, you shouldn't have! The next time you get an idea you run it by me first, understood?'

He smiled pleasantly. 'If you so wish.'

Turning her attention back to Sophie, Miss Harman said suspiciously, 'If you were intending to ask me about the play, why did you not do so when you saw me in the dining hall?'

'I didn't want to get everyone's hopes up in case

you said no, so I thought it best to ask you some-where quiet.'

Miss Harman held her gaze. 'Then why did you run?'

'You started shoutin' at me,' said Sophie. 'You said that I—'

Not keen for Mr Ellis to hear what she had been accusing Sophie of, Miss Harman cut her short. 'Yes, well, never mind that now.' She turned accusingly to Mr Ellis. 'Why send one of the girls to ask me when you could easily have done so yourself?'

Sophie held her breath. Of all the questions Harman had posed so far this was the one where he was most likely to come unstuck.

'Because Sophie has experience with this sort of thing, what with her mother coming from a theatri-cal background and all, so if you had any questions she'd be able to answer them far better than I could.'

Praying with all her might that Harman wouldn't question her on her mother's theatrical experience – of which she had none – Sophie was relieved when the older woman continued to quiz Mr Ellis. 'Plays cost money which we don't have, so you needn't think—'

To her surprise, he'd already begun to speak over her. 'Mr Armitage has already assured me that they'll provide the fundin' should the play go ahead.'

Isla could see by the greedy look that swept Har-man's features that the play was now a done deal. 'You're to run everything past me first, and I have the final say on all decisions. Understood?'

'Of course! I wouldn't dream of doin' otherwise.'

Giving a short sharp 'Hurrumph', Miss Harman left the dining hall. Sophie opened her mouth to thank her saviour, but he was indicating the doors with a jerk of his head.

'Not here. Come with me.'

She gave Isla and Meg a small shrug as she followed in his wake.

Watching them make their way across the hall, Meg opened her mouth to speak, but Isla was shaking her head. 'Come on,' she hissed, and they too left the hall.

'Where are we goin'?' asked Meg as she trotted to catch up.

'Somewhere we cannae be overheard,' said Isla. Pushing the laundry door open, she headed for the drying room. Checking that there was no one else around, Meg asked the question uppermost in her thoughts.

'What in God's name was all that about?'

'I haven't the foggiest! But I hope to goodness he wasn't makin' the whole thing up, because she'll know for sure it was all a lie if he tries to back out.'

'Well, he was obviously makin' up the part about askin' Sophie to help him put on a play, because she'd have told us if that were the case.'

'I reckon it was all true bar the part where he'd asked Sophie to speak to Harman,' said Isla decidedly.

'So you think there really is a play?'

Isla shrugged. 'I'd say so. What do you think?'

'Unless he was making the whole thing up on the spot – which I highly doubt – I'd say there has to be,' said Meg slowly, adding, 'I'd like to know where he's taken her.'

'Somewhere quiet so that he can explain himself, I expect. After all, he's got quite a bit of explainin' to do!'

Meg leaned against a mangle. 'I guess we're goin' to have to be patient and wait for Sophie to come back, cos if there's one thing we've learned from all this it's not to go spyin' on people – they don't like it!'

Sophie was still following Mr Ellis, wondering why he'd created such an elaborate story when Harman was bound to find out he'd made the whole thing up. *And just who is this Mr Armitage*, thought Sophie as they hurried on, *cos Harman looked like she'd seen a ghost at the mere mention of his name*. Deciding that whoever he was he must be important, Sophie nearly cannoned into the back of Mr Ellis when he stopped abruptly outside the door to a storage room, making sure that no one was around before ushering her inside and closing the door behind them. Sophie glanced round the room, which was only slightly bigger than the cupboard in which she'd been hiding from Miss Harman earlier in the day. Wondering if she should say something, she watched Mr Ellis take two chairs from a stack and put them down facing each other.

'We shouldn't be disturbed here,' he said. Indicating that she should sit, he turned his own chair the wrong way round and sat astride it. Folding his arms on top of the back, he spoke matter-of-factly. 'So tell me, Sophie, just why have you and your pals been spyin' on Miss Harman? You must've realised it was a dangerous thing to do, yet you did it anyway. Question is, why take such a risk when you're aware of the consequences?'

Sophie's first instinct was to deny everything, but to do so would be pointless as well as insulting, when he clearly knew that not only had she been watching Miss Harman, but her friends had too. Rather than answer, she turned the question around. 'More to the point, what makes you think we've been spying on her?'

'Because you and your pals aren't the only ones keepin' an eye on what goes on around here.'

Sophie stared at him. Just how much did he know, and was he as suspicious as they were when it came to Harman swindling the government as well as the poorhouse out of money? Not that she could put the question to him outright, of course. *You turned his first question back on him and got an answer*, thought Sophie as she eyed him levelly; *why not do the same again?* She cleared her throat. 'So, you think she's up to somethin'?'

To her disappointment, he flicked the question back on her. 'Do you?'

Sophie leaned back in her chair. *This is like a game of chess. If I answer in a roundabout way, but with facts, not theories, I might be able to put him in checkmate.* 'She was about to burn my hand on the cooker, and no matter which way you look at it, followin' someone doesn't deserve punishment of that nature! Just as she shouldn't have burned Meg with a red-hot poker just for asking whether Madson was workin' at the poorhouse, which on the face of it was a perfectly reasonable assumption what with him spendin' so much time here. So in answer to your question, I find it hard to believe that someone would behave in such a fashion if they hadn't got somethin' to hide.' Pleased with her answer, she hoped that he would reply in kind, but it seemed that he too was holding his cards close to his chest.

'Agreed. But what exactly did you hope to achieve by followin' her?'

Abandoning the game of cat and mouse, she decided to speak her mind. 'To expose her for what she is! The woman shouldn't be in charge of a dog, never mind human beings, and yet everyone turns a blind eye. Well, not any more. We're determined to find out what she's up to so that we can put a stop to her antics.' Her words caught up with her as she realised what she'd said. 'Only you're not turnin' a blind eye, are you?'

'No. So why don't you leave this to me?'

She eyed him shrewdly. They'd said all along that Mr Ellis was unlike any other member of staff they'd ever come across, which meant there was only one response. 'Who are you, Mr Ellis? Or should I say *what* are you?'

He smiled, causing dimples to puncture his cheeks, but ignored her question. 'You say you've been keepin' an eye on Miss Harman. Is she the only one who's been in your sights?'

Miffed at his failure to answer her question but

curious as to where he was going with his own, she simply replied, 'We're almost positive that Madson's in cahoots with her, but it's a tad difficult to keep an eye on someone who doesn't actually work here. We don't know how much the government gives Harman to run this place, but from what we've seen very little of it can be going where it's meant to.'

He gave her a small, silent round of applause. 'My hat goes off to you and your pals. She certainly hasn't managed to pull the wool over *your* eyes!'

She eyed him steadily. 'You still haven't answered my question.'

A soft chuckle emanated from deep in his throat. 'I'm interested to hear your thoughts, seein' as you're quite the sleuth. How about you tell me?'

'I thought at first you might be some sort of inspector, but of course you can't be, because Madson would know if you were. And you obviously know this Mr Armitage, whoever he is, far better than Harman does, but she does know of him, and judgin' by the look on her face when you mentioned his name, he's someone she's wary of. So as she's not scared of anyone, I can only assume that he's one of the bigger bigwigs.' She tapped her forefinger against her chin. 'Bearin' all that in mind, I'd say you work for him, not her, but in what capacity I cannae say.'

There was no mistaking the admiration on Mr Ellis's face. 'How did such an intelligent woman wind up in a dump like this?'

She smiled without happiness. 'Circumstance.'

Shaking his head, he revealed the truth. 'I used to

be a policeman, but now I work as a private dick. With my coming from Liverpool it was thought that no one in Clydebank would rumble me, which is why Mr Armitage hired me to find out what's really going on at Coxhill, in which he has an interest.'

Sophie had to stop herself from crying out in triumph. Until a few minutes ago it would never have occurred to her that Mr Ellis was anything other than a member of staff, but to learn that he had been sent to Coxhill to uncover the truth was like music to her ears. 'So he does know that all is not as it should be, then?'

'A blind man could see she's creamin' money off the top, but gettin' proof has proved difficult when she has someone like Madson in her corner.'

'Well, me and the girls did hope someone like you would be takin' over from Harman, because we think you'd do a smashin' job, but at least you're here to get shot of her, so we cannae grumble at that.'

Flattered that Sophie and her friends appeared to have so much faith in him, he apologised for disappointing her before continuing. 'Now, as we're all singin' from the same hymn sheet, what proof were you hopin' to find that would lead to Harman's downfall?'

'My father was an accountant before he passed, and an honest one at that I might add, but he did tell me stories of people that kept two sets of books, one with the real figures and one for the tax man, and we figure that's what Harman's doin'.'

He eyed her approvingly. 'I have to congratulate

you yet again, because your suspicions are right in line with my own. However, I think it best if you leave the detecting up to me from now on.'

'As you wish, but what about the play? I appreciate you made the whole *Macbeth* thing up to save my skin, but—'

He was wagging his finger. 'Only in part. You see, we need a distraction so that we can search her rooms for evidence.'

'Very clever!'

'It certainly worked out well for you,' agreed Mr Ellis. He paused as an idea occurred to him. 'I know I said leave everythin' to me now, but would you be totally against the idea if I involved the three of you in my plan – when I know exactly what it is?'

Sophie replied without hesitation. 'You can count on us!'

It was much later that evening when Sophie returned to the dorm. Standing in the doorway, she beckoned for her pals to join her, only speaking when they were far from wagging ears. 'Boy oh boy, have I got a tale to tell the two of you!'

'I should jolly well hope so,' said Isla. 'We've been worried sick!'

'That cow Mary's been tellin' everyone that Harman's goin' to sack Ellis, and that she'll be dealin' with you just as soon as she's got rid of him,' muttered Meg.

A smug smile creased Sophie's cheeks. 'That's cos

Mary's not got a clue as to what she's talkin' about. If only she knew the truth!'

Meg and Isla exchanged curious glances, Isla being the first to ask the question on both their minds. 'So come on, then! Don't keep us in suspenders!'

Delighted to put Mary's rumours to rest, and keeping a lookout for eavesdroppers, Sophie told them all about her conversation with Ellis. 'So you see,' she finished, 'it looks as though our plans to oust Harman could actually come to fruition!'

Meg blew out her cheeks. 'I know we were determined to knock her off her throne, but I don't think I ever truly believed we would. Now I do!'

Sophie was watching Isla, who appeared deep in thought. 'Isla?'

Breaking out of her trance, Isla looked up. 'You said somethin' about his usin' the play to create a distraction while he searches her rooms?'

'That's right.'

'Surely it would be easier if we were the ones doin' the searchin'? After all, she's bound to get suspicious if he disappears for too long, what with the play bein' his idea an' all.'

'True, but at the same time she'd miss three people far more than one,' Sophie said reasonably.

'Not if we're hiding in plain sight she won't,' said Isla, her tone heavy with glee.

Meg was looking totally lost. 'Eh?'

'Actors wear costumes,' explained Isla, 'and they quite often have understudies in case they cannae perform for one reason or another. If we take various roles in the play, such as the three witches for argument's sake, Harman wouldn't have a clue who was really under the hair and makeup.'

A slow smile worked its way up Meg's cheeks. 'So we can be off searchin' her room while she believes us to be on stage!'

'Exactly! Ellis cannae do it, cos if somethin' goes wrong durin' the play it'll be him they turn to.'

Sophie clapped her hands together excitedly. 'By Jove, I think you've cracked it – all we have to do now is run it past Ellis, but I cannae see him sayin' no!'

It was the following day, and after having used the play as an excuse to talk to Mr Ellis, Sophie was returning to her friends with the good news.

'He thinks it a brilliant idea,' she said, beaming, 'but he wants to keep our involvement between the four of us, meanin' he won't be tellin' that Armitage feller.'

'Why not?' asked Isla, disappointed to hear they were being kept under wraps.

'He reckons that Armitage would forbid us to take part for fear of what might happen should we be discovered. He said it's one thing him puttin' his neck on the line, but if people found out that we were involved Harman could say that we had a personal vendetta against her and that we'd planted evidence just to get her out, which means any proof he had wouldn't be admissible in court.'

Meg shrugged. 'Doesn't bother me if Armitage doesn't know. It's nailin' Harman that's important.'

'True, but it doesn't solve our predicament,' said Isla, 'cos Coxhill will be no picnic even with someone else in charge, and I don't intend stayin' here till the day I die.'

Meg spoke slowly. 'If distractin' Harman works for Ellis, then why shouldn't it work for us too?'

Sophie gave her an encouraging nod. 'Go on.'

'As she always keeps her room locked, he must be plannin' on getting hold of her keys somehow,' said Meg, 'in which case we'd be able to unlock any door we chose, includin' the front one!'

'But what about money and papers?' said Sophie, who, although excited at the prospect of freedom, was determined to not get overexcited quite yet.

'I'm sure Ellis wouldn't mind bungin' us a few coins to tide us over till we can find work,' said Isla. 'After all, we're practically doin' his job for him!'

'I suppose it doesn't harm to ask,' said Sophie.

Giving a small whoop of joy, Isla flung her arms around her friends. 'We're goin' to get out of here, I just know it!'

JANUARY 1941

A month had passed since Sophie's initial meeting with Mr Ellis, and an awful lot had happened in that time, the most important part being his agreement to turn a blind eye to their escape whilst giving them some money to help them on their way.

Coxhill had gone from a place of pure misery to somewhere that gave people a purpose, albeit a temporary one. Miss Harman's strict rules had been somewhat relaxed, because, as Mr Ellis had rightly pointed out, they could hardly be asked to perform in a play if they weren't allowed to discuss their roles.

'It's as if the play itself has breathed life into the place,' Isla had said as they readied themselves for bath night.

'People are actually smilin' because they've got somethin' to smile about,' agreed Meg.

'Not half as much as they'll smile when Harman's given her marchin' orders,' said Sophie.

Isla beamed. 'Or us when we sneak out the front door.' She glanced to where Sophie was stripping in readiness for her turn in the bath. 'Have you ever thought how fortunate it was for us that Harman caught you spyin' that day?'

'Many times,' said Sophie as she climbed into the tub, 'cos had Mr Ellis not got involved, we'd still be none the wiser as to his real role in Coxhill, and goodness only knows what sort of trouble we could've got into if we'd not taken a step back when we did.'

'I honestly worried that the others would get suspicious,' said Meg, 'but everyone's so excited about the play they talk of nothin' else.'

'Even Harman!' agreed Isla. 'I overheard her tellin' one of the inspectors how she'd come up with the idea for the play when thinkin' about how to best occupy the residents.'

'*Residents*!' echoed Sophie, 'Since when have we been residents? Inmates yes, the convicted even, but *residents*?'

'It was all I could do to stop myself from laughin' out loud,' admitted Isla. 'It makes it sound as if we're livin' in a hotel, but as far as I'm aware even the worst hotels don't serve their guests gruel for breakfast!'

'They'd be out of business if they did,' said Sophie.

'I just hope everyone remembers everythin' when it comes to the night of the play,' said Isla. 'You know what an evil witch Harman can be on a regular day; imagine what she'd be like should one of them forget their lines in front of her precious governors!'

'And they're bound to be more nervous with her starin' at them,' agreed Meg. 'Little do they know that she'll be gone before the curtain's dropped.'

Isla was looking thoughtful as she asked: 'We're doin' all this work, but has Ellis said whether he's got a plan in place for the actual night? Only I cannae help but wonder what we're meant to do with the books should we find them, and will he confront her there and then, or . . .'

'I cannae see why not,' said Sophie; 'he'll have all the proof he'll need.'

'Only against Harman, though,' said Meg. 'Even with both sets of books, we'll still have nothin' on Madson.'

'Surely his constant visits would be proof enough that he's as guilty as she?' said Sophie.

'I doubt it, but does it really matter as long as Harman gets the boot?'

'It's just that I hate to see an injustice, and knowin' that Madson's as much to blame for the state of this place as her it grieves me to see him get away with it,' said Isla.

'Then we'll just have to hope that Ellis can find somethin' to tie Madson in to all of this,' said Sophie, 'cos if anyone can, it's him.'

MARCH 1941

It was the day of the first dress rehearsal and the girls had decided to use the opportunity to treat it as a trial run for the actual night by leaving the hall while the play was on, to see if anyone noticed.

'I don't think I've ever felt this nervous in my life,' Sophie told her friends, adjusting her witch's costume, 'Goodness knows what I'll be like on openin' night!'

Isla, who was also feeling decidedly anxious, agreed. 'I think we're all feelin' the same way. I don't have to do anythin' bar watch Harman and make sure she doesn't leave her seat, yet I still feel as though I've been caught with my hand in the till.'

'Because you know how important it is we get this right,' said Meg as they walked over to Mr Ellis, who was standing in the wings.

He turned on hearing their voices and smiled briefly. 'What's up? You look as though you've lost a pound and found a penny.'

'We feel that way, too,' said Sophie. 'Have you figured out a plan for gettin' her keys yet?'

He indicated for them to draw closer. 'I'm goin' to pick her pocket whilst I'm sitting behind her.'

86

Sophie paled. 'And what will you do if she feels you?' She paused. 'Have you ever even picked someone's pocket before?'

'No-o, but it can't be that hard, and as for what I'll do if she feels me? I guess I'll have to cross that bridge if I come to it.'

Meg placed her hands on her hips. 'Too great a risk. I'll do it.'

Isla scoffed. 'Oh no you won't!'

Meg, however, was resolute. 'Why not? It's not as if I haven't done it before.'

Isla and Sophie exchanged glances. 'Are you sure you know what it means to pick someone's pocket?' asked Isla, convinced that their friend must have got hold of the wrong end of the stick.

Meg felt her cheeks grow warm. 'I only did it a couple of times, and only on my uncle.' Seeing the look of confusion on their faces, she went on to explain that she'd been sent to live with her aunt and uncle after her parents had passed away. 'Mam would never have wanted me livin' with them, because they're a couple of tea leaves,' she finished, 'but it was either live with them or end up here.'

'So you chose Coxhill?' asked Sophie in disbelief.

'God no! But my uncle insisted I help him work the market, meaning he wanted me to pick people's pockets. I knew I couldn't go through with it, but thought I'd buy myself some time if I showed willin' by practisin' on him. I hoped they'd change their minds in the meantime, but they didn't, and when I refused to do as they asked they kicked me out. I lived on the streets for a couple of days, but by the third day I was starvin' hungry and that's when I got caught nickin' a loaf of bread that had fallen on the floor. I knew I shouldn't have done it, but I was desperate. As soon as the authorities realised I had no home or family to speak of, they put me in Coxhill.'

'Are you sure you're still able to do it?' asked Mr Ellis slowly. 'Because we've only got one shot at this.'

'Which is precisely why I should be the one doin' it,' said Meg. 'After all, I have considerably more experience than yourself.'

'She can always practise on me and Isla,' supposed Sophie.

'If you're sure?'

Meg nodded. 'Positive.'

'In that case, it's just the matter of your clothes.'

'What about them?' asked Isla, looking down at her smock.

'You won't get far looking like that, so I've bought you a frock each to get changed into on the night.'

Isla stared at him. 'That's very kind of you, but wouldn't it be easier for us to wear the clothes we came in with?'

'Harman doesn't keep anyone's clothes, on account of not thinkin' they'll ever need them again,' said Ellis leadenly.

Isla's face fell. 'I could kind of understand her sellin' Mam's locket down the pawnbrokers, but what would she do with our clothes?'

'Sell them for rags,' said Mr Ellis bluntly.

'She really is the lowest of the low,' said Isla. 'The sooner we get her out of here the better!'

It was the night of the play and the girls were having a hard time trying to contain their excitement.

'I cannae believe we're goin' to be out of here in less than five hours!' said Meg, who was eager for the off.

'I just hope to goodness that we find somethin',' said Isla, 'cos I'd feel a real heel runnin' off into the sunset leavin' everyone behind to deal with Harman – in fact, I don't think I could!'

'A bit like "I'm all right Jack",' agreed Sophie, 'but I'm sure Ellis will find a way to get rid of her even if we cannae.'

'I'd still feel bad for him, though,' said Isla, 'a bit like we'd let him down.'

'If there's nothin' there to find, then that's not our fault,' reasoned Meg, 'but we all know she's hidin' somethin', and as she won't have a clue anyone's on to her I'm hopin' that she won't have hidden it too well.'

'We'll certainly have plenty of time to have a good root round,' said Sophie, 'and goin' off the size of the ledgers my father used to keep, they're not somethin' that can be easily hidden.'

Isla gave a sharp intake of breath as her eyes fell on Mr Ellis, who was helping some of the actors to prepare. 'Just seein' him gets my stomach turnin' cartwheels. Do you think it will look suspicious if we go over to talk to him?'

'I think it would look suspicious if we didn't!' said Sophie. 'Just look at the people waitin' to speak to him.'

'Nerves,' said Meg. 'They're all lookin' to him for a bit of reassurance. Sophie's right, it'd look odd if we didn't do the same.'

'We'd best join the queue then,' said Sophie, 'because we've still got important matters to sort ahead of tonight!'

Isla tutted as others joined the queue behind them. 'How are we meant to ask him anythin' about this evenin' with so many waggin' ears around?' she hissed to Sophie.

Sophie had been wondering the same thing when Mr Ellis beckoned them over. Excusing himself from the line of anxious actors, he proclaimed in a loud voice, 'There you are, you three. Come with me – I've a job for you to do before curtain up.'

Following him round to the back of the stage, all the girls began speaking at once.

Pumping his hands in a placating fashion, he spoke in a calming manner. 'One at a time!'

Sophie was the first to make herself heard. 'What do we do with the books when we find them?'

'Remember the storage room where we first discussed the play?'

'I do, aye.'

'Leave the books underneath the stack of chairs. You'll find three bags containin' the coats and frocks I bought for you to change into there. I've had to guess your sizes, so I'm sorry if they're not an exact fit, but they'll certainly do for the time being.'

'What happens if we don't find the books?' asked Isla gravely.

'We continue with the plan.'

'But what about Harman?' said Sophie. 'It doesn't seem right that we get to walk away whilst she continues to rule the roost.'

'That will be my problem, not yours,' he assured them, 'and I've every faith that we'll catch her out one way or another.' He looked to each of them in turn. 'Are you still happy to go ahead?'

They all nodded. 'Terribly nervous,' confessed Isla, 'but it would be strange if we weren't.'

Sophie glanced over to where one of the witches was looking for her nose, which had rolled under the cauldron on the stage. 'You've just told a queue of people that you had a job for us before curtain up, so you'd best give us somethin' to do.'

'Good point!' He fell into silent thought before carrying on, 'As you don't have to practise your lines, or have anythin' to do with the play, you can make sure everyone has everythin' they need, that should help me out.' He indicated the queue of people waiting to speak to him.

'Consider it done,' said Isla.

It was much later that evening, and the girls were waiting in the wings with nervous anticipation.

Sophie held up a trembling hand to show Isla. 'I hope Meg's not shakin' like a leaf as well, cos that *definitely* wouldn't be helpful right now.' She glanced towards Ally – the girl who would be taking her place on stage. 'I've told Ally that she has to go on because I've got a nervous tummy.'

Isla followed her gaze. 'How did she take it?'

'I think she was secretly pleased, because I know she worked really hard at rememberin' the lines.'

'Me and Meg did the same, only Meg said she was too nervous to remember her lines, and I told Lucy I had a sore throat so couldn't talk properly.' She demonstrated this by saying the last few words in a croaky voice. 'I reckon they were just as pleased as Ally!'

'Excellent!' said Sophie. 'Does anyone else know about the switch? By anyone else I really mean Mary and Gordon, because they're the main ones we have to watch out for.'

'Don't worry – they haven't the foggiest,' said Isla smugly. 'They're far too nervous to notice what's goin' on around them.'

Sophie looked shocked. 'Mary? Nervous? I didn't think people like her got nervous.'

'Well, she's bitten her nails to the quick, and I think she'd start on Gordon's if he stood still long enough.' Isla jerked her head to a lumbering individual who was pacing the boards. 'I reckon he must've lost a few pounds in sweat alone.'

Sophie looked at Gordon with an air of satisfaction. 'Good! Now they know how everyone else feels when they go runnin' to Harman!'

They both started as Ellis clapped his hands to gain everyone's attention. 'This is it, folks! Has everyone got what they're meant to have?' He glanced around the gathered actors, all of whom were checking themselves over with a general murmur of yeses. 'In that case: places, everybody, and break a leg!'

He hastened past Isla and Sophie, hissing, 'Good luck. I'll be keepin' everythin' crossed for you!'

Sophie swallowed. 'You too,' she said, before jerking her head at Isla, indicating that it was time they were off.

They heard the audience go quiet as they slunk out of the hall. 'Fingers crossed . . .' Isla began, before gasping in surprise. 'What the heck are you doin' here?'

Meg held up the keys. 'Easy as pie! I got them off her as soon as she sat down.'

Instinctively, they looked round to where Harman was sitting, and Sophie jerked her head towards the man who had taken the seat next to her. 'No need for anyone to worry where Madson is, not with him sitting front and centre.'

'What if—' Isla began, but Meg was shooing them off.

'The time for chat has passed. Get you gone, and good luck, and don't worry about who's doin' what cos I'll be keepin' watch to make sure everyone's where they should be.'

Isla gave her a mock salute as she and Sophie headed off. 'Did you see the look on Madson's face?' Sophie asked her. 'He was lookin' proud as a peacock, the slimy git.'

'I'd love to be a fly on the wall when Ellis confronts him with the ledgers – that'll soon wipe the look off his face, especially if they link the books to him somehow!' replied Isla as they trotted along the corridor towards Harman's office. Looking through the keys as they went, Isla felt her heart sink. 'It's goin' to take us for ever to find the right one to unlock her room!'

'Good job we've plenty of time then,' said Sophie as they reached the office door. Testing the handle she tutted. 'Darn! I hoped she might've forgotten to lock it, what with one thing and another.'

Isla held up the keys. 'Some of these have red ribbons, others white, and some green. Why do you suppose that is?'

'I'm guessin' that the white ones correspond to one room, the red another, and the green a third.'

'That should make things a tad easier!' said Isla as she began trying the largest of the red-ribboned keys in the lock. Feeling it turn, she smiled. 'We're in!' Ushering Sophie through, she closed the door softly behind them, making sure to lock it again before they began their search. 'Just in case someone comes along,' she explained to Sophie, who was already determining which drawers were locked and which were open.

'I'll search the ones that are open,' she said. 'You start on the ones that are locked.'

Isla knew which drawer she wanted to search first; it was the one into which Miss Harman had put her necklace when she first arrived. Trying each of the remaining red-ribboned keys in the lock she felt her heart leap as the drawer opened on her fourth attempt – *please be in here* – thought Isla as she began to push the various pieces of paperwork to one side, but a quick yet thorough search soon revealed the necklace to be gone, and any ledger nowhere in sight.

Sophie had turned to ask for the keys so that she could unlock the filing cabinet, when she saw the disappointment on her friend's face. Walking over, she laid a reassuring hand on Isla's shoulder. 'It's the first drawer you've looked in. She could well have moved it, remember.'

'I suppose you're right,' said Isla, but deep down she felt in her heart that the necklace was gone.

Taking the keys, Sophie quickly unlocked the filing cabinet using the smallest key in the bunch before tossing them back to Isla.

The girls continued their search in complete silence, and it didn't take Isla long to ascertain that the rest of the drawers on that side of the desk – all of which were unlocked – were devoid of anything of importance. Swiftly moving to the other side, she was pleased to find that the top drawer was locked. Trying the keys in turn, she spoke to Sophie as one of them turned in the lock. 'I reckon we need only search the ones that are locked,' she told Sophie as she opened the drawer, 'cos if it's goin' to be anywhere it's goin' to be—Bingo!' She pulled out a large book with a red spine, and quickly flicked through the pages, all of which contained several columns, each itemising a sum spent and what on.

'Well done, Isla!' hissed Sophie, before also crying

out in shock, but for a different reason. 'I've found our documents!'

Isla hurried over to join her. 'Are you *sure*?'

'Positive!' said Sophie. She was about to hand them over when she noticed the date on Isla's birth certificate. 'It's your birthday!' she cried. 'Why didn't you say?'

Isla blinked. 'I'd forgotten all about it, what with one thing and another.'

Sophie handed Isla several pieces of paperwork, including her birth certificate. 'Well happy birthday! Seventeen today, eh?'

'It'll be the best birthday ever if we find the other ledger,' said Isla. Pausing, she ran her fingers over her parents' names. 'What do you suppose we do with these? If we take them Harman will know that we had a part to play in outing her, which from what Ellis said wouldn't please Armitage any, but it'll make life a lot easier when it comes to gettin' jobs and the like.'

'It's an easy decision as far as I'm concerned,' said Sophie. 'Life will be a lot easier with documents than without, and I highly doubt Harman will ever be in a position to search through the filing cabinet if we manage to find the other ledger!'

'Agreed,' said Isla, who was already tucking her paperwork into the pocket of her smock. 'Have you found Meg's?'

'Aye,' said Sophie as she locked the filing cabinet. 'I've put them with my own.'

Isla was looking round the room. 'Can you see any-where else she might've hidden the other ledger?'

'Not really,' said Sophie. 'She cannae lodge it up the chimney – for obvious reasons – and apart from the furniture I cannae see anywhere else a large book like that could be hidden.'

'Me neither,' agreed Isla. Tucking the ledger down her front, she headed for the door. Listening to make sure she couldn't hear the sound of approaching foot-steps, she unlocked the door and peered out into the corridor. Giving each other the thumbs-up they both stepped outside, Isla locking the door behind them. 'One down, one to go.'

Trotting along the lengthy corridor, both girls looked anxiously through the windows of empty rooms as they passed. 'I keep expectin' someone to jump out at us,' said Sophie as her own reflection caused her to start.

'Me too!' hissed Isla. 'It's because we know we shouldn't be here.'

'Guilty conscience,' agreed Sophie, as Isla followed her up the flight of steps which led to Harman's pri-vate quarters.

Glancing nervously around, Sophie looked back to Isla, who had reached the top of the stairs and was trying the largest of the five keys marked with white ribbon. To her delight the lock clicked at the first turn. She gave Sophie a grim smile. 'Here goes nothin'.'

Following her into the room, Sophie hurried over to a large chest of drawers, all of which were locked.

'It's got to be in one of these,' she said. Half confident, half praying that she was right, she took the keys from Isla. 'No one has locks on their chest of drawers unless they've somethin' to hide,' she told Isla from over her shoulder. 'It looks to me as though she had these specially fitted.' A minute later, crowing with delight, she extracted a ledger identical to the one they had found in the office. 'I cannae believe we found it so quickly!' she gasped, as a quick flick through the pages confirmed her hopes. 'We've got her bang to rights now!'

She held the book aloft as she turned to face Isla, who was as white as a sheet. His arm hooked around Isla's neck, Madson was grinning. 'What a pity you'll never get to show it to anyone.'

Chapter Four

Sophie clutched the ledger close to her chest as she desperately fought for something to say that would buy their way out of their current predicament whilst still allowing them to escape with both ledgers, but with Madson holding all the cards she only had one choice.

'I'll give you the ledger just as soon as you let her go!'

Madson was shaking his head, an evil smile splitting his lips as he held out his free hand. 'You first.'

Sophie tightened her grip. She might be desperate to see her friend freed, but she also knew better than to hand over the only bargaining chip she had. 'Not until you let her go!'

He gave a disbelieving laugh. 'You must think I come down in the last shower!' He looked at Isla's hands, which were folded firmly around her waist, before glancing round the rest of the room. 'Where's the other one?'

He doesn't know Isla's got it, thought Sophie. Hoping that her face hadn't give the game away she replied in what she hoped was a nonchalant manner. 'What other one?'

'Don't give me that!' scoffed Madson. 'I wasn't born yesterday – now tell me where it is or your little pal here will suffer the consequences!'

'You harm a hair on her head, and . . .'

'And what?' sneered Madson. 'Do you seriously think I can be threatened by a couple of girls? Do me a favour!'

Sophie felt the anger rise inside her. How dare he dismiss them, just because they were women? 'Which only goes to show how ignorant you are!' she seethed, but this only caused him to laugh all the harder.

'You'll be laughin' on the other side of your face when they send . . . you . . . down . . .' Isla began, but his grip had tightened, squashing the words back into her throat. Scared that Madson might take things too far, Sophie hurriedly placed the book on top of the chest of drawers and backed away.

'There! Take it.'

Dragging Isla over to the chest, Madson picked the ledger up with his free hand, but before he could shake it open and look between the pages Isla had kicked back hard with her heel, whilst simultaneously turning her head and biting his wrist. Yowling with pain, Madson ripped his arm from between her teeth, then threw the ledger into the fire. Having fallen during the commotion, Isla was scrambling to her feet shouting 'Run, Sophie!' as he grabbed the poker from the fireplace. 'I'll teach you not to bite, you evil little bitch!'

Terrified that he was about to commit murder, Sophie instinctively grabbed the coal shovel and flung it at Madson's head with what turned out to be pinpoint accuracy. Reeling with pain, he stumbled around blindly, his hands clasped to his head, while Sophie kicked the ledger out of the fire. Stamping on the barely singed pages, she picked it up and yelled at Isla to run.

They were halfway across the room when Meg came rushing through the door. 'Madson—' she cried, only to be cut off by Isla.

'We know! For God's sake run!'

Hurtling down the stairs as fast as their legs would carry them, they heard Madson cry out as he tripped in his haste to pursue them. Tumbling down the stairs faster than they could run, he ploughed into the back of Sophie, who in turn cannoned into Isla and Meg. All three girls landed in a heap at the bottom of the stairs and quickly scrambled to their feet, turning to see that Madson had apparently been knocked out cold during the fall and was lying motionless behind them.

Sprinting down the corridor, Isla spoke between snatched gasps. 'Does Ellis know what's goin' on?'

'I reckon so, cos it was he who brought my attention to Madson's empty seat,' said Meg breathlessly. 'I'm so sorry. I should never have taken my eye off him.'

'Not to worry,' panted Isla, 'all's well that ends well.'

'What worries me is why he came lookin' in the first place,' said Sophie.

'God only knows, but if Harman had anythin' to do

with it she'll know that somethin's up when he fails to come back,' said Meg.

Sophie pointed to Mr Ellis, who was standing in the doorway of the storage cupboard. Ushering them inside, he brought them up to speed as he closed the door behind them. 'Harman's gettin' twitchy, so I'm guessin' she's realised somethin's afoot, which means you have to get out of here *now*.' He looked to Meg. 'Did you find Madson?'

The girls told him of their encounter. 'I don't know how long it will take for him to come to, but at least we managed to rescue this from the fire,' said Sophie, passing him the ledger she had been clutching as she fell.

Ellis smoothed his hand over the cover. 'Is this all you found?'

Isla withdrew something from the top of her smock in answer and handed it to him. 'Ta-dah!'

Breathing a sigh of relief, Ellis began flipping through the pages of both books. He was grinning as he turned to face the girls. 'Identical products, at very different prices,' he told them. 'We've got Harman bang to rights; Madson too with a bit of luck. But we can't afford to hang around. I'll go and open the main door while the three of you get changed.' He took the keys from Sophie and left them to it.

Taking a bag each, the girls took out the frocks and held them up for size. 'Pretty much the same, a bit like us,' said Isla as she changed from the smock into a pale-yellow frock.

'I'm so glad we found both ledgers,' said Sophie

as she donned a navy-blue shirtwaist dress. 'I feel a lot better knowin' we've held up our side of the bargain.'

Meg was doing up the buttons of a gingham frock. 'What should we do with the smocks?'

'Leave them here,' said Isla, slipping her arms through the sleeves of her coat. 'It's not as if they can tell whose is whose.'

The girls fell silent as Ellis knocked gently on the door. 'Are you decent?'

Rather than call out to him, Meg opened the door enough for him to squeeze through, and he jangled the keys as he held them up. 'All done!'

'Do you think Madson will tell them that I attacked him?' asked Sophie. 'Only you know what they're like! They're bound to take his word over mine.'

'Madson admit he had anythin' to do with it?' scoffed Ellis. 'No chance!' He peered through the door to make sure the coast was clear before beckoning the girls to follow him. 'Quick!'

'So this really is it?' said Isla, her tone heavy with disbelief, as they stepped out into the corridor. 'We're actually gettin' out of here?'

Hurrying to the door, Ellis pulled a piece of paper out from his pocket and handed it to Sophie. 'This is the address of my sister Irene, who lives in Liverpool. I've already written to her explainin' everythin', so you needn't worry you'll be turnin' up unannounced.' Taking an envelope from his other pocket he pushed it into her unresisting hand and smiled at all three of them. 'There's enough money in there to cover your train tickets, as well as a bit extra for food and keep – if you're frugal it should last until you find employment.'

Sophie looked at him uncertainly as she felt the weight of the envelope. It far exceeded anything she had been expecting. 'Are you sure?'

'Positive. In fact, you all deserve a lot more than I can afford to give. And as for our Irene? She'll be more than happy to help, because she would never turn away a damsel in distress.'

Sophie shook his hand enthusiastically. 'Thanks for everythin', Mr Ellis. You're a bloomin' hero – I hope you know that!'

He gave an embarrassed smile as he held the door open for them. 'Please, call me Harvey.'

Meg spoke quietly as she followed Sophie out of the building. 'Ta-ra, Harvey! You're a star!'

'We can never thank you enough for all you've done,' said Isla, following Meg outside.

'Nor I you,' he said. Then, hearing a splatter of applause, he began to close the door, saying as he did so, 'Good luck, ladies, and say hello to Irene for me.'

The three women stood looking at each other in stunned silence. Unable to believe that they were really free, it was Sophie who spoke first.

'What are we standin' here for? Let's go!'

Sprinting in the direction of the station, Meg gave a whoop of joy as the wind rushed through her hair. 'We're free!' Isla whooped too, grabbing her hand, and Sophie thought about warning them not to celebrate until their eggs were hatched, but even she had to admit that nothing could go wrong. Not now.

Knowing that time was of the essence, Ellis slipped back into the storage room and retrieved both ledgers. Taking them to Harman's office, he swiftly unlocked the door and hurried inside to place them on her desk, then locked the door again before returning to the hall, where he found Mr Armitage waiting for him along with two policemen. Eyeing him in an interrogatory manner, Mr Armitage asked just one question.

'Well?'

'It's just as we thought – two sets of books, both of which are currently in her office.' They turned as the doors to the hall opened and the audience began to file out. Many of them paused to congratulate Mr Ellis on a job well done, although he was sure most of them had only stopped to ogle at the police presence.

Concerned that Madson might have warned Harman of the girls' activities, he was pleased to see her walking in their direction. Her eyes skimming the policemen, she turned to Mr Armitage. 'What's going on?'

'Ah, Miss Harman! I'd like to have a word with you in your office,' said Mr Armitage, gesturing for her to lead the way.

She glanced to Ellis before looking back to Mr Armitage. 'For what reason?'

'Don't worry, all will soon become clear.' Without smiling, Mr Armitage added, 'Shall we?'

Ellis waited until they had walked off before following on behind. Turning his thoughts to where Madson might be, he very much hoped that the other man would still be where the girls had left him – out of harm's way. Then, seeing Miss Harman plunge her hand into her pocket, a small smile twitched his lips as he watched her frantically feeling for the keys which were currently in his pocket.

She looked to Mr Armitage. 'I cannae find my keys!'

Smiling broadly, Ellis held them up. 'Not to worry, I have them.'

She pointed an accusing finger. 'You *stole* them!'

Ellis shrugged as he unlocked the door. 'Guilty as charged.'

'Well, don't just stand there,' Miss Harman snapped at the policemen. 'Arrest him!'

The constables looked to Armitage, who waved a dismissive hand. 'Harvey is acting under my instructions.'

She looked from Armitage to Ellis and back again, and that's when the penny dropped. For Armitage to call Ellis by his Christian name could only mean one thing – they were working together.

Ushering them inside the office, Ellis pointed the ledgers out to Armitage as he closed the door behind him. 'I think you'll find the answers to your questions in those ledgers.' Stepping forward, Armitage examined both ledgers before asking why one of them appeared to have been slightly scorched. Ellis was about to say untruthfully that he hadn't the foggiest when Madson burst into the room.

Grateful for the distraction, Ellis beamed at the newcomer. 'Mr Madson! How nice of you to join us.'

Taking one look at the ledgers, the policemen and the smug smile on Ellis's face, Madson pointed a trembling finger at Miss Harman. 'She's been rippin' the government off for ages – I was waitin' until I found some evidence before sayin' anythin', but I can see that you're one step ahead of me.'

Ellis eyed him quizzically. 'What do you mean by that?'

Madson gestured towards the ledgers. 'Isn't it obvious? She's runnin' two sets of books.'

Mr Armitage pulled a downward smile. 'I'm curious. Tell me, just how do you know what's in those books?'

Realising that he'd tripped himself up, Madson's eyes darted from the ledgers to Miss Harman and back again whilst he fought for a reasonable explanation. 'Cos she tried to rope me into her little scam, but I refused,' he said with an air of satisfaction.

Miss Harman stared at Madson aghast. 'Me?' she squealed indignantly. 'It was all your idea!'

Mr Armitage's attention had been drawn to the large lump on Madson's head, still black from the coal shovel. 'What on *earth* happened to you?'

Madson gingerly touched the lump on his forehead as he tried to think of an excuse for his appearance, eventually settling on 'I fell. There's no law against that, is there?'

Ellis had begun to speak when his words were lost beneath the wail of the air raid siren.

Chapter Five

The girls were halfway to the railway station when the siren split the night air. Isla rolled her eyes. 'Oh for cryin' out loud! That's just what we need!'

'It's probably a false alarm,' said Meg, crossing her fingers.

Isla looked to the skies. 'Are you willin' to take that chance? Cos I'm not.'

Disappointed that their plan of escape was being thwarted by the threat of an air raid, Meg heaved a sigh. 'I s'pose not. It's just bloomin' typical, that's all.'

'Not to worry,' said Sophie. 'If it's a false alarm we'll be out in no time at all, but if not then at least we'll be in a safe place. If we can find a shelter, that is – there's no way I'm going back to the poorhouse.'

'I haven't a clue where the one nearest here is,' said Meg, but Isla was gesturing towards a group of people all hurrying in the same direction.

'We don't, but I reckon they do,' she said.

Setting off at a brisk pace, the girls caught up with the people they were following just as they disappeared through the curtained doorway of a shelter.

With most of the seats already taken they opted for a bench near the front.

'Keep everythin' crossed, girls,' hissed Sophie, 'cos we cannae afford for anythin' else to go wrong tonight!'

As she spoke the ARP warden entered the shelter behind a young man who strode towards the back. 'Shall I ask the warden if he thinks it's a false alarm?' whispered Meg.

Isla's ears pricked as the dull sound of bombs dropping ever nearer reached them from outside. 'Does that answer your question?'

Hearing the chorus of many voices raised in prayer, Meg sighed heavily before gesturing to the prayers with a jerk of her head. 'I hope He does more for us now than He did when we were in Coxhill.'

'I just hope they don't hit the railway lines,' murmured Isla, 'cos that's the last thing we need.'

'They say that bad luck comes in threes,' said Sophie in an undertone. 'First gettin' rumbled by Madson, now the raid . . .'

Hearing voices begin to remonstrate with someone down the far end of the shelter, the girls looked over to where the young man who'd been the last to enter was striding back towards the door in a determined fashion.

'What's he doin'?' said Sophie, her eyes rounding in horror. 'Surely to God he cannae be thinkin' of leavin'?'

'From what them women were sayin', he thinks his girlfriend's still in one of the tenements,' said Isla quietly. 'You cannae blame him for bein' worried.'

They fell quiet as accusations were thrown between the young man, whose name appeared to be Rory, the warden and the two women about someone called Tammy and her mother, Grace, who had been heard arguing with Tammy's controlling father Dennis Blackwell, prior to the siren.

'Poor bugger,' murmured Isla in reference to the young man. 'I hope those women have got it wrong, and that his girlfriend's safe in a shelter somewhere and not bein' held captive by her rotten father.'

'He must really love her to risk goin' out in the middle of a raid,' remarked Sophie.

Isla watched the young man from the corner of her eye. He was extremely handsome, and had dark curly hair and deep brown eyes. *Whoever this Tammy Blackwell is, she's one fortunate woman to have a man love her the way that Rory obviously does*, she thought. *I hope she appreciates how lucky she is.*

Watching on as the warden managed to persuade the young man to sit next to him and ignore the gossiping women, Isla felt her cheeks grow warm as Rory gave her a fleeting glance. Cutting across her thoughts, Sophie spoke conversationally as she tried to obtain a comfortable position. 'We may as well try and get some kip, cos we could be down here for the night and we'll need to be bright-eyed and bushy-tailed come the morning.'

Averting her gaze from Rory, Isla leaned on one of Sophie's shoulders, whilst Meg leaned on the other. Tired from their stressful day, it didn't take them long to drift off to sleep. Sophie dreamt that she was stepping off the train in Liverpool, her friends by her side, and walking arm in arm into bright sunshine. Meg dreamt she was riding a beautiful palomino through a flower meadow, and Isla dreamt she was comforting the handsome young man by the name of Rory.

Waking with a start as the all-clear sounded, none of the girls remembered their dream, but Isla was reminded of hers when she saw the young man anxiously hurrying from the shelter. Knuckling her eyes, Sophie spoke to her as they made to leave themselves. 'Did you manage to get any sleep?'

'Not much,' Isla began, before exclaiming 'Oh, my giddy aunt'. She stared in horror at the scene of devastation before them. Pointing to a tenement block which had taken a direct hit, she swallowed. 'I hope that Rory's Tammy wasn't in there!'

'You heard the warden,' said Meg. 'Those two old biddies were gossipin' without proof. Tammy will have been down one of the shelters, you mark my words.'

'I hope you're right,' murmured Isla, 'cos poor Rory will be devastated if not.'

'Much as I'd like to help with the clear-up,' said Sophie, who was already walking in the direction of the train station, 'we cannae afford to hang about.'

'I know, but I feel so guilty about walkin' away when we could be helpin',' said Isla, her heart sinking horribly as she heard the desperate cries of people calling for loved ones.

'We all do,' said Sophie, 'but we have to get out of

here as soon as possible, cos we don't know for certain what's happenin' back in Coxhill.'

Meg nodded fervently. 'I know that Harvey was confident he had Harman bang to rights, but not Madson, and I'm guessin' we're not that horrible man's favourite people right now, after Sophie cracked him over the head with the coal shovel.'

'I'd forgotten about that,' said Isla. She paused briefly before continuing as another thought occurred to her. 'You don't suppose Coxhill got hit, do you?'

Sophie held a hand to her stomach. 'Don't say things like that!'

Meg, however, was bringing their attention to the distant building in question, which remained unscathed. 'There you are! Nothin' to worry about!'

'Which is more than can be said for poor Rory,' said Isla.

Sophie gave her a sidelong glance. 'That's the third time you've mentioned him.'

Isla shrugged. 'I felt – feel – sorry for him.'

Sophie held her gaze. 'Is that all?'

'What other reason can there be?'

Sophie shook her head. 'Ignore me. It's been a long twenty-four hours.'

'At least we can have a kip on the train,' yawned Meg, who also hadn't managed to get much sleep.

Walking in silence, Isla turned her thoughts back to Rory. She couldn't quite put her finger on the reason why she wasn't able to keep him from her thoughts, but it seemed as though she was being drawn to him somehow. *It wasn't just that he was good-lookin'*, she thought, *it was more than that, almost like I'm bein' drawn towards him by some sort of invisible force*. She tutted beneath her breath. She was allowing her imagination to run away with her, because of the stressful time she and her friends had been through. She pushed him to the back of her mind and hurried after her friends.

By the time Mary had changed out of her costume and back into her smock, she was one of the last people to leave the hall. Seeing Miss Harman with the police had piqued her curiosity, especially when it was plain to see that Miss Harman was as stumped by their presence as Mary herself. Keen to know what the police were doing at Coxhill, Mary had followed at a distance. Waiting until Ellis had closed the door, she was about to hurry over when she heard someone blaspheming further down the corridor. Hanging back out of sight, she waited until the speaker came into view, and was shocked to see Mr Madson stumbling towards the office with a large black lump on his forehead. Holding back until he was inside and the door closed, she ran over and planted her ear against one of the panels. Her eyes rounding as she heard the accusations unfold, Mary immediately knew that Harman's time in Coxhill had come to an end, and without Harman ruling the roost, Mary would no longer have the privileges she once had. She would be treated the same as everyone else and she would be damned if she was going to let that happen.

Her mind made up to leave the poorhouse, she ran to kitchen to get some provisions for her escape. *No sense in my goin' hungry*, she told herself as she swiped half a loaf of bread along with a large lump of cheese from off the larder shelf. Wrapping the items in a tea towel, she was wondering how she could leave the building when the air raid siren sounded. A slow smile splitting her cheeks, she followed everyone else, but instead of going down to the cellar which served as their shelter she slipped away unnoticed.

Hoping against hope that the air raid was a false alarm she decided to head for the covered market, a place she felt certain the Luftwaffe wouldn't target. Finding the doors locked, she took a rock and threw it through one of the windows, then felt for the latch and brushed the broken glass from the sill and opened the window before climbing through. Glancing round at the various stalls, she made for one that sold bedding and the like and yanked down various sheets and pillows to form a cosy nest in which to shelter from the raid. *As soon as I hear the all-clear I'm out of here*, she thought as she pulled yet another sheet over her.

She wasn't expecting to fall asleep, so she was surprised to see sunshine flooding through the windows when the all-clear woke her. Having no idea as to the time, she jumped up from her makeshift bed and looked around for the nearest clothes stall, where she stepped out of her smock, picked up a pale green frock and slipped it over her head. On the same stall she found shoes and underwear, as well as woollen jumpers and a satchel. Further along she equipped herself with a full wash kit and a comb which she dragged through her hair before placing it inside the

114

satchel, together with everything else. Content that she had all she needed to get by, she was about to make a quick exit when another thought occurred to her. Would any of the stallholders have been stupid enough to leave a float overnight? Crossing her fingers, she searched the stalls nearby, but found only one where the holder had left a small amount of change. Deftly pocketing it, she left the market before she could be discovered.

As soon as she stepped outside she was dumbfounded by the devastation which met her eyes. *They must've come in their hundreds*, she thought as she tossed the satchel over her shoulder and hurried on, but she came to an abrupt halt when she heard someone cry out for her to stop. Convinced that someone knew what she'd been doing, Mary started to run, only to have the young man who'd called out grab her by the shoulder.

'Did you not hear me?' he said. He held out a few pieces of paper. 'You dropped these.'

Mary was about to say that she'd done no such thing when her eyes fell to the identification papers in his hands. Having left without her own documents in her hurry to leave Coxhill, she thanked him with a smile as she took the paperwork and put it in her satchel. *Just what I need – a new identity!*

Desperate to leave the city before the market traders could notice they'd been robbed, Mary didn't stop running until she reached the station, when she took the documents from her pocket and opened them up. *I don't know you from Adam, but your loss is my gain*, she thought as her eyes rested on the birth certificate, *cos you've just made my life a whole lot easier! So thank you, Tamara Blackwell. I owe you one!*

'For goodness sake will you stop lookin' over your shoulder, Sophie,' Isla chided as they boarded the train. 'You look as guilty as sin!'

'I feel it!' said Sophie. 'I know we've done nothin' wrong – apart from whackin' Madson in self-defence – but I doubt the governors will see it that way!'

'As you just said, it was self-defence,' said Isla, 'so I for one don't much care what the governors think, and neither should you, cos but for your actions I wouldn't be here with you now.'

'She's right,' said Meg encouragingly. 'Besides, I very much doubt the governors will care when they hear what Harman's been up to, and if Madson's goin' to tell them what happened in her private quarters he'll have to admit why he was there in the first place.'

Eager to keep their conversation private, Sophie walked to the far end of the carriage before taking a seat. 'I hope you're right, but that doesn't stop me from worrying.' She looked to Isla. 'Which brings me to another matter, and it involves your father.'

Isla looked at her in surprise as she sat down next to Meg. 'Oh?'

'How's he meant to find you should he come lookin'?'

Isla gave a derisive snort. 'That's his worry. If he'd come when he'd promised he wouldn't be in that predicament in the first place.'

116

'If it were anyone else I'd agree with you, but I'm not sure he'd be able to just drop everythin' when he's out at sea,' Sophie pointed out.

'Then he should never have gone!' snapped Isla, before relenting slightly. 'Sorry, Sophie. I know you mean well, but I rather think it's a case of out of sight, out of mind. Quite frankly, he's forgotten he even has a child, if you ask me!'

Rather than press her point, Sophie fell into silent thought. When Isla had first arrived at Coxhill, Sophie had been quick to dismiss her claims that her father would be back for his daughter within a couple of months, but after getting to know Isla better and hearing more about her family she had begun to think differently. *I honestly believe his droppin' Isla off was an act of complete desperation*, she thought now. *He must've been goin' out of his mind with grief, and no matter how misguided his decision may have been, I think he did it out of love.* Not that she would say so to Isla, who was still too hurt and angry to listen to the voice of reason. Uncomfortable with the awkward silence that had followed her friend's response to her last comment, she spoke in reassuring tones. 'My mammy always used to say that time was a great healer; and she was right. It's somethin' you learn as you go through life.'

'I wish my daddy thought so,' said Isla. 'Maybe then he wouldn't have been so quick to act.'

Disappointed, Sophie decided it would be better if she didn't reply to that, and was grateful when Meg put her own thoughts into the mix.

'We may not have our families, but at least we've

got each other,' she said, gazing out of the window, 'and I for one—' She broke off short, her face turning pale as a familiar face passed their carriage on the way to one further along the platform. 'Oh, no . . .'

Sophie tried to follow Meg's line of sight. 'What's wrong? Is it Madson?'

'Worse,' said Meg, 'or it is if I'm right.'

'Worse than Madson?' scoffed Sophie, before adding sharply, 'Is it the polis?'

'No, it's Mary,' said Meg. 'At least I think it was, but if so she's got herself a whole new wardrobe, because she wasn't wearin' her smock.'

Sophie leaned her elbow against the window so that she could hide her face behind the palm of her hand. 'Do you think they've sent her to look for us?'

'I cannae see why else she'd be here,' said Isla, 'although . . .'

'What?' chorused Sophie and Meg when she paused.

'Why would they provide her with different clothes?' finished Isla reasonably.

'They wouldn't. I don't know where she got them from, but there's no way on this earth she got them from Coxhill,' conceded Meg. 'Cos she had a bag too.'

'That makes it sound as though she's run away,' said Isla, 'but why would she do that?'

'For good reason,' said Sophie. 'With Harman out of the picture Mary will have to toe the line the same as everyone else.'

'Which I dare say must have gone down like a brick,' said Meg, who had relaxed a little. 'Cos she'd hardly start obeyin' the rules now, not after havin' her own way for so long.'

'Not to mention those who'd want to seek their revenge on her for sendin' their pals down the river,' said Isla. 'And without Harman to protect her . . .' She widened her eyes before pulling her forefinger across her throat. Sophie shuddered at the thought.

'You cannae blame them,' said Meg. 'I know I'd like a word in her shell-like after dobbin' me in that time.'

'Me too,' agreed Sophie, 'but havin' said that I'd still rather she was on a different train. I don't suppose you saw her actually get on this one?'

'Well, no,' said Meg, 'but even if she did, that guard said we need to change trains at least three times to get to Liverpool, and I can hardly see Mary doin' that. Too much trouble!'

'Aye, she'll probably get off as soon as we're clear of Clydebank,' said Isla. Yawning, she curled up as best she could on the narrow seat. 'I don't know about the two of you, but I feel as though I could sleep for a week.'

'I'm far too excited to sleep,' said Meg. 'Besides, someone needs to stay awake so that we don't miss our stop, as well as keep an eye out for Mary.'

Sophie yawned beneath her hand. 'Good point. Are you sure you don't mind?'

'Not in the slightest.'

The journey out of Scotland proved relatively easy, and even though they were in good spirits when they reached Penrith they were still eager to discover

Mary's whereabouts. Waiting to be served in the station buffet, they discussed what they thought had become of Mary.

'She must've got off at an earlier stop,' Isla suggested, 'because I've not seen her on the platform, and she wasn't in the lavvies a few minutes ago either.'

'And I walked the length of the train while you were both asleep, and there was no sign of her then either,' said Meg.

'She probably got off in Carlisle,' said Sophie, 'and even though I know she cannae harm us now I still don't trust her not to try.'

'She'd certainly do her best to throw a spanner in the works if she were to bump into any of us,' agreed Meg. 'It's in her nature.'

'Once a rat, always a rat,' said Sophie. 'It's as simple as that.'

Isla stifled a yawn beneath her hand. 'All this worry over missin' station signs and connectin' trains is fair wearin' me out. I for one will be jolly glad when we reach Liverpool.'

'It would help if they didn't cancel or reroute at the drop of a hat!' complained Meg. 'You don't know whether you're comin' or goin' half the time.'

'And as for all that business about removin' the signs, it's downright ridiculous considerin' all you have to do is ask a guard,' put in Sophie. She hesitated as the woman behind the counter handed her two buns. 'Are you sure you don't want one, Isla?'

'Not for me, thanks,' said Isla, indicating with a wave of her hand for Sophie to proceed with the payment. 'I'll get somethin' at the next stop. It'll give me an excuse to stretch me legs.' She glanced to Sophie's pocket as they crossed the platform. 'How much money have we got left?'

'Enough for our fares, some sarnies and a couple of days' keep,' determined Sophie, 'so we'll have to get jobs toot-sweet when we arrive in Liverpool.'

'Hopefully Irene will be able to point us in the right direction as far as jobs are concerned,' said Isla. 'You do still have her address, don't you?'

Sophie patted her coat pocket. 'Safe and sound along with the money!'

'Good to know.'

'What's our next stop?' asked Meg as they boarded the train, and entered an empty compartment.

'I'm not sure,' said Isla. 'But I do know this train takes us all the way to Liverpool.'

Sophie smiled happily. 'Our new home.'

Isla was sliding the door to their compartment shut just as the train sounded its whistle before lurching into action, causing a heavily pregnant woman to stumble as she walked past. Rushing to her aid, Isla caught her in the nick of time.

'Heavens to Betsy!' protested the woman as Isla helped her stand up straight. 'Much more of that and I'll be havin' this babby on the train!'

Still holding her by the arm, Isla glanced nervously at the woman's stomach. 'Are you all right?'

'I am thanks to you,' remarked the woman. 'Where on earth did you spring from?'

Isla indicated their compartment with a jerk of her

head. 'I saw you go past as I was closin' the door to our compartment,' Isla told her, indicating Meg and Sophie, who had hurried out to help. 'Is yours close by?'

'It's this one right here,' the woman said, pointing to the one next door.

Side-stepping ahead, Sophie slid the door back, and Meg and Isla helped the woman through.

'Can we get you anything?' asked Isla as their neighbour fanned her face with the newspaper she'd been holding.

'That's ever so kind of you, but I'll be just fine,' she puffed. Sniffing loudly, she added, 'I should know better than to go for a wander, but my ankles swell up somethin' rotten if I sit down for too long.' She smiled brightly. 'I'm Gemma, by the way.'

The girls introduced themselves, and Isla asked the question that concerned her the most. 'Are you travellin' alone?'

Gemma continued to fan her face. 'Much against my better judgement. I know it's not sensible in my condition, but I wanted to see my auntie before the baby arrives. My hubby would've come with me, but he can't leave the farm.'

Sophie glanced at the wall which separated their compartments. 'We've plenty of room in our compartment if you'd care to join us?'

Gemma twinkled at her. 'That's ever so kind of you, but I snore summat awful since I got in the family way.'

'We're not bothered, are we girls?' said Isla.

122

Meg and Sophie agreed with their friend, but Gemma was adamant. 'It's ever so kind of you, but I find it easier to rest when I'm on my own. If it makes you feel any better, I'll bang on the wall should I need you.'

'Just make you sure do,' said Isla, 'cos I'd rather you hollered than tried to manage on your own.'

Gemma held up her crossed fingers. 'I promise.'

Feeling better about the situation, the girls bade her goodbye before returning to their own compartment. 'Somone ought to have a word with the driver,' said Isla as she sat down heavily. 'He should know better than to take off like that.'

'How about you? Are *you* all right?' asked Sophie. 'Only I saw your face, and I'm sure it must have brought back some bad memories . . .'

'I'll not deny she nearly gave me kittens when she stumbled, but she didn't actually fall, so I'm guessin' she's tellin' the truth when she says that all's well,' said Isla, but the others could hear the uncertainty in her voice.

'Well, don't you worry about Gemma, cos I'll keep watch . . .' Meg began, but Isla was talking across her.

'I know it's my turn to get some kip, but I don't think I'll get so much as a wink knowin' that Gemma might holler for help at any moment.'

'I'll wake you . . .' Meg began, but Isla was determined.

'Honestly, there's no point in two of us keepin' watch. You get some sleep.'

Sophie squeezed her hand. 'If it makes you feel

better then by all means. But should you find yourself driftin' off, please don't hesitate to wake one of us.'

'Thanks, girls. I'll feel better knowin' I can be there for her if she needs me. I just wish I could have done the same for my mammy.'

Meg eyed her sympathetically. 'Do you really not think you were there for your mammy?'

'I know I wasn't,' said Isla, 'and I should've been.'

'And do you think your presence would've made a difference?' asked Sophie gently.

'It would've to me,' said Isla, 'cos I'd have known that I did all I could – even if it made no odds to the outcome.'

'If it'll make you feel better, then by all means you keep watch,' said Sophie, 'but for goodness sake make sure you get yourself somethin' to eat at the next stop, cos you've been awake for a long time.' Digging into her coat pocket, she pulled out a couple of coins and handed them over.

'Thanks, Sophie. Do you want me to wake either of you in case you fancy a drink or summat?'

Sophie shook her head. 'I'll be fine, thanks.'

'Me too,' added Meg.

Putting the money in her pocket, Isla watched on as Sophie closed her eyes briefly before standing up and closing the blinds in the compartment. 'Every time I open my eyes I expect to see Madson or Mary staring at me through the corridor window,' she said by way of explanation for her action.

'It'll be that nightmare you had,' Meg commented

without opening her eyes. 'You give me the fright of my life when you shot up out of your seat like that.'

Sophie grimaced apologetically. 'Sorry about that.'

'We're all as bad as each other,' said Isla. 'I keep dreamin' that I'm back in the shelter, and that Rory feller is blamin' me for his belle not makin' it out in time.'

Meg opened one eye and focused it on Isla. 'Do you suppose they get many air raids in Liverpool?'

'No more than Clydebank, I don't suppose,' said Isla. 'It's them poor buggers down south what get it the worst.'

Sophie stifled a yawn beneath her hand. 'The quicker they get rid of Hitler and his rotten Nazis the better.'

'I'm sure the war cannae go on for much longer,' said Isla. 'Now for goodness sake get some kip!' As the words left her lips, they both heard gentle snores emanating from Meg, and it was not long before Sophie joined in, leaving Isla to keep watch. Glancing at the blinds which separated the compartment from the corridor, an image of Gemma formed in her mind's eye. *I'm sure she'll be just fine*, she thought as she raised one of the blinds halfway, *but if she's anythin' like my mammy, she'll be makin' frequent trips to the lavvy.*

Over an hour had passed by the time they reached the next stop, and Isla was famished. *I wish I'd had a bun with the girls at the last stop*, she thought as she descended from the train. Approaching the guard, she asked how long they had at the station.

125

'Ten minutes,' said the guard, 'but don't worry: you'll hear me blow me whistle before the train sets off.'

Hurrying over the bridge to the café, Isla fell into line at the back of the small queue. Keeping her fingers crossed that she would have enough time, she was relieved to find the queue went down quite quickly. Ordering herself a cheese and onion sandwich and a ginger beer, Isla was in the middle of paying the woman when she saw Gemma coming out of the station lavatories. Hastily leaving the café, she caught up with the other woman as she was struggling to get on to the train.

'What happened to wakin' us if you needed help?' Isla scolded as she helped Gemma back on board.

Gemma pulled an apologetic face. 'I know I should have used the lavvy on the train, but it was occupied and I was bustin'.' She held up a brown paper bag containing a sandwich. 'I thought I may as well grab myself a sarnie whilst I was at it.'

Isla nearly jumped out of her skin as the guard blew his whistle. 'Ten minutes my eye,' she tutted irritably. 'It's a good job I saw you when I did, else I'd have missed . . .' She stopped speaking as Gemma slowly slid down the wooden corridor wall. 'Oh my Lord! Are you all right?'

Gemma puffed her cheeks out. 'I never thought that boardin' a train would prove so difficult, but that fair done me in!'

'I'm not surprised!' chided Isla. 'It's a big stretch from the platform to the train. You're lucky you haven't done yourself a mischief.'

'Lesson learned! I'll certainly think twice in future!' As she spoke, Gemma took the sandwich from its bag. 'I'll be right as rain once I've had a few bites of this.'

Isla sank down next to her as the train set off. 'Well, I'm not goin' anywhere until you're safely back in your compartment – no arguments!'

'You can't eat sittin' on the floor,' objected Gemma, as she watched Isla remove her own sandwich from its wrappings.

'Why not? You are, and I've eaten in worse places,' said Isla. An image of the dining hall in Coxhill forming in her mind, she added, 'Much worse.'

'Where do you hail from?' asked Gemma, who was curious to know the places to which Isla was referring to.

'Clydebank,' said Isla, adding conversationally, 'I don't know whether you heard about the recent blitz?'

Gemma stowed the bite of her sandwich into her cheek before replying. 'It was all over the news. Were you caught up in it?'

'Aye, but luckily for us we made it to the shelter in the nick of time.'

'Livin' in the countryside we're not targeted the same way they are in the cities,' said Gemma, 'not that they've seen much action up our neck of the woods – thank goodness.'

'That's good to hear,' said Isla, 'I wouldn't want to think that we were jumpin' out of the fryin' pan into the fire.' She looked to Gemma, who had finished her sandwich. 'Do you think you're ready to have a go at standin' up?'

'Best had,' said Gemma, 'cos I can't sit here all day.' She held on to the rail which ran along one side of the corridor and attempted to stand. 'Dear God!' she grunted as she failed to make progress, 'I think I'm down here for the duration!'

Getting to her feet, Isla held out her hands. 'C'mon, you push and I'll pull.'

Shifting her body so that she was in a kneeling position, Gemma took hold of Isla's hands and pushed, but suddenly she cried out in alarm and snatched her hands away. 'No!'

'How about if I push you from behind?' suggested Isla, but all became clear when she saw the puddle emanating from beneath Gemma's skirt, and she swore quietly before quickly apologising.

'You were only sayin' what I was thinkin',' Gemma assured her, 'but not to worry. I've given birth plenty of times before.'

'On a *train*?'

'All right, so not on a train,' admitted Gemma, 'but it can't be that different, can it?'

Isla's mind immediately leapt to her mother and the staff at the medically equipped hospital who had been unable to save her, but she thrust the thought away. *You cannae think like that*, she told herself, *not when you're all she's got.* Standing up straight, she swiftly took charge. 'I'll let the steward know what's happenin', and he can see if there's a midwife on board while I stay here with you.'

Gemma groaned loudly before muttering 'Good idea' between clenched teeth.

Her heart pounding in her chest, Isla ran to find the steward, who was checking tickets in a nearby compartment. 'There's a lady havin' a baby,' she gabbled, 'you need to get help—' Cut off by the sound of Gemma's contractions, Isla finished her sentence in a hurry. 'And quickly.'

The steward's eyes swivelled to the emergency brake. As he slowly raised his arm, one of the passengers – a woman Isla supposed to be in her thirties – slapped his hand away. 'Good God, man. You can't stop the train here, we're in the middle of nowhere!'

He opened his mouth to protest, but the woman was already on her feet. 'I'm not a midwife, but I am a nurse.' She turned to Isla. 'Where is she?'

'In the corridor,' said Isla, leading the way out of the compartment. 'Her waters have broken . . .'

The nurse's eyes fell on Gemma, who was fighting the urge to push. Sweat pouring down her face, she gritted her teeth as another contraction overwhelmed her, and looking at her wristwatch the nurse glanced to Isla. 'We're goin' to need towels and plenty of warm water.'

Giving her the thumbs-up, Isla looked to the steward, who jerked his head in a backward motion, saying, 'Follow me.'

Isla looked fearfully towards Gemma. 'Can't you go without me? I need to stay . . .'

The nurse smiled kindly. 'She's goin' to be just fine, trust me.'

The steward gave Isla an encouraging smile. 'C'mon, lass, we'll be back before you know it.'

129

'Don't worry, you go with the steward,' Gemma assured her. 'It's not as if I'm goin' anywhere.'

'I'll be back in two shakes of a lamb's tail,' Isla promised.

Hurrying after the steward, Isla followed him to the far end of the train where she waited impatiently for him to fetch towels and water, which took a good few minutes. Taking the towels while he carried the cans of water, Isla called over her shoulder, 'I hope that water's clean!'

'Of course,' replied the steward, only to stop dead in his tracks. 'Is that . . . ?'

Isla beamed as the cry of a newborn baby sounded in the distance. Flooded with relief, she sprinted down the corridor, arriving just as the nurse had finished tidying Gemma up. Tears brimming her eyes, she handed the nurse the towels. 'Thank goodness they're both all right – they *are* all right, aren't they?'

'Yes they are,' said the nurse, as she took the baby from Gemma. 'Gemma's an old hand at this, what with her havin' eight more at home.'

'Eight!' yelped Isla, while the steward simply said 'Blimey!'

Gemma chuckled. 'I did say that I'd given birth plenty of times before!'

Kneeling down, Isla gently stroked the baby's cheek. 'You did, but that doesn't mean nothin' can go wrong. I learned that after losin' my mammy.'

The nurse, who had been busy cleaning the baby, looked up. 'Oh, love, I am sorry. Do you mind me askin' what happened?'

Isla fielded a tear with the crook of her finger as it left her lashes. 'She died givin' birth to my baby brother, who also died.'

Gemma held a hand to her forehead. 'Oh, Isla! No wonder you were keen to keep an eye on me!' Stifling a yawn, Gemma allowed the guard to help her to her feet. 'I'd wager it'll be a long time before I get a decent night's kip with this one to look after!'

'Then you must get some now, whilst I'm here to help,' said Isla, as she followed Gemma and the nurse to the older woman's compartment. The blinds in the adjacent one were still down, and there was no sign of her friends. Isla smiled. 'Good job it was me keepin' an eye out. I cannae believe they slept through that!'

'I can't ask you to help,' Gemma objected, but Isla was holding up her hand.

'You never asked me to do anythin',' said Isla, 'it's me that's insisting!'

'You're a star, Isla, you truly are,' said Gemma. 'You just wait till I tell Tim and the kids all that you've done for me.'

Isla blushed shyly. 'I didn't do much, apart from get some towels.'

'You were there for me, and that means a lot,' said Gemma. Yawning again beneath her hand, she sat down. 'I'm bushed!'

Handing Gemma the baby for its first feed, the nurse turned to Isla. 'Your mammy would be ever so proud of what you've done for your friend.'

'She'd have been tellin' all the neighbours,' chuckled Isla, 'as would my father!'

131

The nurse coddled Isla's hand in hers. 'And quite rightly so. You're a good lass, Isla, with a heart of gold.'

Gemma covered herself up. 'I think this little one's as tired as me.' She looked at Isla. 'Would you like to hold her?'

Delighted at being asked, Isla held out her hands as she settled herself into the seat opposite. Gazing down into the soft pink face as Gemma handed her precious bundle over, she allowed the baby's tiny hand to curl around her forefinger. 'Absolutely perfect.' She smiled up at the nurse. 'You were marvellous!'

The nurse waved a dismissive hand. 'All in a day's work.' The train was pulling into the next station. 'This is my stop.' She smiled at Gemma. 'Will you be all right?'

'I will with this one lookin' after me,' Gemma said confidently.

The nurse slid back the door to the compartment. 'Please pass on my congratulations to your husband.'

Gemma smiled sleepily. 'Will do, and thanks for everythin'.'

Isla gazed down at the perfect bundle in her arms as the nurse closed the door and hurried off the train. 'You're one lucky baby,' she whispered, 'growin' up on a farm with all them siblin's to look out for you.' She looked up to see Gemma still smiling as she drifted off to sleep.

Isla had spent the remainder of the journey cuddling the newborn while Gemma slept soundly. It was only when the steward slid back the door to announce that the train had reached the end of the line that Gemma finally awoke. 'How long have I been asleep?'

'Probably around an hour,' said Isla, 'but I've not got a watch so I'm only guessin'.'

Gemma took her suitcase down from the rack above her seat. 'Thank you so much, Isla. You must be exhausted!'

Isla continued to gaze at the baby. 'Not at all. It's been the best part of my journey.' She stood up and jerked her head in the direction of the door. 'I'll give you a hand off the train, cos you cannae possibly carry a baby as well as that suitcase. Will your husband be waiting for you?' They made their way down the corridor, passing Isla's compartment, the blinds of which were still drawn. Meg and Sophie must be wondering where she was.

Gemma was pointing to a man who was clearly looking for someone. 'That's him! That's my Tim!' Waving to her husband, she descended quickly on to the platform and dropped the suitcase before hurrying into his arms, but Tim was looking to Isla in wonderment. 'Is this . . . ?'

Gemma nodded. 'Meet your new daughter.'

Isla handed the baby to Tim and he smiled lovingly at the tiny bundle, saying softly, 'Does that mean you've still not thought of a name?'

Gemma rolled her eyes. 'I don't know how we'll ever choose.' After a moment, she turned her gaze to Isla. 'What was your mammy's name?'

'Agnes. Why?'

Gemma eyed her husband while rolling the name around her mouth. 'What do you think?'

'I think it's perfect! Plus it's a good Scottish name, so your mammy will approve.'

'You're Scottish!' said Isla, sounding somewhat surprised. 'You don't sound it.'

'Lost my accent when I married this one,' said Gemma, gesturing towards her husband.

'I suppose I get that,' said Isla slowly, 'but my friend Harvey is a Scouser, and neither of you sound *anythin'* like him.'

Tim laughed. 'Why on earth would you expect us to sound like Scousers, when we're not from Liverpool?'

'You're not?' said Isla, looking around to see if she could spy her friends on the platform.

Gemma stared at her as the truth dawned. 'Where do you think you are, Isla?'

'Liverpool, of course,' said Isla promptly. 'The steward did say this was the last stop on the line.'

Gemma clapped a hand to her forehead. 'You boarded the train because you saw me strugglin'!'

'Aye.'

'Only I'd left the train you were on to catch my connectin' one,' explained Gemma. 'I'd put my suitcase in my compartment when the urge of nature took over. When you came over to help, I assumed that you and your friends had caught the same connectin' train as me!'

Isla looked wildly around her. 'Where am I?'

Gemma pointed to where the sign had once stood. 'Ormskirk.'

Chapter Six

Isla threw her hands up in despair. 'I *can't* be! I'd know if I'd got on the wrong train.' She paused, her mind racing for an explanation. 'What about my pals? The blinds of our compartment were still drawn so they *must* be in there.'

'Lots of people draw the blinds to their compartment,' said Gemma. 'Surely you must've crossed the bridge to get to the café that time?'

Isla slapped a hand to her forehead. 'Oh my God! I completely forgot.' Tears pricked her eyes. 'What *am* I goin' to do? My friends will be goin' out of their minds with worry when they wake up to find me missin'!'

'Which is why we're goin' to get you on the next train to Liverpool, as well as send word to your friends lettin' them know what's happened, and that you're on your way.' Gemma jerked her head in the direction of a railway guard who was pacing the platform. 'C'mon, let's go and ask him.'

*

'Liverpool, you say?' The guard was stroking his chin. 'You won't get nothin' goin' to Liverpool until tomorrow.'

Disappointed, but desperate to find a solution, Gemma pressed on. 'What about the buses?'

He pulled a face. 'You'll have to ask down the bus depot.'

'Can we at least phone ahead to let my friends know where I am?' said Isla.

He grimaced ruefully. 'Phone lines are down. Sorry.'

Gemma rolled her eyes. 'For pity's sake!'

A man in RAF uniform slowed mid-step. 'Excuse me, but did I hear you say you were wanting to get to Liverpool?'

Isla turned her attention to the blond airman whose hazel eyes were smiling at her. 'Yes. I don't suppose you know of any buses goin' that way?'

'I can't help you with the bus timetable, but I can get you to Liverpool.' He shifted his kitbag to a more comfortable position on his shoulder as he continued. 'I'm on my way to my base in RAF West Kirby, which isn't far from the city. You're more than welcome to jump in the back of our truck if you'd like?'

'That's very kind of you, but as you can see, I'm not in the services,' said Isla, indicating her frock.

He shrugged in a carefree manner. 'Makes no odds to me, and I know my pals will be more than willin' to help a damsel in distress. We can also radio ahead to let your pals know that you're on your way.'

Gemma was eyeing him dubiously. 'I'm not sure

that I like the idea of Isla travellin' all that way with a truck full of men!'

He smiled in a reassuring fashion. 'Not to worry, there're Waafs as well as men on board.' He turned to Isla. 'But it's up to you at the end of the day. You don't have to come if you'd rather not.'

Isla had made up her mind. 'I do, though. That would be lovely, thank you!'

He held out his hand. 'Aircraftman Theodore Stratham at your service, but please call me Theo.'

'Isla Donahue. Pleased to meet you, Theo, and thanks ever so much. You're a lifesaver.'

He beamed. 'What station will your friends be at?'

Her face fell. 'You mean there's more than one?'

'Four, but not to worry. I'm sure someone in the ticket office here can find out which one your train was due to arrive at.'

'I'll nip and ask,' said Gemma, but Isla was shaking her head.

'You need to get back to your family. *I'll* nip and ask.'

'But I feel so guilty!'

'Why? It's hardly your fault I boarded the wrong train!'

'I know, but . . .'

'But me no buts, as my mammy used to say. I'll be just fine now that Theo's come to my rescue.'

Gemma looked from Isla to Theo and back again. 'I'm sure you will,' she said, with a half-smile.

Seemingly unaware that Gemma was referring to Theo's dashing good looks, Isla smiled back. 'Good luck with Agnes. I hope all goes well.'

Taking a piece of paper from her handbag, Gemma hastily scribbled down her address and handed it to Isla. 'Drop me a line if you find the time. It would be good to keep in touch.'

'I definitely will,' said Isla. 'Thank you.' Waving a brief goodbye, she headed for the ticket office with Theo. 'Are you sure I'm not holdin' anyone up?' she asked anxiously. 'I don't want to be a burden.'

Theo glanced at the watch on his wrist. 'Don't worry. The truck isn't due until seventeen hundred hours – our train actually got in early for once!'

'Our train?' asked Isla, looking over her shoulder.

'We'd been sent to help set up a satellite base,' Theo explained. 'I stopped to use the facilities whilst the others went ahead.'

'As long as I'm not bein' a bother . . .'

'Not in the least.' He held the ticket office door open for Isla, and followed her inside.

Isla gave the office staff the details of the Liverpool train she and her pals had caught, and one of the women behind the desk checked the information thoroughly before coming to a decision. 'Lime Street,' she said with certainty.

Isla held her hands in a prayer-like gesture as she thanked the staff for their help. 'I'll have a word with our driver, who'll get word to Lime Street station,' said Theo as they walked out of the office. 'What are your friends' names?'

'Sophie Garvey and Meg Daniels,' said Isla, who couldn't quite believe how helpful her knight in shining armour was turning out to be.

'We'll ask the staff at Lime Street to put out an announcement over the tannoy system asking them to go to the office,' said Theo, 'and when they do they'll be told to meet you on the steps of the station in around an hour or so.'

'Is that all?' gasped Isla. 'I thought we were hours away!'

'Nah,' he said casually, 'not that bad!'

'I was so worried when I realised my mistake,' confessed Isla, 'but you've put paid to all of that. You really are quite the hero!'

He beamed with unabashed pride. 'Here to serve – especially when the damsel is as beautiful as yourself.'

Isla felt her cheeks warm. He spoke with a silver tongue, and whilst she would never have chosen to board the wrong train, it might all be worth it if she got to spend some time with the charming man by the name of Theo!

Yawning audibly, Sophie looked out of the train window at the platform, which was rapidly filling with the people who were getting off in droves. She nudged Meg awake.

'Hmmm?' murmured Meg.

'I think we're here.'

Meg turned on her side. 'That's nice,' she mumbled, still half asleep.

Sophie looked to Isla's vacant seat. 'Isla's not here, so I'm guessin' she must've nipped to the lavvy.'

Meg knuckled her eyes. 'What do you mean, Isla's

not here? And why didn't she wake us before she went?'

'Maybe she thought she'd be back before we woke up.'

Meg stretched as she got to her feet. 'Call me paranoid, but Isla's a stickler for stuff like this and I cannae see her leavin' the compartment without wakin' us first. You wait here whilst I check.' Nipping out into the corridor, she nearly collided with the steward, who was about to knock on their door.

'Everybody's to get off, miss,' he told her. 'It's the end of the line for this particular train.'

'So we're in Liverpool, then?'

'We certainly are. You'll have to catch another train should you wish to travel on.'

'Yes, we know,' said Meg somewhat exasperatedly, 'but have you seen our friend? She's got long auburn hair . . .'

'Sorry, but no.'

Meg frowned. 'I'm going to check the lavvy.'

'By all means do, but it was empty when I looked a few moments ago – in fact, as far as I'm aware, you two are the last on board.'

Sophie stared at him. 'Are you *sure*?'

'Positive.' Wanting to be helpful, he said: 'Perhaps your friend's usin' the station's facilities?'

Thanking him for his suggestion, the girls stepped out of the compartment. 'I hope he's right,' said Meg, 'cos wherever she is, she's not on this train.'

'I'll check the station lavvies and the caff if you check the waiting room,' said Sophie as they descended on to the platform. 'I don't know why Isla would be in any of them, but she has to be somewhere!'

The girls had checked, double-checked and even triple-checked, but Isla was nowhere to be found. Having done an extensive tour of the platforms, they had decided to check the concourse, even though they were both adamant that Isla wouldn't have left the station, and it was only after a good ten minutes of searching that they reconvened outside the ticket office.

'This is ridiculous,' snapped Sophie irritably. 'She can't have disappeared into thin air!'

'As I see it, there's only one explanation,' said Meg. 'She must have got off the train at the last station to get herself somethin' to eat, and the train's left without her.'

Sophie's face fell. 'Which means she's on her own, with little to no money, and no means of gettin' herself here.'

'I'm sure if she explained the circumstances, they'd allow her to catch the next train,' said Meg, 'especially if ours left early, cos that's their fault and not hers.'

'Why, oh why didn't she wake us?' moaned Sophie. 'We'd not be in this predicament if she had.'

'You know what Isla's like,' Meg pointed out, 'always thinkin' of others before herself. She probably didn't want to disturb our sleep.'

Sophie brightened. 'I've just had an idea!'

'Oh?'

'The people in the ticket office will know where the train last stopped, so if we can get word to the station we can tell them we'll pay for Isla's fare when she arrives!' finished Sophie with a triumphant air.

Meg was opening her mouth to agree when the call came out over the tannoy. *Will Sophie Garvey and Meg Daniels please make their way to the office.*

Both girls locked eyes before hurrying to the office. Bursting through the door, Sophie was the first to speak.

'We're Sophie and Meg. Has this got somethin' to do with our pal Isla?'

The woman beamed at them from the other side of the counter. 'It does indeed. It seems that your friend's been quite the heroine! But I'll let her tell you all about that when she arrives.'

Sophie and Meg were beside themselves with glee. 'You've spoken to her!' cried Sophie.

'Which train will she be on?' asked Meg, who was eager to keep a lookout.

'I've not spoken to her personally, but she won't be on a train. She's comin' with the RAF.'

Meg's jaw dropped as she glanced from the woman to Sophie and back again. 'The RAF?'

'That's what the feller said, yes.'

'What on earth has she been up to?' murmured Sophie.

Meg's heart was singing joyously as she placed her arm through Sophie's. 'I couldn't give a monkey's as long as she's safe.' She hesitated before asking cautiously, 'When you say she's comin' here with the RAF ...?

The woman laughed. 'She won't be arrivin' by

plane, if that's what you're thinkin', but in the back of one of their trucks, so they said for you to wait for her on the steps outside.'

'You've got to hand it to Isla,' grinned Meg. 'When she does somethin' she doesn't do it by halves!'

Feeling rather out of place, Isla joined Theo amongst the other servicemen and women, all of whom greeted her merrily before continuing with their conversations. Listening to the laughter and comradeship between her fellow travellers, she couldn't help but think how wonderful it must be to be part of such a big organisation. *I wonder if it's like this in the merchant navy?* she mused as the truck bumped its way down the road. *I hope it is, for Dad's sake, cos even though I don't think I'll ever be able to forgive him for leavin' me behind, I wouldn't want to think of him as bein' unhappy.*

Sitting on the bench opposite, Theo leaned forward, a twinkle in his eye. 'Penny for them?'

'I was just thinkin' how lovely it must be to be a part of the services,' said Isla. 'Everyone seems so upbeat.'

'You certainly can't beat the camaraderie, it's like one big happy family,' confirmed Theo, 'but it does have its downsides – early mornin's and awful grub bein' the main two.'

'I'm used to both of those,' said Isla. 'Minus the happiness and laughter.'

He pulled a disapproving face. 'That doesn't sound much fun!'

'Good. Cos in that case I've described it correctly.'

143

She glanced at the other travellers before continuing in quieter tones. 'I must say, they've taken my presence ever so well. Not bein' a part of the services, I did rather fear I might be given the cold shoulder, or told to sling my hook even.'

'No chance!' said Theo. 'You're still one of us, uniform or not.'

'He means you're British,' explained a woman who was sitting next to Isla. Smiling, she introduced herself. 'I'm Sally, by the way.'

'Pleased to meet you, Sally. I'm Isla, and for the record I wouldn't mind bein' one of you,' said Isla. 'Not if it's like this I wouldn't.'

'It's hard work, but fun at the same time,' agreed Sally. 'And you soon get used to bein' barked at by the sergeants, who are a pretty decent sort if you toe the line. But as Theo quite rightly said, the food in the cookhouse is pretty rank most of the time.'

'It cannae be worse than sharin' your food with rats and cockroaches,' said Isla matter-of-factly.

Theo stared at her in stunned disbelief. 'Surely you jest?'

'Me and my pals were in the poorhouse before we left Scotland,' said Isla. 'Suffice to say the rumours surrounding such places are true.'

Theo rubbed his chin whilst eyeing her thoughtfully. 'From what I can remember people don't tend to leave the poorhouse unless their families come for them?'

She locked eyes with him. 'That didn't happen in our case. It was more of a self-help kind of thing.'

His eyes glittered with admiration. 'So you left under your own steam? Good for you!'

'I'd rather leave on foot than in a box,' said Isla.

'They're terrible places, and I can only commend you for gettin' yourself out of there,' said Sally. She hesitated. 'Have you thought about joinin' up? Only the services are cryin' out for people with your kind of spirit.'

'I'm not sure I'd be qualified,' said Isla, 'unless the WAAF need people who can sew, of course, because that was my job before enterin' the poorhouse.'

'It may surprise you, but they do. In fact they need all kinds of people from all walks of life,' replied Sally warmly.

Theo was watching Isla with curiosity. 'Feel free to tell me to mind my own business, but I cannot fathom for the life of me how such a lovely, level-headed young woman as yourself ended up in the poorhouse, especially when you already had a job.'

Sally glared at him. 'Theo! You really shouldn't ask . . .'

'It's fine,' Isla assured her. 'I'd be wonderin' the same if I were in his position. After all, it's only the poor and destitute that enter the poorhouse, right?'

'I must admit, that's what I always thought . . .' confessed Sally.

'Me too,' said Isla, 'but we weren't destitute or poor when my father left me there . . .'

Theo and Sally listened in rapt silence as Isla went on to explain the dire string of events that had led to her incarceration. When she had finished, Theo blew his cheeks out. 'And I thought I had it tough being the runt of the litter!'

Isla smiled. 'You have siblings?'

'Six brothers all older than myself, which means I always had everyone else's hand-me-downs,' said Theo. 'Somethin' I've always whinged about – until now, that is.'

'Makes you realise how lucky we are,' agreed Sally.

The driver hit the brakes a little harder than intended, causing Isla to grab hold of the nearest support, which turned out to be Theo's knee. Flushing brightly, she swiftly removed her hand whilst gabbling an apology.

'Don't worry. You can't help what the driver does,' Theo assured her. Peering out of the back of the lorry, he stood up. 'We're here.'

Isla said her goodbyes to her fellow travellers and followed Theo to the tailgate, where he gently lifted her to the ground. 'Can you see your pals?'

Isla stood on tiptoe as she craned her neck for a better view. Eventually spying Meg and Sophie waving frantically as they hurried down the steps, she turned back to Theo. 'That's them over there.' She grinned and waved back.

Theo looked to the driver, who was leaning out of his window. 'Do me a favour and hang on for a minute, won't you?'

The driver rolled his eyes in a good-natured fashion. 'All right, but be quick about it.'

Theo gave a thumbs up. 'There's a good feller!' Turning back to Isla, he spoke hastily. 'I know we don't know each awfully well, but I think you're a smashin' lass, and I'd like to get to know you better – if that's all right with you, of course?'

Isla was delighted. 'I'd like that.'

'Splendid. How about I take you out to dinner tomorrow evenin'?'

'That would be lovely, but you've done so much for me already I feel that I should be the one takin' you out to dinner, not the other way round.'

'I wouldn't dream of askin' a woman out on a date and expectin' her to cough up,' said Theo.

Knowing that her cheeks were burning brighter than a traffic light, Isla wished she had been born with a warmer complexion. 'I didn't realise you meant take me on a date,' she said, embarrassed by her innocence.

'Does that mean you've changed your mind?'

Isla swallowed. 'Not at all.'

'Splendid!'

Hearing someone clear their throat, Isla turned to see that Sophie and Meg were standing behind her. Meg was grinning from ear to ear, but Sophie was eyeing Theo with uncertainty. 'Not that I wish to interfere . . .' she began.

Eager to dispel any concerns she may have, Theo soon put her mind at ease. 'I promise to take good care of her,' he said, 'and to have her back before the clock strikes eleven.'

'Pleased to hear it!' said Sophie.

The driver tooted his horn, bringing them to his attention. 'Time to go, Romeo!' he called out from his position in the cab.

Theo gave him a thumbs up before turning back to Isla. 'I'll meet you at this very spot tomorrow evenin', say six o'clock?'

'I'll look forward to it.' They watched him jump into the back of the wagon, where he was met with a resounding chorus of cheers.

'Why couldn't I have been the one that missed the train?' pouted Meg as they watched the truck drive away.

Sophie laughed, and Isla did too, before saying, 'Only I didn't miss my train,' and going on to tell the girls everything that had transpired since she left them.

'Blimey! Sounds like you did just about everythin' bar solve world peace,' said Sophie with admiration.

'It certainly feels that way,' said Isla, 'but it makes you think, doesn't it? Cos had I not followed Gemma on to the wrong train, I wouldn't have been there to help, nor met Theo, so to say all's well that ends well seems a trifle understated.'

'He seems very confident,' noted Sophie.

'Probably comes from bein' in the services.' Isla glanced around her. 'I wonder how far we are away from Arkles Lane?'

'No idea,' said Meg. Her eyes settling on a young man selling newspapers, she jerked her head in his direction. 'I'll see if he knows.'

Watching the highly animated conversation between Meg and the young boy, Isla grimaced. 'It looks like it might be quite far away, judgin' by the hand gestures he's givin' Meg.'

'We can always ask again if we forget,' said Sophie.

'Although you'd best take note if you're comin' back tomorrow.'

Isla blushed shyly. 'What did you make of him?'

'He's incredibly good-lookin', a blind man could see that, but whilst he says his intentions are honourable we only have his word for it.'

'I'm aware that I barely know him, but we talked a lot on the way here, and he seems genuine to me.'

'What did he say that makes you think so?'

'Nothin' as per se, but he came across as bein' open and honest.'

'I really don't want to be a stick-in-the-mud,' said Sophie, 'but I think it only wise to warn you that he might have somethin' more than dinner in mind.'

'Such as?'

Sophie opened her mouth to respond, then closed it again. She had no idea how clued-up Isla was when it came to the birds and the bees, but now was not the time to be coy, she decided, not when Isla would be going on a date with him unaccompanied. 'Some men use their charm and good looks to worm their way into one lady's boudoir before movin' on to the next after they've had their wicked way.'

Isla couldn't help but giggle. 'My boudoir?'

Sophie rolled her eyes. 'You know what I mean!'

'I do! But they could only do that if the lady allowed them, and believe you me, I've no intentions of droppin' me drawers for any man, no matter how good-lookin' or charmin' they may be!'

'Glad to hear it!' chuckled Sophie as she watched Meg heading back.

'It's ages away,' said Meg as she rejoined them. 'We'd best get goin' before I forget what he said.'

As they walked, Isla mulled over Sophie's words. Was Theo only being nice so that he could bed her? Of course it was possible, but even so, what was the harm in her having some fun, as long as she kept her wits about her? *No harm at all*, Isla concluded. *Cos if Theo even* thinks *about havin' his wicked way with me, I shall tell him he's barkin' up the wrong tree*!

'Never let it be said I don't pay out,' said one of Theo's fellow airmen as he drew some money from his wallet and handed it over. 'I must admit, I didn't think you'd actually go through with it, but havin' seen her I can see why you did!'

Theo pocketed the money with a grin. 'Luck of the draw, I guess!'

Sally stared at him open-mouthed, her eyes narrowing. 'You asked her out for a *bet*?'

He coughed on a chuckle. 'You make it sound as though I did somethin' wrong.'

'Askin' someone out for a bet *is* wrong!' snapped Sally. 'How do you think she'd feel if she knew you'd only asked her out for that?'

'I didn't ask her out *just* to win a bet,' said Theo.

Dominic raised his brow. 'In which case I'll have it back,' he joked.

Theo wagged a finger. 'Sorry, no can do. I'll be usin' this to take Isla out tomorrow evenin'.'

Sally relented, but only slightly. 'I do hope you're speakin' the truth!'

He drew the sign of the cross over his left breast. 'Cross me heart and hope to die!'

She scowled reprovingly. 'You shouldn't say things like that.'

'Does that mean I'm forgiven?' Theo asked with a playful nudge.

'I suppose so.'

'Good!'

As Sally continued to read her book, Theo turned to his own thoughts. He knew that Dominic had suggested the wager because he wanted Theo to move on with his life, but as Theo knew from bitter experience, life didn't always work out the way you wanted it to. *One mistake*, Theo told himself, *that's all it took, yet my life has changed for ever, and no matter what Dom might think, it's goin' to take a lot more than one date for me to escape the ghosts that continue to haunt me.*

Rapping yet another brief tattoo on the door of number thirty-three, Isla turned to Sophie. 'Are you *certain* this is the right address?'

Sophie frowned as she checked the house number against the details Harvey had written down. 'Irene Ellis, number thirty-three Arkles Lane, so unless there's two Arkles Lanes in Liverpool we're definitely at the right place.'

'Maybe she's popped out for the evenin', or even gone to work,' suggested Meg. 'I know the factories run day and night in Clydebank, so I'm guessin' they do here.'

Sophie tucked the paper back into her pocket. 'If she *does* work nights, then it's likely she's in bed.'

Isla stood back from the door to look up at the window above, in the hope that she might see the curtains twitch, but they were wide open. 'So not in bed then,' she concluded. 'Bearin' that in mind, what should we do if she's not in? Cos we can hardly stay out here all night.'

Sophie let out a sigh. 'A B&B will cost us an arm and a leg.'

'But I thought Harvey gave us money to cover our room and board for a couple of nights?' Meg asked anxiously.

'He did, but given that Irene's his sister, I should imagine she won't charge the same rates as a B&B, so what should've lasted a couple of nights will be gone in one.'

Meg looked to the house next door. 'As Irene knows to expect us, maybe she left word with one of her neighbours?'

Isla was already rapping her knuckles on the neighbouring front door. 'Only one way to find out,' she said, before smiling brightly at a woman in her mid-fifties who was eyeing them curiously from behind the curtain of her front window.

'Looks like we've got a taker,' commented Meg as the curtain dropped.

'Let's hope she knows somethin',' hissed Isla as the sound of approaching footsteps neared the other side of the door, which opened slowly to reveal a short, dumpy woman with soft grey hair that hung around her cheeks in waves.

'I'm sorry, girls, but I'm afraid I'm not buyin' . . .' she began, before Isla stopped her with a smile.

'We're not here to sell,' she said quickly, and went on to explain how Harvey had written to warn Irene of their impending arrival. 'So we believe she's expectin' us, only she doesn't appear to be in. I don't suppose she left word with you, did she?'

The woman's face dropped. 'You mean to say he doesn't know?'

The girls exchanged glances, with Sophie being the first to speak. 'Know what?'

'That Irene's joined the WAAF – she's not lived at this address for over a month.'

Isla covered her face with her hands and spoke thickly through her fingers. 'He can't have the foggiest, or he wouldn't have sent us here.'

'The postal service has been pretty rotten since war broke out,' suggested the older woman. 'All I can think is her letter must've got lost in the mail, because there's no way she wouldn't have told him of her intention, not given how close the two of them are.'

Meg looked hopefully towards the house next door. 'Does that mean it's empty?'

'Gosh, no. The Navy commandeered it to house some of their Wrens.'

Isla's brow crumpled. 'They use it to house birds?'

'Birds indeed!' cackled the woman, but kindly. 'The Wrens are the women's branch of the Royal Navy.'

Sophie placed her hands on her hips. 'At the end

of the day it doesn't matter who's in there, cos we're still in the same predicament!'

'We'll have to find somewhere to stay, and sharpish,' said Isla, 'or we really will be spendin' the night on the streets.'

The woman eyed them thoughtfully from over her spectacles before appearing to reach a decision. 'Given that you're friends of Harvey's, and I know he wouldn't send just anybody to stay with his sister, I suppose you could always kip here for the night.'

Isla brightened. 'That's ever so kind of you, but are you sure?'

'Positive.'

Elated that the woman had offered to provide them with shelter for the night, Isla showered her with thanks. 'It really is very kind of you,' she repeated. 'We cannae thank you enough.' Following their host inside, she continued, 'I'm Isla, by the way, and these are my friends Sophie and Meg.' The girls said hello in turn.

Introducing herself as Peggy, the woman spoke to them over her shoulder. 'You say that you're friends of Harvey's, but how did you meet? Cos that's a Scottish accent if I'm any judge.'

'It is indeed,' said Sophie as they followed her through to the parlour. Assuming that Peggy wouldn't know anything about Coxhill she pressed on, 'And in answer to your question, we met Harvey while he was workin' at a place called Coxhill . . .'

Peggy turned to look at them in surprise. 'The poorhouse?'

The girls stared at her open-mouthed, with Meg

being the first to voice their thoughts. 'How on earth do you know that?'

'Irene mentioned summat about her brother workin' in some God-awful poorhouse in Clydebank called Coxhill. I asked what he was doin' up that neck of the woods and she said it was all very hush-hush.' She shrugged. 'I know he'd been sellin' his services as a private dick, so guessed it was somethin' of that nature, only on a bigger scale.'

'And you'd be right,' said Meg, who saw no point in covering for Harvey when the woman clearly knew him far better than they did themselves, certainly enough to guess that he was working undercover.

'Harvey's the salt of the earth,' added Isla. 'He knew the woman in charge of the poorhouse was robbin' the system blind, and he was determined to do somethin' about it – that's where we came in.'

'Sounds like Harvey to me! Always puttin' others before himself.' She eyed their empty hands before continuing. 'Seein' as you've not a scrap of luggage between you, I'm guessin' you had to leave Coxhill in a hurry, but even so . . .' She stopped speaking as she realised the truth. 'You weren't working there, were you?'

Sophie shook her head slowly. 'No. Which is why we had to leave in a hurry, you see, no one was meant to know we were involved, but unfortunately for us it didn't quite work out that way.'

'It's a shame he didn't manage to contact his sister prior to us leavin',' remarked Isla, 'but maybe it was meant to be.'

'Fate,' said Peggy. 'I've an empty house – as you can see – and the three of you are in need of succour, which makes us a perfect match.'

Isla looked at the kitchen chairs, of which there were six. 'You have an awful lot of furniture for someone who lives on their own.'

Peggy gave her an approving glance. 'I can see why Harvey asked for your help – you're as sharp as a tack. Perfect material for his type of work. As for my empty house, I shall tell you that tale as we make a brew. Anyone for tea?'

'Yes please,' said all three girls, Isla adding, 'I've not had a drink in ages!'

Peggy pointed to a shelf containing cups and saucers. 'Can one of you be a dear and fetch me down some cups?' Sophie was the first on her feet, and Peggy pointed to Isla. 'You'll find the milk in the pantry, dear, which is just behind me, and . . .' she hesitated as she looked thoughtfully at Meg, '. . . Meg, was it?' Meg nodded. 'There's some bread and cheese in the pantry, so feel free to make a round of sandwiches each, and one for me too, if you wouldn't mind.'

Pleased to be of assistance, the girls happily set about their given tasks. 'You were goin' to tell us about your empty house that was obviously once full to the rafters?' Isla hinted as she brought the milk from the pantry.

'I've four sons and a husband,' said Peggy, as she placed the kettle on to boil. 'My husband's a merchant sailor, so he's rarely home, and our sons joined up as soon as war was declared.'

Isla looked at the seats of the chairs, which were worn through use. 'I cannae imagine what it must be like for you, going from a houseful to . . .'

Peggy finished the sentence for her. 'Nothing, and it's awful, but it was their choice to join, so I have to respect their decision and pray that they'll come home safe.' She scooped the tea leaves into the pot ready for the water to be added. 'It's good to be makin' a brew for more than one person, I must say,' she told the girls, 'even if it's only for a night or two.'

Meg buttered the bread. 'As long as we're not intruding.'

Peggy poured the boiling water into the pot. 'Not in the least. I'm sick of hearin' my own voice. I actually enjoy goin' to work because I get to see other people.'

'Where do you work?' asked Isla.

'Tate and Lyle,' said Peggy. 'Have done for years.'

'I don't suppose they need any workers?' hazarded Sophie, but Isla was quick to intervene.

'Not for me, I'm goin' to join the WAAF.'

Peggy readied the tea tray with cups and saucers along with milk and sugar. 'Why the WAAF in particular?'

'Our Isla's bagged herself a date with a handsome airman,' said Meg. Chuckling wickedly, she added, 'Not that I'm suggestin' that's the reason for her decision, mind you.'

Isla blushed shyly. 'It was more down to the camaraderie I experienced whilst travellin' with the others in the back of that truck. They were so friendly and chipper, like one big happy family. I know that it won't always be like that, but I think I'd still like to join regardless.' She glanced to Sophie and Meg. 'What do you think?'

'It would certainly hit two birds with one stone when it comes to employment and accommodation,' mused Sophie, 'but I'm not sure they'd accept us when we've no real skills to speak of.'

'That's what I said,' Isla told her, 'but Sally – she was one of the Waafs – reckons they're lookin' for all sorts.'

Peggy poured the tea into the cups while giving her opinion. 'The services will take on anyone who's willing to sign on the dotted line.'

'Because they're desperate?' hazarded Meg.

'I don't like to say so, but yes,' said Peggy. 'Beggars can't be choosers, which is why they take underage boys into the army.'

'Well, that bein' the case, I say we sign up first thing tomorrow mornin',' said Isla, whilst continuing in the privacy of her own mind, *and with a bit of luck I'll be posted to the same camp as Theo!*

Meg, however, was frowning. 'Underage? How old do you have to be?'

'Eighteen,' said Peggy promptly.

Isla's cheeks ruddied, as did Meg's.

Peggy arched a singular eyebrow. 'Had I best not ask?'

'We're both seventeen,' confessed Isla, adding miserably, 'I'm guessin' that means we won't be signin' on the dotted line any time soon!'

'It didn't stop them lads,' said Peggy matter-of-factly.

'If you're dead set on joinin' up, I've got a pen here somewhere.'

Both girls brightened. 'You mean you don't think we'd be doin' the wrong thing?' said Isla.

'It's your life,' said Peggy, who was rummaging in drawer of the writing bureau as she spoke. Turning round, she beckoned the girls over. 'Who fancies chancin' their arm?'

The two girls spent some time practising changing the number three to a two, and with successful attempts at last on their birth certificates, they had settled down to enjoy the rest of the evening.

'What's done is done,' said Meg, as Peggy led them up the wooden staircase to the bedroom they'd be sharing. 'The most they can do is give us a dressin' down for tryin' to pull the wool over their eyes.'

'In which case we'll join the NAAFI,' said Sophie, as Peggy opened the door to the bedroom and led them inside.

'It's lovely, Peggy,' said Isla as her eyes took in the cheerfully patterned wallpaper, and the warm rug which covered most of the bare floorboards.

'It'll be like sleepin' on a cloud, compared to Coxhill,' said Meg as she looked out of the window to the lane below.

Sophie smoothed her hand over the feather eiderdown of the bed nearest the door, her gaze wandering over the large wooden wardrobe with its mirrored door, and the walnut chest of drawers which supported a porcelain ewer and wash bowl. 'We've gone from livin' like cockroaches to princesses, I don't think there're enough words in the dictionary to express our thanks.'

Peggy's face was wreathed in wrinkles as she smiled. 'Your company is thanks enough!'

Chapter Seven

It was the following day and the girls were up betimes, excited about the morning ahead.

'I must say I'm pleased you managed to get hold of your ration books,' said Peggy as she checked the pantry for supplies. 'We're goin' to need more bread, as well as some corned beef, baked beans and potatoes.' She paused momentarily as she added something to the shopping list. 'Is everyone happy with corned beef hash for dinner?'

'We're happy with anythin',' said Sophie, as Isla entered the room with two jugs of milk, 'except tripe, I cannae bear the stuff!'

'And Isla won't be bothered, because she'll be on a date with Theo,' Meg put in.

'What's this?' asked Isla as she placed one of the milk jugs down in the pantry before bringing the other back into the kitchen.

'Talkin' about the corned beef hash that we're havin' for our tea tonight,' said Sophie.

'And I was sayin' how you won't be joinin' us on account of your hot date with Theo,' finished Meg.

Isla rolled her eyes. 'Hot date indeed! I barely know him.'

Sophie stirred the porridge, which was beginning to simmer. 'I'm not sure you have to know someone awfully well in order to go on a "hot date".'

Isla swilled the tea in the pot before straining it into four cups. 'Truth be told I don't even know what's meant by a "hot date".'

'It refers to passion rather than a meetin' of the minds,' said Peggy knowledgeably. 'If you find him as physically attractive as he finds you, I think that's what's meant by a "hot date".'

Isla thought about this for a moment as she poured some of the milk from the big jug into a smaller one. 'I'd be lyin' if I said I didn't find him attractive, but that doesn't mean I intend to smooch the night away.'

'Oh,' said Meg. She wrinkled her nose, clearly disappointed. 'I would if I were you.'

'Meg!' chortled Sophie.

Meg looked up innocently. 'What?'

'Nice girls don't kiss on the first date!' chided Sophie, albeit in a kind tone of voice.

Meg placed the four bowls she'd fetched from the dresser on the table along with the spoons. 'They don't? That's a pity!'

'I can see you're goin' to have fun in the services,' chuckled Peggy, ''cos it doesn't matter which one you join, they're all full of handsome fellers!'

Meg was struggling to control the grin that was splitting her cheeks. 'Where do I sign?'

'Jokin' aside,' said Sophie, 'just think of all the time

we wasted in the poorhouse when we could've been servin' our country. I think it utter madness that folk who would do anythin' to get out of the system are unable to do so just because some greedy woman wants the money!'

Peggy frowned. 'I thought folk ended up in the poorhouse – or workhouse as we call them in Liverpool – because they didn't have any money?'

'They don't. But the government gives Harman a sum of money towards their keep, so the more mouths she has to feed the more money she gets,' Isla explained.

'But if the government pays their keep, then surely it's just as easy and more productive for them to pay them a wage as members of the services? No matter what this Harman of yours wants,' said Peggy as she watched Sophie pour the gently bubbling porridge into the bowls.

'Not if they're not fit enough,' said Sophie. 'Harman tries to make sure the inmates are strong enough to work, but not to join up. Fortunately, she didn't manage that with us.'

Peggy took the empty saucepan from Sophie and placed it in the sink to soak. 'Wicked! There's no other word for it.'

'At least Harvey put an end to all that.'

Peggy laced her porridge with a drizzle of honey before passing the pot to Isla. 'I know it's none of my business, but how on earth did three smashers such as yourselves end up in the poorhouse?'

Each of the girls told her their story, the last to speak

being Isla, who finished with: 'I know some people' – she glanced at Sophie with a wry smile – 'believe I should cut my father some slack, but some things are easier said than done.'

Peggy blew on the spoonful of porridge poised before her lips. 'What happened to your lovely little family was dreadful, but I think it's healthy that you can talk about what happened so openly. Did your father talk about it much?'

Isla's wrinkled her nose. 'Not at all! He always referred to it as "what happened", and as for Mammy? He didn't even like it if I talked about her, which upset me even more.'

'The trouble with men is their inability to handle their emotions,' said Peggy sadly. 'All this stiff upper lip nonsense does no one any good! Cos it only manifests itself in other ways.'

Meg appeared to be confused. 'How do you mean?'

'Grief will always come out in the end, and the longer it festers the worse it will be,' said Peggy simply.

'But what's that got to do with talkin'?' asked Isla, who couldn't see the point to Peggy's cautionary tale.

'Talkin' is good for the soul,' said Peggy. 'It helps you to process what happened and slowly come to terms with your loss; that's why I said it was healthy for you to talk about your mammy so openly.'

'I always tried to get Dad to talk, but he refused,' said Isla sadly, 'which is a shame because he might not have put me in the poorhouse had he done so.'

'Maybe bein' at sea will give him the chance to

grieve properly,' said Peggy. 'Maybe that's why he was so keen to set sail.'

'If I join the WAAF he won't know where to find me,' said Isla softly. 'Cos with Coxhill under new management there'll be no one to tell him where I went or what became of me.'

'Harvey knew what we were plannin' to do,' said Meg reasonably. 'I'm sure he'll let the new people know where you can be reached should your father come lookin'.'

'Only they're bound to ask who I was,' Isla pointed out, but it seemed that Meg had thought of the answer to this too.

'He can say you worked there before joinin' the services – which is true in a way, because we all did, really.'

Isla looked uncertain. 'And do you think that would work?'

'I cannae see why not. Although you won't be able to tell him where you'll be until you've had your papers through.'

'You can give him my address in the interim period,' said Peggy. 'I'm sure Harvey would appreciate a phone call lettin' him know that the three of you made it to Liverpool in one piece and, as I said last night, you're welcome to stay as long as you need – I shall enjoy the company. You can use the telephone box at the end of our road,' she added helpfully.

Isla smiled. 'Thanks Peggy. I'll telephone en route to . . .' She hesitated. 'Where do we go to sign up?'

'The town hall,' said Peggy, and gave them brief

directions on how to get there. Looking at the clock, she gave a small exclamation before jumping to her feet and gathering the empty dishes. 'I'll have to dash if I'm to make it to work on time.'

'We'll do all that,' said Sophie. 'You get yourself off to work.'

Thanking the girls profusely, Peggy handed the shopping list to Sophie then grabbed her coat from its hook by the door. Trilling her goodbyes from over her shoulder, she was halfway out of the house when she remembered the key. 'You can either leave it under the mat or take it with you,' she said, placing it on the hall stand. 'You'll most likely be back before me, so it makes no odds either way. With that bein' said, good luck and goodbye!' The girls rang out a chorus of goodbyes as the door closed behind her.

'I'll wash while you two dry,' said Sophie as she began washing the pots.

It didn't take them long to do the dishes and, with Sophie being the first to finish, Sophie used the dish-cloth to wipe the table down before rinsing it out in the sink. 'I think that's everything,' she said as she cast an eye around the room. 'Are we ready?'

'As we'll ever be,' said Isla, 'although I do feel a tad nervous.'

'Me too,' said Sophie.

'Why?' asked Meg, who was more excited than anything else.

'Don't you think it might look a bit rum when three girls from Clydebank walk into Liverpool town hall askin' to sign up?' Sophie said as they left the house.

'Just because we're all from Clydebank it doesn't mean to say we know each other,' Meg began, but was quickly corrected by Isla.

'When we're all usin' the same address for correspondence?' she pointed out as she slipped the key under the mat.

'Oh, heck. I hadn't thought of that.'

'Half-truths,' said Isla slowly. 'If we tell them that we were livin' in a tenement that got levelled by the Luftwaffe, that would explain why three women with different surnames wound up homeless at the same time. Although with hindsight I hardly think it will matter, when you consider what Peggy said about them bein' desperate for volunteers.'

Meg pointed to the telephone box that Peggy had told them of, and they made their way towards it, Sophie fishing out some coins from the envelope containing their money whilst Isla opened the door and picked up the receiver. Taking the coins from Sophie, Isla asked the operator to put her through to Coxhill.

Waiting with baited breath, all three girls crowed with delight as Harvey's voice came down the line, leaving him in no doubt as to who was on the other end.

'Am I ever glad to hear from the three of you!' he breathed. 'I can't tell you how worried I was when I heard the siren go off.'

'We're fine,' Isla assured him, 'but we're not stayin' with your sister because she's joined the WAAF.' She started to tell him all that happened but Harvey was already talking across her.

'I know. I got her letter the day after you left! As

you can imagine I was beside myself with worry as to what would happen when you discovered you had nowhere to stay. I never meant to send you off on a wild goose chase.'

'Please don't worry,' Isla assured him. 'Peggy Thomas – Irene's next-door neighbour – has offered to put us up for a bit.'

'Has she indeed!' Harvey said with approval. 'I have to say I'm not surprised to hear she came up trumps. Irene's always spoken of her with great fondness, and she was always nice to me whenever I came by to visit.'

'She's an absolute saint,' said Isla, 'but we want to know what happened after we left. Did you get Harman bang to rights as we hoped you would?'

He chuckled softly. 'I did indeed, and she's awaiting trial for defrauding the government.'

He heard Isla give a small whoop of joy before repeating his words to Meg and Sophie. 'That's the best news we could have wished for,' said Isla, adding quickly, 'and before I forget, can you pass Peggy's address on to Harman's successor just in case my father should come for me?'

'Not a problem. Is she number thirty-one or thirty-five? I can never quite remember.'

'Thirty-five,' said Isla.

Sophie caught Isla's eye, gesturing that she would like to have a word with him before her friend hung up. 'I'll just put Sophie on,' Isla said, and passed the receiver over.

'Harvey?'

'Yes?'

'Thanks for everythin'. I know we've said it more than once, but it was all such a rush, and I wanted you to know how much we appreciate everythin' you did for us.'

She could hear the smile in his voice as he replied. 'My pleasure. And if it's all right with you, I'd like to stay in touch, see how you get on and so forth.'

'That would be nice. I think we're all keen to know the outcome of Harman's court case as well as what's happening in Coxhill. Am I to take it that you're in charge for the time being?'

'You are, but they're doin' interviews as we speak, so I'm hopin' to be out of here within the next couple of days.'

'Does that mean you'll be comin' back to Liverpool?'

'I'm afraid not, as my services are required in Birmingham. It seems the governors were quite impressed with the way I handled the Harman case. I must say I feel a bit of a fraud, considerin' you lot did most of the work!'

'Well you shouldn't,' chided Sophie, 'and the governors are right to be impressed with your work! But for you none of this would've happened – and before I forget, what did happen to Madson?'

'I'm afraid we couldn't pin anythin' on him, cos it's his word against hers. He's been sacked, though, because the governors know he can't be trusted.'

'Good! Quite right too!' said Sophie.

The operator cut across, letting them know their time was up. Speaking rapidly, Sophie reminded him of the main reason for the phone call. 'I'm goin' to have to go, but best of British, and don't forget to pass on the message for Isla's father, will you?'

'It'll be my next job,' said Harvey, adding, 'Take care, all.'

Sophie was about to say goodbye when the line went dead. Replacing the receiver, she stepped out of the kiosk to relay the news of Madson's sacking, and finished with, 'Harvey's goin' to pass your message on, Isla, but he won't be comin' back to Liverpool for the foreseeable, as he's off to Birmingham to do another job for the government.'

'This could prove to be a regular stint for Harvey,' said Isla as they resumed their walk to the town hall. 'You never know, they might even give him his own team of private investigators!'

'He's certainly got his work cut out if many institutions are as corrupt as Coxhill,' said Meg, 'and it wouldn't surprise me if they were!'

'It's a shame they couldn't pin anythin' on Madson, but good to hear he's been given the sack. Perhaps he'll think twice in future before tryin' to rip off the innocent,' said Isla.

'We can only hope,' said Sophie.

As the girls made their way to the town hall, the conversation turned to the alterations they'd made to their birth certificates and their alternative plan of joining the NAAFI should the WAAF turn them down.

'We'll still be a part of the services,' said Meg

plainly, 'and we can always apply again once we turn eighteen. But I reckon they'll probably turn a blind eye, just as they do with the lads.'

'You're only a couple of months off being eighteen, so I'd be surprised if they turned you down,' said Isla. 'I, on the other hand, have almost a whole year before I'm of age.' She jumped as Meg emitted a long 'Ooooh' and pointed to the queue of people waiting outside the town hall.

'Will you look at that!' she breathed, continuing with a chuckle, 'The women must've heard about the handsome men in uniform.'

'Good news for you two,' said Sophie. 'They might not be so thorough with their checks given the amount of people they have to get through.'

Isla looked along the queue ruefully. 'Which brings me to another matter. With so many wantin' to sign on the dotted line, do you suppose they might run out of places?'

'I'm afraid I don't think there's any fear of that happenin',' said Sophie darkly. 'There's probably new openin's all the time.'

Isla was about to ask what Sophie meant by this when she cottoned on. 'Oh,' she said weakly, 'that's not a nice thought.'

'Realistic, though,' said Sophie 'and somethin' everyone should think about before signin' up.'

Meg, who'd not given the matter a second thought, turned to her friends. 'Have you both been thinkin' about it? Cos it hadn't even crossed my mind!'

'A little,' said Isla. 'But even though I'm aware of the danger, I still want to do my bit, because I don't know where we'd be if everyone decided against it.'

'We'd be up a certain creek without a paddle,' said Sophie. 'I agree with you; I think we all need to pull together if we're to win this thing.'

Pretending her fingers to be a smoking barrel, Meg blew on them. 'Bloomin' Nazis! Just give me a gun and point me in the right direction.'

The man in front of them turned to look at her with widening eyes. 'What on earth makes you think they'd give you a gun?'

Meg raised her eyebrows. 'Isn't that why they call them the armed forces?' she asked haughtily.

'They arm the men,' said the man. 'Not the women.'

Isla stared at him in disbelief. 'So we'll be no better off than the civilians?'

'I wouldn't say that, not when you're on a base full of weaponry.' He paused to move up the queue. 'I dare say it might be different if they asked you to go to the front line, but you should hope it never comes to that.'

'That would be a dark day indeed,' said Sophie soberly.

Meg, who was now trying to put all thoughts of guns far from her mind, stood on tiptoe to see how far up the corridor the line stretched. 'Can anyone see the head of the queue?'

'Crumbs,' said Sophie, who was craning her neck for a better look as well, 'it goes all the way up to the top of the corridor!'

'That's probably why it takes a couple of weeks to process everybody,' said the man conversationally.

'Two weeks – but that's ages!' moaned Meg. Turning to the others, she added, 'We'll have to get some temporary work to tide us over, cos the money Harvey gave us won't stretch that far.'

'Such as what?' asked Isla. 'We cannae apply to any of the factories, because they'll want someone more permanent.'

'What about one of the laundries?' supposed Meg. 'It's somethin' we already know how to do, so they wouldn't have to waste any time showin' us the ropes.'

'You could try one of the Chinese laundries,' put in the man. 'They're always on the look-out for more workers on account of girls leavin' to sign up.'

'Sounds good to me,' said Sophie, 'so long as they don't mind the fact that we too won't be there for long.'

'Nah, they're pretty easy-goin',' said the man. 'And besides, any help is better than nothin'. You should give Mr Lee a visit; he's got a business on the Scottie Road. Tell him Cuthbert sent you.' He thrust his thumb towards his chest. 'That's me.'

The girls thanked him for the advice as they introduced themselves.

'Do you know Mr Lee well, then?' added Meg.

'I do, yes. He employed my daughters before they signed up; that's how I know he'll take all the help he can, no matter how temporary.'

As they continued to move further up the queue the

girls chatted with Cuthbert about his daughters and the war in general until he reached the front. 'Your turn, Cuthbert,' said Isla as the soldier sitting behind the desk called for the next in line to come forward. She turned to her pals. 'Did you notice? Not once, in the whole time that we spoke to him, did he mention our accents or ask why we were in Liverpool.'

'You're right!' said Meg. She crossed her fingers. 'And if he didn't, maybe the soldier what's takin' everyone's details won't either.'

'We can but hope. I wonder whether it makes any difference which desk you go to?' Isla was looking round at some of the other desks.

'I shouldn't have thought so,' said Sophie. 'It's just to get through everyone quicker.'

Hearing the soldier at the desk to her left shout out 'Next' in a booming voice, Isla asked the girls to wish her luck and hastened towards him. As she had hoped, he showed no interest in her accent, or her address, or her date of birth. She said as much when she reconvened with Sophie and Meg outside.

'The feller who processed my papers looked thoroughly bored,' said Meg. 'Unsurprising, if he's been at it all day.'

'Mine too,' said Isla. 'I asked him how long it would take for our papers to come through and he practically yawned when he said it'd be close to two weeks.'

'So what now, then?' said Sophie. 'The market, or the Chinese laundry?'

'I suppose that depends on which is closer,' said Isla. Seeing Cuthbert leaving the hall, she hurried after him. 'Which is closer? The Greatie, or the laundry?'

He smiled. 'The Greatie. I'm goin' that way meself if you fancy joinin' me?'

'That would be wonderful, thank you,' said Sophie. 'We have a lot to do today and very little time to do it in, so any advice you can give us would be much appreciated.'

'Well, you'll find everythin' you want in Liverpool,' said Cuthbert loyally. 'We've shops to suit every budget, from rags to riches.'

'That's good to know, cos I'm afraid we're more on the rags side of things, which is why we're goin' to the market,' said Meg. 'Cos it's cheap as chips, or so we've heard.'

He grinned. 'It is that, but the stuff's decent, mind. They don't sell you rubbish just because it's cheap.' Chatting merrily away, Cuthbert told the girls of the best places to eat, the different parks, and the good times to be had at the various dance halls.

'He's a mine of information,' said Isla when they eventually bade him goodbye.

'Very handy indeed,' agreed Sophie as they began perusing the stalls. 'I haven't browsed a market like this in years. A shame really, because it was one of Mammy's and my favourite pastimes.'

Isla threaded her arm through her friend's. 'I think all girls like to go shoppin' with their mammy. I know I did.'

'Me too,' agreed Meg dolefully. 'It's more fun when

you've money to spend, though. We're goin' to have to be pretty thrifty until we can secure jobs.'

'That's a point,' said Isla, who was examining a pretty blue frock. 'Isn't this all a bit daft, us splashin' out on clothes and whatnot, when we're goin' to be provided with a uniform in a couple of weeks' time?'

'It's not so much frocks we need but other things,' said Meg as she picked up a comb, 'such as undies, nighties, toothpaste . . .' She blew her cheeks out. 'The list goes on and on.'

'It does indeed,' said Isla. Turning anxiously to Sophie, she glanced to the envelope. 'Are we goin' to have enough, do you think?'

Sophie looked into the envelope before nodding decidedly. 'As long as we get jobs to tide us over, then yes, but we'll have to mind the pennies even so.'

Their reluctance to spend too much had cost them time, but given the savings they'd made the girls weren't too bothered when they arrived outside the Chinese laundry some two hours later.

'Fingers crossed Mr Lee doesn't want to stand and chat, cos we've still got the grocery shoppin' to do,' said Meg. 'And I dare say Isla could do with a bath ahead of her big date tonight.'

Isla rolled her eyes. 'I keep forgettin' about the date. I almost wish I hadn't agreed to meet him now.'

'Why on earth not?' cried Meg.

'Cos it's all goin' to be a bit of a rush, and I'd rather

have time to think things through,' said Isla as they walked through the door to the laundry, where the owner was more than happy to take them on on a temporary basis, starting the very next day.

Outside again, Meg asked Isla just what she had to think through before her date.

'What I'm goin' to say to him,' said Isla. 'We've covered most things, or at least we have as far as my past is concerned.'

Meg pointed to the grocers which Peggy had recommended. 'Who's got the list?'

Sophie waved the scrap of paper as they entered the grocers, then handed it over to the shopkeeper, who placed the listed items in their net bag before marking Sophie's card and taking the money.

'I think that's us done for the day,' said Sophie as she peered into the bag. 'Won't I be glad to put me feet up when we get in!'

Meg agreed wholeheartedly. 'I feel as though I've been dragged through a hedge backwards!'

It was only a short walk from the grocers to Peggy's, and when they arrived Isla slid her fingers under the mat for the key, only to find it missing. 'Peggy must be back already,' she said. Pushing the door open, she called out, 'It's only us!' as they entered the house.

'Did you manage to get everything done?' Peggy asked as they made their way through to where she was sitting in the kitchen.

'Aye, and it's just as well that everythin's so

reasonably priced, because once you start it don't half add up,' said Isla. She raised the three bags she was carrying as proof.

'That's the beauty of the markets,' said Peggy as she took the net bag from Sophie, 'a little goes a long way. How did you manage down the recruitment office?'

'I think it went well,' said Isla, 'cos they said we'll know more in a fortnight when our papers come through.'

'So even though we know you said it was all right for us to stop on for a bit . . .' Sophie began, but Peggy cut her off.

'And I stand by that statement. Goodness only knows, it'll be wonderful havin' a houseful again.'

'Well, you needn't worry about us payin' our way, cos we got ourselves a couple of weeks' work down Mr Lee's laundry,' said Meg.

'I wouldn't have minded in the least had you got permanent jobs at the laundry. I know it's not even been a day, but I've really enjoyed your company, and you'd have been more than welcome to stay on as far as I'm concerned!' She sighed. 'Selfish of me, I know, but I'm goin' to miss you when you go!'

'We can always come back to visit if you'd like us to.'

'I'd like that very much,' said Peggy, 'I only got in half an hour or so before you came back, but even so the silence was deafening!'

Sophie placed the kettle on to boil. 'How often does Mr Thomas come home?'

'It depends. When he went to Africa, I didn't see him for nigh on a year.'

Sophie looked to Isla. 'For all we know, your father could've gone to Africa.'

'I'd say it's highly likely,' said Peggy. 'They have to go wherever there's a need, and right now they're needed everywhere, but there's only so many routes they can take due to the war.'

Isla found herself crossing her fingers below the table. 'Is it dangerous – bein' in the merchant navy?'

'The Krauts don't want supplies gettin' through, so I suppose it's not totally safe, but probably safer than it would be if he were on a warship.'

'Why on earth did he sign up for somethin' like that when he has a daughter waitin' for him back home? I wouldn't mind, but until Mammy died he was in a reserved occupation so he didn't have to go to war, and that's as good as what he's done.' She heaved an exasperated sigh. 'What was he thinking?'

'But isn't that rather the point?' said Peggy softly. 'He wasn't thinkin', was he? Or not with a straight head, at any rate.'

'I know,' said Isla miserably, 'but it doesn't stop me worryin' over him.'

'Of course you're worried – angry too, most probably – but bein' angry and worried won't change anythin',' Peggy pointed out. 'You just need to hope and pray that he comes home safe – that's what I do for my Clive; the boys too, come to that.'

'As do I,' said Isla, 'and you're right: frettin' doesn't help anyone.'

'Well, you've no time to fret when you've a date to get ready for,' Meg reminded her.

An image of Theo sprang to the forefront of Isla's mind. Tall, dark and handsome, he'd certainly prove a pleasant distraction. 'I must admit, it will do me good to let my hair down for a bit,' she said. 'I've forgotten what it's like to have fun, what with bein' cooped up in Coxhill for so long.' Suddenly remembering that they hadn't told Peggy of their conversation with Harvey, she did just that.

'Didn't I say the letter would've got lost?' said Peggy, slapping the table with the palm of her hand.

'You did, and you were right,' said Meg, 'but I have to question whether there was a greater force at play.'

Sophie stared at her. 'You think there was some sort of divine intervention?'

'Is it so far-fetched? Had our paths not crossed with Harvey's, we'd never have come to Liverpool. Isla would never have met Theo *or* helped Gemma in her hour of need.'

'It does seem to have worked out for the best,' agreed Sophie. 'Talkin' of Theo, oughtn't you be gettin' ready, Isla?'

Isla grimaced. 'I still haven't the foggiest what we're goin' to talk about.'

'After the day you've just had?' cried Peggy. 'Surely you jest!'

'Do you really think he'll be interested in our trip down the Greatie, or how we spent an age queuin' in order to sign up?' asked Isla uncertainly.

'After spendin' his day doin' the same sort of thing he does day in and day out,' said Peggy with a hint of sarcasm, 'of course he will! Life in the services can be extremely repetitive, as you'll find out soon enough.'

'A bit like it was in Coxhill,' supposed Sophie.

'Which is why anythin' different will be interestin' as far as he's concerned!' said Peggy.

Isla ran her fingers through her auburn locks. 'Would it be possible for me to wash my hair?'

'I can do you one better,' said Peggy. 'How does a hot bath grab you?'

'Heavenly,' sighed Isla, whilst Sophie and Meg looked on wistfully, something which didn't go unnoticed by their hostess.

'The two of you can jump in after her if you'd like?' she said.

'Oh, yes please – but we'll help you to prepare dinner first,' Sophie told her.

Peggy placed her hands on her hips. 'Part of the pleasure that comes with bein' a mother is cookin' for your children – somethin' I've missed since the boys headed off to war. So whilst I appreciate the offer, I'd be far happier seein' to dinner whilst the three of you have your bath. A bit like old times, you might say.'

'Only if you're sure?' said Meg.

'Positive! You can start by fetchin' the bath from the yard.'

Having done so, and placed several pans on to boil, the girls chatted excitedly. 'Have you thought about how you're goin' to do your hair?' Meg asked Isla.

'Not really. I've always worn it down, apart from when I was in school, when I wore it in a bun. I hated that, because I thought it made me look like Mrs Price from down the road.'

Meg laughed. 'Why, what was wrong with Mrs Price?'

'Nothin' really, but all the kids in my class branded her a witch cos she had a warty chin, and her face was covered in wrinkles, which made her look ancient.'

'And you think you looked like her just because you wore your hair in a bun?' Meg choked.

'Stupid, I know, but as Mrs Price would've been my age at one point in her life I figured she might well have looked like me,' Isla said as they set the bath down.

'So no bun, then?' chuckled Meg.

'Definitely not!' Isla tapped her forefinger against her chin. 'My mammy used to like my hair in a French braid. She said it made me look smart.'

Sophie poured the saucepans of hot water into the bath before coming over to examine Isla's hair. 'I could do you a French braid. I've not done one in a while, but that shouldn't matter any.'

'I'd like that very much,' Isla said gratefully. 'As long as it doesn't give Theo the wrong impression.'

Peggy fetched three fresh towels to hang in front of the fire so that they would be warm for when they'd finished their bath. 'How on earth can a French braid give someone the wrong impression?'

'I don't want him to think I'm desperate,' explained Isla. 'My daddy always used to say that it's the men should be doin' the chasin', *not* the women.'

'And you think by puttin' your hair in a French

braid Theo will think you're desperate?' Peggy shook her head. 'There's a difference between wantin' to look your best and wantin' to look, well, wanton, and you definitely don't fall into *that* category.'

Isla swirled her fingers through the warm water. 'Good, because that's the last thing I'd want to do.'

'Give us a shout when you're finished,' Sophie instructed, 'and Meg can have her bath whilst I fix your hair.'

With the others leaving her to enjoy the first proper bath she'd had in months, Isla was soon revelling in the warmth of the water as it caressed her body. *I wish my mammy were here*, she thought as she lathered the soap between her hands. *I just know she'd have a million questions about Theo and his intentions towards her little girl. On one hand she'd be pleased that he was smartly turned out, but on the other she'd want to know his future plans to make sure that he could take good care of me.* Her thoughts then turned to her father and how he'd react if he knew she was about to go on a date. She puffed out her cheeks as an image of her father, stony-faced, his arms folded across his chest as he eyed Theo with disapproval, entered her mind. *He'd want Theo to jump through hoops before he'd even consider allowin' me to go on a date with him. Which is pretty rich considerin' how he treated his only daughter! Quite frankly it doesn't matter what Theo does, cos it cannae be as bad as what my own father did, and he's meant to love me! Parents might have the best intentions* she conceded, *but even they slip up from time to time, so if anyone's goin' to judge whether Theo's good boyfriend material, that someone will be me. I shan't be askin' him what his plans are for five years' time, because no one knows the answer to that, especially not in this day and age. No, I shall make my own mind up as time goes on, which means that Theo will have to be patient if he wants to be my beau. That will be the best indicator of his worth: not how much money he makes, or what he's got in the bank, but whether he'll be there for me when the chips are down!*

Rinsing the soap suds from her hair and body, she stepped out of the bath, calling to Meg that it was her turn to get in.

'Any more thoughts on meetin' Theo tonight?' asked Sophie as she helped her to dry her hair in front of the fire.

'Aye,' said Isla as she snuggled into the warmth of the towel. 'Theo won't be gettin' the third degree, because talk is cheap. It's actions what speak louder than words, and if he wants to be my beau he will have to prove it by bein' patient and understandin'. If he cannae do that then he's not the feller for me!'

'A rule we should all live by,' said Peggy. 'There's too many men and women throwin' themselves into relationships just because we're at war, but what happens when the war is over and they have to live with someone they barely know?'

'I'm guessin' they're worried they might not make it to the end of the war, hence the urgency to get married,' Sophie suggested as she began braiding Isla's hair.

'Then why marry at all?' said Isla. 'It's hardly a symbol of love when they don't really know each other.'

'It's a symbol of desperation,' said Peggy quietly. 'Of not wantin' to die without at least samplin' summat of life first, and sex and marriage is a huge part of that.'

Isla's cheeks bloomed. 'So they only marry in order to . . .'

'Have their wicked way without tarnishin' their name or reputation,' Peggy supplied.

'But what if the girl gets in the family way?'

'That's why the services discourage relationships,' said Peggy. 'Not only do they make it harder for those who are widowed whilst still in their teens, but they stop women havin' to leave the services due to their condition.'

'What a dreadful world we live in,' said Isla sadly.

'Only whilst Hitler's alive,' said Peggy. 'You mustn't lose heart, queen; the world will go back to the way it was when we win the war.'

Isla glanced up at her from beneath her lashes. 'Do you really think we'll win?'

'No doubt about it,' said Peggy stoutly. 'Good will always triumph over evil, and that Hitler's the devil incarnate.'

'But what about the aftermath?' Sophie asked as she used a piece of ribbon fished out of Peggy's sewing box to fix Isla's hair in place. 'Cos I dare say there'll be countless widows as well as fatherless children – some of whom might possibly be motherless too should luck not be on their parents' side.'

'They don't think of that,' said Peggy. 'It's called livin' in the moment, and that's just what they're doin'.'

'Sad, though,' said Isla. 'Especially for the children.'

Meg came through, wrapped in a towel. 'Bath's free!'

Sophie finished off Isla's hair before standing up. 'The poorhouses will be bustin' at the seams.'

Isla's face fell. 'I hadn't thought of that.'

But Peggy was shaking her head. 'They can't do that to them, not after everythin' their parents did for their country.'

'I hope you're right,' said Sophie stoutly.

Meg was looking bemused until Isla had filled her in on their conversation, when she said decidedly, 'Peggy's right. They cannae do that to them after everythin' they've done for us.'

'I hope not,' said Isla, 'but there's one thing I do know.'

Sophie paused before heading off for her bath. 'And what's that?'

'I shan't be gettin' married to anyone whilst there's a war on!'

Chapter Eight

Isla's tummy was performing nervous cartwheels as the bus approached Lime Street Station. Seeing Theo standing on the steps as he tried to catch a glimpse of his date amongst the crowd, only made her feel worse.

Just remember, she told herself as the bus drew up to the stop, *it's your first date so there's no expectations from his side of things – or at least there better hadn't be.* Remembering the conversation she'd had with her friends before she left the house, she paid attention to Sophie's advice in particular. 'Just be you, and you'll not go far wrong,' Sophie had said as she passed Isla an umbrella in case of rain.

Slightly confused, Isla was pointing out that she could hardly be anybody else when Peggy cut in.

'You'd be surprised at the people who put on a front to impress a potential partner,' the older woman had said knowledgeably. 'Talkin' like they've got a plum in their mouth and money in the bank, when they're scouse through and through without a ha'penny to their name!'

'What's the point in that, when their dates are bound to find out the truth sooner or later?'

Peggy had tapped the side of her nose. 'They're hopin' to have a ring on their finger by that time.'

'But they'd be startin' their married life on a lie!'

Peggy shrugged. 'If you're as poor as a church mouse, I'd wager pennies come before principles!'

'And what about the poor unsuspectin' sod they married?' asked Meg.

'Too late,' said Peggy. 'And besides, who wants to admit they've been taken for a ride?'

Now, as she stepped down from the bus, Isla saw Theo hurrying towards her. 'I thought you might have had a change of heart,' he said as he reached her side.

'I wouldn't say second thoughts exactly, but with this bein' my first ever date I guess I did get a little nervous,' Isla admitted.

Theo smiled at her. 'There's really no need for you to feel that way. Just look at it as two people goin' out for dinner; what could be simpler than that?'

She smiled back. 'Nothin', when you put it that way.'

'There is no other way of puttin' it, or none as far as I can see,' said Theo. 'Now, how about we decide where we'd like to eat? We could have a sit-down dinner in a fancy restaurant, or fish and chips under the stars. I shall leave the choice to you!'

Isla didn't need to think twice. 'In which case I opt for fish and chips under the stars, please.'

He glittered at her affectionately. 'Ah! A woman after my own heart, but I'm curious. What made you opt for the second choice? I only ask because I'm guessin' most women would want dinner in a fancy restaurant – especially if someone else is footin' the bill!'

'For a start I didn't assume that you would be payin' the bill, and secondly eatin' fish and chips by moonlight is more me, if that makes sense.'

'Very much so,' said Theo. 'You can tell a lot about a person by their choices in life, and yours are runnin' parallel with my own so far.'

'Because I said I'd like fish and chips over a fancy restaurant?'

'Yes. Choosin' what you like over what others would deem to be the better choice shows strength of character.'

'I've never been bothered about what others think,' said Isla. 'I am who I am, which is somethin' we were talkin' about before I left the house this evenin'.'

'Oh?'

'Peggy was sayin' as to how some people try to impress others in order to get on in life. Are there many people like that in the services?'

'A few. They tend to be the ones who want to climb the ladder.'

'Do you not want to rise through the ranks?'

'Nah! I'm happy as I am. I certainly wouldn't tread on the heads of others in order to get to the top.'

'That sounds horrible,' said Isla. 'I'm guessin' people like that cannae have many friends.'

'None,' said Theo. 'I'd rather have lots of pals than lots of responsibility.'

'My friends mean everythin' to me,' said Isla,

before changing the subject. 'In the truck you said that you'd been in Liverpool for a while before setting up the satellite station?'

'Just shy of six months, so long enough to be familiar with the dance halls, shops and cinemas. My favourite fried fish shop is just up ahead. I thought we could eat dinner on a bench in the grounds of St John's Gardens, which isn't far from here.'

'That sounds lovely,' said Isla, although she really meant it all sounded very romantic.

Theo beamed at her approval. 'I also thought it might be nice to go dancin' afterwards? Or, if you'd prefer, the cinema?'

Having heard of people who smooched on the back row, Isla said 'Dancin'' with such speed that she took Theo by surprise.

'Am I to take it that you're a good dancer, then?' he asked, hopefully.

Realising that she had given him the wrong impression, she was quick to put him right. 'I know the basics, but I'm no Ginger Rogers.'

'Not to worry, cos I'm no Fred Astaire,' quipped Theo. 'But neither will I step on your toes the whole night long!' Pushing the door to the fried fish shop open, he greeted the elderly woman serving behind the counter with a cheery wave. 'Hello, Celine. And how are you this fine evenin'?'

Celine smiled at him from across the counter. 'I'm very well, thanks. How's tricks?'

'Same old,' replied Theo, adding, 'Please may I have two portions of your finest fish and chips?'

'Comin' right up.' Celine was already scooping chips on to a piece of newspaper.

'Celine's family does the best batter in Liverpool,' said Theo, 'thick and crunchy, just how I like it!'

'Nobody likes soggy batter,' said Isla, 'or no one I know, at any rate.'

Celine deftly wrapped the parcels and placed them on the counter. 'That'll be half a shillin'.'

Handing over two threepenny bits, Theo bade her goodbye before he and Isla headed off to have their dinner.

'If I've said it once, I've said it a hundred times,' Theo began as he sat down on the bench next to Isla, 'you can't beat good old fish and chips!'

'My dad used to call it the food of the gods,' said Isla as she opened her wrappings.

He eyed her thoughtfully. 'I'm guessin' you must really miss him?'

'More than words can express,' said Isla, 'but at the same time I cannae get over what he did, especially given the way he and Mammy brought me up.'

'Which was?'

'To be independent and stand on my own two feet. Yet as soon as I tried he knocked me down.'

Theo popped a piece of succulent fish into his mouth whilst he mulled this over. 'I try not to judge a person until I've walked a mile in their boots. And I cannot imagine what losing your mother must have been like for your father, except that I'm guessin' it must have been a living nightmare for him to do what he did.'

191

'Peggy – that's the lady we're stayin' with – reckons he ran off to sea by way of handlin' his grief. I suppose his puttin' me into the poorhouse was the equivalent of my gettin' caught in the crossfire.'

Theo gave a heartfelt sigh. 'Unfortunately it's very common for people to push their troubles into their boots. Problem is, it doesn't stay there. Instead it works its way back to the surface worse than it ever was before.'

Isla eyed him sharply. 'It sounds as though you've had experience.'

Theo fell silent as he looked to the skies, and only after a period of deep thought did he speak again. 'As a mechanic in the RAF, I've lost people I was close to.'

Isla's jaw dropped. 'I'm sorry, Theo. I didn't realise.'

He shrugged. 'It's all right. You weren't to know.'

'How did . . .' Isla began, before clearing her throat, 'how did they . . .'

'Die?'

She nodded.

'Wrong place at the wrong time,' he said leadenly. 'Although it's hard not to be in the wrong place when the target's your base.'

'RAF West Kirby?'

'No. I'm referrin' to the base I was on before I came to Liverpool.'

'Where was that?'

'Manston,' said Theo. 'Only it's no longer operational on account of the Luftwaffe bombin' the runways to smithereens.'

She stared at him aghast. 'Why would they attack the runways? Surely they'd be better off aimin' for the aircraft?'

'They attack the runways to stop the aircraft from taking off,' Theo told her, 'and to hell with anyone who gets in their way.'

'That's awful,' said Isla softly.

'Agreed, but it's also part of life,' said Theo, 'or at least it is now.'

Isla wasn't sure whether he was purposely changing the subject or not, but either way Theo pointed to her empty wrapper. 'I like a girl with a healthy appetite.'

'Comes from bein' in the poorhouse,' said Isla. 'You soon learn to not turn your nose up no matter how vile the food may be, cos it's either eat it or starve.'

He crumpled her chip paper up in his and popped them in the bin. 'Considerin' everythin' you've been through you seem awfully confident. Have you always been that way?'

'Most definitely, although if anything Coxhill only proved to strengthen it.'

He eyed her curiously as they left the grounds of the hall. 'How can bein' dumped in a poorhouse improve your confidence?'

'Escapin' on top of survivin' proved I can do anythin' I set my mind to.'

Theo held out his hand to hail a passing bus. 'I wish I could've met your mother.'

Isla looked at him in surprise as they waited for the bus to stop. 'What makes you say that?'

'If you take after her, then I'm guessin' she must

have been one hell of a woman!' said Theo, standing aside for her to step up before him.

Isla beamed, delighted to hear her mother being described in such a fashion. 'She absolutely was, and I'd very much like to think that I take after her, because my mammy could move mountains when the will possessed her.'

Theo paid their fares before sitting down next to her. 'A bit like her daughter.'

'I'm pleased you think so, cos I very much want her to be proud of how I've turned out.'

'Then it's mission accomplished,' said Theo, 'cos from what you've told me, I'd say you've not put a foot wrong since the day she passed.'

Isla tried to swallow her smile. 'Let's hope you feel the same way after our first dance.'

He laughed. 'I'm sure you're exaggeratin'.'

'If anythin' I'd say I was doin' the opposite,' said Isla. 'In fact, my girlfriends used to say I had two left feet when it came to dancin'.'

'Then we shall practise until you're perfect,' said Theo. 'By the time we're finished, you'll be givin' Ginger Rogers a run for her money!'

Isla smiled but said nothing. She knew from her past attempts that dancing was not her forte, and she very much doubted that her long absence from the dance floor had done much to improve matters, something which was confirmed during their first waltz.

Rubbing his shin, Theo smiled as Isla continued to apologise profusely.

'Please don't worry,' Theo assured her as he hobbled

over to their table. 'It's not as though you didn't warn me.'

'I know, but I'm sorry, truly I am,' Isla apologised yet again. 'I swear I've never kicked anyone in the shins as much as I have you.'

He looked up sharply. 'You mean you've done this before?'

She smiled guiltily. 'Only when my dad tried to teach me, and that's because I wasn't used to havin' to follow someone's lead, so I kept lunging forward, a bit like I was with you tonight.'

Still rubbing his shin, he took a sip of his drink. 'I hope you'll get the hang of it before you do me a permanent mischief.'

'I bet you never thought you'd need shinpads to go dancin'.'

Theo roared with laughter. 'Now there's an idea!'

'I'm fine if you'd rather sit the rest of the evenin' out,' said Isla, who was worrying she might actually draw blood if they continued to dance.

Theo drained his drink with a smack of his lips. 'I'd like to think I'm made of sterner stuff than that.' He held out his hand. 'Once more unto the breach?'

She drew a deep breath. 'You're no quitter, I'll grant you that.'

He placed his arm round her waist and grinned. 'No pain, no gain, that's what they say.'

Determined not to kick him, Isla did her best to surrender herself to his guidance, whilst gazing into his eyes. 'You seem to know an awful lot about me, yet I know very little about you.'

He wrinkled a nostril. 'My life's pretty borin' compared to yours – not that I'd call bein' dumped in a poorhouse excitin', you understand.'

'You might think your life mundane,' said Isla, 'but I'd do anythin' to be considered borin'.'

He laughed out loud. 'If anyone else were to refer to me as mundane, I'd feel thoroughly insulted, but comin' from you I rather take it as a compliment!'

'Thank goodness for that. I certainly wouldn't intend to insult you!' As she spoke, her toe whisked past his trouser leg.

'You're improvin',' said Theo. 'No connection that time!'

'Aye, and you're digressin',' said Isla. 'Are you doin' that intentionally, or . . . ?'

He glanced in the direction of the band before meeting her eyes once more. 'Only because there isn't a lot to tell. You already know I have siblings and parents, and that I'm in a mechanic in the RAF. What more would you like to know?'

'What were you before you joined up?' asked Isla.

'Mechanic,' said Theo. A small smile twitching his lips, he added, 'Told you I was borin'.'

'You said you're the youngest of seven – somethin' I find hard to imagine, bein' an only child – but does that mean your brothers are also in the services, what with them bein' older an' all?'

'They are that – much to my mother's despair.'

Isla thought of Peggy and how she felt about her sons joining up. 'Empty house,' she said.

He leaned back in order to view her properly.

'That's what she always says. She must mention it in every letter and phone call, which makes me feel guilty, but what's done is done.'

'But she doesn't see it that way?'

'No, and of course she's especially upset with me, so I get it in the neck every time I go back on leave.'

'Because you're the youngest?'

His eyes left hers briefly before returning. 'Summat like that, yeah.'

Isla smiled. 'You're her baby. You cannae blame her for feelin' the way she does.'

'I know, which is why I feel guilty.'

She frowned. 'Why would you feel guilty?'

'Just because I know how worried she is,' he said, pulling a downward smile.

She gave a cynical chuckle. 'I wonder whether my daddy would be as worried about me if he knew what I'd signed up for.'

'Sounds like you don't think he would,' Theo observed.

'He left me in the poorhouse, which is far worse than the services,' said Isla. 'Bearin' that in mind, he should be pleased that I've joined up.'

'I bet my mother won't feel that way when I go to Africa.'

Isla's stomach dropped horribly. She may not know much about the ins and outs of the war, but she did know that Africa was a dangerous place to be. 'You're goin' to Africa?'

'I've not had anythin' confirmed, but I have put my name down.'

'I suppose it's commendable to volunteer, but what made you do so?'

He shrugged. 'A chance to see a bit of the world before I turn up me toes?'

'And you haven't told your mammy you might be going?'

He baulked at the very idea. 'God no! She'd go bananas, especially if she knew I'd volunteered.'

'But if you do get sent to Africa, won't she know that you volunteered?'

He was shaking his head. 'One thing you'll learn is that people get posted to different bases all the time – there's every likelihood I'd be posted anyway in due course, so why rock the boat?'

She eyed him uncertainly. 'So you're goin' to lie to her?'

'Not lie exactly, just fail to tell the truth.'

'Same thing,' said Isla. 'But I suppose I can see why you'd fib. It would be different if you were married.' Something in the way he averted his gaze gave her cause for concern. 'You're not married, are you?'

'No, and nor will I be whilst there's a war on.'

'Very sensible! There are too many young people jumpin' into marriage just because they're scared of what the future holds. That's no reason to get married, not in my opinion.'

'Youth makes fools of us all,' said Theo grimly.

'And desperation,' supposed Isla. 'Cos let's face it, you'd have to be desperate to marry someone you barely knew.'

'You'll hear no argument from me.'

Isla looked down at their feet. 'It's been a while since I kicked you last. Do you think I'm gettin' the— Damn and blast!'

Theo let go of her hand to rub his shin. 'Talk about famous last words!'

She pulled a disappointed face as the music stopped and the lights went up. 'I bet your shins are glad the evenin's come to an end.'

'Nonsense! If anythin' they were just beginnin' to go numb!' He grinned. 'How about I take you dancin' again, see if we can get through at least half the evening without any casualties?'

She giggled. 'That would be nice.'

'I'm free on Saturday evenin' if that's any good?'

'I'll have to check with my new boss, but if he's all right with it, then so am I.'

'New boss? I thought you'd signed up?'

'We have, but we need jobs in the interim period and the man ahead of us in the queue to sign up suggested the Chinese laundry.'

'Blimey! You don't let the grass grow, do you?'

'We cannae afford to.'

'How about you telephone my base as soon as you know what's what?'

'I won't ask straight away, cos it seems a little cheeky,' said Isla. 'I'll leave it a few days, and then ask.'

'Perfect!'

As they left the building, he held out his arm. 'The RAF are goin' to pick me up outside the town hall in about half an hour's time, but I'd rather see you safely home first.'

'That's awfully sweet of you, but I'll be just fine on my own. Besides, I rather fancy you won't have time to do the two.'

He shot her a sidelong glance. 'I could see if the driver wouldn't mind droppin' you off.'

Isla's eyes nearly left her skull. 'You will not! I'm not havin' everyone thinkin' I use the RAF as my personal taxi service.'

'Blow what they think,' he began, but Isla was adamant.

'No, Theo. I do have my pride, you know.'

'I do indeed, but I also know that pride comes before a fall.'

She chuckled softly. 'You worry too much!'

'At least let me put you in a taxi.'

'That'll cost the earth . . .' Isla began before he interrupted.

'Worth it, if it means I sleep well tonight.'

'Honestly, Theo, Peggy's home isn't far from the bus stop.'

'A taxi from the town hall will drop you off outside the door. Plus I promised Sophie that I'd look after you and I intend to stand by that promise,' said Theo matter-of-factly.

She half raised her hand to object, but he could tell by the smile on her lips that she'd given in. 'All right! But just this once.'

He squeezed her arm in his. 'Fine by me. I'll make sure I have sufficient time to walk you home on Saturday.'

He hailed the approaching bus, and paid the clippie

before leading the way to a seat near the back where it was quieter.

'I've had a wonderful evenin',' Isla said as she looked out of the window. 'Liverpool's a beautiful city.' She paused. 'I know you're from Yorkshire, but not whereabouts.'

'Fangfoss.'

Isla wagged a chiding finger. 'Pull the other one, it's got bells on!'

'I swear to you it's true! But if you think that's bad, it used to be called Fangfoss-with-Spittle.'

She shot him a wry glance. 'Now I know you're definitely pullin' my leg!'

He held his hand to his heart. 'I swear on my life.'

'Who on earth came up with a name like that? It sounds like somethin' out of Dracula.'

'Maybe that's why the village has such a small population,' he said with a wink. 'I'll have to invest in some stakes!'

Isla chuckled softly before continuing on a more serious note. 'The RAF must've been a real eye-opener after a small village.'

'It was, but I soon got used to it. I enjoy bein' part of a crowd; it makes me feel alive. And Liverpool is a fantastic city with plenty to see and do, not to mention the fact it's close to the sea.'

'Do you swim?'

'Like a fish,' said Theo. 'You?'

'Like a stone,' quipped Isla. 'But better than I dance.'

'That's good to hear,' said Theo. 'After all, bein' able to swim can save your life.'

She eyed him curiously. 'Where did you learn to dance?'

'At my local village hall,' grinned Theo. 'Bein' the handsome young chap that I was, I had plenty of volunteer teachers, and even though they were all pushin' sixty they sure knew a thing or two when it came to dancing.' He stood up. 'This is our stop.'

Stepping off the bus, they headed towards a line of taxis. 'Are you sure you don't mind?' Isla asked as they approached the cab at the head of the queue.

'As I said, I'd rather get you a taxi than worry whether you'd got home safely,' said Theo. He spoke briefly to the driver before turning to Isla. 'What was the name of your street?'

'Arkles Lane.'

The taxi driver stubbed his cigarette out with the toe of his boot and accepted the fare from Theo.

'Your carriage awaits,' smiled Theo as he opened the back door of the car. 'My ride won't be too much longer, so I shall say goodnight to you here. Oh, and thanks for a lovely evenin', by the way. I really enjoyed myself.'

'Me too,' said Isla as she slid into the back of the car.

'And don't forget to let me know if you're free on Saturday.'

'Will do, and thanks again!'

Having been on tenterhooks waiting for Isla to get back from her date, Meg and Sophie fired a multitude of questions at her before she'd had a chance to close the door.

'Did he keep his word, and was that a taxi I heard

just now?' was Sophie's first question, followed by, 'Wasn't that expensive?'

'Theo paid for it,' said Isla, adding, 'He paid for everything – and yes, he kept his word.'

Meg gave an excited squeal. 'So how was it? We know you didn't kiss – did you?'

Isla laughed. 'No we did not!'

Looking slightly disappointed, Meg continued, 'So what did you do and where did you go?'

Isla looked around for Peggy, who was nowhere to be seen. 'Where's Peggy?'

'Bed,' said Sophie. 'But you can fill her in over brekker, now spill the beans!'

Isla did just that as they readied themselves for bed. 'I bet you cannae wait for Saturday,' said Sophie after Isla had finished describing her evening. 'I'm sure Mr Lee won't mind you havin' a few hours off.'

'Me neither,' agreed Isla, adding conversationally, 'So what did the three of you do with your evening?'

'Not a lot,' said Meg. 'We had dinner, which was delish; did the washin' up, then listened to the wireless.'

'The corned beef hash really was scrummy,' agreed Sophie, 'but you'll find that out for yourself tomorrow, cos there's plenty left over.'

'Aye, Peggy reckons we need feedin' up,' said Meg, rubbing her tummy contentedly.

Isla stifled a yawn beneath her hand as she slid between the sheets. 'If I don't get some shut-eye, I'll be fit for nothin' come the mornin'.'

Agreeing that they should call it a night, the girls settled down to sleep. Picturing Theo in her mind's eye Isla envisaged him dancing with an old lady who failed to stand on his toes or kick him in the shins. A smile creased her lips as she drifted off to sleep. *You're a lucky girl, Isla Donahue, cos but for the fact you got on the wrong train you and Theo would never have met, and where would you be then?*

Back in RAF West Kirby, Theo entered the Nissen hut he shared with Dominic and a few others. Leaning up on one elbow, Dominic knuckled his eyes. 'How'd it go?'

'Good.'

'Are you seein' her again?'

'Saturday night,' Theo confirmed.

Dominic peered at him through the darkness. 'So why the long face . . .' There was a pause. 'You didn't tell her, did you?'

'Of course I didn't tell her!' snapped Theo, 'cos I wouldn't be seein' her again on Saturday had I done so, would I?'

'You never know.'

Theo tutted irritably. 'I should never have listened to you.'

'As I remember it, I didn't hold a gun to your head.' Dominic frowned. 'So what's the problem? You obviously like her, else you'd not have asked her out again, so . . .'

'Of course I like her,' said Theo gruffly. 'That's part of the problem.'

Dominic stared at him incredulously. 'There's nowt wrong with likin' someone.'

'Maybe not in your case.'

Dominic sat up. 'What *is* your problem? I know you've been through the mill lately, but I thought this would be good for you.'

Theo kicked off his shoes. 'It's not as easy as all that.'

'Then call it off!' huffed Dominic as he lay down again. 'Honestly, Theo, if you're that bothered, why did you arrange to see her again?'

'Because I like her. I know I shouldn't, given the circumstances, but I can't help myself.'

'You need to stop worryin' about the past and get on with your life whilst you still have one, cos none of us know what's round the corner. You should know that better than most.'

Theo took his jacket off and hung it up. 'Which is why I'm findin' this so difficult.'

'You need to give yourself a break, mate,' said Dominic sleepily. 'Life's tough enough as it is without beatin' yourself up for somethin' you did when you were just a kid!'

'Easier said than done. And I'm sorry for snappin' at you just now.'

There came a mumbled ''S okay' from Dominic.

Theo took his shirt and trousers off and hung them up next to his jacket. *I wish I could be like Dom*, he thought, climbing into his issue pyjama bottoms, *but then again, Dom's in a very different position to me. He can say and do whatever he likes with no repercussions, whereas every time I open my mouth I find myself tellin' another lie. It's not as though I don't want to move on and be like everyone else – I do! But that won't happen unless I tell her the truth, and if I do that she'll run for the hills, and what's more I don't blame her!* He sighed. Whilst he didn't like lying, he felt he had no choice if he were to stand a chance of having a decent relationship. *I'll leave sleepin' dogs lie for now and see what happens. Maybe once she gets to know me better . . .* He hesitated. Would she be angrier being told later rather than sooner? Trying to imagine himself spilling the beans to Isla, he pulled back the covers and slid between the sheets, but the look of shock and anger on her face forced him to turn his thoughts to Africa and what life would be like in that foreign land, where nobody knew the truth.

The girls had only been in Liverpool for a week but it was already beginning to feel like home.

'Everyone's so friendly,' remarked Isla as they made their way back from the laundry.

'A real sense of community,' Sophie agreed, 'somethin' I didn't expect in such a large city.'

'I'm goin' to be quite sorry to leave,' said Meg, 'as much for Peggy as for myself.'

'I love to hear her singin' away to herself in the mornin's,' said Isla. 'It's better than any alarm clock.'

'Did you manage to get in touch with Theo?' Sophie asked.

'Aye, but only to say that I'd meet him outside Lyons caff at fifteen hundred hours.'

'Fifteen hundred hours!' Meg grinned. 'You're speakin' the lingo already!'

Isla shrugged. 'May as well get used to it, cos that will be our life in a fortnight's time.'

'I hope so,' said Sophie. 'Some of the women in the laundry reckon it can take up to three weeks dependin' on what they're after when you sign up.'

'Aye, but they also said it might be sooner,' Meg reminded her. 'Besides, are you really bothered if it's longer? I know I'm not. Don't get me wrong, I'm not sayin' I regret signing up, but neither am I in a rush.'

'It's not so much that I'm eager for the off,' said Sophie slowly, 'but I don't like the feelin' of livin' in limbo. At the moment we're neither laundry girls nor servicewomen, and I want to be one or the other. I suppose it comes from bein' institutionalised. Almost as though there's safety in routine, which is ridiculous considerin' none of us were safe in Coxhill.'

'I agree with you,' said Isla. 'I don't like not knowin' what's around the corner, but I think that's because of losin' Mammy so unexpectedly. I thought my life was goin' in one direction only to find myself doin' a complete U-turn through no decision of my own. And Dad dumpin' me in Coxhill has made me anxious to know what's comin' up way before I get there, if that makes sense.'

'Perfect sense,' said Meg. 'Not knowin' where your life is headed is a bit like playin' blind man's buff, when you're the only person in the room!'

'At least we know we only have a couple of weeks or so to wait,' said Isla as she opened the door to the house on Arkles Lane.

'True,' said Sophie, before calling out to Peggy, who they knew would already be home.

'In here,' said Peggy, but there was something about the way she said it that gave the girls cause for concern.

'Is everythin' all right?' asked Isla as they hurried through to the parlour. Peggy's eyes fell to a brown envelope on the kitchen table, and Isla covered her mouth with her fingers. 'I hope it's not bad news,' she said thickly.

Peggy looked pointedly at Sophie. 'It's for you.'

'Me?' squeaked Sophie. She picked up the envelope. 'Oh . . .'

Staring at the envelope in Sophie's hands, Isla and Meg looked for their own, but Peggy was shaking her head. 'Only Sophie, I'm afraid.'

Taking a knife from the cutlery drawer, Sophie slid it along the envelope. 'I dare say yours will arrive tomorrow,' she told the other girls as she took her papers out of the envelope. Her eyes scanning the contents, she drew in a breath. 'I'm in the Wrens.'

'The Wrens,' Isla repeated, her heart sinking horribly. 'I wanted to be in the WAAF.'

'You might well be,' said Peggy. 'Just because you were standing together in the queue, doesn't mean . . .'

Sophie's jaw dropped. 'I was called to a different desk from Isla and Meg.'

'Oh,' said Peggy in such a manner that they could only draw one conclusion.

'We might've signed up for different services, mightn't we?' said Isla hollowly.

'I'm afraid you could well have,' said Peggy.

'Did they ask whether you could swim?' Sophie asked Meg, but Peggy was quick to dismiss the implication. 'Half the bloomin' Navy can't swim.'

Meg stared at her aghast. 'But that's ridiculous!'

'Maybe so, but true nonetheless.'

Isla looked to Sophie, who was still staring at her instructions. 'When do you leave?'

'A week today,' Sophie said hoarsely.

Meg crossed her fingers. '*Can* you swim?'

Much to their collective relief, Sophie nodded.

'Thank goodness for that,' breathed Isla, adding, 'Oh, Sophie,' as a tear escaped Sophie's lid.

'It's all right,' said Sophie. Dabbing her eyes with her handkerchief, she waved away their concerned faces. 'It's just a bit of a shock, that's all.'

'We don't know that our papers won't be on that mat first thing tomorrow mornin',' said Meg optimistically. 'For all we know, we could all be in the Wrens.'

'And even if we aren't it doesn't mean that this is the end,' Isla assured her.

Sophie chuckled as she fielded more tears. 'Good! Because we've come too far to part ways now.'

'We can write and telephone, and meet up whenever we have the opportunity,' said Isla. She glanced to the papers in her friend's hand. 'Are you trainin' nearby?'

'Plymouth,' said Sophie. 'Which is about as far south as you can get!'

'On the plus side, you might well end up here in Liverpool!' Peggy rallied her. 'If you do, then you'll need a place to stay and I'd be more than happy to put you up.'

'That would be wonderful, Peggy, but if this whole experience has taught me one thing, it's not to count my chickens before they've hatched!' Hoping to change the subject, Sophie added, 'I dunno about you lot, but I'm famished, so how about we make a start on dinner?'

Peggy was pointing to the oven. 'Way ahead of you, kiddo. There's a fish pie ready to serve.'

Isla rubbed Peggy's shoulder as she passed by. 'You spoil us, Peggy!'

Peggy beamed proudly. 'And there's bread and butter puddin' for afters too, if anyone fancies it.'

Sophie automatically began setting the table, while Meg fetched the condiments from the pantry and Isla took the pie out of the oven. 'Bread and butter puddin' will go down a treat after the news I've just received,' Sophie remarked.

'It's kind of excitin' though, don't you think?' said Isla, beginning to dole out the delicious-smelling pie.

'Dauntin' is how I'd describe it,' said Sophie. 'I've no idea what they'll expect of me, plus I've never been on a boat in my life. What if I'm seasick?'

'From what I've heard, most Wrens don't leave dry land,' said Peggy. 'But why don't you pop next door and have a word with the Wrens livin' in Irene's old house? They'd be able to give you a good idea of the sort of duties you'll be asked to perform.'

'That's a good idea,' said Sophie. 'I'll nip by on my way home from work tomorrow, see if anyone's in.'

Peggy bowed her head to say grace as the girls took their seats around the table. When she had finished they all whispered a brief 'Amen' before tucking into the delicious fare, but Isla had a question for Peggy. 'You know how you like to say grace before every meal?' she asked as she pushed her fork into the mashed potato.

'Yes?'

'Don't you ever question God's existence with all that's goin' on?'

Peggy eyed her quizzically. 'You mean the war?'

'Aye, that and other things.'

Peggy too pushed her food around the plate before looking up. 'What's the alternative?'

'Sorry?'

'When I go to bed at night, I ask God to watch over my family,' said Peggy, 'because I can't.'

Meg looked from Peggy to Isla and back again before voicing her thoughts. 'I know where Isla's comin' from, but at the same time I'd like to think there's someone up there lookin' after us, because we need all the help we can get.'

'Which is why I pray,' agreed Peggy. 'They say that God moves in mysterious ways, and even though I have a hard time understandin' how he can allow Hitler to do the unspeakable things he does I have faith that it's all part of his greater plan.'

'Even though I'm not sure that I'm a believer, it didn't stop me prayin' that I would escape Coxhill one day,' said Sophie. 'Whether it was an answer to prayer or simply chance, I suppose it doesn't really matter as long as I'm free.'

'But what about poor Kayleigh?' Isla responded. 'She didn't deserve to leave Coxhill the way she did.'

Peggy looked up sharply. 'What's this?'

'Kayleigh was a friend of mine who fell out with Harman,' said Sophie, and went on to explain her theory behind the other girl's disappearance.

Peggy shook her head in sorrow. 'But without proof, you can't be sure that it wasn't just an accident, and even if it wasn't, how do you know that there wasn't somethin' worse lined up for poor Kayleigh?'

'Worse than death?' Isla choked. 'What can possibly be worse than that?'

'Livin' with pain,' said Peggy decidedly. 'My father died of lung cancer, and he was beggin' for death a long time before he finally passed.'

Isla wanted to point out that God should have come to Peggy's father's rescue when he needed him the most, but she knew that doing so would only be churlish. Besides, if belief gave you comfort, what was the harm in that? 'That's awful, not just for him but for you too,' she said eventually.

'It was, but he's at peace now, which is a godsend,' said Peggy, continuing a little more cheerfully, 'So how's the fish pie?'

Isla indicated her empty plate. 'It was delicious, Peggy. Your boys are very lucky havin' such a wonderful cook for a mother!'

'It's one of their favourites, but they like scouse best. I'll make that tomorrow.'

'But I won't be here tomorrow evenin',' Isla protested. 'Will it keep?'

'It'll keep all right, but I reckon it's best fresh so I'll do summat else tomorrow . . . maybe toad in the hole? And have the scouse on Sunday.'

'Oooo, I do love a bit of toad in the hole,' said Meg, 'my mammy used to do the cheese so that it was a whisper away from bein' burned.'

'Best way,' agreed Peggy. Seeing the empty plates, she added, 'Are we all up for a bit of bread-and-butter puddin'?'

There was a resounding 'Yes please' from all three girls.

'We never got puddin' the whole time we were in Coxhill,' Meg told Peggy as she collected the empty plates. 'It's somethin' I've definitely missed.'

'And birthday cake,' said Sophie suddenly. 'I've not had a birthday cake since bein' in Coxhill.'

Peggy looked determined as she doled the pudding into four bowls. 'Then I shall make one to make up for the ones you've missed. It won't be like the ones I made *before* rationin', but I'll do my best.'

'Thanks, Peggy, but it's really not necessary—'

'*Everyone* deserves a slice of cake on their birthday,' said Peggy. 'My sons might not come home often, but when they do there's always a cake here waitin' for them.'

'You remind me of a mother hen, the way you cluck and fuss over everybody,' Isla smiled. 'It's nice.'

'Good! Cos I won't be stoppin' any time soon!'

Chapter Nine

Isla gazed out of the window as the bus neared the town centre. It had taken a while for the news of Sophie's imminent departure to sink in, but the more it did the more the gravity of her new reality hit home. It wasn't so much that she thought she wouldn't be able to function without Sophie's presence, but more that it was marking the end of an era, something they had all agreed as they left the Wrens' accommodation next door to Peggy's earlier that day.

'It's been the three of us for so long,' said Isla. 'It will be strange to wake up knowin' you're not in the bed next to mine – or under mine, as was the case in Coxhill.'

'Accordin' to those girls, Sophie will be just fine, though, which is quite a weight off my mind,' said Meg as they entered number thirty-five.

Sophie smiled. 'Mine too. And at least with my bein' the first of us to go, I'll be able to give you both some idea of what to expect, cos even though the girls next door gave us a good idea, it's always better hearin' these things from someone you know well, don't you think?'

'Definitely!' agreed Isla. 'For a start you can tell us what it's like compared to Coxhill – somethin' which they couldn't do.'

Now, as the bus neared its stop, Isla stood up. *I just hope the other Wrens are nice to her*, she thought as she made her way down the aisle, *and that there's no little sneaks like Mary in there*. This new thought turned her mind to Mary, and where she might have ended up. As the obvious answer entered her mind, she tried to banish it from her thoughts, but it kept coming back. Mary had no family – or none that Isla knew of – which meant she'd more than likely be heading straight for the services. *All she'd have to say is that her documents perished in the fire and she'd be good to go. And it doesn't matter where she joins up*, thought Isla as she stepped off the bus, *cos she could be posted anywhere in the UK, an' knowin' our luck she'll end up on the same station as one of us*. Even the thought of having to spend the war in Mary's company was just about more than she could stand, and she was certain that Sophie and Meg would feel the same way. On the other hand, could she really see Mary obeying orders? No. Mary was the sort that liked to give orders, not take them, and if that was true of Mary it would also be true of women like her, which would mean that the forces were the last place they'd be likely to end up, and that could bode well for Sophie, Meg and herself.

Heading along the pavement towards Lyons, she was pleased to see Theo outside waiting for her.

Waving a cheery greeting, he walked towards her. 'How's tricks?'

'I would say "same old" if it weren't for the fact that Sophie received her papers for the Wrens yesterday.'

'The Wrens?' he said with surprise. 'That must've come as a shock.'

'It did.'

'How does she feel about it? I only ask because I know you all had your hearts set on the WAAF.'

'She was apprehensive at first, but she feels a lot better after speakin' to the Wrens who live next door – in fact we all do.'

'How would you feel if you found you were signed up to the Wrens?' he asked, as he opened the door of the café for her to pass through ahead of him.

'Now that I know a little bit more about the services and the way things work, I don't think it really matters which one you join – it's more where you end up. For example, I'd be happy in the Wrens, the ATS or the WAAF if it meant I could stay in Liverpool – especially if I get to stay with Peggy.' She paused. 'How about you? Did you want to join the RAF service in particular?'

'Like most others I had my heart set on becomin' a pilot,' said Theo, pulling a chair out for her. 'But of course the reality is very different to fantasy! You've got to have qualifications comin' out of your ears to be even considered as a pilot – either that or be born with a silver spoon in your mouth, neither of which applies to me, unfortunately.'

She shuffled her chair closer to the table. 'Does

that mean that you regret your decision to join the RAF?'

'Not in the least,' said Theo as he took the opposite chair. 'I find bein' on the ground just as important as bein' in the air – safer, too, or at least it is most of the time.'

'So you're not envious when you see pilots fly off into the wide blue yonder?'

'No. Not only has that ship well and truly sailed, but I've seen the state of some of the planes when they come back. The sight of that alone is enough for me to be grateful I didn't pass muster.'

She felt her tummy lurch unpleasantly. 'It cannae be nice, watchin' your pals leave and wonderin' if you'll ever see them again.'

'I hate to say this, but it's somethin' you get used to. I'm not sayin' it gets easier, mind, but I suppose you toughen up after the first few. That's why it's important to get away from the base for a while,' he said, handing her a menu. 'A change of scenery does you the world of good.'

Seeing the waitress hovering in the background, Isla glanced at the menu before her, and the girl approached, her pencil poised over her pad.

Theo looked expectantly to Isla. 'Tea for two?'

'Yes please.'

The girl made a note before looking back up. 'Will you be ordering anything to eat?'

'We will indeed,' replied Theo, and turned his attention back to Isla. 'Have you decided, or would you like a little more time?'

'I'd very much like a slice of your minced beef and onion pie, please,' said Isla, smiling at the girl, 'and can I have it with chips?'

'You can indeed,' said the waitress, before turning to Theo. He ordered the same, only with mashed potato.

'I thought we could go to the Rialto after dinner,' Theo said as the waitress left to fetch their order, 'unless you'd prefer to go back to the Grafton, of course?'

She smiled. 'I don't mind where we go. What is the Rialto? A hippodrome?'

'What makes you think that?'

'I thought it might be your polite way of saying you didn't fancy any more bruises on your shins.'

'Oh ye of little faith!' Theo chortled. 'I told you it would take more than a few bruises to put me off and I meant it.'

'So another dance hall then? Is it as nice as the Grafton?'

'If anythin' I would say it was a bit grander,' said Theo. 'Certainly from the outside.'

'Well, I shall endeavour to keep my feet on the floor where they belong!'

He rolled his eyes. 'You honestly weren't that bad – it's not as if I needed stitches or owt like that.'

'I hope you're not speakin' too soon!'

He waved a dismissive hand. 'Don't you worry about me! I've dropped all manner of tools on me toes in the past but it didn't put me off becomin' a mechanic.'

'I suppose pricking my finger with a needle never put me off wantin' to become a seamstress. Did you always want to be a mechanic?'

'Very much so. I've always loved tinkerin' with engines – well, anythin' mechanical really – since I was a nipper. It's the whole reason why I left school early. I knew I'd never want to be anythin' else, and bein' as my father owned his own garage . . .'

'It made perfect sense.'

'Exactly!'

'You said you joined the RAF because you dreamed of becomin' a pilot, but didn't you think they'd put you straight in as a mechanic what with your background and all?'

'You'd think so, but no. You see, I'd been drivin' a car since I could reach the pedals and I rather stupidly thought that would make me a good pilot!'

'Are they very different?' said Isla.

'Entirely! You use the pedals on the plane to steer rather than slow down or speed up, and the yoke – that's what they call the thing that looks a little like a steerin' wheel – to pitch and roll.'

'I'm not even goin' to ask what that means,' said Isla, before stopping for the waitress, who'd returned with a tea tray that she expertly unloaded before hurrying off to take another order. Pouring the tea into first her cup, then Theo's, Isla glanced towards the milk jug. 'Just milk, if I remember rightly?'

'You do indeed.' He grinned at her. 'I'm sweet enough as it is!'

Smiling, she poured a small amount of milk into each cup. 'So, how's life at RAF West Kirby?'

He took a sip of his tea before answering. 'Very

much the same as it was the last time I saw you. It's only the faces that change.'

She placed her own cup back on the saucer. 'I suppose it must be hard to keep track, what with people bein' posted to pastures new.'

'Most of the time, but it's not so much that with the air crew.'

Her face dropped. 'Oh . . .'

He glanced around at their fellow diners, most of whom were happily chatting away. 'For most people this far north the horrors of war are mainly down south, or across the Channel, but for the RAF it's very much on our doorstep – somethin' which you'll soon get used to.'

'At least they have you to make sure their planes are fit to fly,' said Isla.

'Of course – it's paramount that we maintain the aircraft properly, what with the crews' lives bein' in our hands.'

'I hope I'm never given a role with that much responsibility!' said Isla fervently. 'But I dare say they don't have female mechanics.'

'Only they do. In fact, there aren't many roles now that women don't do.'

'Unless it involves guns.'

'The ack-acks are guns. And whilst the women may not fire them, they're the ones responsible for spottin' the planes, and givin' the coordinates to the fellers what pull the trigger – or whatever they do to fire the bullets.'

'But given that most air raids take place at night,

how on earth can they be sure whether they're firin' at the Luftwaffe or the RAF?'

'Excellent trainin',' said Theo succinctly. 'But if truth be known, it's very rare for them to hit anything . . .'

She tutted. 'Let me guess. Because they're female?'

'Sex has nothin' to do with it! Hittin' a movin' object is hard enough at the best of times, but when it's thousands of feet up in the air?' He pulled a negative face. 'Nigh on impossible!'

'Then why bother?'

'It forces Jerry to fly higher to escape the guns, which in turn makes it less likely that they'll hit the targets *they're* aimin' for.'

A slow smile brightened her cheeks. 'Clever!'

'Very. The ack-acks have saved many an airbase from bein' hit.' Theo paused before continuing darkly, 'Although it doesn't always work. Certainly not in the case of a surprise attack.'

'Is that what it was at your last base – a surprise attack?'

He lowered his gaze. 'They sounded the sirens only seconds before the attack. Not enough time to get the fellers in their kites, let alone anything else.'

'Easy pickings for the Luftwaffe,' said Isla sadly. 'It must've been dreadful.'

'Up until that point I'd never even seen the Luftwaffe. Apart from the newsreels, of course.'

'I cannae imagine how terrifying it must have been for you.'

He lowered his gaze. 'I came off lightly compared to some.'

'I know you said you lost friends. Were any of them close?'

'All of them.' He cleared his throat. 'But you have to get over it and move on no matter how tough that might be, cos you can't afford to let your concentration lapse, not even for a second.'

'I'm guessin' it must've affected your outlook on life, though?' said Isla, adding as an afterthought, 'Was the attack behind your decision to sign up for Africa?'

He turned his attention to the salt cellar, which he seemed to take great interest in. 'Without question. I just wanted to run away, and you can't get much further than Africa.'

His statement reminded Isla of her father's reaction to losing his wife and son. 'You do know that runnin' away doesn't help, though?' she said in the tones of someone who wanted to remain sympathetic whilst being realistic.

'It depends on what you're runnin' from.'

She furrowed her brow. 'The loss of your friends, or so I'd have thought, cos you'll not outrun the Luftwaffe, not in Africa. That would be more like jumpin' out of the fryin' pan into the fire.'

He smiled softly as they locked eyes. 'Unless you're runnin' away from yourself.'

Her frown deepened. 'How can you possibly run away from yourself?'

'I'll let you know if I ever find out.'

Uncertain as to what he meant, she turned the conversation back to his friends, in the hope that it might

222

cast some light. 'Have any of your pals at the base signed up for Africa?'

'Just me. It seems I was the only one sufficiently desperate to get away.'

'I very much doubt that. We all handle situations differently – you've only got to look at me and my father to know that. I dare say your friends are hurtin' just as much as you, just dealin' with it differently.' She hesitated, reflecting on the similarity between Theo and her father before swiftly moving on. 'Do you still see any of them?'

'The majority got posted to Lincoln, but Dominic was sent to West Kirby with me.'

'How's he coping?'

He shrugged. 'Better than me, but then . . .' He hesitated for a moment. 'It was just different for Dom.'

'Was he not as friendly with those you lost as you were?'

'Summat like that.' Theo turned his attention to the waitress, who was bringing their meals over. 'Now that both looks and smells delicious,' he said as she put the plates down in front of them.

'Doesn't it just!' Isla agreed as she gathered her knife and fork.

Slicing the shortcrust pastry, Theo smiled as the smell of beef and gravy filled his nostrils. 'So, what's your favourite food? Personally I'm a meat and two veg kind of guy.'

Isla chewed thoughtfully before swallowing. 'I was quite the fussy eater before I went into Coxhill, but since comin' out I'll eat just about anythin' and everythin'. Even the stuff I never used to like tastes delicious to me now.'

'I've always loved my grub,' said Theo through a mouthful of pie, 'but the food in the cookhouse is questionable, to say the least.'

'In what way?'

'I think by tryin' to make a little go a long way they water down the ingredients until it ends up nigh on tasteless, and what little flavour it does have never seems to match what it's meant to be. So, for example, summat like this pie would taste more of onion than it did of beef, and the pastry would be like a brick, although I'm not sure of the reason for that.'

Isla stifled a laugh with her fingers. 'That good, eh?'

'I'm sure it's not as bad as the stuff you had in Cox-hill, and I feel bad for whingin' when I know you've had it so much worse, but I have to speak as I find.' He hesitated. 'Do you cook?'

Her cheeks warmed as she envisaged her one and only attempt at a caramel custard, which for some unknown reason had come out with a layer of cooked egg white on the bottom. 'Do I cook? Yes. Am I good at it? No. Although I do make a mean egg and bacon sarnie – or so my father tells me.'

'What more could a man want, apart from a good old dollop of brown sauce?'

She feigned shock. 'Ketchup, surely?'

He laughed. 'The age-old debate, but I'm afraid it's brown sauce for me every time.'

She gazed thoughtfully out of the café window. 'I suppose if they send me to the cookhouse I'd at least

224

learn the basics, and whilst the food might not be the best I dare say it's a darned sight better than anythin' I could produce!'

'Have you given any consideration as to what you'd like to do, if not cook?'

'I quite fancy drivin', because it looks like great fun, but other than that, no.'

'Can you ride a bicycle? Some of the girls who've come to our base ride motorcycles.'

She shook her head fervently. 'No balance. My father tried his best, but Mammy said he was to stop before I broke somethin'.' There was a slight hesitation before she added, 'I wonder if my lack of balance has anythin' to do with my inability to dance?'

He chuckled good-humouredly. 'I wouldn't have thought so. I'd say that was more to do with coordination than owt else – and you're quite good at dancin'! With a bit of practice you'll be even better.'

'I hope so. But what happens if they send me off to do something that I just cannae do – such as ridin' a motorcycle?'

'They train you for somethin' else,' he said matter-of-factly. 'An' they'll keep tryin' until they find somethin' you are good at.'

'That's good to know,' said Isla, watching Theo finish his last mouthful. 'My mammy used to say that I was good at everythin', but I suppose all parents think that about their kids.'

'Do you not think she'd have been worried knowin' you'd signed up?' he asked, sounding mildly surprised.

'Oh, she'd have been beside herself with worry,'

she said frankly, 'but she strove for women's rights in the workplace, and knowin' that I was doin' a man's job in a male-dominated society would have made her cock-a-hoop.'

He eyed her thoughtfully as he watched her finish the remainder of her meal. 'You definitely get your fightin' spirit from your mammy, then,' he said decidedly, 'and possibly your daddy too.'

'They were both keen for me to be independent – ironic, really, considerin' he dumped me in the poorhouse rather than give me a chance to prove I could make it on my own.'

'Perhaps he thought it the best way of makin' sure you were looked after,' said Theo. 'Understandable in theory, not so much in practice, as it turned out.'

She glanced at the menu, something which was not unnoticed by Theo. 'Pudding?'

'Is that a term of endearment?' she asked, tongue-in-cheek.

He laughed. 'If it was, I dare say I'd be nursin' a sore nose by now.'

She raised a quirked brow. 'To go with your sore shins, no doubt! If I'm not careful I'll be done for GBH.'

He twinkled across the table at her. Isla was unlike any other woman he'd met, which was both a positive and a negative. Positive because he was lucky to be in her company, but negative because he knew he risked losing her should she find out the truth about his past. But would that ever happen? Dominic was the only other person in West Kirby who knew what had happened, and Theo knew for a fact that Dominic wouldn't say anything. He tried to think if there was any other way she might possibly learn what had happened on that fateful night, but apart from the women at his former base he could not imagine anyone who might be in a position to tell her. And even if she were to bump into any of them, why would they see fit to put their oar in rather than leave the past where it belonged? So deep was he in thought, he didn't notice the waitress who'd come to collect their plates until she cleared her throat. Bringing himself back to the present, Theo looked straight to Isla. 'Is there anything on there that takes your fancy?'

Her eyes flared. 'Everything! But I've done my eeny meeny miny moes, and the treacle tart has it!'

He nodded his approval. 'Good choice. I'll have the gooseberry crumble with custard.'

'Crumble was goin' to be my second choice,' said Isla, as the waitress loaded her empty tray with their plates.

'You can always have a bit of mine,' said Theo gallantly.

'Deal! But only if you do the same?'

'As you've twisted my arm, how can I refuse?' He glanced at his wristwatch. 'Once we've finished here, we can catch a bus to the Rialto.'

'I'd like to take the girls to the Grafton before Sophie leaves for Plymouth, but I might change that to the Rialto if I think that they'll like it better there.'

'Can they dance, then?'

Isla hesitated. 'I'm not sure. I haven't run it past them yet.'

When the waitress arrived with their puddings, they each had a bite of the other's before passing them back.

'Both equally delicious,' said Isla after trying a spoonful of her own.

'Agreed,' said Theo. 'We'll have to do this every time we go out.'

She smiled mischievously. 'You're plannin' on takin' me out again? Aren't you worried that people might start to talk?'

He flashed his brows. 'They'll do that no matter what we do, so we may as well give them summat to talk about!'

She grinned. 'That's the sort of thing my father would say.'

'And he's right. No matter what you do in life there's always someone waitin' in the wings to pronounce judgement. Sad, really, when you think about it, because none of us are perfect.'

'I guess it's in our nature.'

'You're not like that, though,' said Theo, 'and neither am I.'

'Ah, but only because we've both been through the wringer, so we know better than to waste our time casting aspersions on others.'

'Exactly! Why don't more people see it from that point of view? Instead of actin' all high and mighty, makin' it look as though you're doin' something wrong just because you've dared to continue living your life!'

A little uncertain as to what he was referring to, Isla assumed he was talking about his view that you have to get on with things rather than dwell on the past. 'Life's too short,' she said, picking up the last piece of treacle tart. Theo motioned to the waitress that he was ready to settle the bill.

'That was delicious,' he said as he handed over the money. 'Please pass our compliments on to the chef.' Thanking him for the deliberate overpayment, the waitress cleared their plates whilst they headed for the door, where Theo pointed to a bus which was heading their way. 'If we hurry we might just catch it.' He jogged Isla over to the bus stop just in time to hop aboard.

'Puddin's and joggin' do *not* go hand in hand,' Isla said as she plumped down in a window seat.

'I must admit it's more usual to exercise *before* havin' something to eat, but we can always have us a drink before we hit the dance floor,' said Theo as he collapsed beside her.

Remembering their previous night out, when Theo had steered clear of alcoholic drinks, she asked, 'The last time we went dancin', you stuck to soft drinks. Was there a reason for that?'

He wrinkled his nose as if smelling a foul odour. 'I don't like the taste – somethin' which the other fellers constantly rib me about.'

'Why do they do that?'

'They consider you a bit of a wuss if you don't drink alcohol, cos that's what real men drink.'

'How ridiculous!' snorted Isla. 'It's actions that determine whether you're a man, not what you drink. Not to mention the fact that many women like the odd ale – or short, for that matter. Not me though. I had a sip of my daddy's whisky when I were a wee lass.' She pulled a face. 'It was utterly vile and I don't know how anyone can claim to like it.'

'Ginger beer is the closest I get to actual beer,' said Theo, continuing in the privacy of his head, *which is just as well as it means I'm less likely to say anythin' I shouldn't.*

'The only alcohol I allowed to pass my lips was the sherry my mammy used to put in the trifle,' chuckled Isla, 'but you couldn't really taste that.'

'I do love a good trifle,' said Theo, adding, 'I swear I never used to talk about food this much before the war, but nowadays it seems to be my main topic of conversation.'

'The more you cannae have somethin' the more you want it,' supposed Isla. She glanced at some of the bomb-damaged buildings they were passing by. 'Judgin' by the look of some of these, I'd say Liverpool seems to have had its fair share of bombing raids, yet my pals and I haven't heard a peep since we arrived. Is that just luck?'

'I don't wish to tempt fate, but what I will say is that the Nazis appear to be concentratin' their efforts further down south at present. Which is lucky for us but tragic for them.'

'What will you do after the war? Go back to your father's garage?'

'I don't think I could ever go back to Fangfoss, not after seein' what the rest of the country has to offer. I suppose it depends on where I end up. You?'

'Ah, that depends on what role I play in the services,' said Isla, 'and whether there's something similar waiting for me on the outside.'

The bus was slowing, and they made their way to the back of the bus before stepping on to the pavement. 'This,' said Theo, pointing to the impressive façade of the building in front of them, 'is the Rialto.'

'It's magnificent,' said Isla as he led her inside. 'Dare I say, much more impressive than the Grafton.'

'I'm glad you approve!'

Handing their coats over to the clerk, Theo got them both a drink and they made their way over to a table near the dance floor. Watching the other couples, many of whom were women dancing together, Isla pulled a disgruntled face. 'Why can't I dance like them?'

Theo held out his hand. 'By the end of the night you'll be dancin' *better* than them.'

Isla's dancing had definitely improved since her debut in the Grafton, but she still found herself occasionally stepping forwards when she should have been stepping back.

'You'll master it when you least expect it,' said Theo, 'and once you're there you'll wonder why you ever found it difficult in the first place.'

'I hope you're right.' She glanced over to a small

group of women who appeared to be watching them with interest. 'At least I'm providin' entertainment . . .'

Theo barely gave the women a moment's glance. 'Let them stare. They're only jealous.'

Isla, who was watching one of the women in particular, glanced up at Theo's face. 'Do you know that woman? Only she cannae keep her eyes off you.'

Theo glanced at the woman standing at the side of the dance floor, her arms folded across her chest. His heart sank horribly as he swept Isla over to the other side of the room. 'Unfortunately, yes.'

Isla looked back to the woman in question, who was glaring at Theo with an expression of pure hatred. 'What on earth have you done to deserve her wrath? She doesn't seem at all pleased to see you.' She hesitated. 'If I were to guess, I'd say that she looks like a woman scorned. Have you . . .' She purposely left the sentence hanging.

'Not if she were the last woman on earth.'

Isla averted her gaze. Was it her imagination, or was Theo protesting too much? After all, the woman was certainly attractive, even when scowling. Could it be that Theo was the one who was scorned? She dismissed the thought almost immediately. Whatever had gone on between the two, it was he who had offended her, not the other way round. She watched as the woman went off with her friends, although where they were going to exactly Isla couldn't be sure. She looked back to Theo, who was looking considerably relieved to see the woman walking away. *Whatever Theo might say, she's clearly unhappy with him, yet I believe him when he says that she's the last person he'd go for.* Whatever the reason, it was clear that Theo wasn't keen to share his thoughts, so Isla turned her attention back to the dance. 'Will you look at that!'

'What?' yelped Theo, whose nerves seemed to be considerably frayed by now.

'I haven't stepped on your toes nor kicked you in the shins for at least five minutes.'

'See?' he said, his voice heavy with relief. 'Didn't I say that you'd master it?'

Praying that the woman who had made it plain she knew him all too well had left the building, Theo kept a keen eye out for her for the rest of the evening, but she was nowhere to be seen, or at least not until he was making his way to the men's room.

Hurrying over from where her friends stood waiting for her, the woman grabbed him by the elbow. 'You don't let the grass grow, do you?' she spat waspishly.

Glancing over to where Isla sat, Theo was relieved to see that she wasn't looking in their direction. 'I know what this must look like, but we're just friends.'

She arched a cynical eyebrow. 'Pull the other one – it's got bells on.'

Theo shook his head. 'I can understand why you'd be angry, Caroline, but do you seriously expect me to live the rest of my life as a recluse . . .'

Her voice became a high-pitched squeal. 'The rest of your life? It's not even been a year!'

'So what? I can't have friends now? Is that what you're sayin'?'

'Of course not! But—'

'But nothin',' snapped Theo. 'Isla's a friend, nothin' more, nothin' less. If you don't believe me you can go ask her for yourself!'

Still staring at Isla, the woman sighed heavily before averting her gaze. 'That won't be necessary.'

Theo shoved his hands into his trouser pockets. 'It's been hard for me too, you know.'

She looked at him with a face full of regret. 'I just don't want to see you make the same mistakes.' She paused. 'Have you told her? Because if not, you should.'

'No. Because she's only a friend,' said Theo. 'I dare say you don't go tellin' your pals every single detail of your life?'

She looked down to the floor. 'No.'

'There you go then.' He paused. 'Whilst we're about it, would you tell a potential beau?'

Caroline's jaw flinched. 'I certainly wouldn't lie to him, but—'

Theo cut her off before she had a chance to continue. 'But nothin'. I understand you're havin' a hard time, but don't go judgin' me when you're not prepared to tell the truth yourself.'

'Like I said, I don't want to see anyone gettin' hurt,' said Caroline. 'But if you do become an item, I hope you're honest with her, because the truth will always out in the end.'

'And if that becomes the case, then I will,' said Theo. 'Now if you don't mind?'

She cast him a rueful look before leaving to join her

friends. Glad that the uncomfortable encounter was over, Theo continued about his business before returning to Isla. 'Fancy another turn on the floor?'

Isla patted the seat beside her, inviting him to sit down. 'I know it's none of my business, Theo, because we're not a couple, but is there somethin' I should know about the woman you were just talkin' to?'

Theo froze. He had had no idea that Isla had witnessed any part of their conversation, but now was not the time for hesitation. 'There is. If I tell you, I just hope you understand why I did what I did.'

'Oh, dear. I'm guessin' this isn't goin' to be good.'

Theo half-smiled. 'If you got the impression she hates my guts, you'd be right.'

'But why? I mean, I know I don't know you very well, but I cannae imagine anyone takin' against you so.'

'It's cos I know somethin' about her which she doesn't want to come to the surface, and the same could be said about me.'

Isla lowered her gaze. Whatever it was he was about to say, the prelude definitely didn't bode well. 'Oh.'

Knowing that he would have to spill the beans, if only in part, he drew a deep breath. 'How old do you think I am, Isla?'

She shrugged. 'You've been in the services since the start of the war, so I'd reckon you must be, what . . .' she fell silent as she did the arithmetic in her head, 'nineteen or twenty?'

He leaned on his elbow. 'That would be if I joined when I was eighteen.'

Her head whipped round. 'Just how old were you?'

He grimaced. 'Sixteen.'

Isla's eyes nearly left her skull. 'Sixteen! But that means you're . . .'

'I'll be eighteen in September.' His stomach dropped as he watched her cast a scrutinising eye over him. Would she decide that he was too young; would she walk away and never see him again?

Instead, a look of realisation dawned on her face. 'So that's why your mammy was so angry at you for joinin' up!'

'As fire,' said Theo. 'Not made any better when the Luftwaffe targeted my last base.'

'And is that woman threatening to tell the RAF your true age if you reveal her secret?'

'She thinks I've nothin' to lose the closer I get to eighteen, and as a result she's worried that I'll tell everyone *her* business, but I'd never do that! As I told her, we all have our secrets, some worse than others.'

Isla knew better than to ask what the woman's secret was, even though she was dying to know. Theo stood up. 'I'll get our coats . . .'

But Isla laid a hand on his arm. 'There's no need for us to leave.'

'I'm not goin' to lie to you, Isla. I didn't ask you to come out with me because I wanted another friend; I asked you out because I wanted to know if you'd be my belle. But all that seems pretty pointless now.'

'Why? Because you're younger than I thought? It's not as if you lied to me, Theo, cos I never actually asked your age. Quite frankly, you look – and act – much older than your years.'

'That's as maybe, but it was obvious that you would assume me to be at least eighteen, so I should've been upfront with you from the start.'

She leaned forward, taking care to speak in hushed tones. 'Truth be known, I'm not eighteen myself until next March. The day I escaped Coxhill was my seventeenth birthday, so you aren't the only one who's told a few fibs to get into the services.'

Relief flooded Theo. 'You're not angry, then?'

'Not in the slightest. After all, I was hardly truthful with you – not that you asked.'

He brightened. 'Bearin' in mind what I've just said about wantin' somethin' more than friendship, *will* you be my belle?'

Isla answered without hesitation. 'Of course I will!'

Beaming from ear to ear, he leaned forward and gently brushed his lips over hers. 'I reckon I must be the luckiest man alive!' he whispered, before kissing her properly.

Surrendering to the touch of his lips, Isla wished that the kiss would last for ever, and was disappointed when he broke away. 'It's later than I thought,' he said as the house lights went up.

'Time flies when you're havin' fun,' she said dreamily.

Taking her hand in his, he led her over to collect their coats. 'You know, I'm almost glad I bumped into Caroline tonight – that's the Waaf you saw me talkin' to earlier – cos I don't know whether I'd have had the courage to ask you to be my girl otherwise.'

'Why do I somehow doubt that you lack courage around the ladies?' Isla asked with a wry smile.

He shrugged. 'I'll not deny that I've kissed a girl before, but it's different with you – you're special.'

'I don't know about that,' said Isla, blushing. 'Maybe if I were rich, or—'

'That wouldn't make you special, or not to me it wouldn't,' said Theo. 'Do you think your folks would approve of us gettin' together?'

'Mammy would, but you know what fathers can be like. No man is ever good enough for their little girl.'

'And quite right too.' Standing back so that Isla might board the bus before him, Theo paid the clippie. 'I'm afraid I shan't have time to pop in when I take you home but hopefully I will the next time.'

'That would be nice, especially with Sophie goin' off to Plymouth.'

Still holding her hand in his, he rubbed his thumb over the backs of her knuckles. 'I wonder if you'll get your papers before she goes?'

'I hope so, cos I'm not keen on livin' in limbo,' said Isla. 'There's nothin' worse than not knowin' where your life's headed.'

'Even then things can come along to turn everythin' upside down,' said Theo. 'That's why I try not to plan too far ahead.'

'Quite wise too,' said Isla, adding, 'Thanks for this evenin', by the way. It was lovely.'

He smiled. 'You're welcome. And whilst I know it goes without saying, you won't mention our earlier discussion to anyone, will you? Only I wouldn't want word gettin' out, cos even though I don't think they'd do owt about it now, you never know; they might want to punish me for lyin' to them.'

'My lips are sealed,' said Isla, making a zipping motion along the line of her mouth.

'I knew I could rely on you.' Seeing her smile softly while gazing out of the window, Theo couldn't help but feel a bit of a heel. He may have told Isla the truth, but only in part. Would she be as understanding if she knew the whole? He very much thought not, but then again, what she didn't know wouldn't hurt her.

By the time Isla got in that evening the other girls were already in bed.

'How'd it go?' yawned Sophie as Isla tiptoed stealthily across the bedroom floor.

Leaning up on one elbow, Meg squinted at the alarm clock. 'I'd say it went well considerin' the hour!'

'It was wonderful,' Isla confirmed, before going on to tell them everything that had happened that evening except the part about Theo's age and his uncomfortable encounter with the Waaf; after all, a promise was a promise.

'I *knew* you'd end up as a couple!' Meg crowed excitedly.

Slipping her nightie over her head, Isla spoke thickly. 'How could you possibly know somethin' like that?'

'Because it was obvious he thought a lot of you – he'd not have gone out of his way to help you otherwise – and because you'd have to be nuts to turn him down.'

Isla slipped between the cold sheets. 'And that's your theory on relationships, is it?'

'Aye,' said Meg succinctly. 'All relationships are based on mutual attraction.'

'Maybe at first,' conceded Isla, 'but looks aren't everything.'

'They must help, though,' Meg supposed.

'Most definitely,' put in Sophie, 'but it doesn't matter how good-looking someone is if they're a pig inside, and you can only find that out through time.'

Isla blew out the lamp which the girls had left on for her. 'I might not have known Theo for very long, but I know he's not a pig.'

'I hope not,' said Sophie. 'And as long as he treats you right, then that's all that matters.' She paused momentarily. 'And I must say that I too thought he would ask you to be his belle, but it does seem awfully quick. Did anythin' happen to prompt this sudden relationship?'

Knowing that she couldn't tell Sophie how he'd confided in her, Isla shrugged the question off. 'It's not as if he's asked me to marry him!'

'Aye, it's only a bit of fun,' said Meg, 'and you can always break it off should you find you're not suited over the course of time.'

'Exactly!' said Isla.

'I didn't mean to upset you,' said Sophie softly, 'I just worry about you, that's all.'

Isla smiled. 'I know you do, but I'll be fine.' She

stifled a huge yawn beneath her hand. 'Golly, am I whacked! It must be all that dancin'.'

'And smoochin',' giggled Meg.

Isla wagged her finger. 'We only had one kiss.'

'That's one more than I've had,' said Sophie, 'and you're younger than me!'

Yawning for the second time, Isla brought the conversation to a close. 'G'night, girls.'

Saying their goodnights, they all settled down to sleep, but Isla was still mulling Sophie's words over in her mind. Theo had asked her to be his belle not long after the incident with the other Waaf; could that have prompted his decision? He'd more or less hinted that it had, but was it more than that? Or was it down to Isla's acceptance of his age? Thinking back to the heated discussion he'd had with the Waaf, there was something about the whole encounter which gave Isla pause. For a start, why would the Waaf confront Theo in the manner she did if she was scared of him tellin' tales on her? Surely she'd try to avoid him if that were the case? And why was it that he gave vague replies when she asked a question he didn't really want to answer? Because using the term 'summat like that' was as good as replying with 'kind of', which replied without replying. *More to the point*, Isla told herself, *why didn't you push for a proper answer instead of lettin' him fob you off like that?* She knew why. *Because I love being in his company. He makes me feel safe, just like Daddy used to before we lost Mammy. And he makes me laugh – a lot – somethin' else Daddy used to do. Is it really so bad that he doesn't want to tell me every detail of his life? No.*

That sort of thing takes time. He trusted me enough to tell me the truth about joinin' up under age. But on the other hand he's going to be eighteen in a few months' time, so it didn't really matter who he tells, not any more. The services are desperate for volunteers, so they'd hardly throw him out when he's done all his training. No, this is a case of 'too good to be true'. You're finding fault when there's none to find because you cannae believe your luck. Stop tryin' to put a spanner in the works and enjoy yourself! Thinking back, she recalled that at least one of his replies of 'summat like that' had been before she knew his real age. *So there you are!* she concluded. *Now for pity's sake get some sleep or you'll be fit for nothin' come the mornin'!*

Closing her eyes, it wasn't long before Isla drifted into sleep, but the Waaf and the way she was staring at Theo remained in her mind's eye. Dreaming that she was back in the Rialto, Isla watched the woman whom he'd been having a heated conversation with come over to interrupt their dance, only instead of arguing with Theo she was fixated on Isla.

'You don't know him,' she said, her eyes resonating the pain she felt, 'because if you did you'd run a mile!'

'You've got him all wrong,' dream Isla protested. 'He'd never tell on you – he's not like that!'

But the other woman was shaking her head sadly. 'You need to take my advice and forget about Theo Stratham, cos he's bad news.'

Dream Isla had opened her mouth to retort when the vision of the woman faded before her eyes. It was replaced by Isla's father, who also gave her a warning.

'He's no good for you, Isla,' he said. 'He's a wrong 'un through and through.'

'He wouldn't dump me in the poorhouse!' dream Isla snapped. 'You're just jealous because he's a better man than you.'

The pain her remark had caused was clear to see in her father's eyes, and was too much for her to bear. Isla woke from her dream with tears pouring down her cheeks, but for the life of her she couldn't think what had caused her to cry.

Rolling over, she went back to sleep, and dreamt of the moment she and Meg got their papers and how happy they were to be starting their new lives as Waafs in RAF West Kirby. Celebrating their news in the Rialto, dream Isla failed to see the Waaf who had argued with Theo watching her with growing concern from a nearby table.

Chapter Ten

It was the afternoon prior to Sophie's departure and the girls – including Peggy – had arranged to have the day off so that they might spend some time together.

'You've not done any of the really touristy things,' said Peggy, 'so how about we visit the Palm House in Sefton Park? We can go for a row on the lake, feed the ducks and have a stroll through the park itself.' Thinking it a splendid idea, the girls had made a picnic to take with them, which they were currently eating whilst beside the lake.

'It's beautiful here!' breathed Isla as she looked out over the sun-kissed waters.

'I wish we'd had more time to do this sort of thing,' said Sophie, selecting a corned beef and tomato sandwich. 'We'll definitely have to do more when we come back on leave.'

'Dancin', too,' said Isla. 'I know we've all been busy with work and what not, but I still cannae believe tonight will be your first night at the Rialto.'

'I'm really lookin' forward to it,' said Meg, 'but not

as much as I'm lookin' forward to goin' dancin' in the WAAF.'

'What's the difference?' asked Sophie as she put the greaseproof wrappings from her sandwich back into the wicker basket.

'We'll be on a base full of single fellers,' said Meg. 'There'll be men aplenty to dance with, so findin' a boyfriend should be easy.' Another thought hit her. 'And if he's on the same camp as me it would sort of be like we were livin' together, only without the hanky-panky, of course.'

Inhaling sharply, Sophie began to choke on her mouthful of sandwich. After much back-patting by her friends, her eyes were still watering when she eventually managed: 'I should hope not!'

Giggling an apology, Meg continued to dream about her ideal boyfriend. 'Do you reckon I could bag myself a pilot?'

Sophie gave her a wry smile. 'And why would you want a pilot in particular?'

'Because they're rich and handsome!' said Meg, wiping some breadcrumbs from the skirt of her frock.

Peggy laughed out loud. 'Maybe I've been mis-informed, but I don't think money and looks are requirements for becomin' a pilot.'

'Ah, but a man always looks good in uniform,' said Meg, who was basing her knowledge on the posters she'd seen on the outer walls of the hippodromes.

'So it doesn't matter what rank they are as long as they're in uniform?' said Isla, who wanted to be clear.

'I wouldn't say that exactly,' mused Meg, before

coming to a snap conclusion. 'I *knew* there was a reason why pilots were more handsome than the others!'

'Which is?' asked Isla, who was intrigued to hear her friend's theory.

'They have the money to look after themselves! Nice teeth, well cut hair, clear skin . . . all that stuff costs money.'

Isla frowned slightly. 'I suppose I'd agree with some of that, especially the teeth bit, but clear skin . . . are you sure?'

Meg started to nod, but Peggy cut across her. 'They have clear skin because they're rarely spotty little oiks who've only recently shed their nappies!'

All three girls burst into laughter at Peggy's description. 'Blimey, Peggy!' gasped Sophie as she regained her breath. 'What an image that conjures up!'

'True, though,' said Isla, who was wiping the tears of laughter from her eyes. 'Theo was sayin' that he wanted to be a pilot, but couldn't due to his lack of education.'

'Either a university degree or a silver spoon,' said Peggy knowledgeably, 'and whilst the latter doesn't require them to be a certain age it does mean they've had an extensive education, so it comes to the same thing.'

'Why does everythin' always come down to money?' sighed Sophie. 'It's so unfair.'

'Because you need money to do just about anything and everything,' said Peggy.

'Not this, though,' said Isla, looking to the lake. 'This is free.'

Peggy pulled a downward smile. 'Not necessarily.

Someone somewhere will be payin' for all of this.' As she spoke she was pointing to the perfectly manicured gardens.

'And they won't be doin' it unless there's somethin' in it for them,' said Sophie. 'That's one thing my father taught me – you get nothin' in life for free, even if it looks that way.'

'It's wrong, really,' Meg began, but Peggy interrupted.

'You're right but wrong at the same time. Nobody likes payin' taxes, but where would we be without the money to fight the war? Or to pay the firemen to extinguish the fires? Not to mention the scuffers who keep the streets safe.'

'I hadn't thought of it like that,' admitted Meg, 'but you're right, cos without the money from taxes this country would have no way to defend itself.'

'I shouldn't imagine them planes come cheap, neither,' said Isla. 'Nor the ships.'

'And someone has to pay for the trainin', not to mention the weapons, as well as the food . . .'

'They should do what Harman did and outsource,' said Meg dully.

'They do,' said Peggy, continuing darkly, 'It's called arms-tradin'.'

The girls stared at her in stunned silence until Isla stammered, 'Are you seriously tellin' us that our country has been sellin' weapons to other countries?'

'And we aren't the only ones,' said Peggy.

Isla stared at her, agog. 'But not to Germany, surely to goodness?'

Peggy gave a half-shoulder shrug. 'I hope not, but

it wouldn't surprise me, cos nothin' does any more, not where money's concerned.'

'Dear God,' was all Isla could say.

'Well, I hope this teaches them a lesson!' huffed Meg.

'It probably will,' said Peggy cynically. 'They'll probably ask for more money next time.' She opened the bottle of lemonade and poured it into their mugs. 'I'd like to think there won't be a next time, but if history is anything to go by . . .' She pulled a grim smile before swiftly changing the subject. 'I reckon we finish up here then see about hirin' a boat.' She glanced at Sophie. 'You never know – the practice might come in handy!'

The rest of the afternoon had been filled with laughter as the four women did their best to row their boat without colliding with anyone else's. Their time finally ended when Meg lost an oar whilst endeavouring to push them away from the bank.

'I hope I do better than this in the Wrens,' chuckled Sophie as she ran her fingers along the surface of the lake. 'Goodness only knows where we'll end up if I'm in charge.'

'Not far from where you started if you keep rowin' in circles like you did this afternoon,' laughed Isla.

Thanking the man who had towed them back to the jetty, the girls scrambled out of the boat one by one, with Sophie being the last. 'I know it's an obvious statement to make, but they're so darned unsteady,' she said as she practically leapt into Isla's arms, nearly sending them both into the water.

'So, what now?' asked Meg.

'By the time we've got home and had our dinner, it'll be time for the three of you to head to the Rialto,' said Peggy.

'Three of us?' said Isla, her voice heavy with disappointment. 'Why aren't you coming?'

'All this fresh air has fair taken it out of me! Besides, I'd feel out of place bein' the only old fogey amongst a bevy of beauties!'

'You're not an old fogey!' Isla chided as she held her hand out to stop the bus. 'And besides, I hate the thought of you sitting in the house on your tod.'

'Don't worry about me, I'll be fine,' said Peggy. 'If it's any consolation, I've had a fabulous day and I'd very much like it if we could do it again when you come back on leave. And if my Clive's home I'll even come dancin'.'

They each paid the clippie before taking a seat further down the bus. 'I must admit I'm rather lookin' forward to meetin' Clive and your boys,' said Meg, sitting down next to Peggy. 'They won't be cross with us, will they?'

'Why would they be cross?'

'They might think we've taken advantage of your hospitality,' said Meg, 'what with you bein' on your own and all.'

'They think no such thing,' said Peggy firmly. 'I've already told each and every one of them how you girls have kept me company as well as paid your way – in fact more than paid your way – and they're delighted to know their old ma's not on her own.'

'I just wish we could stay for longer,' said Sophie. 'I feel guilty walkin' out on you.'

'I shan't be alone for long, though,' said Peggy. 'What with the three of you havin' leave, I would hope to have at least one of you around for a while every couple of months or so.'

Isla was eyeing Peggy in a thoughtful manner. 'Have you ever thought about joinin' up, even if it's just the NAAFI?'

'Often, but I want my boys to have a home to come back to,' said Peggy emphatically. 'And I wouldn't have that if I joined the war, cos likely as not the house would be taken over by one of the services, as they did with Irene's.'

'Keep the home fires burnin',' said Isla. 'Who was it that said that?'

'John McCormack,' said Peggy. 'It was a song about the Great War, and a beautiful one at that.'

The mood was turning sombre, so Isla changed the subject with a cheery smile. 'So, who's lookin' forward to takin' a turn on the floor?'

Meg glanced at Sophie. 'You'll have to lead, cos I ain't got a clue what I'm doin'.'

Sophie's face dropped. 'That makes two of us. In fact, it's the reason why I haven't pushed to go dancin' before.' She looked to Isla. 'Quite frankly, we've all heard about Theo's shins, and I don't like the idea of havin' my toes stepped on.'

'Theo's an excellent teacher,' said Isla. 'He's going to be more than happy to show you the ropes.'

'We cannae do that to him,' protested Meg. 'He'll never want to take you dancin' again!'

Isla waved a dismissive hand. 'He's made of stern

stuff, is my Theo. Besides, you might be a natural on the dance floor. Not only that, but he was a tad concerned that he'd be spoilin' our last evenin' together, so I told him we all wanted him to be there.'

'Why—' began Meg, before letting out a gasp. 'Cripes! We were so busy natterin' we nearly missed our stop!' Hurrying down the aisle, they thanked the clippie for spotting them in time to signal the driver to brake by ringing the bell.

'Why would he think he'd be spoilin' our last evenin' together?' resumed Meg as they stepped down on to the pavement.

'Because he'll be the only man,' said Isla. 'So maybe givin' you two some dance lessons will assure him that he's very much welcome.'

'On the other hand, I don't want to spoil your time together,' said Sophie, 'cos I dare say learnin' to dance isn't done in five minutes!'

'You'll soon get into the swing of things,' Peggy assured her as they walked arm in arm towards the house. 'It's easy once you get the hang of it.'

'Are you *sure* you won't change your mind about joinin' us at the Rialto? I bet you'd make an excellent teacher.'

Peggy took a deep breath before letting it out with a whoosh. She was really going to miss her time with the girls, and refusing their invitation that evening would be a reminder of what was to come. 'Fine. But I ain't dancin' with no fellers, mind, and that includes Theo!'

The girls whooped with joy, causing Peggy to

chuckle. 'You'll have the neighbours wonderin' what's goin' on,' she said, leading the way into the house.

'Let them wonder!' cried Meg. 'This is goin' to be the best night ever!'

The four women ate the remainder of their picnic whilst getting ready for the evening ahead, and it wasn't too long before they were stepping off the bus outside the Rialto.

'There's Theo,' said Isla, waving to gain his attention.

He gave a little wave back as he walked towards them, a look of uncertainty etched upon his face. 'I hope I'm not intrudin' . . .' he began, but Sophie cut him off.

'You're really not,' she said. 'Besides, I've only met you once, and briefly at that. I'd like to reassure myself that my Isla's in good hands before I head off to Plymouth!'

His eyes twinkled. 'Ah! So I'm bein' vetted?'

'Of course.' Sophie smiled. 'Plus there's the added bonus of getting to spend the evenin' with four lovely ladies.'

'Then I am a lucky chap indeed.'

Isla swiftly introduced Theo to Peggy and, after a quick hello, Peggy joined Sophie and Meg who were already entering the building.

'I take it there's still no news on your postin'?' Theo asked Isla as they followed them inside.

Isla wrinkled her nose. 'More's the pity.'

'I'm sure you'll hear soon enough, but in the meantime let's show your friends how far you've come!'

A short while later, with their drinks on a table

near the dance floor, Isla was dancing a slow waltz with Theo whilst the others had a break. Gazing at the other dancers as they swept past, Isla found herself looking for the woman who'd been arguing with Theo in the Rialto. *I don't know what it is*, she thought, *but I just can't shake her from my mind. Theo explained the situation, but I'm sure there's more to it than he's letting on.*

'You're doin' really well,' said Theo, cutting across her thoughts.

'Don't jinx it!' chuckled Isla. Chastising herself for allowing her attention to wander, she tried to put her doubts firmly from her mind.

Despite Sophie's original fears, Meg had proved to be an excellent student who never put a foot out of place.

Taking a seat with Peggy whilst Meg and Isla took a turn on the floor, Sophie looked in the direction of Theo, who was standing by the bar getting the drinks. 'So, what do you think? Do you approve?'

'Hard to say,' said Peggy slowly. 'And funnily enough, not because of anythin' he's said or done, but more for the way Isla is around him.'

Sophie looked surprised. 'But she likes him a lot. She'd not have agreed to be his belle otherwise.'

'She might well like him, but I'm not convinced she trusts him,' said Peggy decidedly.

Sophie's frown deepened. 'But we've talked about it and Isla is adamant that he's a lovely feller.'

Peggy eyed her sharply. 'Who was suggestin' otherwise?'

253

Quickly running through the conversation the girls had had regarding Theo's hasty proposal for Isla and him to become an item, Sophie ended with: 'I honestly think you've got this wrong, Peggy, Isla herself assured me that she'd know if Theo were a pig or not.'

'Unless your words gave her food for thought,' said Peggy. 'Because somethin' doesn't sit right to me.'

'I suppose she might've decided to slow things down a little, but I think that would just be Isla bein' sensible.'

Peggy pulled a brief downward smile. 'Could be, but I still think there's more to it than that.'

'But if there is, why hasn't she said anything?'

Peggy gave her an understanding smile. 'She's hardly likely to do that when she knows you're goin' off tomorrow, now is she? You've got enough on your plate as it is.'

'Well, if not to me, then why not Meg?'

'Maybe she's worried Meg will say something to you? You can't blame her, really; she's only lookin' out for her pals.'

'Do you think there's anythin' to worry about?'

Peggy shrugged. 'Isla's a sensible girl. If she's got any real concerns she'll back out of the relationship.'

'I don't think it sensible to agree to be someone's belle when you've only met them a few times, and neither did Isla before she met Theo. She even said that folk were daft for leapin' into marriage when they didn't really know each other.'

'Maybe she thinks that way about marriage but not about courtin'?'

Theo was coming towards them carrying a tray of drinks, which brought their conversation to an end, and seeing refreshments arrive Isla and Meg left the dance floor to join them.

'I swore I'd never take the role of the man again,' said Isla as she selected her drink from the tray, 'but apart from the odd slip-up I'm doin' quite well. Not as well as Meg, though – she's taken to this dancin' malarkey like a duck to water.'

'I could dance all night,' said Meg with a happy sigh. 'I hope they have dance halls nearby wherever we get posted.'

Theo spoke knowledgeably. 'They hold dances in all the NAAFIs, so even if there's nowhere nearby – although there always is – you've still got that to fall back on.'

'The camps have their own cinemas, too,' Peggy put in.

'As well as a shop to buy the necessaries,' Theo added. 'I suppose bein' on camp is a bit like livin' in a small village.'

'Have you been in the services long then, Theo?' asked Peggy.

'Since the beginning, but I've only been in Liverpool a short while.'

'Where were you before that?'

'Manston,' said Theo, 'but we had to move after the Luftwaffe paid us a visit.'

Peggy quickly drew the sign of the cross over her left breast. 'I'm guessin' it must've been pretty bad if they had to relocate you.'

'They flattened the place,' said Theo distantly.

Peggy was eyeing him sympathetically. 'Oh, I'm sorry to hear that. Did you lose many pals?'

He rolled his tongue around his cheek. 'I'm afraid I did rather.' His eyes flicked up, locking with Peggy's, before he looked back to Isla. 'Ready to go again?'

'I certainly am.' Isla got to her feet as Meg left to use the conveniences, and Sophie turned to Peggy. 'I didn't realise he'd had it so rough.'

'Mmm,' said Peggy.

Sophie eyed her quizzically. 'What?'

'There's something he's not tellin' us about his last base, although I don't know what.'

'Such as?'

Peggy lowered her gaze. 'A lot of people carry guilt for makin' it when their pals didn't. It's perfectly plausible he's doin' just that.'

'Poor Theo. Do you think we should say anything to Isla?'

Peggy shook her head fervently. 'Best not to get involved. Besides, what would you say? It's not as though Isla isn't aware of what happened in Manston. No, if she needs help she'll come to you when she's ready.'

Next morning the girls were up betimes, ready for the day ahead.

'How're you feelin', Sophie?' Isla called over her shoulder as she slowly descended the staircase in front of her pal.

'Nervous and excited at the same time, a bit like the night of the play,' Sophie confessed.

'You'll be just fine. I bet you'll . . . ooooh.'

'You bet I'll what?' Then Sophie saw that Isla was staring at the two brown envelopes on the hall floor. 'Oh!'

Picking the envelopes up, Isla called up the staircase to Meg, who was still getting her dressing gown on. 'Meg! Our instructions have come.'

The bedroom door swished open, followed by what sounded like a herd of elephants descending the stairs. Her eyes rounding, Meg took the envelope from Isla's outstretched hand and stared at it.

'It's not goin' to explode,' chuckled Isla as she headed into the kitchen to find a knife.

'Maybe not, but this envelope holds the answer to my future,' said Meg, 'and I'm not sure I'm ready to learn what that is this early in the morning.'

'Leave it until teatime, then,' teased Isla.

Meg held the envelope to her chest. 'I cannae do that. The suspense would kill me!'

Taking a knife from the cutlery drawer, Isla slit her envelope open and offered the knife to Meg, who took it reluctantly.

Pulling out her own instructions, Isla gave a small whoop of joy and handed them to Sophie to read. 'I've been accepted into the WAAF, and they're sending me to RAF Bridgnorth in a week's time!' Her eyes dancing with delight, she looked to Meg, who was jiggling with joy as she shouted 'Snap!'.

'I wish we could all be together,' Isla told Sophie,

'but I think we knew that was never goin' to happen once we realised the desks were for different services.'

'I know, and whilst I'm disappointed, I'd already resigned myself to the fact that we were goin' to be separated,' said Sophie. A tear forming in her eye as she looked at Meg's papers too, she continued, 'I cannae begin to tell you how proud I am of the pair of you. You're like sisters to me, and I couldn't have wished for better siblin's, I really couldn't.'

'Same here!' cried Isla.

'Closer than sisters,' said Meg, 'cos we've been through more stuff together than most families would in a lifetime.'

'What's this about sisters?' asked Peggy, who after hearing the whoops of joy was making her way down the stairs. Sophie handed her the papers whilst Meg and Isla gabbled their good news.

Looking slightly glum, Peggy handed the papers back to their prospective owners. 'I'm glad you two aren't bein' split up, but sad to learn that I've only a week left with a full house.'

'I know you were dreadin' the thought of us leavin',' Isla told her, 'so I asked Theo when he thought we'd get our first bit of leave, and he said after we've completed our trainin'. It won't be for a few months yet, but it's somethin' to took forward to.'

'It is,' said Peggy. Realisation hitting her, she looked to Sophie. 'But doesn't that mean your leave will be different, what with you finishin' your trainin' a week before the others?'

Sophie sagged visibly. 'I hadn't thought of that! Oh, I do hope that won't be the case.'

'Maybe it'll depend on what we're trained to do,' supposed Meg. 'After all, it cannae take that long for someone to teach us how to make a stew, or not compared to teachin' someone how to drive it can't.'

'Very true,' said Peggy. 'Some of the top jobs take months and months of training.'

This didn't sound any better to Sophie, who said as much before adding, 'We'll just have to arrange to have some leave together further down the line.' She looked to Isla. 'Don't forget to phone Harvey to let him know you an' Meg've been accepted into the WAAF. It's good to keep him abreast of the news.'

'And we'll let him know that you're in the Wrens whilst we're about it,' said Isla.

'Talkin' of which, we'd best get the porridge on,' said Peggy, 'I wish I could've come and seen you off at the station, Soph, but I'm afraid I have to work. Cos, as my Clive likes to say, the bills won't pay themselves.'

Sophie appeared to have an epiphany. Rushing off to fetch her handbag, she was fishing around in her purse when she came back. Pushing some money into Peggy's resisting hand, Sophie ordered her to take it, as she herself wouldn't need to pay for her keep in the Wrens. 'And you'll miss the extra income when we're all gone,' she finished.

Peggy looked at the coins in her hand. 'You're a good, sweet, kind-hearted girl, Sophie, but whilst I appreciate the gesture you're goin' to need this for supplies such as soap and what not.'

'I've kept a little back, so there's no need for you to worry about that,' said Sophie firmly.

Isla, who had already set about making the porridge, called over her shoulder, 'You were a lifesaver when we first came to Liverpool, Peggy. I don't know what we'd have done without you!'

'We'd have been in dire straits, that's for sure,' added Meg, who was spooning leaves into the teapot.

Giving in, Peggy put the money in her purse. 'Well, thank you. I shall use it to buy summat nice for when you come back on leave.'

Seeing the steam begin to wisp up from the spout of the kettle, Meg took it from the stove and poured some of the water into two jugs before placing it back on to boil. 'You can have the first wash, Sophie.' She passed the second jug to Peggy. 'This one's yours.'

'It should be me doin' the brekker whilst the three of you get ready,' Peggy protested, but was quickly corrected.

'You're the one who's got to go to work in an hour's time,' Isla chided her. 'Meg and me don't have to go in until we've seen Sophie off on the train, so no arguments!' Reluctantly agreeing, Peggy followed Sophie up the stairs.

'It's goin' to feel very strange here without Soph,' said Isla. 'A bit like losin' an arm.'

'I know exactly what you mean. Cos even though we've got each other, Sophie's always been the voice of reason, and we'll miss that with her gone.'

'First I lose my mammy and my baby brother,

then my daddy, an' now Sophie,' sighed Isla. 'I hope you're not next!'

'Me too, but even if I am you'll make new friends; we all will. Only we'll have an advantage over most, because we've already lived away from home, and in far worse circumstances,' said Meg as she poured the now boiling water into the teapot.

'I hadn't thought of it like that, but you're right,' conceded Isla. 'Bein' in the services should be a piece of cake in comparison.'

'I hope you're right,' said Sophie as she re-entered the kitchen, 'cos I feel like a cat on a hot tin roof!'

'Blimey, you were quick,' said Meg, heading for the stairs.

'I just wish I was on the train already. Not because I want to leave, but it's horrid to be waitin' for the inevitable.'

'Waitin' is always the worst part,' agreed Isla. 'I found that out when we were leavin' Coxhill.'

Sophie held a hand to her stomach. 'I'm not sure I'll be able to eat any breakfast.'

Looking disappointed, Isla wagged the large wooden spoon she was using to stir the porridge at Sophie. 'I'm not havin' you leave this house on an empty stomach.'

Sophie laughed. 'You sound like my mammy.' She paused. 'When are you goin' to tell Theo about your postin'?'

'On the way home from work tonight, after I've called Harvey. Why?'

Sophie shrugged. 'Just wondered.'

Isla eyed her affectionately. 'Are you still worried about the two of us gettin' together so soon?'

'Not if you're not.'

'I like him a lot, he's a smashin' feller and I'm lucky to have him,' said Isla, continuing to stir the porridge. 'But I'm not in love with him or anythin' like that, if that's what you're wonderin'.'

Sophie found herself relaxing a little. 'I just worried you might do what so many others before you have done, especially after experiencin' the kinds of loss you have.'

'You thought I was goin' to leap into marriage rather than risk losin' Theo?'

Sophie grimaced. 'You wouldn't be the first.'

'Would you be awfully insulted if I were to say that I look upon you a bit like I did on my mammy?'

Sophie felt her cheeks tinge with colour. Flattered beyond words, she fought for something to say. 'Not at all. In fact I'm honoured to know you think of me like that.'

Isla smiled. 'I thought you might imagine I was implyin' you were old enough to be my mammy.'

Sophie laughed. 'I might look it, but . . .'

Isla tutted with good humour. 'You look nothin' of the sort, but you did take me under your wing, and that's the sort of thing my mammy would have done in the same situation.'

Sophie's cheeks coloured further. 'You needed help, it's as simple as that,' she said modestly.

But Isla wouldn't allow it. '*Everyone* in Coxhill needed help, but no one else was willing to stick

262

their necks out for fear of what might happen if they did.'

Sophie gently took the spoon from Isla's unresisting hand. 'Maybe I did that because you were different from everyone else.'

Peggy entered the kitchen, her nostrils flaring as she walked over to the stove. 'Gosh, that porridge smells good.' Taking this as her cue to go and wash, Isla trotted up the stairs.

Her brow raised, Peggy eyed Sophie in a questioning manner. 'Is everything all right?'

'I think so. We talked about Theo . . .' Seeing the older woman's eyes round, she was quick to put her at her ease. 'Not what we were saying – only about how Isla feels.'

'And?'

'She likes him a lot, but she's not in love and she won't be rushin' into marriage any time soon,' said Sophie in a satisfied voice.

Peggy smiled. 'Good! Cos I'd hate to have to take my rollin' pin to 'im!'

Saying goodbye to Peggy had proved hard enough for Sophie, but when it came to bidding farewell to Isla and Meg on the platform she was only just about holding herself together. 'I cannae believe this is it!' she said, taking both her friends in a tight embrace.

'Me neither,' sniffed Meg. 'I wish we were comin' with you.'

Isla remained quiet, fearful that she might choke on her tears if she attempted to speak.

Jumping as the guard yelled 'All aboard who's goin' aboard', Sophie wiped her tears with the backs of her hands and smiled bravely. 'Take care of each other, won't you?'

'Always,' said Isla. 'And you must write to let us know how you're gettin' on just as soon as you can.'

'Will do! And—'

But the guard was slamming the carriage doors as he made his way along the platform, so there was no time for Sophie to do more than peck them both on the cheek before hurrying to board.

'We're really goin' to miss you, Sophie,' cried Isla as they strode after her.

'And I you,' said Sophie as she leapt up the last carriage steps. Standing back to allow the guard to close the door, she pushed the window down. 'Smile for me, girls, and don't forget, we'll be together soon!'

Isla and Meg forced themselves to smile even though their hearts were aching. 'We'll be countin' the days!' Meg called as the train blew its whistle to announce its imminent departure. They both saw Sophie mouth something back but it was lost under the squeal of the train's wheels as they gained traction. Standing arm in arm, Isla and Meg waved frantically from the platform until the train was out of sight.

'That's it,' said Isla, dabbing her tears. 'She's gone.'

'Only for now,' Meg comforted her. 'We'll be back together soon, and we can write and phone in the meantime, so it's not as if we're losin' her altogether!'

'I know, but that doesn't stop me from wishin' she was comin' with us instead of goin' off on her own.'

'We're lucky, cos we've got each other,' said Meg. 'And you're even luckier cos you've got Theo.'

'Only for the time being,' said Isla, 'cos we're goin' to be headin' off to Bridgnorth in a week's time and he might well be in Africa before I get any leave.'

'In which case you'll cope, just as you always have,' said Meg with confidence. 'Now let's get off to work so that we can tell Mr Lee the news!'

Isla and Meg had stopped to use the telephone on their way home from work, and Isla was currently talking to Harvey, who, as luck would have it, was still in the poorhouse.

'Nobody wants the ruddy job!' he said gloomily. 'They take one look at the place and practically run for the hills – not that I blame them, mark you.'

'They cannae expect you to stay on indefinitely,' said Isla uncertainly.

'That's what I said, but they keep on makin' excuses; sayin' that they've got loads more candidates, and that I'll be on my way soon. But they've been sayin' that for ages!'

'Oh, dear.'

'At least you can console yourself with the fact that Harman will likely as not soon be behind bars,' said Meg, who was sharing the receiver with Isla.

'There is that, I s'pose,' he said, before continuing in lighter tones. 'As for your joinin' the WAAF, I'll give your details to the girls in the office so that they can pass them on to your father. I've already given them Peggy's address, but I think it best if they have the two just in case.'

'In case of what?' asked Meg innocently.

Isla covered the mouthpiece with her hand. 'In case she gets bombed,' she hissed.

Meg grimaced. 'I hadn't thought of that.'

Apparently talking to someone over his shoulder, Harvey could be heard distantly before turning back. 'I've got to go, but don't worry – I'll pass your message on.'

Thanking him profusely, the girls said their goodbyes and called Theo's base. Hearing his voice come down the line, Isla told him their news.

'Bridgnorth!' he said approvingly. 'I believe it's a beautiful part of the country, although I've never been myself. How do you feel about it?'

'Glad that the wait is over, but sad that we won't be sharing the journey with Sophie.'

'Granted, but on the other hand you'll have plenty to talk about when you see each other next!'

'That's a good way of lookin' at it,' said Isla. 'Will I get to see you before I go?'

'Wild horses wouldn't keep me away!' said Theo. 'I'm guessin' you'll pretty much have your nose to the grindstone every day between now and then, but would you be able to come out the evenin' prior to your posting?'

'I don't see why not.' She looked to see if Meg had any objections, but she was nodding encouragingly. 'What time, and where?'

'Seein' as it'll be our last evenin' together, how

about we meet outside the Grafton at say nineteen hundred hours?'

'Perfect!'

Their last week in Liverpool had gone by in a flash, and Isla was waiting for Theo outside the Grafton, thinking about the phone call she'd had with Sophie earlier that day.

'It's certainly nothin' like Coxhill,' Sophie had told her and Meg, who had once again been sharing the receiver. Hearing their cheers come down the line, she had paused briefly. 'There's a real community spirit, and the girls I'm with are lovely! We've done lots of marching, as well as exercise in general, and I now own more clothes than I have in a long time – even if they are mostly uniform!'

Isla had been beside herself with relief. 'I cannae tell you how glad I am to hear it's all workin' out for you!'

'Well, if the WAAF is anythin' like the Wrens you're goin' to have a whale of a time!' was Sophie's reply.

'Have you met any sailors?' said Meg, leaning in to the mouthpiece.

Sophie laughed. 'Not as many as you'd think, but a few, aye. Have you any plans for your last evenin' in Liverpool?'

'I'm goin' dancin' with Theo, and Meg's goin' to play cards with Peggy,' said Isla.

'Very nice. What time's your train tomorrow?'

'Zero nine hundred hours, as they say in the services. Or should I say as *we* say in the services.'

'Are you lookin' forward to it?'

'Very much.'

Now, Isla waved to Theo who was walking towards her, a broad smile on his face. 'Hello there, Aircraftwoman Donahue!'

Isla rolled her eyes. 'Trust you to be the first one to call me that!'

'Sounds well, don't you think?'

'Very formal,' said Isla, 'but also very grown up.'

Taking her by the hand Theo led her into the Grafton as they continued to chat. 'Have you heard from Sophie?'

'Aye, and she's doin' just fine. In fact better than fine.'

'That's splendid news,' he said, heading towards the bar. 'And how are *you* feelin' about your impending departure for pastures new?'

'Not as apprehensive as I was before speakin' to Sophie, but still a tad nervous, based on the theory that just because service life suits her doesn't mean it will suit me.'

'You'll take to it like a duck to water,' said Theo with conviction. 'I reckon you could do just about anythin' you turn your hand to.'

'I dunno about that, but what makes you think so?' said Isla, although she was smiling with pleasure at his faith in her.

'You're not scared to stand up to those in authority, which takes real gumption, and whilst I wouldn't recommend tellin' your NCO where they can stick their job as you did with your boss in Clydebank, people with a lot of backbone tend to go far in the services.'

268

Thinking back to a comment that Sophie had made when Isla first entered Coxhill, Isla spoke slowly. 'Sophie said I had a lot of gumption not long after we first met. She seemed to think it was a good thing to have.'

'Undoubtedly,' agreed Theo. Seeing the barmaid approach he checked with Isla and ordered two ginger beers before continuing, 'I doubt you'd be here today without it.'

'In which case I'd never have met you.'

'And you only met me because you'd jumped into the fray to help a stranger,' said Theo as he paid for the drinks.

'Gemma! I had a letter from her the other day.'

He gestured for her to follow him to a nearby table. 'You did?'

'Aye. She and Agnes are doin' just grand!'

'You'll have to go and see them when all this is over,' said Theo. 'I'm sure they'd love to see you.'

'Gemma's already invited me. I've said I'll go just as soon as I find the time.'

'Time is precious in the services,' said Theo. 'You have to make the most of what you have, so you must make sure you spend it wisely.'

'I intend to! We've already agreed to spend our first week's leave at Peggy's, but from what I gather it'll be a long time before we get a whole week off after that.'

'It'll be what they call forty-eights, as in forty-eight hours,' said Theo as he placed their drinks on an empty table. 'Not much time to do an awful lot, so you have to be quite strategic in gettin' everyone together at the same time.'

'Which is why we're so lucky to have Peggy's house as a base,' agreed Isla.

The band struck up a waltz and Theo held out his hand. 'May I have the pleasure of this dance?'

'You may,' she said, a smile creasing her cheeks as she felt his arm encircle her waist. 'I wonder where I'll be the next time I step on to a dance floor.'

'Or whose shins you'll be crackin'.'

Isla giggled. 'I feel sorry for Meg.'

'Meg might have a beau of her own to dance with by then,' Theo pointed out.

'Well, I shan't be dancin' with another feller!' said Isla loyally.

'I wouldn't mind, cos I trust you,' said Theo genially. 'Besides, I'd rather that than see you sitting on your tod twiddlin' your thumbs.'

She rested her head against his chest. 'Does that mean you'll be dancin' with other women?'

He shook his head firmly. 'No, but just because I don't doesn't mean to say that you shouldn't either.'

She smiled. 'As the RAF cannae afford to have half the aircrew down with broken shins, I'll stick to dancin' with Meg or not at all!'

He rubbed his hand along her waist in an affectionate manner. 'As long as you don't miss out. And speaking of shins, you've not so much as scuffed my trouser leg the whole time we've been on the floor.'

Isla immediately looked down at her feet. 'Well, I'll be!'

'Didn't I say you'd get there in the end?'

'You did, and you were right,' said Isla, 'but a lot of that is down to your patience, not to mention resilience.'

Laughing gently, he pulled her close. 'You're worth every bruise.'

She laid her cheek against his chest. 'How is it that you've not been snapped up already, Theo Stratham? I'd have thought a man such as yourself would've been bagged a long time ago.'

He faltered mid-step before replying, tongue in cheek, 'I guess you're just lucky. And so am I, cos if we'd not met before you entered the forces there's no way you'd still be single!'

'Charmer!'

He grinned. 'I do my best!'

She closed her eyes as they continued to dance, 'I know we've not known each other long, but I won't half miss you when I'm away.'

'As I will you,' said Theo, continuing with a sigh, 'I just wish I'd met you earlier.'

She looked up at him, a frown forming. 'What do you mean by earlier?'

He shrugged. 'Oh, when I first entered the forces.'

'Why? What difference would that have made?'

'We'd have got to spend more time together, instead of a couple of measly weeks.'

'If you believe in fate then there's a reason why we didn't meet sooner – especially when you take into consideration that I might've been at your previous airbase, in which case I could well have been pushin' up daisies by now.'

She felt his arms stiffen as the last words left her lips. 'You shouldn't say things like that,' he said heavily.

Realising that her response might have appeared disrespectful to those he'd lost, she immediately apologised. 'Sorry, Theo. I should've been more sensitive.'

'You don't have to say that you're sorry. I'm the one at fault.'

'You?' she said, her voice full of surprise. 'How do you work that one out?'

'Because there's nothin' wrong with what you said. I was bein' overly sensitive.'

'You cared for your pals,' said Isla, 'which is understandable. When Sophie left, we were talkin' about how we're closer than family. I should imagine that was the case with you and your pals.'

'It was – is, even – and you'll find the same in the WAAF.' He eyed her thoughtfully. 'Do you ever feel as if you're doomed?'

She gave a sarcastic laugh. 'Are you kiddin'? With everythin' I've been through I'd be daft in the head *not* to think like that. But why do you ask?'

'Cos I feel that way too sometimes,' said Theo softly, 'only my doom's of my own making.'

There it is again, thought Isla, *the feeling of guilt that he carries around with him.* 'Is there somethin' you regret in particular?' she asked cautiously. 'I only wonder because you seem to blame yourself a lot for no reason at all, or at least none that I can see.'

He opened his mouth, closed it, then opened it

again. 'I guess it's just the war,' he sighed, sounding resigned. 'I feel guilty just for bein' alive sometimes – especially when it comes to those I lost.'

Isla knew from the conversations she'd had with the women down the laundry, as well as Peggy, that survivors carried this kind of guilt. 'You should be celebratin' the fact that you're alive, not blamin' yourself,' she said kindly.

'It's not always that easy,' said Theo dully. 'But I don't want to ruin your last evenin', so let's draw a line under the past and leave it where it belongs, shall we?'

'Good idea. Why dwell on somethin' you cannae possibly change?'

It seemed to Isla as if no time had passed at all before the lights went up. 'I've got to be on a train in less than twelve hours!' she cried in dismay.

Apologising sincerely for not keeping a closer eye on the time, Theo helped her on with her coat. 'If we rush we can make the next bus, but I think all things considered it would be better for you to catch a taxi.'

'And more expensive,' said Isla. 'The bus will be just fine!'

But Theo was shaking his head. 'I'm not havin' you miss your train tomorrow cos I kept you out too late. If nothin' else I don't want Peggy chasin' me with her rollin' pin!'

Isla chuckled at the image. 'It's very kind of you,' she said as they headed outside, 'but it's really not necessary.'

'I'll decide what's necessary and what isn't,' said Theo as he hailed a cab, 'especially when I'm the one to blame.'

Isla stood back as he opened the door of the cab. 'Next time I speak to you it will be over the telephone, and you'll be in Bridgnorth,' said Theo, twinkling down at her.

'I'll call as soon as I can,' said Isla. 'And thanks for another wonderful evening, Theo. You've been a star!'

Leaning forward, he kissed her lightly on the lips. 'Goodbye, Isla, and good luck for tomorrow.'

'Goodbye, Theo.' Settling herself into the back seat, she waved as the cab drove off. Only when Theo was out of sight did she turn her thoughts back to how he'd seemed determined to blame himself for her staying so late. Which was odd to say the least, especially as she was just as much to blame as he. *Why would he choose to think he was the one at fault?* thought Isla as the cab turned down Belmont Road. *It's almost as though he holds himself responsible for everythin' that goes on around him, but why?*

Back outside the Grafton, Theo congratulated himself on doing the right thing and putting Isla into a cab instead of satisfying his own selfish desires by prolonging the evening. *You've finally grown up*, Theo told himself. *I just wish you'd done it sooner!*

Chapter Eleven

'Are you sure you've got everything?' Peggy fussed as they hurried to the train station.

'Positive!' Meg and Isla called over their shoulders as they took the steps two at a time.

'I swear I'll never natter again,' huffed Peggy as she did her best to catch them up. 'Talk about lettin' time run away with you.'

'I seem to be makin' a habit of it lately,' said Isla. 'We'll have to buck our ideas up from now on, cos I dare say they won't put up with tardy behaviour in the WAAF.'

'Is that it?' cried Meg, pointing to a train full of seated passengers.

Isla rushed over to the guard. 'Will this train take us to Chester?'

'If you're quick about it,' the man replied.

Isla ran back and threw her arms round Peggy, planting a kiss on her cheek. 'Thanks for everythin', Peggy.'

'Good luck and take care!' cried Peggy as Meg too took her in a fierce embrace.

'We will!' Isla called back as she boarded the train. Turning, she saw that Meg was still holding on to Peggy. 'Come on, Meg!'

Giving Peggy's cheek one final kiss, Meg ran full pelt, only just reaching the carriage in time. Tutting his disapproval, the guard closed the door behind her, blew his whistle, and waved his flag.

'Talk about makin' it by the skin of your teeth,' gasped Isla. 'I'm not cut out for this kind of excitement!'

Agreeing wholeheartedly, Meg slumped herself down in an empty seat, and looked out of the window for Peggy, who spotted her and waved to them both.

Waving back, Isla sat in the seat opposite Meg's. 'If I get out of breath runnin' for the train, how am I goin' to cope when they get us doin' star jumps and the like?'

'The same way you do everythin' else,' said Meg. 'Practise, practise, practise! Just as you did with the dancin'. Talkin' of which, I never got the chance to ask you how it went last night.'

Isla gazed out of the window as her breathing returned to normal. 'It was good, but he's got a dreadful habit of blamin' himself for everythin'. Almost as if he feels responsible for every situation, even when it's nothing to do with him.'

'He probably feels the need to be in control after his base got bombed,' said Meg wisely. 'Even though he couldn't have done anythin' to prevent it, he might still feel guilty, much like you did when your mammy died.'

Isla's mouth fell open. How could she have not seen it before? 'That's exactly how I felt!'

'So you should understand how he feels. After all, you got on the wrong train in your determination to make sure no harm came to Gemma, and you did that out of your need to be in control.'

'You're right, I did, but this is different. I cannae put my finger on how, it just is.'

'So, how did it go apart from the blame thing? Did he get down on one knee and beg you not to look at another man?'

Isla cast her a fleeting glance. 'Quite the opposite. He encouraged me to dance with anyone I wished, because he didn't want me to feel left out.'

Meg wrinkled her nose. 'That doesn't sound very romantic! Surely he should become a raging inferno at the very thought of another man lookin' at his belle?'

'He says he trusts me.'

Meg eyed her cynically. 'Forgive me if I'm speakin' out of turn, but how can he possibly trust you, when he barely knows you? Sorry, Isla, but do you think he might be givin' you the green light because that's what *he* intends to do?'

'No,' said Isla. 'He was quite emphatic about that.'

'What did he say that makes you so sure?'

'It was more the way he said it,' said Isla decidedly. 'He looked as if he'd rather chop his right arm off than dance with anyone else.'

'Blimey! He's got it bad for you, hasn't he!'

'It seems that way, but . . .'

'But what?' asked Meg, averting her gaze from the window back to Isla.

'I still think there's something he's not telling me.'

'Such as?'

'I don't know, cos he's not telling me!'

Meg eyed her friend thoughtfully. 'You're worried, aren't you?'

'I told Sophie that I wasn't in love with him and that was the truth, but I'm very, *very* fond of him, and I'm worried that he might not be what I think he is.'

'But even if he's not, there're plenty more fish in the sea,' said Meg. 'So why's he so special?'

'He makes me feel safe. If it turns out I'm wrong, I'll feel as though I've been betrayed by the two men who've meant the most to me in the world. Stupid, I know, because I've only seen Theo a handful of times, but . . .'

'If it's any comfort, from what I've seen he's true blue,' said Meg, 'and I truly cannae see why you're suspicious.'

Isla leaned back in her seat. If she were to tell Meg that he'd lied about his age to get into the RAF, she'd be breaking a confidence, something she was not prepared to do. 'You know when you can see somethin' out of the corner of your eye, but when you try to look it's gone?'

Meg nodded. 'Always gives me the heebie-jeebies, does that.'

'That's what it's like with Theo. I know summat's not right, I just don't know what.'

'Have you mentioned any of this to him?'

'In a roundabout fashion, but he's got an answer for everything.'

'Do you think you maybe regret sayin' yes to bein' his belle and now you're tryin' to throw a spanner into the works?'

Isla dismissed the idea without hesitation. 'No. I'd not have agreed to be his belle if I wasn't sure.'

'There is one thing . . .' said Meg slowly, then shook her head. 'No, forget I said anything.'

Isla leaned forward eagerly. 'Too late now! Go on, say what's on your mind.'

Meg sighed before speaking reluctantly. 'Could it be that you're scared of bein' happy?'

Isla eyed her in disbelief. 'Is that a serious question?'

'Think about it logically. You must have been over the moon when you thought you were goin' to be a big sister, and then you lost your mammy as well as your baby brother,' said Meg gently. 'If that wasn't bad enough, your father then left you at Coxhill. You finally get out, and meet the man of your dreams, but he's in the RAF and he's already had one near miss when he lost his pals at his last base. Are you worried that bein' happy could mean you lose him too?'

Isla was about to deny this out of hand, but the more she thought about it the more it made sense. 'But why would I try to sabotage my own happiness?'

'If you get in first, you're the one in control, something that hasn't been the case for a long time. Or not until we broke out of Coxhill, at any rate.'

There was a pause. 'I think you might be right,' Isla said at last. 'Cos I cannae see any other reason for feelin' the way I do, because he's been nothin' but genuine and honest with me, even when he didn't have to be.'

Meg's forehead crumpled. 'What do you mean, bein' honest with you when he didn't have to be?'

Isla blinked. The overwhelming sense of relief had caused her to inadvertently tell a truth.

Meg pressed on. 'Isla?'

Isla glanced around the empty compartment as though scared someone might overhear what she was about to say. 'It's daft really, but I've still got to swear you to secrecy.'

Meg performed the sign of the cross over her left breast. 'Cross my heart and hope to die.'

Isla let the words out in a rush. 'Theo won't be eighteen until September.'

Meg looked perplexed. 'And?'

'And how old do you have to be to get in the services?'

Meg placed both hands over her mouth as though trying to stop herself from speaking out loud. Glancing around, she hissed, 'But he's been in the RAF since the beginning!'

'He signed up when he was sixteen,' Isla confirmed. 'He told me the night we got together.'

Meg grinned. 'Is that it? I thought you were goin' to say somethin' truly terrible, such as him bein' wanted for murder.'

'I must admit I thought somethin' similar!'

'So why the secrecy? It's not as if the forces would chuck him out now.'

'That's what I thought,' said Isla. 'But he insisted I

say nothing, even though he knows the truth about me too!'

Meg rubbed her chin. 'I can see why you've had your doubts, but in all honesty I think he's probably spent the past two years livin' with paranoia, and now he finds it hard to let go. A bit like he's drummed it into himself.'

Isla decided it was time to tell Meg of Theo's encounter with the Waaf. Listening in rapt silence, Meg didn't speak until Isla had finished her tale.

'What do you think he's got on her?'

'Goodness knows, but that wasn't my worry,' said Isla. 'I was more concerned with his explanation.'

Meg was looking confused. 'I think I'm missin' your point.'

'Why would she hang around to have a go at Theo if she was scared he was goin' to blow her big secret?'

Meg mulled this over. 'On the other hand, he has to be tellin' the truth, else she'd not have upped and left the way she did.'

'So, you don't think there's any hidden meaning?'

'If he'd done something really wrong – and I mean *really* wrong, not just fibbed about his age – she'd be the one with the upper hand and it would be Theo leaving the Rialto with his tail between his legs.'

Isla threw her hands up in despair. 'You're right! I'm doin' it again!'

'Not necessarily,' mused Meg. 'He's lied once, and to an authority much bigger than you, so who's to say he couldn't do it again? I'm not sayin' he would or that he has, but I can see why it would sow a seed of doubt in your mind.'

'I'm overthinkin' things, because I want to be ready for anything that comes my way,' said Isla decidedly. 'I wasn't prepared to lose my family – which nigh on killed me inside – so I want to make sure I'm on the ball for anything else life has to throw at me.'

'Only you cannae control the world around you,' Meg pointed out, 'so you're goin' to have to learn to let go and relax!'

'Easier said than done.'

'It's either that or push away anythin' good that comes your way because you're frightened of losin' it, and you're doin' that already!'

Isla drew a deep breath before letting it out slowly. 'How can I learn to trust people again?'

'By givin' them a chance to prove you can,' said Meg. 'In other words, trust them until they give you cause not to. Has Theo given you cause not to trust him?'

'Not if feelin's and hunches don't count . . .'

'They don't,' said Meg firmly.

'Then no, he's not given me any reason to distrust him.'

Meg clapped her hands together. 'There you are, then!'

Isla smiled. 'I wish I'd told you all this before.'

'So do I,' said Meg, looking a tad hurt, 'cos that's what friends are for, but I think I know why you didn't.'

'Oh?'

'You already knew the answer, but hearin' it from someone else can be a tough row to hoe.'

'The truth hurts,' said Isla. 'It's never nice to hear that the problem lies with you.'

'Aye, but in this case it's not because of who you are,' said Meg kindly. 'You've been made this way by the actions of others.'

'You're right there, cos I was *never* like this before. I always took people at face value, and I reckoned myself to be a good judge of character, but all that changed when my father took me to Coxhill.'

'Quite understandable,' said Meg. 'As the old sayin' goes: if you cannae trust your family, who can you trust?'

'Exactly! Stabbed in the back by my own flesh and blood. It's no wonder I find it hard to trust people!' Isla hesitated. 'I trust you, Sophie and Peggy, though. Why's that, do you think?'

'Maybe because you had no choice but to trust me and Sophie if you wanted to get out of Coxhill; and Peggy – well, she was givin' us a place to stay when she didn't have to,' said Meg, before continuing more quietly, 'Or maybe it's because we're not men.'

'I'm beginnin' to think it could be that,' said Isla miserably.

'Me too, because it would make sense,' agreed Meg. 'However, you've just got to bear in mind that all men aren't bad, and that your father was acting out of a moment of desperation and quite frankly madness. It's impossible to imagine what it must be like to lose the love of your life as well as your baby if you haven't been in that position, and thank goodness we haven't.'

'I'm so glad we've had this chat,' said Isla. 'I was really startin' to fall for Theo, but held back just in case.'

Meg smiled. 'Glad I could be of assistance!'

Having spent the last four weeks being poked and prodded by all manner of doctors, nurses and dentists, as well as being set the same mundane tasks day in day out, Isla and Meg had completed their initial training and were currently waiting to be told what their jobs as Waafs would be.

'Any ideas as to what you'd like to do?' Meg asked as they waited to be called forward to receive their instructions.

'Anythin' that will make a real difference,' said Isla. 'Maybe somethin' such as a driver – like Sophie's doin'? You?'

'I think everythin' the WAAF does makes a difference,' said Meg, 'but I'd like to have some sort of trade to turn to when I leave, so perhaps a mechanic?'

Isla cast her a cynical glance. 'They might be willin' to have you work as a mechanic in the WAAF, but can you really see some feller lettin' a woman service his car once the war's over?'

Meg wrinkled her nose. 'Probably not, but—' She was interrupted by the sergeant, who had called out her name. 'Here goes nothin'!'

When she headed back to Isla, she was pulling a downward smile. 'Balloon operator in RAF Titchfield in Portsmouth. I was rather hopin' we might be posted within reach of London so that we could be near Sophie.'

The sergeant called out Isla's name, and when she returned a few seconds later she was grinning from ear to ear. 'At least you've still got me!' she said.

Meg gave a small squeal of delight as she took Isla in a warm embrace. 'I honestly thought they were goin' to split us up,' she said as they left the hut. 'Let's call Sophie to let her know.'

Hurrying off to the NAAFI, the girls were greeted by a long line of people all waiting to use the phone. 'It would seem that great minds think alike,' said Isla as they joined the back of the queue.

'Portsmouth's a fair way from Liverpool,' said Meg, 'but bein' balloon operators means we're needed pretty much everywhere there's an RAF base, so you never know your luck – we might well end up back in Liverpool. Sophie too, what with her bein' a driver.'

'And pigs might fly,' said Isla cynically.

Meg wrinkled her nose. 'I suppose you're right; no one has that sort of luck.'

'We'll have to telephone Harvey, too, to tell him of our new posting,' said Isla.

'I wonder if he's been replaced yet?' mused Meg, before tutting impatiently. 'You can see why they only allow each caller three minutes. We'd be here all night otherwise.'

'Oh, darn. I'd forgotten they limit your calls,' said Isla. 'We'll have to phone Harvey tomorrow before we leave for Portsmouth.'

When the girls eventually reached the top of the queue they were delighted to find that they didn't have to leave a message for Sophie: she was having her break in the NAAFI when they called.

'Isla! Meg!' she cried. 'How are you?'

'Brilliant.' Meg was smiling. 'We've been given our instructions and we're goin' to be trainin' as balloon operators in Portsmouth.'

There was a brief disappointed silence before Sophie spoke again, and the girls could tell by her tone of voice that she was trying her best to remain upbeat. 'That's a really important job – well done to the two of you! I just wish it was closer to London.'

'Us too,' said Isla, who was sharing the receiver with Meg. 'But at least we'll be able to meet up at the end of our training, which is better than nothing.'

'Now *that* will be somethin' worth waitin' for!'

'How's life on the road?' asked Meg, aware that they didn't have long.

'I'm lovin' it! My instructor said he'd swear I'd been drivin' my whole life!'

'I hope we have the same luck on the balloon sites,' said Isla, 'but there again, I can't see it bein' harder than drivin' a car—'

The operator cut across, letting them know their time was up.

'We'll ring you from Portsmouth,' said Meg. 'Good luck with the rest of your course!'

'And you—' Sophie managed before they heard the line go dead.

Standing back, Meg handed the phone to Isla. 'All yours.'

Crossing her fingers that the operator wouldn't recognise her voice from their call with Sophie, Isla was delighted when she was put through to Theo's base, and his voice eventually came down the line.

'Isla! Am I to take it you've had your instructions?'

'We have indeed, and we're bound for Portsmouth, where we'll be learning the barrage balloons.'

'Excellent news! And as you said we I take it that Meg's also goin' to Portsmouth?'

'She is,' said Isla. 'Quite frankly, we cannae believe our luck!'

'It's about time you had some good luck,' said Theo. 'Does this mean you'll be comin' back to Liverpool in six weeks' time?'

'It does and we cannae wait!'

He gave a small cheer. 'Me neither! We'll have to celebrate with a dance at the Rialto, and a moonlit walk with fish 'n' chips under the dockers' umbrella.'

'That sounds wonderful! Have you had any news about your voluntary posting?'

'Not a dickie bird. Which I'm rather hopin' means I've not made the grade.'

'Poppycock!' cried Isla loyally. 'They'd be hard pushed to find a better mechanic.'

She could hear the smile in his voice as he replied. 'You're biased!'

'Maybe just a little.'

Theo sighed as the operator cut across their conversation. 'Caller, your time is—'

'We know!' Isla huffed.

'Call me once you're settled in Portsmouth,' said Theo.

'Will do. Take c—'

The line went dead, possibly payback for Isla cutting the operator off mid-sentence, or at least that was Isla's theory. Hanging up the receiver, she went off to join Meg.

'Any news?'

'He's not heard anything, so he's hopin' he won't have to go.'

'You never know your luck!' said Meg. 'Now, let's get somethin' to eat!'

Lying in his bed, Ian Madson heard the letterbox snap shut. The past month had been like a living nightmare. No longer employed by the government, he was paranoid that they'd find something to tie him in with Harman, and as a result he lived in fearful anticipation of the long arm of the law landing on his shoulder whenever he was out and about. Not only that, but he was regarded with contempt by many, and treated accordingly. He remembered one such occasion as he swung his legs out of bed.

'Coward!' an elderly woman had screeched at him, whilst thrusting a white feather into his hands. 'Why aren't you on the front line with the rest of them?'

His cheeks had ruddied, because he knew her to be correct. The easiest option would have been for him to join the queue at the recruiting office and sign on the dotted line, but he'd rather work down the docks than do that. He grimaced as an image of himself working with the rest of the dockers entered his mind.

Hell will freeze over before I join the likes of them, he told himself as he slid his feet into his slippers. Slowly plodding down the stairs to the front door, he looked at the brown envelope on the mat. *Another bleedin' bill that I cannae afford to pay.* He leaned down to pick it up, tearing the corner of the envelope open, as he took it through to the kitchen to fetch a knife from the cutlery drawer. Sliding it into the hole he'd made, he slit the envelope open and pulled out the contents within.

Sinking on to one of the kitchen chairs, he stared in horror at his conscription papers.

With their training nearing an end, Meg entered the Nissen hut with a fistful of envelopes, most of which were addressed to Isla.

'The usual culprits,' she said, handing Isla hers. 'One from Peggy, one from Sophie, one from Harvey, and *two* from Theo! How often does that boy write to you?'

'At least twice a week,' said Isla as she put her envelopes in order, Theo's being the last to be opened and Harvey's the first. Slitting his envelope, she pulled out the epistle which lay within.

Dear Isla, I do hope the WAAF are treating you well! I can't go into too much detail for obvious reasons but my latest case is coming along nicely and I must say it feels good to be back doing what I do best!

I'm afraid I have some good and bad news regarding Coxhill, the good news being the government have decided it's too costly to run, and as a result have chosen to close it down. However, that's where the good news ends. I asked what would happen to the remaining inmates and they said that they would be 'cared for' although they didn't go into any detail as to what that actually meant. The bad news is that there will be no point of contact for your father should he come back for you. I asked what would happen if people returned for their loved ones, and there was a general shrugging of shoulders. I'm so sorry, Isla, because I know how much you hoped that you and your father would be reunited one day. I'm sure you will be, but just not through Coxhill. I've left your details with the local police – a lot easier to do now that the poorhouse has been disbanded – and they've said they'll pass them on should he call by, but I'm afraid that's all I can do.

Isla looked up from the letter, her face radiating disbelief, and spoke directly to Meg. 'Did you get a letter from Harvey as well?'

Meg looked up solemnly from the sheet of paper in front of her. 'I'm so sorry, Isla.'

Pulling a grim smile, Isla tried to appear unfazed. 'I doubt it'll make any odds, cos it's been close to a year since he saw me last and he still hasn't come back.'

'If he's at sea . . .' Meg began carefully, before being cut off by Isla, who was waving Harvey's letter back and forth like a flag.

'He could write! And whilst I wouldn't trust Harman to respond, I know damned well that Harvey would have done, and I'm sure his successor would too, if a letter had arrived before Coxhill was closed, but I've not had so much as a hello!'

'True, but—'

'But me no buts,' said Isla. 'I've been makin' excuses for that man for a long while now, and it's about time I stopped!'

Whilst Meg very much wanted to comfort Isla by suggesting that her father might still come for her, she knew when to quit.

Glad that her friend wasn't going to argue the point, Isla opened the letter from Peggy.

Dearest Isla, I do hope this letter finds you well. I've had a wonderful surprise visit from Gregory – my eldest – who's home on leave. I've no idea where he's been or what he's up to, what with it being top secret and all, but it's been wonderful to have him home. It's a shame his leave didn't coincide with yours, because I know he wanted to meet you all, but I'm sure that will happen one day. I must say I do feel blessed to have had him for a whole week, and can't wait to see the three of you in a fortnight's time.

The city is still finding its feet after the May blitz, and there are many folk who head out into the country every night now for fear the Luftwaffe will come back, but I'm not one of them. Home is where the heart is, and not being here would make the distance between myself and my sons feel even greater!

Isla turned her mind to the urgent telephone conversation she'd had with Theo after hearing about the latest attack on Liverpool. 'I'm fine, and so is Peggy,' Theo had told her. 'It wasn't as bad as some of the previous nights, but they were still pretty relentless.'

He had gone on to list some of the buildings affected, and she'd been sad to hear that Blacklers – one of her favourite shops – had been burned to the ground and that the Palm House in Sefton Park had lost most of the glass from its roof.

'As long as you and Peggy are all right then that's all that matters,' Isla had said thankfully. 'Buildings can be rebuilt, and at least it didn't happen in daylight when Blacklers would've been full to the seams with shoppers.'

Now she turned her attention back to Peggy's letter. *Clive has written to say he's hoping to be back in Liverpool sometime within the next six months, so I'm keeping my fingers crossed.* Isla gazed at the letter unseeingly. What she had just said to Meg was true. If Peggy's husband had managed to get word to her from his ship, then Isla's father could have done the same, which was a painful thing to have confirmed. Banishing the thought from her mind, she read on. *I must say it will seem strange to have him home again, yet wonderful at the same time.* Peggy went on to write about her other sons and the Wrens from the house next door, and when she had finished reading it Isla tucked the letter back into its envelope and turned to Sophie's.

Dear Isla, I'm so glad to hear you're conquering the course – Meg too come to that – because I know you had your concerns early on. I must say it sounds awfully hard work, and whilst I'm envious of your extra rations due to the sheer physicality involved, I don't think I'd be capable of doing your job! I drove my first lorry the other day, and it really is just like driving a car, only bigger! Oh, and of course you have to take into account that you're quite often carrying lots of men and women in the back, so you have to go easy on the brakes! I can't wait to get my first proper posting. If I'm really lucky I'll get the chance to drive some of the bigwigs around. Wouldn't it be a feather in my cap if I were to find Churchill in the back of my car?

Isla broke off from her reading. Sharing a car with Churchill might seem an exciting prospect to Sophie, but the very idea of it filled Isla with dread. Shivering, she turned her attention back to Sophie's letter. *I doubt it'll happen, though*, it continued. *There must be hundreds of girls who are more qualified than I am to undertake such a task. Before I forget, how's Meg getting on with her beau?*

Isla's face was split by a smile. Meg had met Kenny the first day of training and the pair had been practically inseparable since.

'Isn't he dreamy?' Meg had sighed as she entered the hut after their first official date.

'I take it things went well, then?' said Isla, patting the space beside her.

Sitting down on Isla's bed, Meg smiled wistfully. 'He was everythin' a girl could wish for. Polite, attentive, charming and above all gentlemanly.'

'No kissing?' Isla assumed, who knew how worried her friend had been that her beau might expect a goodnight kiss – something Meg felt she wasn't ready for just yet, despite her earlier comments.

'Only the back of my hand,' breathed Meg. 'Just like they do with princesses.'

Isla had to admit she was envious of Meg's ability

to see her beau on a daily basis when Theo was so far away, but she was also delighted for her. Meg deserved a good man in her life, and Isla hoped that Sophie too would find happiness with the opposite sex. She turned her attention to the remainder of Sophie's letter, which finished: *Any road, as some of the girls from Lancashire like to say, I'd best dash, as I'm due for another lesson! Hope all's well. Much love to you both, Sophie xx*

Isla placed Sophie's letter with the ones she'd already read, and turned to Theo's. Given that he wrote often, his letters were often short but sweet. Taking both of them from their envelopes, she started to read the earlier one first.

My Darling Isla, Life in West Kirby – or at least Isla guessed it was West Kirby, because the censors had blanked it out – *is still as dull as ever. I went for a walk around the city the other day with some of the boys, and golly has it changed! Fritz really did a number on us, not that it's done anything to dampen the Scouse spirit, mind you! They're still as gung-ho as ever they were, if not more so! It never ceases to amaze me how resilient folk can be when faced with such atrocities, and I admire each and every one of them for their fighting spirit. Whilst I remember, I've been asking around and there's lots of balloon bases close by, so with a bit of luck you* There was a break in the flow of writing, with a quickly scribbled explanation below. *I'll have to sign off for now, because they're calling for the mail, and I don't want to miss it. Will write again in a couple of days. With much affection, Theo xx*

Isla picked up the next letter, which started off much like the first.

Darling Isla, Boy have I had a lucky escape! Two of the fellers in my team have been sent to Africa. Or rather Isla thought it had been Africa before the censors had their way. *When they told me the news, I really thought I'd be next, but it's been several days and I've still not heard anything, so I'm guessing they've filled their quota as it were.* Isla breathed a sigh of relief. *I'm hoping they won't be looking for any more recruits for some time yet. I did think about having a word with my NCO to see if I can retract my words, but I figure leave sleeping dogs lie; with a bit of luck they might forget about me. Anyhow, I'd best be off – after all, the more useful I am here the less likely they are to send me elsewhere! Much fondness, Theo xx*

'Any news?' said Meg, who'd finished reading her own letters.

'Not really. Sophie asked how you were gettin' on with Kenny, and Theo's been for a walk around the city and it sounds much like Peggy said – not that it's dampened the spirits of the locals any, which is good.'

'They're a breed of their own, the Scousers,' said Meg. 'It'd take a lot more than the Blitz to break their bulldog spirit!'

'You're biased because Kenny's a Scouser,' said Isla. 'Not that I don't agree with you, mind.'

Meg grinned. 'I cannae stop thinkin' about him – which my mammy once said was one of the first signs of bein' in love. Would you agree?'

Isla's eyes rounded. 'How on earth would I know?'

'Well, you did say that you were awfully fond of Theo . . .'

'Bein' fond of someone is not the same as bein' in love with them,' said Isla, 'and whilst I think about Theo a lot, I wouldn't say I think of him any more than I do about Sophie or Peggy. I expect you think about Kenny all the time because he's your first boyfriend and it's all still new to you.'

'Could be,' supposed Meg, 'but it's only a little newer than your relationship with Theo. In fact, when you think about it, I've seen a lot more of Kenny than you have of Theo.'

Isla eyed her with cautious inquisitiveness. 'When you say you've seen a lot more of Kenny . . .'

Meg rolled her eyes. 'I mean that I've seen him more often.'

'Ah! Good. And yes, I suppose you're right, I hadn't thought about it like that, but you probably know Kenny far better than I know Theo.'

'Yet you don't think about him all the time even though you're hundreds of miles apart,' said Meg curiously, 'and as they reckon absence makes the heart grow fonder, logically you should be thinkin' about Theo far more than I do about Kenny.'

'I dare say not everyone falls in love at first sight,' Isla began, and Meg squealed excitedly.

'So you do think we're in love, then?'

'You and me?' quipped Isla, but Meg pressed on obliviously.

'Kenny says he cannae stop thinkin' about me either!' She sighed happily. 'His friends reckon he's smitten!'

Isla gave this some thought before answering slowly. 'I suppose it's hard to tell between love and infatuation.

In fact, I'm not sure how you differentiate between the two, although I dare say time has a lot to do with it.'

'How so?'

'If it's infatuation you'll get bored over a period of time, and if you don't then you'll know it's love.'

'So if you don't fall in love at first sight, what does happen to make you fall in love, do you suppose?'

'Again, I think the answer is time,' said Isla. 'The more time you spend together the more you don't want to be apart. Theo and I have had hardly any time together, so maybe that's why I only feel fondness towards him.'

'You'd be sad if anythin' happened to him, though?'

'Of course. And not just because he's someone I know, but because he's someone I care for – a lot!'

A Waaf poked her head round the door to their hut. 'They're goin' to run a drill, so Sarge wants everyone out pronto.'

The girl disappeared, presumably to tell others to get ready. 'Why do they warn us before they do a drill?' said Meg. 'It seems to be rather missing the point if you ask me.'

Isla smiled. 'That's the WAAF for you! Although I'm sure they'll do drills without warning us first, as we get closer to passing out, but after that dreadful accident the other week you can hardly blame them for being cautious.'

'She's lucky she's still got her hand!' agreed Meg. 'It certainly taught me a lesson.'

'Aye,' said Isla. 'When Sarge bellows at you to let go, you let go!'

Chapter Twelve

Meg and Isla could barely contain their excitement when their train pulled into Lime Street Station. Seeing Peggy and Sophie frantically waving to them from the platform, they hurried along the corridor to the end of their carriage in readiness for the guard who was opening the doors as he strolled up the platform. Passing her kitbag to Meg, Isla jumped down and turned to take both bags so that Meg could join her.

'It's so good to see you both,' cried Sophie as she hurried towards them. 'It might've only been a few months, but it feels so much longer!'

'I second that,' said Peggy. 'Especially when I look at the three of you. Cos whilst I thought Sophie had altered a lot when I met her off the train a couple of days back, so have the two of you, and for the better I might add!'

'Cos we've got muscles now,' said Meg, thrusting her chest forward as she added, 'I'm even gettin' a bust!'

Isla laughed. 'Join the WAAF and get a bust! They should put that on the posters; they'd have women flockin' in from all four corners of the kingdom.'

Eyeing her pals fondly, Sophie beckoned them over for a group hug. 'I'm sick of hearin' myself sayin' that I've missed the two of you, but I have!'

'And we you,' said Isla. 'You cannae go through the things we did and not feel the ache when you're split up.'

'We're in love,' said Meg, much to the others' amusement.

'I think you mean we love each other,' said Sophie, 'which we do!'

Knowing that Meg was referring to the conversation she and Isla had had two weeks before, Isla explained this to Peggy and Sophie as they walked out of the station. 'So would you agree, Peggy?' she asked as she finished.

'I would indeed. Based on the fact that I fell in love with my boys as soon as they were born, but I fell in love with Clive over a period of time.'

'So you think you're in love, then, Meg?' Sophie asked.

'I reckon so. It's only been a few hours but I miss him terribly already!'

'I can vouch for that,' said Isla with a resigned sigh. 'It's all I've heard since we left Portsmouth – Kenny this and Kenny that. I know more about his likes and dislikes than I do about Theo's!'

'Talkin' of whom, when are you seein' him?' asked Peggy.

'Tomorrow evenin',' said Isla. 'I anticipated it would be a dreadful journey gettin' here – which it was – so I thought it best if we didn't meet up until tomorrow, when I'll be feelin' bright-eyed and bushy-tailed.'

Meg stifled a yawn beneath her hand. 'Fair point! I know I wouldn't want Kenny to see me right now either.'

Isla tutted audibly. 'Don't give me that! You'd be off like a shot if I told you he were waitin' for you on the concourse!'

Meg giggled softly. 'You're probably right.'

'No probably about it,' Isla chuckled.

'Which does rather beg the question why you aren't just as keen to see Theo?' said Sophie, after glancing quickly at Peggy. 'You've plenty of time for an afternoon nap as well as a catch-up with the rest of us, so I see no reason why you're not chompin' at the bit to say hello.'

Isla was about to reply when she saw the girl with whom Theo had had his heated exchange on the other side of the road. 'That's her!' she hissed to Meg.

'Her who?' asked Meg, genuinely perplexed.

'The girl I was tellin' you about – the one with Theo in the Rialto. Don't stare!'

Sophie frowned. 'What girl's this?'

Isla glanced at Meg, who nodded encouragingly. 'It was the first time that Theo had taken me to the Rialto . . .' Isla went on to tell her friends everything she had told Meg. 'I know it's all down to my paranoia,' she said eventually, 'and I've tried to dismiss my doubts, but I just cannae shake the feelin' that somethin' doesn't sit right. And even if everythin' is kosher with Theo, that's not the only issue. I think the reason for my not fallin' in love with him has more to do with me than it does with him. I cannae explain what I mean by that because I don't know myself, but even knowin' what a nice chap he is, and how thoughtful he can be, there's just no spark between us.'

Sophie was looking surprised. 'What sort of spark were you expecting?'

Isla nibbled the inside of her bottom lip. 'You're goin' to think I'm bein' silly.'

'I won't,' said Peggy with verve, 'because I've felt the spark you're talkin' about. It's when you see someone for the first time and feel an instant connection even though you've never spoken to them directly and don't even know their name.'

'That's it!' cried Isla. 'That's exactly what I mean.' She looked to Meg. 'Is that what you have with Kenny?'

Meg thought about it for a moment before replying hesitantly, 'I'm not sure.'

'Then the answer's no,' said Peggy. 'Not that I'm dismissin' your feelin's or implyin' that they're not real, or that you're not in love. But every now and then you meet your soulmate, and that's the spark that Isla's referring to. It's not the same as love at first sight, or instant attraction; it's more a sense of belonging, as though you're meant to be together.' She looked pointedly at Isla. 'And if you know that feelin' it can only mean that you've felt that way yourself!'

'Who on earth have you met that made you feel that way?' asked Meg curiously.

A look of realisation dawned on Sophie's face. 'Oh my God! It's that feller from down the shelter, isn't it?'

'You've no need to tell me how stupid I am for feelin' that way about a man who's in love with another woman,' said Isla miserably, 'but I cannae help myself! I'm not sayin' it's either Rory or no one, I'm just sayin' that I should feel that way about Theo and I don't even come close.'

'I'm not sure whether Kenny's my soulmate,' said Meg slowly, 'but I know from what you're sayin' that I do have stronger feelin's for him than you appear to have for Theo, yet you're still with him. Why is that, do you suppose?'

'Because there's somethin' drawin' me to him,' said Isla. 'I gravitate to him like a moth to a flame, but with none of the attraction, if that makes sense?'

'Not really. Unless . . .'

'Yes?' said Isla, who was desperate for answers.

'Maybe you're attracted to him in a brotherly sort of way.'

'It's definitely not that,' said Isla, 'because I'd rather hope I wouldn't find my brother physically attractive, the way I do Theo. But before you start, that's not what's drawin' me to him either.'

Unable to work out what her friend was feeling, Sophie asked the question on all their lips. 'So what do you intend to do about it? Keep seein' Theo and hope the feelin's develop?'

'I don't know!' wailed Isla. 'The sensible side of me is sayin' I should stay with him and see where it takes me, but the fanciful side says I should set myself free to find my soulmate, and I'm *not* talkin' about Rory.'

'I suppose it stands to reason that there has to be more than one possible soulmate for each of us,' said Peggy slowly.

Meg looked to Isla. 'So what will you do when you see him tomorrow?'

'See whether my feelin's have grown any stronger? Cos I don't see what else I can do!'

'At the end of the day you've done nothin' wrong, cos you're not leadin' him on by pretendin' your relationship's progressin' when it isn't,' said Peggy, 'and at the same time you've not been together too long, so *his* feelin's won't be crushed should you decide to end it.'

'I hope you're right, cos that's the last thing I'd want to do,' said Isla.

Peggy arched an eyebrow. 'Do you think he likes you more than you like him?'

Isla pulled a downward smile. 'Hard to say.'

'Well at least you haven't done anythin' daft like got yourselves married,' said Sophie. 'That really would have been a disaster!'

'Wouldn't it just,' agreed Isla.

'I must say, all this indecision rather makes me glad I'm still single,' Sophie put in.

Peggy cocked her head to one side. 'Is there *no one* on the horizon?'

Sophie wrinkled her nose. 'There was one feller I met, but he's away at sea a lot, a bit like your Clive, I suppose.'

'What feller's this?' asked Isla, grateful that the attention had moved away from her and Theo.

'Just some feller I met down the docks,' said Sophie, 'but that was when I was in Plymouth. I'm hardly likely to see him again what with bein' in London now. Besides, I don't think he was particularly interested in me, and on top of that I don't want to start a relationship with someone who spends most of their life sailin' the seven seas!'

'You're after a landlubber,' chuckled Peggy, 'and whilst I love my Clive dearly, I don't blame you. A seaman's wife has a lonely marriage.'

'You never know; you might fall in love with one of your passengers,' said Isla.

'I did rather fancy one of the fellers who was teachin' us how to drive the lorries,' mused Sophie, 'but he was too young for me.' Isla gave her a surprised look before remembering that Sophie was a good few years older than she and Meg were.

'Most of the instructors are young lads,' continued Sophie, 'and when I say young, I mean probably around twenty, which is far too young for me.'

'Twenty years physically, but still in their teens mentally,' said Peggy wisely. 'Men always mature at a slower rate than women.'

'That explains a lot!' said Meg. 'Some of the fellers on our base act like schoolchildren half the time!'

Peggy grinned. 'Sounds about right.'

'It also explains why men like Theo join the war underage,' said Isla. 'War is excitin' to youngsters; glamorous even.'

'Do you think Theo still sees it that way?'

'Not after his last base got bombed,' said Isla. 'I can tell by talkin' to him that that was a turnin' point in his life.'

'Kudos to him for not tryin' to run,' said Peggy, 'cos he could've used his age to get back home.'

'Whereas instead he volunteered to go to Africa, which is a definite sign of his age,' said Isla cynically.

Peggy gave an involuntary cough. 'Talk about runnin' in the wrong direction! Does he not realise that Africa's just as dangerous as it is over here, if not more so?'

'He does now, which is why he regrets his decision.'

'Hence the need to be a fixed age before you can join up,' remarked Sophie.

Isla shivered. 'I wonder how many poor souls will die before even reaching the age of signing up?'

'Too many,' said Peggy. She stopped speaking as the gasps of Meg and Isla reached her ears. Following their line of sight to what used to be Blacklers, Peggy sighed. 'A sorry sight indeed,' she said. 'Unfortunately, a lot of the city looks that way.'

As they progressed the girls were dumbfounded by the extent of the damage.

'Theo said it was bad,' said Isla in hushed tones, 'but I didn't realise it was this bad.'

'Being down London way, I'm sorry to say I'm used to it,' said Sophie. 'If anythin' Liverpool got off lightly in comparison.'

'I just thank the Lord they stopped when they did,' said Peggy, 'else there'd be nothin' left!'

'And we thought Clydebank was bad,' Meg reminded Sophie.

'Sophie told me about Coxhill,' said Peggy. 'It just goes to show how bad the place was that no one's willin' to take it on!'

'Probably saw the cockroaches and rats in the kitchen,' said Isla. 'Thank goodness Portsmouth wasn't like that, because from what I've heard some of the bases aren't far behind Coxhill when it comes to rats and the like.'

Peggy eyed her thoughtfully. 'I know that Sophie's been posted to a base in Scarborough, but what about the two of you? You've not said yet.'

'We only found out yesterday,' said Isla. 'I'm off to RAF Immingham, but Meg's stayin' in Portsmouth to train the trainees.'

Meg beamed. 'I think Kenny swung it for me so that we wouldn't be parted.'

'There's no "think" about it,' said Isla. 'He definitely put in a good word for you!'

'So we're goin' to be spread far and wide across the country,' said Sophie, 'which can mean only one thing.'

'What's that?' queried Meg.

'Having plenty of forty-eights, as little holidays,' said Sophie.

'You're all welcome to come to me at any time,' said Peggy, 'although it'll doubtless be a short stay given the time it will take for you to get to Liverpool and back.'

'You could always come to us,' suggested Isla. 'Everyone deserves a break, and I dare say it's been a while since you last had one.'

'I've never been on holiday without the family before,' said Peggy slowly. 'No children arguin' amongst themselves, or grumblin' hubby complainin' about the price of everythin'? Count me in!'

'When was the last time you went on holiday, Peggy?' asked Meg. 'I only ask cos you called your sons children.'

'It doesn't matter how old or big they get, they'll always be my children,' said Peggy. 'Especially as they act like kids half the time!'

'I'm already lookin' forward to it and we've not finished this leave yet!' Meg smiled.

Isla feigned shock. 'What? And spend even more time away from Kenny?'

'Oh, ha ha! But jokin' aside, they do say that absence makes the heart grow fonder. Maybe I want to test that theory.'

'Don't mind me,' said Isla. 'I'm only teasin'.'

Turning the corner into Arkles Lane, Peggy rummaged in her handbag for the key. 'Not leavin' it under the mat any more?' asked Isla.

Peggy produced the key and slid it into the lock. 'It hardly seemed worth my botherin' when it's just me what lives here,' she said as she led the way into the house. Meg's nostrils flared as she took in the scent of what she hoped to be scouse, and she said as much to Peggy, who nodded. 'It is indeed!'

'My favourite,' declared Isla, as she dropped her

kitbag at the bottom of the stairs. 'Is there anythin' we can do to help?'

'All taken care of,' said Peggy. 'You don't think I'd let you travel all that way and then expect you to help cook the dinner, do you?'

'You wouldn't allow us to cook dinner after walkin' home from work,' said Sophie, 'never mind halfway across the country!'

'I do enjoy bein' in the WAAF,' said Isla, 'but nothin' beats comin' home.' Realising what she'd said, she held a hand over her mouth, but Peggy was delighted.

'This *is* your home,' she said. 'For ever and always! Even when the boys come home – although I doubt they'll ever come back to live here – it'll still be yours too!'

Isla smiled, but apologised for her slip-up just the same. 'Sorry, Peggy. I didn't mean to be overfamiliar – it's just . . .'

'This is the first proper home that any of us have had in a long while,' said Meg, with a half-smile. 'It's your own fault for bein' so accommodatin'!'

'I'm honoured that you think of me that way,' said Peggy as she took the scouse out of the oven, where it had been keeping warm. 'As a mother myself I know how I would feel if my children had no one to turn to when they were far from home, and that makes my role here all the more important!'

'I think I speak for all of us when I say our mammies would be very much relieved to know we had someone such as yourself lookin' after us,' said Isla.

'Aye, she's right there,' said Sophie, and Meg also agreed.

Isla had begun laying the table while Sophie put the kettle on to boil. 'So what are we goin' to do with our leave?' Isla asked them. 'Any ideas?'

'We're bound to go dancin' a couple of times,' said Sophie, 'and we just have to have fish and chips from the pierhead – they're my favourite. Other than that, walks through the parks and the odd trip to the cinema?'

'Sounds good to me,' said Meg. 'What about you, Peggy? Have you got any time off work?'

'A couple of days,' said Peggy, 'but I can muck in with your evenin' plans no problem.'

'Then that's us sorted out,' said Sophie, adding, 'Who's for tea?'

There was a show of hands and Sophie fetched down four cups, whilst Peggy dished out the delicious-smelling stew.

Hoping against hope that he wouldn't pass the medical, Madson had been bitterly disappointed to learn that he had been signed off as being fit for purpose. Having spent the following weeks exercising relentlessly under orders from a man who was far younger and – in Madson's opinion – inferior to himself, he was now waiting to learn his fate. His fingers tightly crossed, he had sent up a prayer that he would be offered some sort of desk job – after all, he had told them that he was in an office job before being called up, so it would only make sense that they used his administrative skills. Hearing the sergeant call out his name, he went up to receive his orders.

A man by the name of Lawrence leaned over Madson's shoulder as he read his instructions. 'The ack-acks! You lucky sod.'

A frown etching his brow, Madson turned to face him. 'What makes you say that?'

Lawrence shrugged. 'Better than bein' shipped off to Africa.'

Madson felt a small wave of gloomy relief pass through him. 'If you look at it that way.'

Lawrence clapped his hand on Madson's shoulder. 'What other way is there to look at it? Besides, just think of all the lovely crumpet.'

Lines formed on Madson's forehead. 'Sorry?'

'The ATS!' cried Lawrence.

'Every cloud, eh?' said Madson glumly.

Lawrence shook his head as he walked away. 'There's no pleasin' some people!'

A one-way ticket to my old life is the only thing that would please me, thought Madson miserably. *I rue the day I ever met them bloody girls. If I'd stopped in my seat instead of tryin' to find out what they were up to, I'd probably be runnin' Coxhill by now.* Leaving the hut, he kicked a stone with the toe of his boot, sending it ricocheting off a nearby truck. He held his breath as he waited for the backlash, but it turned out the truck was empty of personnel. Walking on, he pushed his hands deep into his pockets. He had no idea where the girls had gone, but he thought it highly likely that they'd joined the services. *They'd better hope they haven't joined the ATS*, he thought grimly, *else they might have an accident.* A wicked smile creased his cheeks. Wreaking his revenge wouldn't get him out of the services, but it would make him feel better.

After spending the day perusing the shops and various markets, Isla was currently on her way to meet Theo. Having spoken at length to the girls about her feelings towards her beau, she was in two minds as to whether they should continue their relationship. On one hand she thought the world of him; he was kind, caring and fun to be with, and he gave her a sense of protection. But on the other, there was no spark. If it wasn't for the kissing she would have said their relationship was more of a friendship than anything else, and she didn't know whether it was fair to continue when she was already having doubts about a future together. True, she had demons of her own to contend with, and that would probably be the case whoever she was with, even Rory. She envisaged Rory in her mind's eye. Was she using the memory of him as an excuse to run away from her relationship with Theo? Maybe the idea of commitment was scaring her because she was frightened of being let down. Glancing through the bus window at the façade of the dance hall, she felt a sense of relief because Theo wasn't there yet, which meant she had more time to think. Or it would mean that if her attention hadn't been drawn to the young Waaf Theo had called Caroline. *Why do I see her nigh on every place I go?* thought Isla curiously as the bus drew to a halt. *I know it's only coincidence, but even so it does seem rather strange, almost as though fate was wantin' our paths to cross.* Stepping on to the pavement, she glanced at the Waaf, who noticed, smiled and looked away, before looking back with an air of curiosity.

'Sorry, but do I know you? Only your face looks awfully familiar.'

Isla shook her head. 'You don't know me, but I believe you know Theo Stratham?'

Caroline's face immediately clouded over. 'More's the pity.'

Not wanting to get pulled into something which had nothing to do with her, Isla began to examine her fingernails, hoping that either Theo or Caroline's friends would soon arrive and they could go their separate ways. However, after waiting a good fifteen minutes it seemed that neither of them was going anywhere soon and when a further ten minutes had elapsed and they were still the only two standing outside, Isla caught Caroline's attention by making eye contact. 'I know that nothin' runs on time any more, but I'd have thought another bus would've been here by now,' she commented.

Seeming to relent slightly, the Waaf moved closer. 'Me too. I've been runnin' errands most of the day, so I said I would meet my girlfriends here.' She glanced at her watch, tapping the glass casing with her index finger and holding it up to her ear, before saying, 'There's nothin' wrong with my watch, so it must be the bus.'

Isla shrugged. 'Perhaps it's broken down? Theo was meant to be here nigh on half an hour ago.'

Caroline rolled her eyes. 'I'm not sure I would rely on Theo if I were you.'

Isla pulled a downward smile. 'He's normally pretty good when it comes to time-keepin'.'

The girl eyed her sharply. 'Do you see a lot of each other?'

'Gosh, no. I've not seen him in months.'

'Oh.' Looking slightly sheepish, the Waaf shrugged. 'So he was tellin' the truth, then.'

'Sorry?'

The Waaf waved a dismissive hand. 'Ignore me. I'm bein' churlish.'

'I know you don't like him – I saw you quarrelling with him once – but he's not as bad as you seem to think.'

Caroline rolled her eyes. 'If you believe that, you don't really know him.'

'I know that he's never betrayed your confidence,' said Isla. 'Doesn't that mean anything?'

'It means he's keen to save his own skin, no more, no less,' said Caroline. 'He's certainly not done it for me!'

'He has, you know.'

Caroline heaved a sigh. 'I don't mean to be rude, but you know nothin' about Theo.'

'I know his secret,' said Isla. 'He told me that night, after the two of you exchanged words.'

Caroline swallowed. 'You mean to say he actually

told you? I mean, I did say he should, but I didn't think he'd actually go through with it.'

'Well, he did.'

'And you don't mind?' Caroline said incredulously.

Isla shrugged. 'I'll not deny I was a bit surprised at first, and I can understand why his mammy was so upset, but what's done is done, and there's no sense in cryin' over spilt milk, is there?'

Caroline's jaw was practically on the floor. 'Spilt milk? Are you insane?'

Isla was indignant. 'No I am not! You're the one blowin' everythin' out of proportion.'

Caroline placed her hands on her hips. 'I know the two of you are only friends . . .'

Isla stiffened. 'We were until that evening. That was the turnin' point, and even though he was still doubtful I didn't see why we should hold back over some silly mistake.'

Caroline was practically beside herself. 'I reckon the two of you deserve each other! And to think I was worried he might be pullin' the wool over your eyes! More like a match made in heaven!'

'Us?' cried Isla, her voice rising with fury. 'What about you? I've no idea what you've done, but it must be bad for you to act the way you did that night!'

Caroline looked as though she'd been hit over the head with a shovel. 'I know I'm hardly innocent in all of this, and I very much regret doin' what I did, but I was only Maggie's friend. It was Theo that was her husband!'

314

Chapter Thirteen

Isla rocked on her heels. Had she really just heard what she thought she'd heard? Blinking, she looked at Caroline, who, seeing the shock on Isla's face, had both hands pressed firmly over her mouth.

'Theo's *married*?' Isla repeated.

Taking her hands away, Caroline swallowed. 'You said you *knew*!'

'About him bein' underage when he joined up,' said Isla. 'I know nothin' about his—' She broke off, speechless for a moment before pressing on, 'Are you sure we're talkin' about the same Theo?'

'Theo Stratham,' said Caroline, her voice barely above a whisper. 'Yes, I'm sure.'

'But he *can't* be married! I mean, where is she?'

Caroline was looking at the pavement. 'She was killed when our base got bombed by the Luftwaffe.'

Unable to believe what the other girl was saying, Isla looked around as though expecting someone to jump out and say it had all been a joke. 'None of this makes any sense! He told me that *you* were the one with the big secret, not him!'

Caroline gave a joyless laugh. 'That's a bit rich, considerin' we were havin' an affair behind poor Maggie's back.'

Isla stared unblinkingly at the other Waaf. 'I don't believe I'm hearin' this.'

'I'm not proud of what we did!' said Caroline, tears forming in her eyes. 'In fact I'm thoroughly ashamed. That's why I was so angry at Theo for carryin' on with his life as though nothin' had happened – that and the fact that we were responsible for her death.'

Isla's jaw flinched. 'I am *not* condonin' what the two of you did, but surely you cannae blame yourselves for Maggie's death.'

To her horror, Caroline was shaking her head. 'Only we can. Cos we wanted to have some time together alone, so we got her out of the way by sendin' her off on a wild goose chase to look for Dominic, claimin' that he wanted to have a word with her.'

Isla spoke through thin lips. 'Not nice, but not . . .'

'She was still lookin' for Dominic when the air-raid siren sounded.' Caroline was wringing her hands as she continued. 'Theo had told her to look for Dominic by the aircraft, knowin' full well that he wasn't on the base, which meant she'd be searchin' for quite some time.'

Isla gazed numbly at her. 'The Luftwaffe bombed the runway . . .'

'. . . where we'd sent Maggie,' said Caroline, her voice thick with tears. She dabbed her eyes with her handkerchief. 'Of course we didn't mean it to happen, but had we not sent her off on a pointless mission she'd have been in the shelter . . . with us.'

Isla was silent as the words sank in, and several moments had passed before she spoke again. 'You don't know that though, do you?' she said at last. 'Even if you hadn't intervened, she might've been in the cookhouse, or the NAAFI, or takin' a stroll around the camp, and not got to the shelter in time. You can't know for certain that you contributed to her death.'

Caroline sniffed. 'It's very charitable of you to say so, but I'm afraid it will never ease my guilt. Theo, on the other hand . . .'

Isla blew her cheeks out. 'Grief can affect people in many different ways. I just wish he'd told me the truth from the get-go, because no matter what, Maggie deserves to be acknowledged.'

A bus was trundling towards them, and Caroline dried her eyes. 'I'm sorry. I should never have said anything.'

'And let me live in a lie?' cried Isla. 'I should cocoa! I'm *glad* our misunderstandin' brought out the truth. And I was right in thinkin' that our paths were meant to cross for a reason.'

Caroline looked confused as the bus came to a halt beside them. 'Sorry?'

'I saw you yesterday walkin' down the Scottie,' explained Isla, 'and then again today. It's almost as if things were being orchestrated so that we'd meet up.'

Caroline's face paled, as Theo stepped down from the platform. 'I think it's time I faced the music—'

But Isla was shaking her head. 'You've told the truth, for which I'm grateful. It's time for Theo to do the same, and for that he and I need to be alone.'

Theo was walking towards them in a somewhat stilted fashion, as though he wasn't sure whether he would be welcome or not, and Caroline gave Isla a quick smile. 'Thank you for not makin' me feel any worse than I already do.' She hurried off to join her pals, who had travelled on the same bus as Theo.

'You're late,' said Isla, as Theo arrived by her side. 'What happened?'

Theo spoke distantly. 'The bus got a puncture, and there was no spare wheel.' He pointed to Caroline's retreating back. 'What was she doing here?'

Isla's features remained impassive as she replied, 'She was waitin' for her friends, and we got talking.'

'Oh?'

'Aye, we had quite the catch-up. You'll laugh when I tell you about our misunderstandin'.'

Looking highly doubtful about that, he gazed at her through soulless eyes. 'Will I now?'

'Well, I say you'll laugh,' said Isla, 'but I rather suspect you won't. But I'm a great believer in fairness, so why don't you tell me your version of what happened to your wife the night she was killed by the Luftwaffe?'

She had half expected him to get distraught, or to protest at the way she delivered the words as though they were meaningless, but he did neither of those things. Instead he pushed his hands deep into his pockets, whilst hanging his head in shame. 'I know how bad it must look, and you're right. We should never have sent her off the way we did, but . . .'

'But what?' said Isla in clipped tones. 'But you didn't realise the Luftwaffe were on their way? Or but you were in love with the wrong woman?'

He looked up with dull eyes, and spoke without feeling or emotion. 'Maggie and I were just sixteen when we met. Knowin' that I was goin' to join the services, we decided to marry before I left so that we could show our love to the world.' Isla drew in a sharp breath, and he paused for a moment before pressing on. 'We'd barely known each other more than a month when we tied the knot, so when Maggie said that she too had lied about her age and joined up I was cock-a-hoop.'

'That was short-lived,' said Isla, not quite beneath her breath.

'Of course it was short-lived,' snapped Theo. 'We were kids who'd never lived away from home before, and what's more we barely knew each other, or not in the married sense of the word at any rate. Prior to entering the services, we'd held hands but that was it! Spending all our days together we quickly realised the mistake we'd made, but by that time it was too late.'

'If you both knew you'd made a mistake, why sneak around behind Maggie's back with Caroline?' said Isla tartly.

He raised his hands above his head as if in despair. 'Because even though I wasn't *in* love with Maggie, I did love her as a friend, and as such would never do anythin' to hurt her or make her look or feel foolish! She knew our relationship was on the rocks, but it would've wounded her deeply to know that I'd started seein' Caroline, especially with the two of them bein' friends.'

'You still should've told her.'

He stared at her in disbelief. 'Do you think I don't know that? Do you think I don't regret sendin' her off to look for Dominic when I damned well knew he wasn't even on the base? Of course I do!'

She folded her arms across her chest. 'Really? So why start datin' me less than a year after her passing?'

He pinched the bridge of his nose between forefinger and thumb. 'I don't know! Maybe I was on the rebound, maybe I was confused, or maybe I was tryin' to fill the hole left in my heart from when I lost my first love, cos even if it was only a platonic relationship, I *did* love Maggie.'

'So why aren't you with Caroline?'

'Because I don't love her, and never have,' said Theo. 'She was fun to be with, excitin' even, but that's all.'

She stared at him open-mouthed. 'So you volunteered for Africa because you felt guilty about your wife?'

'Exactly! And now I feel guilty about you, because I've not been honest, and even though I like you – a lot – I don't have the first clue as to where our relationship is goin'. Or I didn't, but I do now.'

She responded slowly. 'I swear what I'm goin' to say has nothin' to do with anythin' I've learned this evenin' . . .'

He gave a snort of disbelief. 'Yeah, right.'

'Think what you will, but I've had a nigglin' doubt at the back of my mind for some time, and after speakin' to Caroline I now know what it is.'

'That I'm a filthy rotten liar?'

Ignoring the remark, Isla drew a deep breath. 'You remind me of my father. He too ran away after losin' the woman he loved, just as you did after losin' Maggie.' She sighed heavily. 'In short, you both have a tendency to leg it when the goin' gets tough!'

'I'm sure your father is twice the man I am.'

'You were young, Theo, and as such your mistakes can be forgiven. When he left me at Coxhill my father was a grown man—'

'—who'd had his world ripped out from under him,' said Theo. 'I can't imagine what that must have been like, but I think I can see why he reacted the way he did.'

'I'm sure you can,' said Isla waspishly, and was about to apologise when he held up a hand.

'I deserved that. As for your father, I can only compare his actions to my own experience, and quite frankly I truly believe he was puttin' you first even if it didn't feel that way.'

'How can condemnin' me to Coxhill possibly be puttin' me first?' said Isla, angry tears of frustration forming in her eyes.

He drew a deep breath. 'If I was runnin' away from what happened to Maggie, why do you think I volunteered for Africa instead of hunkerin' down in West Kirby? Cos they're both a long way away from where it all went wrong.'

She pulled a fleeting downward smile. 'It's hotter in Africa?' she said, somewhat sarcastically.

'Because I didn't care whether I lived or died, not after what I'd done to Maggie. In fact death would've been preferable to livin' with the guilt.'

The comment floored Isla, but only temporarily. 'So what? Askin' me out was a way of gettin' over your grief?'

He eyed her incredulously. 'You *never* get over the grief; you should know that better than most. Instead you find a way to deal with it. Mine was to try and forget what happened by pretendin' it never did.' He hesitated, before eyeing her sadly. 'I'm truly sorry for the way I've treated you, Isla, I really am. If I could turn back the hands of time . . .'

He had spoken the raw truth, and she knew it. 'For what it's worth, I believe you.'

'You do?'

'Aye. You speak with a passion that only comes when someone's bein' truly honest.'

'So where do we go from here?'

'My father turned his back on me, and I swore I wouldn't do that to anyone else,' said Isla. She smiled grimly. 'I hope you get over the past, because we were all young once, and we shouldn't have to pay for mistakes arising from our youth for the rest of our lives.'

His eyes were glassy. 'Thanks, Isla. It means a lot to know that you understand why I acted the way I did. It really does.'

'If I can forgive you for lyin' to me, then you should forgive yourself for bein' young. You're not the same person you were back then. None of us are, so stop bein' so hard on yourself.'

His lower lip trembled as he fought to regain his composure. 'You're one in a million, Isla Donahue, I hope you realise that.'

'Look after yourself, Theo.'

He responded with a mock salute. 'I truly hope you find a man who can look after you the way you deserve.' He paused. 'Would it be a step too far for me to ask if we could stay in touch? Only you're the only person I've ever been able to speak to about this.'

'I'm fine with that, cos talkin' is a good way of dealin' with your grief.'

A small smile twitched his lips. 'Thanks, Isla.'

She smiled back. 'Goodbye, Theo, and good luck.'

Meg stared at Isla in disbelief, a spoonful of porridge poised before her lips. 'He *what*?'

'I couldn't believe it myself at first,' said Isla as she sprinkled the tiniest dusting of sugar over her porridge, 'but he didn't even try to deny it.'

'Well, he's certainly not the man I thought him to be,' huffed Meg, 'and it just goes to show that all that glitters is *not* gold!'

Isla smiled faintly. 'That's just it though, don't you think? He's not a man, but a boy, who threw himself in at the deep end only to find he couldn't swim.'

Sophie stared at her aghast. 'How can you take this so lightly?'

'Because my father is a lot older than Theo, yet look how he dealt with my mammy's death. In short, he didn't! At least Theo can blame his stupidity on his youth. He made a mistake, even though he didn't think so at the time, and once he realised the size of the hole he'd dug himself, it was too late for him to get out! A divorce takes years, and – God forbid – Theo might not have that long should luck not be on his side, plus I don't think he'd even know how to go about gettin' one.' She dug her spoon back into the porridge. 'I'm not condonin' the way he handled things, but we all make mistakes, especially when we're young.'

'It's a tough row for him to hoe,' agreed Peggy, 'and he's goin' to have to live with the consequences for the rest of his life. And all because he thought he was in love.'

Meg was watching Isla curiously. 'Thinkin' back, I remember the conversation we all had about folk marryin' when they barely even knew each other. I seem to recall you were aghast at the very thought, so it surprised me somewhat when you agreed to be his belle after just two dates.'

Isla shrugged. 'I think I was super keen to have the sort of relationship what my parents had, and with Theo remindin' me a little of my father, my feelin's were somewhat confused.'

'You knew somethin' was up, though,' said Peggy. 'Sophie and I noticed it that time we met him in the Rialto.'

Isla tilted her head to one side. 'You did?'

'Aye. There was somethin' about the way you looked at him which we both found a bit odd.'

Isla gave them a bewildered smile. 'How was I looking at him?'

'Hesitantly, as though somethin' was wrong ...' said Peggy, '... and you didn't quite trust him,' Sophie agreed.

'You didn't say anythin' to me,' said Isla, looking from one to the other.

'Because it wasn't our place to do so,' Peggy told her.

'Besides, what were we meant to say? We didn't know that Theo had done anythin' wrong, and if it hadn't been for the way you looked at him we'd have thought everythin' was hunky-dory,' Sophie added.

'Exactly!' said Peggy. 'We figured that if you *did* think somethin' was awry, then it was up to you to come to us should you feel the need, not to us to go stickin' our beaks into your business.'

'Well, it was very astute of you,' said Isla, 'because I *did* think somethin' was amiss, and as it's turned out I was right.'

'Do you really think it's wise to stay friends with him, though?' asked Meg uncertainly, 'especially when you know you cannae trust him?'

'Theo needs a good friend,' said Isla, 'someone he can relate to, and strangely enough that's me. Because I understand why he did what he did, because my dad did the same – if that makes sense?'

'It does,' said Peggy. 'And I for one think that he's

lucky to have you. Most women would've wanted to wash their hands of him, but not you, and that's what I call strength of character.'

'Thanks, Peggy. I did worry you might all say I was mad for agreein' to stay friends, or think I was lettin' him walk all over me with a view to wormin' his way back into my heart, but the truth is, he's already in my heart. I'm awfully fond of Theo, and what Caroline told me hasn't changed that. We've talked about it, and if anythin' I feel closer to him now than I did before.'

'That's because you weren't in love with him, though,' Peggy pointed out. 'You'd have felt very differently if you had been.'

'And I guess a big part of you feels relieved that he wasn't heartbroken when you broke things off,' Sophie added. 'I'm sure you didn't want to hurt his feelings.'

'Very true,' Isla conceded. 'I think we were destined to be friends, so that we could put each other on the right path.'

'Talkin' of paths, how fortuitous was it that the bus got a flat the very day you and Caroline were waitin' outside the Grafton together?' said Sophie pointedly.

Isla snapped her fingers as a memory came flooding back. 'Those were my thoughts exactly! And that was before I'd even spoken to her.'

'No!' breathed Meg, both surprised and shocked.

Isla nodded. 'I even told her that it was almost as if someone wanted our paths to cross, because I'd only come back to Liverpool the day before, yet I'd already seen her twice.'

Sophie pointed to the ceiling. 'Your mammy again, if you ask me. I said she was lookin' out for you when we was in Coxhill, and I reckon this proves it!'

'So you did,' said Isla. 'And there's not a doubt in my mind now that you were right.'

Meg was looking awkward. 'But if your mammy is watchin' over you why on earth did she let your father leave you there? Surely she wouldn't have wanted to see her daughter in the poorhouse.'

'Or maybe Dad and I had to go on that journey in order to be happy,' said Isla, and went on to tell them the real reason behind Theo's volunteering for Africa.

'I'm glad you're keepin' in touch,' said Meg soberly. 'But . . .'

'He's payin' a huge price for followin' his heart,' said Isla. 'The last thing he needs is for me to turn my back on him.'

Meg appeared to be in deep thought, and when she didn't reply Sophie asked if there was anything wrong.

'Theo totally believed that he was in love with this Maggie, only to find out further down the line that he wasn't . . .'

'That's about the size of it,' Isla agreed. 'So what are you saying?'

'Well, I don't even know if I love Kenny or am just infatuated with him. So how on earth am I meant to know whether I'm truly *in* love with him when the time comes?'

Peggy picked up her bowl and headed for the sink. 'Now the answer to that is easy, or at least I think it is.'

They all eyed her eagerly.

'You'll know,' Peggy said simply.

There followed a deathly silence, broken by Meg's disappointed cry. 'That's it? You'll know?'

Peggy laughed. 'What were you expecting me to say?'

'Somethin' more specific,' said Meg, who was clearly disappointed. 'Such as *you'll get sweaty palms*, or *your heart will beat nineteen to the dozen . . .*'

'Or the earth will move when you kiss, or angels will appear with harps,' Peggy chuckled kindly. 'But that's the stuff of movies and fairy tales. And I can think of a dozen reasons for sweaty palms and fast heart rate, none of which include bein' in love! And if you ever start hallucinatin' about angels and harps I suggest you get yourself to the doctor toot sweet!'

'And I thought that bein' in love was meant to be as easy as fallin' off a log!' Meg pouted.

'Whatever gave you that idea?' cried Peggy. 'Love is *far* from easy. In fact it's extremely complicated, and it can be easily broken if you're not careful. It's the same with marriage. Folk think you get married and that's the end of that, but you have to work at a marriage if it's to survive the test of time.'

'Which makes it all the more important to wait

until you know what's what, cos only fools rush in,' Sophie added.

Peggy addressed Isla directly. 'And how do you feel now that the two of you are no longer an item?'

'I actually feel quite good, because my misgivings have been validated, and neither of us got hurt in the long run. And I've come to a realisation regarding my own life.'

Sophie looked up interestedly. 'Oh?'

'I've been tryin' to get back to the way things were before Mammy passed, and even though I knew it to be impossible I just wanted that feelin' of love back, you know? The love that comes with havin' someone say "call me if you need anythin'", or "I'll always be here if you need me".'

Peggy eyed her sympathetically. 'You're lookin' for someone who'll always be there for you no matter what.'

'But you've got that with us!' cried Sophie. 'We'll always be here for you!'

Isla smiled gratefully. 'I know you will, but . . .' She pulled an awkward face, and was relieved when Peggy finished her sentence for her.

'Isla wants that security to come from a man.'

'I'm not sure why exactly . . .' Isla confirmed hesitantly.

'Men are physically stronger than women,' said Peggy. 'That's why they go off to war whilst we keep the home fires burning.'

But Sophie, who'd lost her own father, had a different idea. 'Were you a daddy's girl?'

Isla was about to reply, when the tears came from nowhere. 'Oh, Isla!' cried Sophie in distress, whilst Meg and Peggy rushed over to comfort her.

'I think that's why what he did affected me so badly,' gulped Isla. 'It was like havin' someone you idolise turn on you for no reason. When Mammy passed it was Dad I looked to for comfort and reassurance, but he had nothin' to give.'

By now Sophie had joined her friends round Isla's side of the table. 'My daddy was always the one who let me get away with things,' she said, 'and if Mammy went to shout he'd tell her to leave me alone, and say we was only havin' a bit of fun. He snuck me sweeties when I wasn't meant to have any, and he'd plonk me on to his shoulders as though I was as light as a feather.'

Tears continued to trickle down Isla's cheeks as she locked eyes with Sophie. 'That's *exactly* what my dad was like! I was his princess, who could do no wrong! We were more like pals than father and daughter.'

To Peggy the tale was all too familiar. 'All fathers are like that. It's the mammies what discipline, and set the rules, while the daddies turn up at the end of a hard day's work and play with the kiddies!'

Isla thought back to her own parents. 'You're right. Mammy was the glue what held our family together, but I thought my daddy was the be-all and end-all. Something I quickly learned to be untrue when she passed.'

'He must've feared that you'd seen him as a failure,' said Peggy sadly. 'He wasn't used to bein' the disciplinarian – that was your mammy's job – but with her gone he'd have had no choice.'

'He probably wanted you not to see him in a different light,' said Sophie.

'By marchin' me to the poorhouse?' Isla huffed. 'I'd rather he'd shouted at me until the cows came home than did that to me.'

'As we've all discovered, love is a strange and complicated thing,' said Peggy.

'It's a wonder anyone gets married!' said Meg, much to Peggy's amusement.

'Ah, but when you fall in love you'll want to be with that person for ever no matter the ups and downs.'

'Which clearly wasn't the case for Theo,' said Isla sombrely.

'Well, at least you're free to find the real love of your life, Isla,' said Sophie. 'It will be interestin' to see who it is!'

It was Sophie's last day of leave and the girls had gone to wave her off at the train station. 'It's rotten that we didn't get to spend the full week with you,' pouted Meg. 'It's not like we get to see much of you as it is.'

'There'll be plenty of opportunities in the future,' said Sophie, putting her kitbag down to give them all a hug goodbye.

'But Scarborough's miles away!' cried Meg.

'We could meet halfway,' supposed Sophie. 'Maybe somewhere near Nottingham?'

'By the time I got there, it'd be time for me to head

back,' wailed Meg. 'It's all right for you and Isla; Immingham's not too far from Scarborough.'

'It's a fair old trek by train,' said Isla. 'There's no direct line.'

'Still closer than Portsmouth,' Meg mumbled.

'In which case we'll have to save our leave so that we can get a whole week off at a time,' said Sophie sensibly. 'That way we could spend it with Peggy.'

'I suppose that's better than nothin',' said Meg. 'I just wish we could be together all the time!'

'You've got Kenny,' Isla pointed out, 'which is more than Sophie or I have.'

Meg brightened. 'That's true.'

Sophie turned to watch the stragglers who were boarding the train. 'I'd best shake a leg, or I'll be left behind.' Taking each of her friends in a one-armed hug, she smiled through her tears. 'Good luck with everything, and take good care of yourselves!'

'We will,' said Isla, who was now dabbing her eyes. 'Just make sure you do the same.'

Sophie ripped off a mock salute. 'Yes ma'am!' Picking up her kitbag, she headed for the train, her pals by her side.

'Don't forget to write,' said Isla as Sophie boarded the nearest carriage.

'And don't forget to drop by should you ever find yourself drivin' down our neck of the woods,' said Meg.

Standing back so that the guard could close the door, the girls waved tearfully to Sophie, who smiled bravely back. 'Ta-ra, you two! Best of British!'

Chapter Fourteen

If Isla had thought the training tough, it was nothing compared to being on a fully operational balloon site. She knew that Meg and she had been chosen for their stature and strength, and even though they'd been told they'd get extra rations for the sheer physicality of their work she had no idea just how physical it was until she reached Immingham.

'I've got muscles growin' on my muscles,' she said to Shirley, one of the Waafs sharing her hut. 'I'll be lookin' like Popeye soon enough.'

Shirley laughed as she swung her legs out of bed. 'I think it comes as a shock to most new recruits. These things are always more intense when done for real – your pal doesn't realise how lucky she is!'

Isla knew that Shirley was referring to Meg's still being at the training station. 'She does!' she said firmly, 'cos I've told her!'

'I wish I'd been lucky enough to find me a feller like that Kenny,' Shirley remarked as she shuffled her feet into her boots. 'She properly fell on her feet there.'

'I know. I wish I was as lucky as her when it comes to love!'

Shirley frowned. 'Who's that Theo bloke that writes to you? I got the feelin' the two of you were close?'

'My ex,' said Isla, much to Shirley's surprise.

'Blimey! I'd use my ex's letters to light the fire if he tried writin' to me.'

Isla laughed. 'He's not that bad. Just a bit young.'

'He can't be that young!' Shirley remarked.

Remembering Theo's secret, Isla gave further explanation. 'Not so much physically, but more wet behind the ears type of young!'

'I see! Oh well, that goes for half the fellers in here,' Shirley said matter-of-factly.

Isla had started to laugh when the door opened and Mary walked in.

Stunned to her core, Isla stared at the woman she had not seen since they had fled Coxhill many moons before. Not yet having seen Isla, Mary was about to put her kitbag on one of the empty bunks when she turned to ask if it was free. It was then that her eyes met Isla's. Her face dropping in a flash, Mary paled as her glance darted from Isla to the only other Waaf in the room and back again. Swallowing, she started for the door, but Shirley, who had seen that exchange of looks, had already made her excuses and left the two women to discuss their apparent differences in private.

Isla's initial reaction had been to tear more than a strip or two off Mary for the way she'd behaved back in Coxhill, but given that it seemed they would have to live together she reined herself in, asking in clipped tones, 'Is this a fleeting visit, or are you here to stay?'

Mary shot Isla a look of pure loathing. 'The latter, unfortunately, although had I known they let the likes of you in I'd have told them to go take a runnin' jump!'

'Oh, would you now?' asked Isla, her brow rising slowly. 'That should be worth seein'.'

Ignoring Isla's response, Mary turned her attention back to the bed. 'Is this bunk taken?'

'No,' said Isla, and would have left the conversation at that had it not been for the look of disdain that continued to crease Mary's brow. 'If you think I'm cock-a-hoop to have you here, then you're sadly mistaken – especially after what you did to the rest of us in order to gain favour with Harman.'

'Trust you to hold a grudge!' snapped Mary. 'I did what I had to do in order to survive in that hell-hole. It's not my fault you didn't have the nous to follow suit.'

'I'd rather have gone without than spy on my friends!' cried Isla.

Mary gave a short, patronising laugh. 'More fool you!'

Isla was about to respond in anger when she thought better of it. Arguing was only exacerbating the situation. It was obvious that one of them was going to have to be the bigger person, and as that someone clearly wasn't going to be Mary it would have to be her. 'I think it best if we agree to let bygones be bygones. Being on a balloon site means we *have* to work as a team, and I for one am not goin' to let the past stand in the way of anyone's safety.'

'We don't have to talk just because we're on the same base,' sniffed Mary haughtily.

'Oh, for goodness sake, Mary, grow up!' snapped Isla. 'You know darned well that we have to talk to each other if we're to do our job properly. If either of us has the right to be miffed with the other, then I think you'll find that person is me, because it was my pal that you shopped to Harman that day, not to mention countless others.'

Mary's lips tightened. 'It's your fault I broke my toe! Cos I'd bet a pound to a penny you knew where Sophie was all the time.'

'Of course I knew where she was!' Isla told her with satisfaction. 'And it's your own fault you broke your toe. You were bein' spiteful and vindictive, just to gain favour with Harman. You'd have sold Sophie down the river quite happily if it got you a few brownie points.'

'She shouldn't have been spyin'—'

'Yes she should!' cried Isla defensively. 'That woman was a no-good liar who was stealin' the food from our mouths, and what's more you knew it!'

Mary's cheeks coloured. 'Are you goin' to tell the others?'

'No, and not only because we need things to run like clockwork, but because everyone deserves a second chance – even you.'

Mary gave a short sharp reply. 'Thanks.'

Curious as to whether it had been Mary they'd seen on the day they left Coxhill, Isla put the question to her.

'I knew things were goin' to go pear-shaped, so I jumped on the first train out of Clydebank.'

'And where have you been until now?'

'Findin' my feet,' said Mary.

Another Waaf entered the hut, her eyes settling on Mary. 'ACW Blackwell?' she said.

'Aye?'

'You're wanted in the office.'

Mary followed her out, leaving Isla on her own. Taking a piece of paper from her belongings, Isla immediately set pencil to paper. *Dear Sophie, You aren't goin' to believe who just walked in . . .*

As she continued to write, Isla couldn't help but focus on Mary's surname. *I've only ever known her as Mary*, thought Isla as the pencil continued to flow over the page, *but her surname seems familiar somehow?* Should she mention it to Sophie? She decided against it. *It hardly matters what her surname is*, she thought. *It's the fact that she's here at all that matters!*

Hurrying into the office behind the Waaf who had collected her, Mary's heart was racing nineteen to the dozen as she arrived at the desk.

Looking up, the woman on duty clicked her fingers and pointed to Mary's neck. 'I hear you have an item of jewellery?'

Relieved that she hadn't been outed for using a false identity, Mary swiftly removed her necklace. 'How did you know?'

The Waaf eyed her levelly as she handed it over. 'Never mind that. You know the rules.'

Happy that the summons had proved to be of no matter, Mary stepped out of the office feeling considerably better than she had when she went in, but she also knew that she wasn't completely out of the woods. Isla knew her to be Mary, yet her papers claimed her as Tammy. It hadn't been an issue until now, and Mary preferred to keep it that way, but how could she explain a change in name?

Screwing her lips to one side, she went for a walk to the NAAFI, where she could think without being disturbed. *I cannae confide in that rotten cow because she'll not be sympathetic. Everyone refers to me as ACW Blackwell, which is fine, and Isla certainly didn't bat an eye when the Waaf called me that. As long as nobody refers to me as Tammy*, thought Mary, before stopping in her tracks. All the girls she had trained with called her Tammy, because that's what happened when you got to know each other properly, and no doubt they would expect to do the same here. Turning on her heel, she headed back to the office. She would demand to be moved, or leave the WAAF altogether. If they asked why, she would say that she and Isla didn't get on to the point they couldn't be on the same base. But what reason could she give that would make them sit up and listen? They didn't move folk unless there was a real concern. Steeling herself, she opened the door to the office and caught the attention of the woman behind the desk.

'I need to leave.'

It was much later that same day, and when Isla came back to the hut after supper it was to find it a hive of gossip. Turning their heads as one, the girls stared at her.

'Just so you know, we don't believe a word of it,' said Shirley as she made her way over to where Isla stood.

'Believe what?' Isla began, until commonsense caught up with her. 'Let me guess. This has summat to do with the new girl?'

'She told us in the office that the two of you were in the poorhouse together,' said Elsa, a tall Waaf with curly brown hair.

Isla lowered her gaze before looking back up. 'For what it's worth, she was tellin' the truth.'

Elsa looked slightly stunned. 'So you did break her toe?'

Isla rolled her eyes. 'She did that all on her own . . .' She explained the whole scenario, finishing with, 'Honestly! Why she was so worried that I would say somethin' when she went ahead and spilt the beans anyway is beyond me!'

Shirley grimaced. 'Only she didn't tell quite the tale you just did. She said that it was you what was runnin' to that Harman woman, and that you'd broken her foot whilst hidin' a fugitive.'

Isla couldn't help but burst into laughter. 'She said what?'

Elsa – who had been in the office when Mary had spun her web of lies – repeated to Isla everything Mary had told them.

Isla sank down on to her bed. 'It's all true, but the other way round,' she said. 'She's the one who smarmed up to Harman, not me. They can ask Harvey Ellis if they need proof – he's the feller that ran Coxhill after Harman. He knows exactly what Mary's like!'

'Mary?' said Elsa, blinking. 'Who's Mary?'

'The girl we're talkin' about,' said Isla. A confused frown forming, she added, 'Why? What did you think her name was?'

Elsa's cheeks coloured. 'I think I'd best have a word with the girls in the office . . .'

Isla caught up with her as she left the hut, leaving the other girls chattering excitedly behind them. 'I'm comin' with you!' she said.

'I'm afraid that won't be possible,' Elsa began, but Isla was adamant.

'I'm not havin' everyone talkin' about me behind my back when none of it's true!'

'Only I shouldn't have told you what she said . . .' protested Elsa.

'Well what a good job you did,' said Isla. 'Because Mary's been lyin', and not just to you, but to the services in general!' A thought occurred to her. 'Where is she, by the way?'

'Gone,' said Elsa, a tad shamefacedly. 'I'm not sure where, but possibly to another base?'

Isla shook her head angrily. 'I cannae believe I said I'd keep shtum for the sake of the team, when she was plannin' on tellin' a pile of porkies the whole time!'

'If it's any consolation, I don't think she got on well with the women in her last base either.'

'Oh?'

'We had an anonymous phone call to say she had an item of jewellery, which as you know isn't allowed.'

'Where on earth would Mary get jewellery from? I never seen her wearin' any the whole time we was in Coxhill,' said Isla. 'In fact we weren't allowed personal possessions, for fear they'd get nicked, or that's what Harman told us, at any rate. She confiscated my necklace and sold it to a pawnshop, or at least that's what we think she did with it.'

Elsa tutted. 'What a rotten thing to do!'

'You think that's bad? It was the last thing I had of my mammy's, so thanks to her not only have I not got the locket, but I've not got a photo of my mammy or daddy either!'

Elsa faltered mid-step. 'A locket, you say?'

'Aye. Why?'

'Was there anything special about this locket, apart from the photos, of course?'

'Aye. It had tiny blue enamel forget-me-nots on the front. It was a present from my daddy . . .' Her voice trailed into silence.

Elsa swallowed. 'I think we might have found where your necklace went, and it wasn't to any pawn shop.'

Isla blinked. 'You mean . . . Mary . . . ?'

'It would appear so. I mean, it would be one heck

of coincidence for Mary to have an identical locket to yours.'

Tears of joy were tracking their way down Isla's cheeks. 'I cannae tell you what this means to me, Elsa. I never thought I'd see that necklace again.' She sniffed as she dabbed her eyes. 'I know it's a tad bittersweet . . .'

'Why bittersweet?'

'I might know where my locket is, but you cannae give it me back, because that's the rules,' said Isla, but Elsa was looking at her in a determined fashion.

'I'm the only one who knows about the locket – well, me and Mandy Spires, at any rate. As long as you promise to keep it out of sight, I see no reason why you shouldn't have it back.'

Isla thanked her profusely, promising, 'Mum's the word!'

It was some time later when Elsa was able to return Isla's locket to her.

Holding the precious treasure in her hand, Isla ran her forefinger over the delicate blue enamel forget-me-nots that adorned the front and gently opened the clasp. A tear trickled down her cheek as her eyes fell on the images of her mother and father facing each other across the hinge.

'I cannae thank you enough, I truly can't,' she whispered. Fastening the clasp, she tucked the locket beneath her shirt. 'I shall *never* take it off!'

Choked to see Isla's reaction, Elsa cleared her throat. 'Glad I could reunite you with somethin' so special.'

Feeling happier than she had in a long while, Isla returned to the hut, and despite having sent off two letters earlier in the day she was soon asking whether she could borrow more paper as well as a pencil sharpener from her comrades. Having achieved both, she once again set pencil to paper.

Sophie stared in disbelief at the letter before her as she read it through for the second time.

Dear Sophie, Have I got news for you! Subsequent to my earlier letter – which was already winging its way to you before I'd found out the whole truth – I am now able to update you fully on the whole Mary business!

Remember our time in the shelter when we were fleeing Clydebank? As it turns out, Mary must have got hold of Rory's girlfriend's papers some how, and she used them to get into the services!

Sophie scanned over the rest of the letter, learning how Isla had come back into possession of her locket, as well as how Mary had disappeared without trace before reaching her next base.

They think she must've realised that I'd spill the beans, because she legged it as soon as the driver stopped at a set of traffic lights! Apparently there was a right kerfuffle whilst the other Waafs ran around the streets trying to find her, but as she'd chosen to make her escape close to a train station, they're fairly certain she would have jumped aboard one of the trains without first purchasing a ticket. I'm not sure whether they can do anything about her going AWOL, but I do know that the polis are after her regarding the stolen documents!

Sophie wondered what would've happened had Mary not bumped into Isla when she did. *I've said it before, but I'll say it again*, thought Sophie as she hunted for a piece of paper, *someone's up there lookin' out for our Isla and I'll be a monkey's auntie, if that someone isn't her mammy!*

Isla was reading a letter from Meg which made it sound as though she had been beside herself when she got the news about Mary's arrest.

As if some feller gave her them papers, Meg had written. *It's obvious she nicked them! Question is, how did she come into possession of documents belonging to a dead person? I had a word with Kenny, and we're guessing that Mary must've found her documents lying around outside somewhere. I must admit, I thought that to be highly unlikely until Kenny told me that all manner of things end up where you'd least expect them after an explosion. With that being the case, it's quite possible that Mary really did happen across them whilst on her way to the station and just made up that bit about the feller giving them to her so that people wouldn't think she'd nicked them, cos there's no such thing as finders keepers when it comes to someone else's documents!*

Isla thought of the bittersweet moment when Elsa had rushed into the NAAFI eager to pass on the news regarding Mary's arrest.

'They've found her!' she gasped, before half falling, half sitting in the seat opposite Isla's.

'Mary?'

'She was trying to board a ferry for Ireland when a police constable recognised her,' said Elsa.

Isla gaped at her. 'Just how far-ranging was the search to find her?'

'Nationwide,' said Elsa. 'The RAF don't take what she did lightly!'

'So what's the outcome, do you know?'

'No, and I doubt we ever will, because it's in the hands of the civilian police now. But I do know that she fessed up to havin' used documents that didn't belong to her, and it's been confirmed that the documents belonged to the woman you told us about.'

Isla felt her heart skip a sickening beat. 'And is she . . . ?'

Elsa responded solemnly. 'I'm afraid it would appear so.'

Isla hung her head. 'Poor Rory . . .'

'Who?'

'Rory's the feller I was tellin' you about, the one down the shelter, who was shoutin' the odds regardin' Tammy's father.'

'What a thing for that Mary to have done!' said Elsa reprovingly. 'Imagine if he'd got wind that his belle was alive and well in the WAAF, only to find that it was Mary, and she'd stolen Tammy's identity.'

'Mary wouldn't think of that, though,' said Isla, 'cos people like her only think of themselves.'

'Do you think it was the poorhouse that made her that way?' asked Elsa innocently.

Isla shot her a reproving glance. 'No, cos neither Sophie, nor Meg, nor myself turned out like Mary! There's two kinds of people in this world: ones who'll trample over others to get what they want, and ones that'll give you a helpin' hand in times of trouble. Mary definitely falls into the first category.'

Isla sighed inwardly. The conversation had taken place a week or so after Mary had gone AWOL, and Isla still couldn't shake Rory from her thoughts, mainly because she worried he might've done something rash, like Theo after losing his wife, or her father after losing her mother. *If he signed up for the army he might be over in Africa already*, she thought as she gazed unseeingly at the page, *or even worse . . .* She tried to shake the last thought from her mind, but found she kept harping back to it, much to her shame. *Rory's nothin' to do with you*, she reminded herself, *so put him out of your mind and get on with your life, because you're usin' him as an excuse to live in the past instead of movin' on, which is ridiculous considerin' he doesn't even know you exist!*

Shirley called out to her as she entered the hut. 'Penny for them?'

Isla sighed. 'I've had a letter from my pal, the one that's in Portsmouth.'

'I remember – the lucky duck! Everything all right?'

'Aye. It just came as a bit of a shock, the business about Mary I mean. There we were never expectin' to lay eyes on her again, and wham! She lands on our doorstep all guns blazin', as it were.'

Shirley sat down on her bed to undo her laces. 'The past has a nasty habit of sneakin' up on you when you least expect it.'

'I just hope there's no more surprises to come out of the woodwork,' said Isla. 'I think I've rather had my quota for one year, thank you very much.'

'Does that mean you have other skeletons in your closet?'

'I didn't think I had this one!' said Isla.

'So there's no more like her in that poorhouse you were in, then?' said Shirley as she used her toes to push her shoes off.

'I'm afraid there were, but I had very few dealin's with any of them. Mary was the main one.'

'What about that ex of yours? Is he likely to spring any nasty surprises?'

'No. I know all there is to know about him, and I'm rather hopin' he'll be able to put the mistakes of his past firmly behind him!'

Chapter Fifteen

Theo stared at the papers in his hand. 'Is it too late to say I've changed my mind?'

'Yes it ruddy well is, so stop yer bellyachin' and start sayin' yer goodbyes.'

Theo looked back to the papers, which confirmed his departure to Africa in a month's time. Nodding solemnly, he headed for the NAAFI.

Thankful that there was no one in line for the telephone, he quickly dialled the operator and asked to be put through to RAF Immingham. Asking the Waaf who'd answered the phone if he could be put through to ACW Isla Donahue, he was relieved to hear her voice come down the line.

'Hello?'

'Hello, Isla. How's tricks?'

'Theo! It's not like you to telephone. Is everything . . .' her voice faltered, and Theo was about to tell her of his overseas posting when she beat him to it. 'You're goin' to Africa, aren't you?'

'I'm afraid so.'

'When?'

'September fifteenth.'

Isla felt her heart sink. 'How do you feel?'

There was a tingling silence before he said quietly, 'I don't really know. Numb, maybe?'

'What did your mammy say?'

'I haven't told her, because I don't know how to do so without breaking her heart.'

'Oh, Theo!'

'Each time I try to rehearse what I'm goin' to say, I see the look on her face, and the words stick in my throat.'

'I'm afraid there's no good way of puttin' it,' said Isla. 'You'll just have to tell her straight.'

'I thought I'd telephone—'

Isla cut across him without apology. 'No! This has to be done face to face. I know it'll be tough – probably harder than goin' to Africa itself – but you cannae shy away from it. Your mammy will want a cuddle from her boy after hearin' news like that.'

He smiled. 'That's why I rang you. I knew you'd know what was best, and you're not afraid to call me out for bein' a coward either.'

'You're not a coward!' snapped Isla. 'There's nothin' wrong with not wantin' to hurt the ones you love.'

'I've always managed to make a right pig's ear out of it in the past,' said Theo, 'despite not wantin' to.'

'Which is why you're doin' the right thing now,' said Isla. 'When will you have time to go and see her?'

'They've given us a forty-eight this weekend,' said Theo. 'That's why I rang you straight away.'

349

'You mean you've only just found out?'

'Within the past five minutes or so,' said Theo. 'You were the first person I wanted to contact.'

'I'm glad you called me first,' said Isla, 'and I'm sure your mother will have an inkling what's comin' when you surprise her with a visit.'

'She's an intelligent woman,' said Theo. 'I dare say she'll know just by the look on my face when I walk through the door.'

Envisaging the face that had only just reached eighteen years of age, Isla felt her heart go out to him. 'It's amazin' what a kiss and a cuddle can do.'

'I thought I might buy her some pansies,' said Theo distantly. 'They always were her favourites.'

'That would be nice.'

'Thanks, Isla.'

'What for?'

'For being there for me, despite everythin'.'

'I said I would, didn't I?'

'You did that.'

The operator let them know their time was up, but Isla noticed the softness in her voice and suspected she'd been listening in on their conversation.

'I'm always here should you need me,' said Isla. 'Give your mammy my best.'

'I will.' There was a short pause before he added, 'Do you remember my sayin' how I wished I'd met you a long time ago?'

'I do.'

'I still wish I had, because maybe, just maybe, we'd still be together.'

Uncertain as to how she should reply, Isla was grateful when the operator finally cut them off.

Theo stood by the back door to his parents' house, trying to summon up the courage to enter. His hand was on the door handle when it twisted in his palm, and his mother opened the door from the other side. Tears cascading down her cheeks, she flung her arms around his neck, whispering, 'You'll be fine. I bet it'll be no different from bein' in Liverpool.'

He heard his father clear his throat. 'It'll be hotter, mind, so be careful you don't burn!'

Theo smiled weakly. 'How did you know?'

'A mother knows,' she said, as she brushed the back of his jacket free from imaginary pieces of lint.

His father settled back down behind his news-paper. 'I've been keepin' abreast of the news just in case, and I agree with your mother, it's no worse out there than it is here. Crossin' the sea's goin' to be your biggest challenge.'

'Victor!'

'I'm only sayin'—'

'Well don't!' Tutting at her husband's insensitiv-ity, she indicated that Theo should take his jacket off 'before it gets stained', she said.

Doing as his mother instructed, he followed her through to the kitchen and handed her the flowers. Taking the small bouquet, she lifted it to her nose before placing all the flowers but one into a vase.

'What's wrong with that one?' asked Theo, point-ing to the single bloom.

'I shall press it, as a reminder of today,' said his mother. She paused as she gathered her composure once more to say brightly, 'Would you like a slice of my Victoria sponge?'

He smiled. 'Have you ever known me turn it down?'

Patting the chair by the kitchen table, she fetched a side plate and a knife from the unit. Cutting a thick slice of the cake, she handed it to Theo. 'Will you be leavin' any broken hearts behind?' she asked, adding silently *aside from mine*.

'No. There was one girl, but that's all over now.'

She smiled kindly. 'You'll meet someone special one of these days.'

Theo gazed at the slice of cake. 'I already have, but she found out about Maggie, and that was the end of that.'

'Oh, son!'

'It's all right, Mam, really it is. Meetin' Isla was the best thing that happened to me, because she forced me to face some home truths.'

'She wasn't mean to you, was she?' Concern was etched in her brow.

'No. Far from it – in fact we're still friends. It was her I rang for advice, when they told me I'd been called up.'

'It sounds as though the two of you are close?'

'We are, but we both come with too much baggage. She's had a bit of a rough time as well, only hers wasn't down to her own makin', unlike mine.'

'You followed your heart,' said his mother defensively.

He grinned. 'You've changed your tune!'

'Well, time changes things, as does circumstance.'

'You mean you're worried I might cark it whilst in Africa.'

Her cheeks paled. 'Please don't say that!'

He gently apologised, before continuing, 'I realised I was in love with Isla way too late, but even if I'd known sooner I don't think it would have made any difference. Not until she's found her father and squared things with him, at any rate.'

She cupped his chin in her hand and gazed lovingly down at him. 'If she's the one for you, she'll find her way back.'

He held her wrist in his hand. 'So I shouldn't try chasin' after her?'

She shook her head. 'Time will tell whether the two of you are meant to be together or not, and in the meantime you should concentrate on yourself, cos you don't need distractions, not in your job!'

SEPTEMBER 1941

Isla had scarcely been able to believe her luck when she received her new posting to Fazakerley.

'I'll be able to come and wave you off in person,' she told Theo the week before her move.

'I couldn't think of a better send-off,' said Theo: 'you, my mam and my dad.'

'I don't want to step on anyone's toes. I'm only a friend, not family.'

'A very good friend,' said Theo, 'and I want you

there. Mam will too – she knows you've been good to me.'

'As long as you're sure?'

'Positive.'

Now, as she stood on the docks with his parents, Isla felt a lump form in her throat as Theo's mother kissed her son goodbye. Straightening a tie that didn't need straightening, she smiled weakly. 'You'll be back before you know it.'

Smiling back, he pecked his mother's cheek. 'I'll write every day, I promise.'

Mrs Stratham beckoned Isla to join them. 'I'd quite like to write to you too, Isla, if that's all right with you, dear? Only it would help to ease my mind if I know that you've heard from him when I haven't.'

'It's absolutely fine with me,' said Isla. 'I'm at RAF Fazakerley.'

Mrs Stratham smiled. 'You are kind.'

Theo's NCO called out to him to board the ship, and Mrs Stratham held on to Isla with one hand and her husband with the other.

Surprised by the speed with which the ship put to sea after Theo had boarded, Isla could only watch in sympathy as the tears which his mother had managed to hold back till now fell freely, and his father wept also. Quietly bidding them goodbye, she was about to slip away when Mrs Stratham caught her sleeve. 'I really am truly grateful to you for keepin' in touch with our boy,' she said between sobs. 'He looks up to you, you know.'

Isla smiled. 'I know he does, and there's really no need to be grateful. Theo's a good friend.'

'A bit misguided,' said his father, after blowing his nose, 'but his heart's in the right place.'

Fearful that they might be hinting she rekindle the flame that never was, Isla smiled politely. 'I'd best be off. I'll let you know should I hear anythin' from Theo.'

Hurrying away before they could say something to change her mind, Isla was grateful when she saw her bus approaching. *They only want their son to be happy*, she told herself as the bus trundled along the street, *but do they really think that the two of us gettin' back together would make him so? More to the point, has Theo said something that has given them that impression?* She recalled his words on their last phone call, and thought, *He's just like me, wanting to live in the past rather than face the future, but I'm sure that's all it is.* She turned her attention to the aircraft flying overhead. Theo was frightened at the prospect of going abroad, and he probably reasoned that if they were together he'd never have volunteered in the first place. Confident that she had found the answer to her concerns, she settled into her seat.

Sitting in the layby, Sophie examined the map. As long as there were no surprise diversions the route to RAF Fazakerley was a relatively easy one. Putting the map to one side, she checked for oncoming traffic before pulling back on to the road. One of the perks of her job was getting to travel round the country, and when they had asked for a volunteer to drive some files from her base in Scarborough to RAF Fazakerley she had jumped at the chance. Telephoning Isla, she was pleased to learn that her visit happened to coincide with Isla's scheduled day off, because it would give them a chance to discuss Theo's posting to Africa. *Isla's got a heart of gold*, thought Sophie as she turned on to the main road that would lead her to the balloon base, *and she doesn't like to upset people or see them unhappy, especially if she knows she can do something to prevent it*.

Sophie's worry had been that Isla would rekindle her relationship with Theo because he was going to Africa, not because she wanted to give the relationship another go, and that wouldn't be fair on either of them, but especially not on Theo, who Sophie believed still had feelings for Isla.

Seeing the base loom before her, she pulled up at the gate and flashed her identity card to the guard, who waved her through. She parked the car alongside some others and headed for the office, her arms brimming with the files that were the reason for her visit. There she was told to wait whilst the necessary officer was called through, and it wasn't long before she was returning to her car with a fresh set of paperwork to take back to Scarborough.

'Hello, stranger. Long time no see!'

Sophie turned at the sound of the familiar voice, a beam stretching her cheeks. 'Isla!' Closing the boot of her car, she took her friend in a warm embrace. 'Golly, it's good to see you! How's tricks?'

'Same old. It's a shame you won't have a chance to see Peggy whilst you're down in this neck of the woods.'

'I'm afraid I've only got a few hours before having to head back,' said Sophie ruefully, 'but at least you and I can have a good catch-up.'

'So where do you fancy goin'? As you've not got too long, would you prefer to stay on camp or take a drive into the city?'

'A wander round the city, if that's all right by you,' said Sophie. 'I prefer to get away from the bases as much as I can, otherwise it never feels as though I've had a proper break.'

'Will it be all right to use your car? Only I know you're not meant to use it for recreational purposes.'

Sophie waved a dismissive hand. 'I've driven here all the way from Scarborough; a few extra miles won't make any difference. Come on, get in.'

Jumping into the passenger seat, Isla admired the deftness with which Sophie cranked the car into life and drove them round to the gate. 'Quite the professional,' she commented. 'I'm very impressed.'

'It's old hat now,' said Sophie as she glanced both ways before pulling out. 'You'd not have been as impressed had you had to suffer me kangarooing down the road the way I did in the early days.'

'Meg would be ever so impressed,' said Isla. 'She's always wanted a ride in a car with you behind the wheel.'

'Her own personal chauffeur.' Sophie smiled. 'Have you heard from her lately?'

'Aye, she wrote the other day to say that nothin's really changed, and she's beginning to get bored with trainin' folk instead of bein' out in the thick of it all. I told her she doesn't know how lucky she is, and she should be grateful for small mercies.'

'And what about Theo?'

Isla, who hadn't finished talking about Meg, shot Sophie a sidelong glance. 'Why do I get the feelin' that Theo is the main reason for your wantin' to visit me?'

Sophie smiled guiltily. 'That obvious, eh?'

'It is to me, but only because I know you so well!'

'Look, whilst I can understand how you can forgive his past and still remain friends, I'm not sure I'm comfortable with how close the two of you are, given the feelin's he still has for you.'

Isla gazed out of the window to the tall verges thick with wild flowers. 'As I do for him, which is why I cannae turn my back on him, not knowin' him as I do.'

'And that's fine. I just worry that you might get pressured into doin' somethin' you don't want to do because you feel sorry for the guy.'

'I can see why you'd think that might happen, and I'll admit I did rush off before his mother could say anythin' that might have been awkward . . .'

'So you get the impression that he's told his mother about the two of you?'

'I know he has, but there was something about the way she looked at me that made me think he'd given her reason to believe that he still had romantic feelin's for me. And whilst I know that I'm precious to him, it's not in a romantic sense.'

'Are you sure about that?'

'I think so. He did say somethin' about how he wished we'd met earlier because if we had we might still be together, but I put that down to him not wantin' to go to Africa, cos had he met me before Maggie we might still be together and, with that bein' the case, he'd never have volunteered for Africa in the first place.'

'Ah!'

'Do you think it's more than that?'

'I'm sorry to say I think it might be.'

'So what do I do?'

'Now that is a tricky one! You don't want to upset him, but neither do you want to give him false hope.' She pulled the car into a parking spot and applied the handbrake. 'What are his letters like?'

'Interesting, because he talks about Africa – a lot.'

'And what about you? Does he talk about his feelin's for you?'

'No. And when I reply I steer clear of anythin' personal, because I don't want to give him the wrong impression.'

'Then I think that's all you can do for the time bein',' said Sophie, getting out of the car. 'Now, what shall we have for our lunch?'

'Fish and chips,' said Isla promptly. 'That way we can eat them in the grounds of St John's Gardens.'

Sophie linked arms with her friend. 'I'm sorry if I've been bombardin' you with too many questions about Theo, but I don't want to see you fall into a hole in order to make him feel better.'

'I won't,' Isla assured her. 'I promise.'

Sophie held the door of the fried fish shop open for Isla to passed through. 'Good!'

Their fish lunch procured, the girls headed for the grounds of St John's Gardens, nattering happily. 'So how's life on the road?' Isla wanted to know. 'I should imagine you get to meet lots of people on your travels.'

'Aye, but even so it can be a bit lonely at times, cos you're never in one place more than twenty-four hours.'

'Not long enough to find yourself a beau, then,' Isla teased.

'I'm not interested in fellers,' said Sophie, as they sat down on a park bench. 'Or not ones that show an interest in me, at any rate.'

'What do you mean by that?'

Sophie grimaced. 'Most of the men I meet are after a quick kiss and cuddle on the back row of the picture house, but I want more than that.' Isla stifled a giggle, causing Sophie to roll her eyes. 'When I say I want more, I mean commitment-wise!'

'Have you seen anyone that takes your fancy?'

Sophie began to shake her head before reconsidering. 'There was one feller. Do you remember me tellin' you about the sailor I met down at the docks, the one who wasn't interested in me?'

Isla had a vague recollection of the conversation and tried to recall more as she unwrapped her parcel of food. 'You were in Plymouth at the time, if I remember rightly?'

'That's the one.'

'Flippin' 'eck, Sophie, you've not seen hide nor hair of him in ages! Whatever made you bring him up?'

'Because I saw him again in Scarborough.'

'Blimey, he gets about a bit!'

'As do I,' said Sophie, before waving this off as inconsequential. 'Point bein', I think he remembered me from the time I saw him in Plymouth!'

'Oh? What did he say?'

Sophie finished the chip she was eating before replying. 'He didn't say anything. It was more the look he gave me.'

Isla tried to swallow her smile. 'And just how did he look at you?'

Sophie wrinkled her nose. 'As if he recognised me.'

Not wanting to show her disappointment, Isla pressed on. 'I thought you weren't keen on courtin' a fisherman, or a sailor or whatever he was, because they spend their lives at sea?'

'True, but on the other hand I spend my life on the road, so in some respects we'd be perfectly matched.'

'The odds of you both bein' on the same patch of dry land at the same time must be hundreds if not thousands to one!' cried Isla. 'And is he even interested? You didn't seem to think so when you were in Plymouth!'

Sophie broke open her fish, allowing the hot steam to penetrate the air. 'He smiled, and he didn't do that the first time I saw him.'

'Why on earth would you want a relationship with a feller you'll never get to see?' said Isla. 'Or is that the attraction?'

Sophie laughed. 'He just seems favourable over the spotty oiks or stuffed shirts the Navy seems to be endowed with.'

'Favourable, eh?' Isla smirked. 'Does that translate into "good-looking"?'

Sophie grinned. 'Maybe.'

Isla shuffled on the bench so that she was face to face with her friend. 'Go on, tell all!'

Sophie stared at a patch of sky as she envisaged the handsome sailor. 'He's probably around six foot tall, jet-black hair and a beard to match, sparkling—'

Isla was chuckling beneath her breath.

'What?' said Sophie crossly, failing to see what was causing her friend such mirth.

'He isn't a pirate, is he?'

'What? Why . . . oh, I see. Blackbeard. No, he isn't a pirate, cos I don't think pirates are handsome dashin' chaps . . .'

'Have you not seen Errol Flynn in *Captain Blood*? Cos I have . . .' Isla fanned her face in the pretence of being hot. 'What a corker!'

Sophie rolled her eyes. 'I don't think real pirates look like Errol Flynn! But whether they do or not is beside the point. Yes, I do think he's good-lookin' – handsome, even.'

'So now that we've established why you're so keen on him, why don't we get back to the crux of your problem?'

'Being?'

'That you'll never see him!' cried Isla. 'Or hardly ever, at any rate.'

'I've seen him twice already,' Sophie pointed out, 'and we weren't even trying!'

Isla gathered her thoughts. 'But you didn't seem to think he was interested. And before you say he smiled, lots of people smile at me, but it doesn't mean to say they want to take me out to dinner!'

'I s'pose not,' said Sophie reluctantly.

'There are plenty more fish in the sea,' said Isla. 'You need to cast your net a bit wider!'

'Or wait until the war's over,' said Sophie with a resigned sigh. A sudden thought occurred to her. 'Hold on a mo. How can you lecture me on waitin' on one feller when you've been doin' the same with that Rory bloke?'

'I dated Theo,' Isla pointed out.

'Wrongly,' said Sophie, 'cos he wasn't the one for you.'

'Ah, but I didn't know that until I'd dated him,' said Isla smugly, 'whereas you've not so much as been to the Hippodrome with a feller!'

'What's the point when I may never see them again?' said Sophie. 'I could be sent to Inverness tomorrow and Botany Bay the day after that! It's different when you're actually based somewhere, but I'm very rarely in Scarborough, to the point where I'm lucky if there's anyone left that I recognise on my return!'

'I s'pose you've got a point.'

'That's possibly what's drawin' me to this sailor or fisherman or whatever he is,' said Sophie. 'As well as the fact that he's drop-dead gorgeous, of course!'

'Or the fact that there'll be no expectations, because you'd both be away a lot?' mused Isla. 'I can see the attraction.'

'It would make for an easier life,' said Sophie, 'but in all honesty I like to keep it as a pipe dream, cos no one gets hurt that way.'

Isla grinned. 'Does he smoke a pipe? Most sailors do, don't they?'

Sophie was shaking her head. 'I have no idea. But I hope not – they smell dreadful!'

They spent the rest of their time together wandering the streets of the city before returning to the car and heading back to drop Isla at her base.

'I've had a wonderful time,' she said as she got out of the passenger seat. 'I cannae wait until we're all together in January.'

'Which reminds me, I've asked for the leave, but not had it confirmed, so I'll make sure they haven't forgotten about it when I go back to Scarborough tomorrow.'

'Tomorrow? Aren't you goin' back today?'

'I wish! But I've got a few more stops to do yet.'

'Where will you stay?'

'I'm booked in at some God-awful tavern in York.'

'Why'd you book it if it's so horrid?'

Sophie smiled. 'Because the Navy booked it, not me!'

Madson had been crossing the street when a pretty Wren caught his eye, but for the wrong reason. Staring open-mouthed, he stopped in his tracks. Were his eyes deceiving him? He frowned. Everyone looked different in uniform – or rather they all looked the same, but certainly nothing like they did before they entered the services. However, there are some faces you don't forget, especially if their owner nearly killed you with a coal shovel. His mind racing, he looked about him to see if she had any friends or colleagues nearby, but everyone else was dressed in civilian clothing. His jaw tensing, he made his way towards her in a determined fashion, and took great pleasure in shoulder-barging her as he swept past.

Spinning round to face him, Sophie shouted an objection. 'Mind where you're goin'!'

He stopped in his tracks, and turned very slowly to face her, a wicked grin sweeping his cheeks as he saw her face fall in horror.

'Well, well, long time no see,' he said, his lips barely moving as he spoke. 'I bet you never expected to see me again.'

Sophie swallowed. Unsure how to respond, she remained quiet.

He shot her a look of surprise. 'What's up? Cat got your tongue? Or are you too much of a coward to speak without a shovel to hand?'

Sophie glared at him. 'You were goin' to thrash my friend with a *poker*! What did you expect me to do?'

'You shouldn't have been stickin' your noses in where they didn't belong,' spat Madson.

'Harman was robbin' the food from out of our mouths – you too, come to that,' protested Sophie.

'You should've been grateful there was someone willin' to look after you,' he bellowed, 'because in case you didn't know, Coxhill has closed, and those that had a roof over their heads are now livin' on the streets – and the blame for that lies at *your* door.' He stood back and began to clap his hands together in a slow, sarcastic fashion. 'Well done!'

Sophie's cheeks reddened. 'Don't you dare try and make out that we were the ones in the wrong.'

'You left me for dead,' seethed Madson, 'and if it weren't for the people around us now I'd repay the favour.'

Sophie's face went from red to white within a heartbeat. 'You were . . .' she began, but he was already speaking.

'You'd best hope I don't bump into you again when there's no witnesses, cos if I do, I promise, it'll be the last time we meet – and that goes for your pals too!'

Sophie stared after him in shock as he turned on his heel and continued on his way. Standing for a second or two in stunned silence, she looked around for a telephone box, and spying one across the street she hastened over and called Isla's base first.

'I didn't expect to hear from you so soon!' said Isla, worry clearly present in her voice. 'Is everythin' all right?'

Sophie hastily relayed the encounter with Madson, not pausing until she'd finished.

'Oh my good God,' Isla breathed. 'Are you all right?'

'A bit shaken up, and I dare say I'll be lookin' over my shoulder for some time to come,' Sophie confessed. 'Scarborough is a long way from the two of you, but I thought you and Meg should know in case you run into him at some stage or other.'

'Thanks, Sophie; forewarned is definitely fore-armed. Are you goin' to report him for threatenin' behaviour?'

Sophie briefly mulled this over before shaking her head. 'He'd only deny it, so what's the point?'

'You'd have somethin' on record should he carry out his threat,' said Isla, 'cos we both know he's cap-able of violence.'

A smile twitched Sophie's lips. 'He's not the only one. I reckon he'd not dare attack me no matter what he may say, cos he knows I'll hit him with the first thing that comes to hand should he try! He even mentioned the coal shovel.'

Isla chuckled. 'I bet he's still got the lump.'

The operator cut across, letting them know their three minutes were up, so they swiftly bade each other goodbye and Sophie asked to be put through to Meg's station.

'Cheeky so-'n'-so,' Meg said, after hearing Sophie's tale. 'It's him who should be worried about encoun-terin' you when there's no witnesses around, not vice versa.'

'Aye,' Sophie agreed. 'I reckon he only confronted me in the first place because there were people around.'

'And I'd wager his threats towards me and Isla are just as empty as his threat to you,' said Meg. 'After all, birds of a feather and all that.'

'I hope so,' said Sophie. 'Isla thinks I should report him just in case. What do you think?'

'I think the Wrens will say they have enough to deal with – especially as it's just your word against his.'

'I agree,' said Sophie. 'He just wanted to air his grievance, and put the frighteners on us.' Satisfied that his threats were empty, she put the encounter far from her mind.

JANUARY 1942

It was the first time the girls had been together since they had last been in Liverpool, and Peggy was over the moon to have a houseful once more.

'I can't tell you how pleased I am to be cookin' for more than one person again! Cookin' at all, in fact, cos I rarely bother to do scouse or Woolton pie when I'm on my own; I just haven't the heart for it.'

'I wish they had cooks like you in the RAF,' said Meg as she rolled out the pastry for the pie topping. 'We never get anythin' as good as this in the cookhouse – *or* the NAAFI, come to that.'

'So my boys tell me,' said Peggy. 'That's why I like to spoil you all when you come back for a visit.'

'And much appreciated it is too!' said Sophie, her mouth watering as the smell of Peggy's homemade bread filled the kitchen.

Beaming under their praise, Peggy turned the subject to the evening ahead. 'So, have you decided where you want to go dancin' yet?'

'The Grafton,' said Sophie. 'I hope you're goin' to be joinin' us, Peggy.'

'Wild horses wouldn't keep me away,' said Peggy.

'I really enjoyed myself when we went dancin' last. It took me back to my youth, when me and my pals would let our hair down in pursuit of the boys!'

Isla laughed out loud. 'Peggy! I thought young women weren't meant to pursue boys!'

Peggy shrugged. 'Why else do young girls do their hair and makeup if not to impress the boys?' She wagged a reproving finger. 'Not that we asked them out, mind you; we just baited the hook to see if we got any bites!'

'I bet a night on the tiles with you and your pals was a right good laugh,' Sophie chuckled.

'Only behind the scenes,' said Peggy, tapping the side of her nose in a conspiratorial fashion. 'On the surface we were as prim and proper as the day is long.'

'So where did you meet Clive?' said Meg, placing the pastry carefully on top of the pie filling.

'I knew him from school initially,' said Peggy, 'but with him being a few years older than me we never actually spoke until I bumped into him at the Grafton one Saturday night. He was watchin' me and my pal Ethel doin' the foxtrot. The next dance was an excuse me, and that's exactly what Clive did!'

'And was that it?' Isla asked.

'Pretty much. We started seein' each other on a weekly basis until we were married a year later.' She opened the oven door for Meg, who was ready to place the pie inside, and then removed her pinny and swigged the last of her tea. 'That's dinner in the oven, girls. How about we go and get ready?'

The four of them headed upstairs to do their hair and makeup ready for the night ahead, and it was some time later when they reconvened in the kitchen, the girls smartly dressed in their respective uniforms and Peggy in a neat two-piece suit of pale blue. 'I shall feel very special walkin' into the Grafton with the three of you dressed like that!' remarked Peggy.

'I must say, I always feel very smart in my uniform,' said Meg as she opened the oven door, releasing the delicious scent of the Woolton pie into the kitchen. 'Far more so than I do in the frock Harvey found for me.'

'How is Harvey?' Isla asked the room in general. 'I've not heard from him in a while.'

'I have,' said Sophie, who was laying the table. 'He's still enjoyin' his job, but he's keen to get together with us at the first opportunity.'

'It would be lovely to see him after all this time,' said Isla, her nostrils flaring as Peggy started to plate up the pie. 'That smells and looks fit for a king! My mouth's waterin' already.'

'Mine too,' said Sophie. 'I'd best not have too much, though, not if I'm goin' to have a dance later.'

'It does look good, if I do say so myself,' said Peggy. 'Fetch the veggies off the stove, Sophie, there's a luv.' That done, Peggy passed the jug of gravy round and said grace, and a companionable silence fell as everyone concentrated on the delicious dinner placed before them. Meg was the first to clear her plate.

'I know you've done spotted dick for afters,' she said, 'but I'm goin' to have to give it a miss this time.'

'Me too,' agreed Peggy. 'I reckon I must've been thinkin' of my boys when I dished the portions out!'

'Delicious, though,' said Isla as she finished the last piece of pie crust.

'So are we agreed that we're all too full for pudding?' Sophie asked.

There was a general murmur of concurrence, so Sophie put the pudding back in the oven to keep warm. 'We might change our minds after an evenin' of dancin',' said Meg, 'and whilst I wouldn't normally want to go to bed on a full stomach, I'll make an exception for Peggy's spotted dick!'

Collecting the plates from the table, Isla began to wash the dishes, leaving the others to tidy up. 'I had a letter from Theo the other day,' she said conversationally. 'I rather think he's enjoyin' himself out in Africa.'

'Enjoyin' himself?' said Peggy doubtfully. 'Are you sure?'

'Aye. He writes non-stop about the difference in culture, as well as other things. And whilst a lot of his words were blotted out, I reckon I got the general gist of it.'

'I bet the food out there is heaps better than what we get in the cookhouse,' said Meg as she wiped a plate dry.

Isla laughed. 'Actually, accordin' to Theo he's not brave enough to eat the local fare, which in his own words looks decidedly dodgy. Instead he survives on food sent out from Britain, which he says is worse than the stuff we get over here, on account of havin' travelled for months on end before hittin' dry land.'

'Blimey!' said Sophie. 'And I thought we had it bad!'

'I'd definitely try the local food if I were out there,' said Meg, 'just to give it a go.'

Peggy wrinkled her nose. 'I've heard they eat all manner of peculiar things in Africa, so it's hardly surprisin' that Theo's decided to stick with meat and two veg.'

'Such as?' asked Isla, who was keen to learn more about African dietary habits.

Peggy placed a hand to her mouth. 'I don't want to think about it, not on a full stomach!'

'Does he say much about the war over there?' asked Sophie, putting the last of the dishes away.

Disappointed at the change of subject, Isla used a dishcloth to wipe the crumbs from the cleared table. 'Only that the work's ten times harder due to the heat.'

'I bet he'll have a lovely tan when he comes back,' said Meg, looking at her own pale hands. 'I reckon everyone looks better with a bit of colour.'

'Not me,' said Isla as she fetched her jacket from its peg. 'I go red then white, but never brown.'

'My Clive comes back lookin' like a foreigner when he's been at sea for a few months,' said Peggy, as they all headed out into the street. 'He reckons it's the sun's rays bouncing off the waves that gives him such a good colour.'

'If my father's been to foreign lands he might look like that too, Peggy,' Isla suggested, adding as an afterthought, 'Not that I suppose I'll ever get to see him that way, unless there's a miracle, that is.'

'Is he not a redhead like yourself?' asked Meg curiously.

'Nope. I've got my mammy's hair and complexion.'

'Porcelain skin,' said Peggy approvingly. 'Quite beautiful!'

'Not when it's red,' said Isla. 'I'd much rather have the type of skin that tans.'

Sophie held her hand out to stop the bus that would take them to the Grafton, and continued the conversation while they took their seats. 'Gettin' back to Theo, has he mentioned when he's comin' home?'

'No. If anythin' he seems to think he might be out there for the duration – however long that may be.'

'If the Great War is anythin' to go by, I can't see this one endin' any time soon,' said Peggy solemnly. 'In fact, I believe the Krauts are better prepared this time around, so it may well go on for even longer.'

'Loose lips!' barked a man sitting two rows up from the girls.

'I'm makin' an observation, you daft old sod!' snapped Peggy. 'I ain't tellin' nobody anythin' they don't already know.'

'I'm just glad that the Americans have joined the war,' sighed Isla. 'We've a much better chance with them on our side.'

Forgetting his words of warning regarding careless talk, the old man in front of them agreed wholeheartedly. 'They should've jumped in from the start, but better late than never.'

'And certainly better than the three years it took them to join durin' the last lot,' said Peggy.

'The Krauts will never beat us Brits, with or without the Yanks,' said the old man stoutly, 'cos they ain't got our spirit!'

'It'll be a cold day in hell before the Swastika flies above Buckingham Palace!' said another man further along. He was greeted by a general murmur of agreement from the other passengers.

'Everythin' comes to an end sooner or later,' said Peggy, 'and this war is no different.'

'We never thought we'd see the back of Coxhill, or that it would cease to operate,' said Sophie. 'Yet look at it now!'

'I suppose if you look at it that way,' Meg began, before pointing out of the window. 'We're here!'

Joining the queue of passengers all heading for a night out, the girls reminisced about their first time in the dance hall, and discussed how much had changed since then.

'We're all grown up now,' said Meg, 'or at least it feels that way!'

Sophie smiled. 'I find it flatterin' that you still think of me as the same age as you two, even though I'm a good few years older!'

'It's a compliment,' said Peggy. 'Take it while you can, cos no one ever says that about me!'

'Theo looked older than his years,' said Isla as they headed into the venue, 'but I guess a lot of that was down to his joinin' up so young.'

'And his height,' said Meg. 'He was ever so tall for his age.'

Heading for the bar, the girls bought drinks for themselves and Peggy before selecting a table near the dance floor.

'Thank you, all. Drinks first, or . . .' Peggy left the question hanging.

'Drinks,' said Isla. 'I like to people-watch before I take to the floor; see who's here, and whether there's any Ginger Rogers or Fred Astaires knockin' about the place.'

'Only us!' chuckled Meg, before emitting a long 'Oooooh.'

'What?' cried Sophie.

'Who've you seen?' Isla chimed in.

'He's a bit of all right,' said Peggy, who was following Meg's line of sight.

'Oh my God, it *can't* be,' said Isla. Her voice barely above a whisper, she added, 'Only it is!'

'Who?' asked Sophie curiously.

Isla was staring open-mouthed. 'It's Rory!'

Chapter Sixteen

'Who's Rory?' said Peggy, her eyes fixed on the young man with the dark curly hair.

'He was the one that lost his girlfriend the night of the March bombings,' said Isla. 'She was Tammy Blackwell, the girl whose identity Mary stole.'

'Well I never!' breathed Peggy. 'Fancy him bein' all the way down here, and in RAF uniform too.'

'I bet he joined up not long after that night,' said Isla.

'I wonder what made him choose the RAF?' said Meg, who was still staring. 'Or do you think the RAF chose him?'

Isla turned sombre eyes to her friends. 'I'm wonderin' whether he's heard tell of a Tammy Blackwell from Clydebank servin' in the WAAF – cos if he has . . .'

'Someone should tell him the truth,' said Sophie, nudging Isla's elbow.

'Why me?' cried Isla. 'I don't want to be the bearer of bad news!'

'You know him better than we do,' Meg whispered.

'I do not!'

Sophie whipped round to face her. 'You were the one to tell us about Mary, so it's only right that you tell him!'

'Aye, cos we don't know the ins and outs as well as you do,' Meg agreed.

'Well, one of you should tell him,' said Peggy, 'because someone needs to.'

'What will people think if I approach a man I don't know?' Isla cried.

Meg frowned. 'That you have somethin' to say?'

'I thought you liked him,' said Sophie quietly. 'And this would be your perfect opportunity to speak to him.'

Isla stared at her in horror. 'And say what?' She put on a sarcastic voice. 'Hello, Rory! You don't know me, but I'm sorry to say that your girlfriend is dead after all, and the woman pretending to be her has been arrested!'

Sophie rolled her eyes. 'Well, obviously you don't put it quite like that!'

'How else can I put it?' said Isla in frustration. 'I cannae approach him for no reason, and he might think me to be overly keen if I say I recognise him from the shelter. Cos it does look a bit odd, my rememberin' him after all this time.'

'Don't see why,' said Meg evenly. 'I recognised him, yet I'm not in the least bit keen.'

'You see?' said Sophie, pointing to Meg. 'Just tell him the truth! That Mary had stolen Tammy's documents, and was pretending to be her.'

'What if he decides to shoot the messenger?' said

Isla in a last-ditch attempt to wriggle out of an embarrassing situation.

'Then you'll know you did your best,' said Sophie. Suddenly taking hold of Isla's arm she squeezed it tightly. 'Oh my good God. He's comin' over!'

Her mouth drier than the Sahara, Isla stared at Rory, who was walking towards them in a determined fashion. Smiling as he approached, he looked at each of them in turn, finishing with Isla.

'Pardon me for askin', but do I know you? Only your face seems familiar.'

Isla swallowed. 'We've never really met, but I did see you down the shelter the first night of the Clydebank blitz.'

His smile vanished in an instant. 'Oh.'

'We didn't mean to eavesdrop,' said Isla quickly, 'but we overheard your conversation with the two women regarding your belle, and there's something we think you should know.' She went on to tell him how Mary had come to her base, and everything they had learned as a result of that encounter. 'We worried that you might hear rumours that Tammy was servin' in the WAAF,' said Isla, adding meekly, 'I'm sorry.'

He eyed her sympathetically. 'What for? Bein' in the wrong place at the wrong time? As far as I can see you've nothin' to feel sorry for. You weren't the one who entered the services under a deceased person's identity, that was Mary.'

'I know, but the last thing I wanted was to be the bearer of bad news,' said Isla.

He laid a reassuring hand on her shoulder and Isla

felt her spirits rise. 'Better that I find out now than further down the line. Unfortunately, I've already had someone try to tell me that Tammy's still alive.'

Isla gasped. 'No!'

'It was hogwash, of course, but it hurt just the same.'

'I bet it did,' said Isla. 'Do you suppose they'd bumped into Mary?'

'No. The woman who told me was an old school acquaintance of ours, so she'd know that Mary wasn't Tammy.'

Meg pulled a downward smile. 'Maybe she'd heard it from someone who had bumped into Mary?'

He shook his head. 'To cut a long story short, she'd heard tell that Tammy and her mammy were on the run after havin' attacked Tammy's father.'

'A likely story,' snorted Isla. 'We all heard what them women said about Tammy's father, and if anyone was the aggressor it was him, not them. By all accounts he had a horrific temper when roused.'

'Exactly!' said Rory. 'That was the whole reason behind my helpin' them to run away, cos Dennis had threatened to kill them should they even *think* about leavin' him.'

Sophie stared at him open-mouthed. 'Blimey!'

'It does make you wonder how Mary got hold of Tammy's documents, though, now that we know everythin',' said Meg, 'cos surely Tammy would've had them herself, given she was intendin' to run away?'

Rory was shaking his head. 'No, she wouldn't,

because I'd arranged for her and her mammy to have new identities to stop Dennis from trackin' them down.'

'Well that's that, then,' said Isla. 'There's no way she'd have run off after all you'd done for her.'

'Agreed,' said Rory. 'I blame the polis, cos it was them what put the idea in Ella's head in the first place.'

Isla lifted her gaze. 'The polis?'

'Aye. Accordin' to Ella, Dennis had gone into the police station claimin' they'd attempted to murder him before leggin' it.'

'Goin' off that basis,' said Isla slowly, 'and I hope you understand I'm only playin' devil's advocate here, but if he really did go to the polis, do you suppose there could be a grain of truth in the rumour that Tammy and Grace were on the run?'

He heaved a sigh. 'If there was, and they really did run off, where does that leave me? Cos at the end of the day they *knew* I was waitin' for them, and even if they didn't know about Jellicoe House gettin' hit it doesn't take away from the fact that they'd disappeared leavin' me to wonder what the heck had gone on.'

'That must be awfully tough,' said Peggy. 'Never knowin' the truth – because I dare say you never will.'

'Which is why I have to stick with what I do know,' said Rory. 'Tammy was in the buildin' when it got bombed and Dennis is a filthy, rotten, lyin' murderer.'

'You're right, and I'm sorry for rakin' up the past.'

'Not at all . . . Isla, is it?'

She smiled before holding out her hand. 'Pleased to meet you, Rory, and properly this time.'

He glanced at her empty glass. 'Can I buy you a drink?'

'Thanks for the offer, but we've taken up enough of your time.'

'Nonsense! You've been very helpful, and I appreciate your comin' forward, especially when I'm guessin' it couldn't have been easy for you.'

Isla nodded guiltily. 'We practically drew straws.'

He laughed. 'And you drew the short one?'

'Something like that.'

'So you definitely need another drink.' He glanced around the remaining glasses. 'Anyone else in need of a top-up?'

They all politely declined, but thanked him anyway, and Rory held his hand out in front of him, indicating that Isla should go before him. 'So what made you join the RAF?' she asked as they weaved their way through the crowd.

'I wanted to get my own back on the Krauts for what they'd done to Tammy,' said Rory. 'You?'

She gave a short mirthless laugh. 'I don't think you want to hear my life's story.'

He looked at her in surprise. 'Boring, is it?'

She laughed again. 'I wish!'

'Sounds intriguing.'

'You'll be sorry you asked.'

Having gained the barmaid's attention, he ordered himself a shandy before turning to Isla, who asked for a lemonade. 'Try me,' he said as the barmaid left to get their drinks.

Isla told him everything, from the moment her

mother had been carted off in the back of the ambulance to the moment he came up to her earlier that night. The conversation had taken quite some time, and they were currently back at the table, watching Meg and Peggy dance together whilst Sophie danced with one of the Waafs from Isla's base.

'And I thought I'd been through the mill!' said Rory.

'But we've both come out the other side,' said Isla optimistically, adding, 'Between the two of us and my ex, I reckon we could write a book!'

He frowned. 'Your ex?'

Isla filled him in on how Theo came to be a widower, and the consequences thereafter.

'I know he was young, but if there's one thing I cannae bear it's infidelity,' said Rory. 'Lying is the worst thing you can do to someone you supposedly love.'

'And I agree,' said Isla, 'but we all make mistakes, and you cannae punish someone for the rest of their lives for somethin' they did when they were barely out of nappies!'

He shot her a look of admiration. 'You're one hell of a woman, Isla, I'll give you that!'

She raised her brow. 'You tellin' me that you never made a mistake?'

'Plenty! In fact it's all I seem to have done since joinin' the RAF.'

She eyed him cynically. 'Why do I find that hard to believe?'

'Because you never got to see me at my worst,' said Rory flatly, 'and I'm glad you didn't cos it wasn't pretty.'

She turned to face him, a look of curiosity on her face. 'As you've not been dishonourably discharged, I cannae see how you've done anythin' *that* bad.'

'I've toed the line as far as the RAF's concerned,' said Rory, 'but I'm ashamed to say I haven't treated the women so well.'

'Oh?'

'My pals were convinced that I needed to move on from losin' Tammy, and they thought I should do that by datin'. In truth I wasn't ready to start courtin' again, so I made sure the women I took out knew that I only wanted friendship, but with them wantin' more I sort of ended up workin' my way through them.'

She chuckled beneath her hand. 'The unintentional gigolo!'

'That's what it looks like to people who don't know me,' said Rory, 'but even though I'm ready to start datin' again I cannae be bothered explainin' my past to every woman I meet. They'd probably run for the hills, so what's the point?'

'You told me,' Isla reminded him.

'You're different.'

'Because I don't want to be one of your conquests?' she said, with tongue-in-cheek cheeriness.

'Oh, ha ha!' he said, before chuckling softly to himself. 'I think it's because you don't have a hidden agenda.'

'Such as gettin' you to propose before the night is through?' Isla quipped.

He smiled. 'I know you're only jokin', but I'm sure that's what some of them had in mind.'

She pulled a downward smile. 'You only have to see what Theo went through to know how hasty people can be. If anythin' the thought of marriage makes me want to run for the hills!'

'And that's what makes you different,' Rory supposed. 'Well, that and the fact that we've got an awful lot in common when it comes to love and loss.'

'Birds of a feather . . .'

'We are indeed.' His eyes locked with hers, and Isla knew that he was interested in her without him so much as speaking another word.

The band began to play, and Rory stood up. 'Would you like to dance?'

'Very much!' Isla felt her heart quicken as he led her to the dance floor, and when his arm slipped around her waist a shiver ran through her body.

'I must say I never expected my evenin' to turn out this way,' he murmured as he guided her expertly around the floor.

'Me neither,' said Isla. 'Mainly because I never expected to see you again, yet here you are!'

'I'm surprised you remembered me at all,' said Rory, 'although I suppose that night was pretty memorable what with one thing and another.' Leaning back so that he could look down at her, he added, 'Though havin' said that, I did think you looked familiar when I first came over.'

Not wanting to point out that he had actually glanced at her in the shelter, albeit fleetingly, for fear of sounding strange, Isla spoke airily. 'You must have seen me during the raid – although I'd be surprised if you remembered anythin' from that night, given you had so much on your mind at the time.'

He looked into her eyes. 'I'd normally agree with you, but . . .'

'But what?'

'I don't want to sound cheesy, but whenever I look into your eyes I get a sense of déjà vu, as if I've met you before. But more than that, it feels as if I already know you.'

Isla's heart sang, for she felt exactly the same way, but if she were to say that now she might well be leaping out of the frying pan and into the fire. *You got together with Theo too quickly*, she reminded herself, *and look where that got you.*

'I suppose you do know me in a way, cos I've told you my life story,' she said in a bid to keep things light.

'I get that, but this is something more, something soulful, as if we've met in a past life – if you believe in that sort of thing, of course.'

Isla gave a half-shoulder shrug. 'I believe that my mammy's keepin' an eye on me, cos I'm not normally lucky!'

'And what about fate? Do you believe in that?'

Isla mulled this over before answering cautiously. 'I'm not sure whether it's fate or my mammy, but I thought it pretty remarkable when I bumped into Caroline twice in two days, especially as I wasn't even based in Liverpool at the time.'

'Not to mention the chances of us bein' in the same venue hundreds of miles from where we grew up, nigh on a year after spendin' a few hours together down the same shelter the very night I lose my Tammy. And I'm not even goin' to start on Mary!'

'So what are you sayin'? That fate has coordinated a string of events for us to end up at this point?'

'Either that or your mammy's playin' matchmaker.'

'I – I . . .'

He hugged his arm around her waist. 'Relax! I'm teasing – but only the bit about your mammy playin' at matchmaker.'

She smiled with relief, because she hadn't known how to respond. 'I suppose it does seem odd, but with all of us choosin' the same service . . .'

He smiled. 'I thought you said the WAAF chose you, not the other way round, and that's how you and Meg got separated from Sophie.'

'Good God, you're right!'

'I reckon I should stick by you, Isla . . . ?'

'Donahue.'

'Donahue, because you've got one heck of a guardian angel in your mammy!'

Isla became aware of the locket around her neck. Was it her imagination or was it slightly heavier than it had felt a few moments ago?

'She always was the best,' she said. 'I just wish I could've been there for her as she's been for me.'

'Your daddy was there for her,' said Rory, 'so she wasn't on her own.'

'True.'

'Do you think you'll ever see him again, what with your mammy pullin' the strings as it were?'

'If Mammy's orchestrating my life, then most definitely,' said Isla confidently.

He ran the tip of his tongue over his bottom lip as if he feared what he was about to say might not go down too well. 'Only if that is the case, why do you suppose she hasn't got the two of you back together before now?'

'Because he's not ready yet,' said Isla, almost without thinking. She stopped dancing to look up at him. 'Why does it take a stranger to make me see what I've known all along?'

'And what's that?'

'My daddy was going through hell when he put me in the poorhouse, and when he said he'd be back for me in a couple of months I didn't believe him, not deep down.'

'And why do you suppose that was?'

'Because I knew he wouldn't be ready,' said Isla. 'Because to put me in such a vile place showed how low he'd sunk, and I knew it would take more than a couple of months for him to find himself again!'

'So you don't think he was running away, then?'

'No! He was protecting me from being dragged down alongside him.' Her eyes were searching his as she gabbled through her thoughts. 'Theo talked of not carin' whether he lived or died after what happened to Maggie. I reckon Daddy was the same, and he was frightened that I might follow suit, as it were, so he put me somewhere he thought I'd be safe until he could come back for me. Trouble was he underestimated how long that would be!'

Seeing Isla talking in such an animated fashion, her friends came over.

'Is everything all right?' Sophie asked, keeping her eyes fixed on Rory.

'Better than all right!' cried Isla. 'I've finally seen the light!'

Peggy, Meg and Sophie exchanged glances before looking back to Rory and Isla. Peggy was the only one to speak. 'And that is?'

'Daddy hasn't written to me because he doesn't know how to tell me that he isn't ready to come back for me yet. He didn't run away, he was tryin' to save me from goin' through what he was goin' through. Cos whilst Coxhill was the pits, I'd wager it was nothin' compared to how Daddy felt when he watched my mammy pass.' She looked up at Rory. 'Rory's right, or rather we've all been right! Mammy's been lookin' after me all this time! Too many coincidences, too many similarities! Me getting together with Theo helped me see the torture my father was going through when Mammy passed, and meetin' Rory again—' she stopped, trying to work out her mother's reasoning for her being with Rory, 'has shown me that my father isn't ready to come back to me yet, but he will just as soon as he is!'

One of Rory's pals came over to see why everyone was standing on the dance floor talking instead of dancing. 'Is everythin' all right?'

'Just chattin',' said Rory, 'but maybe we should make a move, as we appear to be causin' a bit of a jam!'

Apologising to the other dancers, the small group headed back to their table along with Rory's friend, who was keen for the off. 'The lads want a fried fish supper before headin' back to base. Are you comin'?'

Rory rubbed his stomach enthusiastically. 'You know me! I never turn down a fish supper.' Taking Isla's hand in his, he lifted it to his lips and kissed her knuckles. 'It's been an absolute ball, as well as an eye-opener. We must do this again sometime.'

Isla smiled. 'I think you and I both know that you're just bein' polite.'

He looked at her in true surprise. 'I'm really not, you know. I very much enjoyed myself this evenin', and whilst I've learned a lot about you already, I'd like to get to know you better. For instance, who is the Isla that has left her past behind and joined the WAAF? Cos I'd wager you're not the same girl you were down that shelter.'

'I'm not even the same girl I was a few months back,' admitted Isla, 'but I'm guessin' the same can be said for you.'

'I'm definitely not the same girl,' Rory quipped, before adding, 'Seriously, though, I'm a very different person from the one I was when you saw me last. In fact I don't know how many facets I've discovered about my character and personality thus far, but I'd wager there're many more yet to be revealed. So what do you say to havin' dinner with me one evenin'? It'll be my shout, of course.'

'I suppose it cannae harm to have dinner.'

He beamed. 'Splendid. Where would you like to meet?'

Her first thought was somewhere they would both know such as St George's Hall or Lime Street Station, but as she'd met Theo at both places she plumped for somewhere different. 'How about the Lyceum café on Bold Street?'

'Perfect. When are you free?'

'I cannae do this week . . .'

Sophie spoke over her. 'Oh yes you can! You've got a whole week to be with us; one evenin' won't harm.'

'Sophie's right,' Meg agreed.

Isla looked to Rory. 'In that case, whatever suits you.'

'How about Thursday evening, say eighteen hundred hours?'

'I'll see you there!'

The girls waited until Rory and his pals had left the dance hall, before bombarding Isla with questions. 'Calm down!' giggled Isla. 'I cannae make out a single word either of you are sayin'.'

Meg was the first to ask her question. 'Do you think he might be your soulmate?'

Isla took a cautious breath. 'If he's bein' honest with me, and I've no reason to think otherwise, then yes, I do!'

'What did he say exactly?' asked Sophie. 'And when I say exactly, we want a blow-by-blow account!'

Peggy laughed. 'Young love, eh?'

Isla told them everything, but when she got to the part about Rory saying that looking into her eyes was like a déjà vu experience Meg and Sophie lost the plot altogether.

'I knew it!' cried Meg. 'He's the one for you! I'd lay my life on it!'

'That's the kind of stuff you see in the flicks!' swooned Sophie, before looking slightly cautious. 'You don't think he's only sayin' it to get into your drawers, do you?'

Isla laughed out loud. 'No I do not! I always knew when there was summat Theo wasn't tellin' me cos he'd only give vague answers, but not Rory. He speaks from the heart no matter what the question.'

Peggy was watching Isla carefully. 'So what's the problem? Cos you seem hesitant, a bit like you did with Theo once.'

'Peggy's right,' said Sophie. 'There's somethin' you're not sure about.'

Isla screwed her lips to one side. 'What if those rumours about Tammy being alive are true? I don't want to fall in love with Rory just to have Tammy come along at the last minute and sweep him out of my arms.'

'And do you really think that could happen? Given the hurt and betrayal she made him suffer?' Peggy asked uncertainly.

'Love is a powerful force,' said Isla. 'One look from her and he could forgive her on the spot! And for all we know she might have had a damned good reason for runnin' off the way she did.'

Sophie shrugged. 'Such as?'

'I don't know, but if I were Tammy I'd not rest until I let him know that I was all right.'

'So if she is alive, it's possible she might not have loved him as much as he loved her,' Peggy suggested.

'Perfectly possible,' said Isla.

'I think you're goin' to have to suck it and see,' said Sophie. 'If you're meant to be together, you'll know soon enough, but if you let him slip through your fingers on the back of "what ifs" you'll never forgive yourself.'

'I'd trust your mammy if I were you,' said Meg. 'She's gone to a lot of effort to get the two of you together. You don't think she'd have done that if she thought he'd go runnin' back to Tammy at the drop of a hat, do you?'

'No. But that's only if we're right. Some might say the idea of my mother guidin' me through life is a fanciful notion, and that I shouldn't base my life around such nonsense.'

'And what do you say?' asked Peggy mildly. 'Cos your opinion is the only one that counts.'

'I say I trust my gut,' said Isla. 'Rory is the second to last missing piece in my jigsaw.'

Meg was clasping her hands to her cheek in a prayer-like fashion. 'How romantic!'

'And what about Theo?' Sophie asked. 'Are you goin' to tell him about Rory? It seems only fair, seein' as he still holds a torch for you.'

'I will, but I don't know whether it would be better said in a letter or over the phone.'

'Letter,' said Peggy. 'That way you can break it to him gently, whereas you could get cut off on the phone before you've had time to explain yourself properly – not that you should have to explain yourself, of course.'

Isla would far rather not tell Theo anything at all than risk upsetting him when he was so far away from home, but she knew it would only take someone from West Kirby to see them together and he might find out anyway. 'But what should I say? It's not as if Rory and I are even courting! Meeting for a dinner is hardly the news of the century.'

'Don't say anything just yet,' advised Peggy. 'Wait until you've been out with Rory a few times first and go from there.'

'Peggy's right. You don't want to go countin' your chickens before they've hatched, even if we are all certain that you and Rory are a perfect match,' said Meg.

'Right, I'll wait and see what happens first,' said Isla. 'There's no point in jumpin' the gun.'

Sophie wrinkled her nose. 'For all you know Theo might've found himself another belle,' she said, 'what with him bein' a bit of a ladies' man an' all.'

'That would be ideal,' said Isla, 'so why do I get the feelin' it won't be the case?'

Chapter Seventeen

It was the evening of her planned dinner with Rory, and Isla thought she had never felt so anxious in her life. 'How does my hair look?' she asked the girls for what felt like the umpteenth time.

'Perfect, just like it did when you asked two minutes ago!' sighed Sophie. 'Honestly, Isla, you're goin' to have a nervous breakdown if you carry on like this!'

'I just want everythin' to look as perfect as it can,' said Isla, as she blotted the lipstick which Peggy had lent her. Turning round, she bared her teeth at her pals whilst saying 'Lipstick?' in the sort of voice used by bad ventriloquists.

'Nope,' said Meg, without raising her eyes from the paper she was reading.

'You never even looked!' cried Isla.

Smiling, Meg put the paper down. 'You've just looked in the mirror for yourself. Why do you need me to confirm what you've already seen?'

'Because I'm nervous!'

'Really? I'd never have guessed!' Meg said with good-humoured sarcasm.

'You seem to forget that you were just like this when you began courtin' Kenny!' Isla reminded her.

'I wasn't! Was I?'

'You reapplied Mandy's lippy that many times, she took it back off you whilst there was still some left!'

Meg's cheeks bloomed. 'She did, didn't she? I'd forgotten about that!'

'And you tore a hole in your stockin's by trying to straighten the seams.'

Meg smiled wistfully. 'It all seems a long time ago now, but you're right, I do remember what it was like. My stomach was jumpin' about like a box of frogs!'

'Which is just what mine's like now,' said Isla. 'I don't remember feelin' this nervous when I went out to dinner with Theo.'

'You weren't,' said Peggy bluntly. 'Your only concern was to not appear wanton.'

'You weren't anywhere near as eager to see Theo as you are Rory,' said Sophie.

Isla nodded. 'This is different.'

'Cos you actually care this time,' Peggy told her, 'and that's because he matters to you.'

'He really does,' said Isla. 'I just hope our date's everything I want it to be.'

'Angels playin' harps, no doubt . . .' said Meg.

Isla laughed. 'I'm not that naïve, or not any more, but I do know it'll be special when – or rather if – we kiss, cos even the touch of his hand makes me . . .'

'Makes you what?' asked Peggy sharply.

'Makes me feel all warm and fuzzy,' replied Isla,

seemingly unaware of the sharpness in Peggy's tone. 'Like everything's all right with the world.' She looked at Meg. 'Do you feel like that when you and Kenny kiss?'

'He has soft lips and he tastes of mints,' said Meg, much to the amusement of her friends. 'What's wrong with that?'

'Nothing!' Peggy laughed. 'It's just a typical Meg answer, that's all.'

'Is that good?' asked Meg, eyeing them suspiciously.

'The best!' cried Isla.

'We wouldn't want you any other way,' agreed Sophie.

'Perfect as you are,' Peggy confirmed, 'so don't ever change!'

Isla glanced at the alarm clock on the bedside table. 'Cripes! I'd best shake a leg!'

'Have you got everything?' Sophie asked as she passed Isla her handbag.

Pulling the zip back, Isla glanced inside. 'Purse, comb and handkerchief. Do I need anythin' else?'

'Nope,' said Peggy. 'Now get you gone, and good luck!'

Isla swung her handbag over her shoulder and took one last look in the mirror. 'I hope I manage to calm my nerves before I meet him!'

'You'll be fine,' Sophie assured her. 'You've already broken the ice.'

'Exactly! We've already said everythin' there is to say,' said Isla anxiously, 'so what are we meant to talk about tonight?'

'You'll find something,' said Peggy. 'Now for goodness sake go before you talk yourself out of it!'

Isla left the house to a flurry of good wishes from her friends. Seeing that the bus was already at the stop, she hurried down the road waving frantically to the clippie, who was about to ring the bell. Jumping on board, she thanked the middle-aged woman fervently before taking a seat and gazing out of the window, her imagination conjuring up an image of Tammy, who in her mind was as beautiful and glamorous as any movie star. *I bet she was stunning compared to me*, Isla thought as the clippie rolled off her ticket in exchange for the fare, *with big blue eyes and blonde curly hair, and no doubt an hourglass figure!*

Ashamed of herself for being jealous of a dead woman, Isla turned her attention to the evening ahead, and what might be expected of her. *He's only taken girls out on a friendly basis as yet*, she reminded herself, *and even though he hinted that he was ready to begin dating again he never suggested that this was a date, so you needn't worry that he might try to kiss you.* She hesitated. *Was* she worried he might try to kiss her, or was she more worried that he might not? After all, it would be the difference between her and the other girls he'd taken to dinner, which would be a good sign indeed. On the other hand, nice girls didn't kiss on the first date . . . she hesitated. What was she thinking? She wasn't even on a date! Tutting under her breath, she told herself that she was jumping the gun because she felt so at ease with him, and she was pretty sure he felt the same way.

And it's very different from when I went to meet Theo, she told herself. *He was a charmer who reminded me of my father, but Rory . . .* She envisaged Rory, who was the complete opposite of Theo, not so much looks-wise, because they were both very handsome, but in the way that he conducted himself. *Theo was sweet, but that's not what I want from a man. I want someone who can look after me and guide me through the rough times, and Rory's already shown me he can do that within the first couple of hours of gettin' to know him.*

The bus pulled up on the street where the café was, and she was pleased to see that Rory was standing outside waiting for her with a beautiful bouquet. 'Flowers?' she said as he handed them to her.

'Aye. I thought you could do with a bit of cheerin' up,' said Rory. 'Our first meetin' was a little intense to say the least, and I wouldn't want you to think that I was always so morbidly sincere.'

Thanking him for the beautiful posy, she noted that the gesture, along with his words, showed that he cared about what she thought of him as much as she cared what he thought about her. Holding the flowers to her nose, she smiled. 'You could very well think the same of me. Is that part of the reason you wanted to meet again? So that you could set the record straight?'

'That and the fact that I very much wanted to see you again,' said Rory. 'Despite spendin' most of the evenin' discussin' our various misfortunes, I really enjoyed our time together, and I wanted to repeat the experience, only with more smiles this time!'

She chuckled quietly as he opened the door of the café for her. 'So what would you like to know?'

'For a start, where would you like to sit? Here by the window, or more towards the back?'

'The back,' said Isla. 'We can chat better there.'

Indicating that she should go before him, Rory followed her to the table of her choice, where he pulled a chair out for her and beckoned to draw the attention of the waitress. 'What would you like to drink?' he said, as he also sat down.

'Tea, please,' said Isla. 'You cannae beat a good cuppa, or not in my opinion at any rate.'

Rory looked up at the waitress, who was waiting with pencil poised. 'A pot of tea for two, please,' he said, and the woman made a note of the order before leaving them to chat.

'How are you findin' life in the WAAF? As you thought it would be, or completely different?'

'Very much as I thought it would be,' said Isla. 'Only probably better, because I love it.'

'Given that you were a seamstress before it all went wrong, what do you think you'd be doin' now if your mammy was still around?'

'Oh, good question.' She fell into silent contemplation before looking up. 'I reckon I'd still have joined the WAAF, because it's the right thing to do – plus I was bound to tell old Branning to stick his job sooner or later. What about you?'

He grinned. 'I don't think the WAAF would have me.'

'Oh, ha ha!' said Isla, her eyes crinkling with

amusement. 'You know full well I was referrin' to the RAF!'

He chuckled softly before replying to her original question. 'As a dockworker, I was exempt from call-up, but had I stayed there who's to say I'd still be alive? What with them bein' the main target for the Luftwaffe and all, I reckon you're in as much danger down the docks as you are on an airbase.'

She grimaced. 'What a thought!'

'True, though.'

'Do you think you might have joined up just to do your bit, based on those grounds?'

He screwed his lips to one side. 'I was a very different person back then, and I rather think my decision would've been swayed by Tammy and what she thought.'

'Do you think she'd have joined up?'

'I doubt it. She'd have wanted to stay with her mammy. They were very close.'

She leaned back as the waitress placed the tea things down on the table. 'Can I get you anything else?'

Rory glanced at the four choices on the menu before picking his favourite. 'Yes, please, I'll have the pie and mash. Isla?'

'Sausage and chips, please.' Taking the tea tray, the waitress headed back to the kitchen

Cursing herself for being bothered enough to ask her next question, Isla did so anyway. 'What was Tammy like?'

'She reminded me a bit of you or I suppose I should say you remind me a bit of her.'

'How so?'

'She'd never back down from a fight – even when the odds were stacked against her – and she was intelligent as well as beautiful.'

Isla bit the bullet. There was no point in pinning her hopes on Rory if he was still in love with Tammy. 'Do you think you'll ever get over her loss?'

Rory gave the question some consideration before replying. 'I didn't think so at first, but I soon learned that time moves on regardless of your feelings, and if you don't move on with it you'll end up not just lonely but bitter, and life's too short to be feelin' that way. As a result I've stopped lickin' my wounds, and I must say I'm already feelin' a lot better for it.'

'Which is brilliant!' said Isla. 'But it's a lot easier said than done, don't you think?'

'Heaps! And but for my pals I don't know where I'd be right now, cos they were the ones who stopped me from wallowin' in self-pity, for which I'll always be grateful cos that's not the kind of man I am. Prior to losin' Tammy, I always used to try to see the light in any situation, but I allowed the grief to fester in my gut. Somethin' I'll never do again, cos it's a truly rotten way to live.'

'I hope my daddy finds good pals like yours,' said Isla fiercely.

Far from nodding his agreement, Rory looked decidedly doubtful, causing her to question why.

'Workin' down the docks I've met my fair share of seamen, and I guess the nature of their job tends to make them quite gruff characters, not the sort to talk about their feelin's,' he said. 'Not that I'm sayin' the men in the RAF spend all day chattin' about their feelin's but they do look out for one another, and if one of the team is bringin' the rest down they try their best to do somethin' about it, or at least that's what they did with me.'

'How, exactly?'

'By pointin' out the hardships that some of the younger men had been through, and how my sombre mood was affectin' the rest of the crew. Lookin' at things from someone else's point of view really made me see the light, and even though I'm not sayin' it was an overnight cure, it did set me on the right path.'

'There's a lot to be said for havin' good friends,' said Isla. 'I doubt I'd be here without mine.'

'Nor they without you,' Rory pointed out. He decided it was time to turn the conversation to something a little lighter, and went on, 'We've talked about what we might have done before things went pear-shaped, but what do you want to do after the war?'

Isla smiled as she poured out the tea, letting Rory add his own milk. 'That changes on a daily basis! Some days I think I'd like to work as a seamstress again – but for myself, not some cantankerous old sod! Other days I think I'd quite like to go back to work down the laundry, because I enjoyed the company of the other women. How about you?'

He grinned. 'I can safely say I've never wanted to become a seamstress.' Isla tapped his hand in a playful manner, and still beaming, he continued, 'I've always loved tinkerin' with engines and the like, but never had the qualifications to back me up, which is why I worked down the docks. Since joinin' the RAF, though, I've achieved the necessary certifications that mean I could work in any garage that takes my fancy – maybe even start my own business one of these days.'

'Gosh! I wish I was as decided as you!'

He shrugged. 'Unfortunately, I think we've still got plenty of time to make our minds up.'

The waitress returned with their meals, which she placed on the table. Rory broke the pastry casing of his pie with a satisfying crunch. 'I can see why the lads recommend this place.'

With Isla in agreement that the food did indeed look delicious, they ate in relative silence, with only the occasional remark on how the food tasted as good as it looked, or how the café was able to serve such fine food with rationing being so tight.

'I wish the cookhouse turned out food as good as this,' said Isla, 'although I've no room to talk, cos I'm not exactly gifted in the cookery department.'

Rory emitted a low chuckle. 'That makes two of us. Just how bad are you?'

'I'd love to say that I'm not bad at all, but that wouldn't be altogether true. I'm all right when it comes to everyday cookin', but I cannae make edible pastry like that to save my life!' she said, indicating the last piece of his pie with her fork.

'How about egg and chips? Can you cook that?'

'Anyone can cook egg and chips,' said Isla. 'It's anythin' bakery related I seem to struggle with.'

'Well you're doin' better than me,' said Rory, 'cos I

cannae even cook egg and chips, not unless you like your eggs hard all the way through, of course.'

'A hard yolk is equal to blasphemy,' Isla told him, 'or so my daddy used to say. In fact the only time he ever used the Lord's name in vain was when mammy overcooked his eggs. He always said you had to have a runny yolk to dip your—'

'Chips into,' Rory finished.

'Ah! Another man who likes to dip his chips, then?'

'No point in havin' an egg otherwise.'

'Well, if it's egg and chips you're after, or sausage and mash, then I'm your girl every time,' said Isla. 'Not pies or scones, though, unless you want chronic indigestion.'

He laughed. 'That's what I like about you. Honest as the day is long!'

'No point in bein' anythin' else,' Isla commented. 'Lies will always out in the end, just as they did with poor Theo.'

'You have to be the only woman I know who'd sympathise with a liar and a cheat!' said Rory. 'Which makes you one remarkable lady, Isla Donahue.'

'Goin' through everythin' I have has taught me to be patient, and to see things from other people's point of view,' said Isla. 'To judge Theo would mean I have to do the same to my father, and even though I did judge him at first, hearing Theo's point of view only went to show me how wrong I was.'

Rory was gazing at her with a mixture of affection and admiration. 'You really are special, do you know that?'

Isla gave a small embarrassed smile. 'I cannae take all the credit. Life's experiences have made me who I am today, cos I wasn't always this understanding. Had I met Theo before losin' my mammy, I would've read him the riot act before sendin' him off with a flea in his ear!'

'It doesn't matter what made you the way you are,' said Rory, 'you're you, and that's the important thing.'

'Would you say that you've changed a lot since losin' Tammy, or have you come full circle?'

'Good question!' He fell temporarily silent as he thought this through. 'I suppose I'd say that I'm the same person I always was, with no real changes except that I'm happier in my job, because I'm doin' somethin' that I love. I didn't like workin' down the docks – I only did that because I was desperate for the money, and when it's a case of sink or swim you'd best learn to doggy paddle toot-sweet!'

'It's rotten bein' stuck in a job you don't like,' Isla sympathised. 'I enjoyed sewin', but I really hated working for Mr Brannin'.'

Their attention turned to the waitress who'd come to collect their empty plates. 'Anyone for pudding?' she asked, piling crockery and cutlery on to her tray.

'Always,' said Rory, before quickly browsing the menu. 'Treacle tart for me, please. Isla?'

'Not for me, thanks, although I would like a glass of lemonade, if that's all right?'

'Of course.' Making a mental note of their order, the waitress hurried off with her tray.

'Where were we?' asked Rory. 'Ah yes, our current roles!'

'I love workin' as part of a team,' said Isla. 'Workin' on the balloon site suits me down to the ground. And knowin' we're forcin' the Luftwaffe to fly higher than they'd like gives me a real sense of accomplishment.'

'Hard graft, though,' noted Rory. 'It's not for everybody. I believe they're quite particular in who they choose?'

She smiled. 'You've got to have strength and determination, two things which I have oodles of!'

He eyed her thoughtfully. 'Where do you see yourself living after the war?'

To Isla the answer was simple. 'Liverpool. I love it here, and quite frankly Peggy is the closest thing I've got to family left. You?'

'I'll never go back to Clydebank, so I guess I'll settle wherever I'm working at the time and go from there. I might even stay in the RAF for a while whilst I make my mind up.'

'What about your parents? Won't they want you to go back to Clydebank?'

He gave a cynical chuckle. 'They didn't want me in the first place, so I should imagine they won't give two hoots where I choose to settle as long as it's far away from them.'

Isla's face became a mask of sorrow. 'Trust me to open my big mouth!'

He waved away her concerns. 'Don't be daft. It's a perfectly natural question.'

She eyed him curiously. 'When you say they didn't want you . . . ?'

'I was a foundling. Abandoned on the steps of the orphanage as a baby.'

Not sure quite how to respond, she tried to remain upbeat. 'You've done well for yourself in spite of that, which is pretty impressive.'

The waitress returned with their order, which she promptly unloaded on to the table before asking, 'Is there anythin' else I can get you?'

'Not at the moment,' said Rory, adding as the waitress walked away, 'Fancy a bite, Isla?'

She held up a hand. 'I wouldn't dream of deprivin' you!'

'Go on!' he encouraged. 'Everyone deserves a little sweetness in their lives!' Rolling her eyes, she leaned forward whilst Rory fed her a small piece of tart. 'Nice?'

She gave him the thumbs up. 'Very! But one bite is more than enough, thank you.'

'Not watchin' your figure, I hope,' said Rory reprovingly.

'No, my teeth,' Isla chuckled. 'I'm not keen on the dentist as it is, and I've no desire to give him cause to start drillin' holes!'

'Very sensible!' noted Rory. 'I wish I had your restraint, but I've always had a really sweet tooth.'

Isla watched as he savoured every mouthful of his tart. 'Good job it's not me what made that pastry, otherwise you'd need a dentist just for that,' she joked.

He held his hand in front of his mouth as he laughed. 'I'm sure you're not that bad!'

'Put it this way: if the RAF ever runs out of bombs, I'll make them some of my pastry!'

Chuckling, Rory glanced at the clock on the wall behind the counter. 'Is that really the time?' Checking against his wristwatch, he shook his head. 'I cannae believe how fast the time goes when I'm with you. It feels as if we've barely been here five minutes.'

'They do say that time flies when you're havin' fun,' said Isla, 'and I've not had this much fun in a long while.'

'Me neither,' agreed Rory. 'So when are we goin' to do it again?'

Isla couldn't help but feel slightly disappointed that he hadn't asked her out on an official date, but at the same time she knew Rory would only break his golden rule of 'just friends' for someone very special.

'I'm off this week . . .' Isla began, but Rory was shaking his head.

'I'm afraid I'm goin' to be busy until Friday week. Would that suit?'

'I think so, but I'll have to check my diary.'

Rory signalled to the waitress, indicating that he was ready to pay. 'It's a shame we cannae meet up sooner, but I'll keep my fingers cross for a week on Friday.'

'Me too,' agreed Isla. 'Where would you like to go next time?'

'How about the flicks?' he suggested, before instantly changing his mind. 'On second thoughts scrap that. You cannae have a real conversation when folk are tryin' to watch a film. How about dinner again, but followed by dancin' this time?'

She beamed. 'That would be perfect!'

The waitress approached them with the bill, which Rory insisted on paying.

'Thank you so much for this evenin',' said Isla as he walked her to the bus stop. 'I've really enjoyed myself.'

Rory opened his mouth to say something, thought better of it and changed his mind. 'I shall look forward to seeing you on Friday week. Good night, Isla.'

Isla wished him good night and boarded the bus, which had just pulled up. *I could've sworn he was goin' to say somethin' else just now; you could tell by the way he hesitated*, she thought as she exchanged the exact fare for her ticket. *And when he did speak it was as though he was only bein' polite, rather than speakin' from his heart.* As the bus set off, Isla mulled through the possible reasons for his change of mind. Had he been about to ask her out on a proper date? She couldn't be sure, but figured that if he hadn't done so by the end of their next evening together it was likely that he did only want to be friends.

Back in Arkles Lane, Isla wasn't surprised to find that the girls were having a late night playing cribbage with Peggy. 'Well?' asked Meg as soon as she entered the parlour.

'It was the best non-date I've ever been on,' said

Isla, 'but before you ask, no he hasn't asked me to be his belle, or to go on a date with him. We are meetin' for dinner again, though,' she finished lamely.

'I reckon he wants to make absolutely sure before he asks you out properly,' said Sophie, 'and quite right too.'

'I hope you're right,' said Isla, 'because I think I might be fallin' in love with him, if I'm not already.'

Meg practically jumped out of her seat, grinning at Sophie. 'Didn't I say?'

'You did,' smiled Sophie, 'and you were right.'

'What did you say?' asked Isla, intrigued.

'That you were in love,' said Meg. 'You've got it written all over your face!'

Isla looked aghast. 'You don't think Rory can tell, do you?'

'I haven't the foggiest,' said Sophie, 'but do you think he'd be the sort of feller to string a girl along knowin' she had feelin's for him?'

'He'd never do that,' said Isla resolutely. 'I'm certain of it.'

'In that case, I think Sophie is right,' Peggy pronounced. 'And Rory's makin' sure that you're the girl for him before he even *thinks* of askin' you out on a date.'

It had been a tearful farewell when Isla had waved Meg off at the train station.

'I cannae wait until we're all together again,' Meg sniffled as she picked up her kitbag.

'It's a shame that Sophie had to leave earlier than planned,' Isla sighed.

'Aye, but at least she gets to drive rather than sit in a packed carriage with screamin' kids and sweaty old men,' Meg wailed.

'That's one way of lookin' at it,' Isla had agreed, chuckling in spite of herself.

Now, as she entered her hut, she was approached by the young Waaf who was handing out the mail.

'Did you have fun on your leave?' she asked, casually handing Isla a letter.

'Very much so,' said Isla. 'Has anything changed whilst I've been away?'

There was a general murmur of 'no's as Isla slit the envelope open. Pulling out the letter within, she saw straight away that it was from Theo.

Dearest Isla, They all told me that the novelty would soon wear off, and boy were they right! I'm sick to death of the sight of sand, and even sun's beginning to take its toll. Quite frankly, I can't wait to get back to good old rainy Blighty!

Being away from everyone you know and love gives a chap lots of time to think, and I've been doing a lot of that lately. I know that I really messed up as far as you and I were concerned, and I truly rue not being truthful from the get-go. That being said, I would very much like it if we could be more than friends one day.

Isla felt her heart drop. It was the letter she'd been dreading, and her friends were no longer here to give her advice. *Peggy!* thought Isla as she scanned the remainder of the letter, which spoke of dry heat and rats. *She'll know what to do!*

*

411

Peggy blew her cheeks out as she read the letter, which Isla had hurried over with at the first opportunity.

'You can't let him think there's hope when there isn't,' said Peggy, 'but I understand your dilemma.'

'It feels like such a ruthless thing to do,' said Isla miserably. 'What if I tell him there's no hope and he gets bombed the very next day? He'd have died with a broken heart and it would have been my fault!'

Peggy wagged a reproving finger. 'No it would not. You're not responsible for what them Nazis do, and it's hardly your fault that Theo has hooked his star to your wagon. And just for clarity, this is nothin' to do with him tellin' a few porkies, it's simply because you're in love with someone else.'

'Someone who may not even reciprocate my feelin's,' said Isla dolefully.

'And would that make any difference to how you felt about Theo?'

'Well, no.'

Peggy leaned forward. 'I know you don't want to hurt his feelings, luvvy, but that's exactly what you'd be doin' if you didn't tell him the truth.'

'So how do I break it to him? I cannae just say *sorry, but I'm in love with someone else*, cos that would be a right kick in the teeth.'

'Just tell him that you're sorry, but you don't feel the same way, and that you'd like to remain friends.'

Isla gave a resigned sigh. 'I hope he doesn't take it too badly. I know his mammy won't be pleased: she asked me to look out for him, not break his heart.'

'Again, it's not your fault,' said Peggy, 'so stop

beatin' yourself up over somethin' which is out of your control!'

Isla had done as Peggy suggested, which felt terrible because she truly cared for him, albeit in a platonic way.

'I feel just dreadful,' Isla told Sophie down the phone the evening she had written to Theo, 'but he must've known we had no future.'

'He probably does,' said Sophie, 'and just thought he'd take a punt in case you said yes. At least now he can lick his wounds before movin' on, and he will, given the fullness of time.'

'I hope so, cos he really is a nice chap underneath it all.'

The operator had cut across them with her usual warning that their time had come to an end.

'I'd best be off anyway,' Isla told Sophie. 'I'm meetin' Rory for dinner and dancin' in an hour.'

'Ah! So Operation Hair and Makeup it is, then?' Sophie chuckled.

'Somethin' like that, although I'm not goin' to get my knickers in a twist this time.'

Now, as the bus trundled to a halt, Isla waited for the passengers in front of her to disembark before following suit.

'I've never known a week to go by so slowly!' said Rory, as he greeted her with a smile.

'And yet I bet tonight will pass in a flash,' said Isla.

'Probably,' said Rory. 'I thought we could start the evening with dinner at the Adelphi, followed by dancin' at the Rialto?'

'The Adelphi!' gasped Isla. 'Isn't that a bit . . . well, posh?'

'I rather hope so. Have you any objections?'

'Well, no, but are you sure?'

'I wouldn't have suggested it otherwise,' said Rory. Holding out his arm for her, he added, 'Shall we?'

Taking his arm, Isla wondered why Rory was taking her to such a prestigious venue, when he could easily have gone for a cheaper option. *Unless he fancies a posh meal out*, she supposed, as they walked the frosty pavements. When they stepped into the hotel lobby, she couldn't help asking, 'Do you often eat in establishments such as this?'

'Never! Which is why I thought we deserved a treat,' said Rory. 'How about you?'

'Oh aye,' she said with good-humoured sarcasm, 'they're sick of the sight of me at the Ritz!'

Laughing, Rory acknowledged the smartly dressed woman who had come over to take them to their table. 'It's ever so nice,' said Isla as they threaded their way through the dining room. 'I've never been anywhere that has napkin rings before!'

Holding her chair out for her, Rory made sure that she was seated before sitting down in the chair opposite. 'What would you like to drink?'

'Lemonade, please,' said Isla.

Rory gave their hostess the order and requested ginger beer for himself before turning his attention back to Isla. Seeing the look of uncertainty on her face, he leaned forward. 'Are you all right?'

'Yes. It's just . . .' She paused. Why did she feel so

uncomfortable? He'd brought her to a lovely restaurant in a posh hotel . . . Isla sighed inwardly as the penny dropped. *It doesn't mean anythin' though*, she thought; *it's not special because it means nothing*. Aware that Rory was waiting for more, she waved a dismissive hand. 'I'm fine. Ignore me.'

'Would you rather we went elsewhere?' Rory was looking for the woman who'd taken their order. 'I can cancel the drinks, if you'd prefer.'

Not wanting to create a scene, Isla spoke her thoughts. 'I just think this might be wasted on me,' she said. 'Shouldn't you save somewhere like this for someone, well, special?'

'You are special!'

'That's very nice of you to say, but I had to break Theo's heart a few days ago when I told him I didn't feel the same way about him as he did about me.'

Rory looked surprised. 'I assumed the two of you were through?'

'We were – are, even,' said Isla, 'but Theo said he'd like to give it another go.'

'And you don't feel the same?'

'No!' said Isla, a little frustrated, 'but I hate that I have broken his heart, cos I'd hate to have that done to me.'

Rory stretched out an arm and took her hand in his across the table. 'Rather than let you continue, I think I should explain why I brought you here.'

'You said it was because you thought we deserved a treat,' said Isla dully.

'True, but I also wanted to bring you somewhere

memorable so that you'd always remember the time and place when I asked you if you'd consider bein' my belle.'

Isla felt as though someone had pulled the rug out from under her. '*Oh!* I . . . I . . .'

He smiled. 'I thought it must be obvious how much I like you, and why I wanted to bring you somewhere special. I don't want us to just be friends, and I don't think you do either. So how about it? Will you be my belle?'

Isla's brain was shouting at her to be sensible and turn him down, but her heart disagreed and answered with a resounding 'Yes!'

Smiling from ear to ear, Rory squeezed her hand across the table. 'I'm sorry if I gave you the wrong impression.'

'Ever since my mammy passed, I've not known whether I'm comin' or goin' as far as my feelin's are concerned,' Isla told him. 'And whilst I'm terrified of havin' my heart broken, to walk away would be doin' just that.'

He frowned. 'Why on earth do you think I'd break your heart? We're like peas in a pod, you and me. I'd never do anythin' to hurt you.'

'Not intentionally,' said Isla, 'but what if the rumours are true and Tammy really is—'

'They aren't,' said Rory quickly, 'so you can put that thought right out of your mind, because it's never goin' to happen.'

'It's just, after my daddy . . .'

'I know, you find it hard to trust, especially when

the first man you agree to date betrays your trust all over again, but I promise you, Isla, I will *never* do that. I'd still want to be with you even if Tammy were to walk in right this minute.'

'When I first saw you down the shelter it felt as though I was bein' drawn to you,' said Isla, 'which was wrong, especially under the circumstances, and I felt the same way the day I saw you in the Grafton.'

'It was the same for me – in the Grafton, I mean – and I guess that's what I meant when I said that bein' with you was like some kind of déjà vu. I honestly believe that we're meant to be together, and I'm not goin' to let the ghosts of my past stand in the way of our future!'

Reassured by his words, she smiled. 'I'm so glad that you feel the same way, because I couldn't have agreed to keep seein' you as a friend whilst secretly hopin' it would lead to more than that.'

His eyes sparkled as he looked into hers. 'I cannae make any promises, because none of us know what lies in store – you and I know that better than most – but I can tell you this: no one will ever get between us. Oh, and your mammy does a crackin' job at matchmakin'!'

Isla chuckled softly. 'Doesn't she just? I only wish my daddy . . .' Her voice trailed off with a sigh.

'. . . was here with you,' said Rory. 'He will be, one of these days, I'll make sure of it!' As he spoke, he got up from his seated position and motioned for her to do the same. Leaning forward to take her in his arms, his lips brushed against hers before kissing her softly, only breaking away as the waitress entered the restaurant with their drinks.

Isla looked up at him dreamily. 'Why is it that I don't doubt for a minute that you will?'

'Because I would do anythin' to make you happy,' said Rory, 'no matter how long that takes!'

Pressing his lips against hers, he kissed her again, this time with a passion she had never experienced before. For the first time in a long, long while, Isla was truly happy.

Dear Readers,

I do hope you had a smashing Christmas surrounded by those you love the most! We had a houseful this year and I have to confess, I thoroughly enjoyed the madness and mayhem that comes with so many people living under the same roof. Ever since I moved to Anglesey, I've been promising myself that I shall keep swimming throughout the winter months, and this is the first year I've kept that promise. With spring just around the corner now, I'm excited for more fair-weather swimming, though I am sure the water will still be cold for a while yet. . .

New Year was spent at home, but we did pop down to the sea at midnight to hear the ships sound their horns to welcome in 2025. It was a truly magical experience!

I'm so pleased that you have now read my latest book, *Forgotten Child*, the second novel in my Runaways trilogy. Rather than follow on from the characters in *The Winter Runaway*, *Forgotten Child* introduces us to a whole new set of characters who exist within the same timeline as those in the previous story. I love writing this sort of book as I find it intriguing to see how people from different walks of life cope when they're thrown together due to circumstance. Having to take strangers at face value can be difficult, because you're vulnerable to what they decide to tell you about their past, something which our heroine, Isla, discovers to her detriment.

As always, I hope you enjoyed reading the book as much as I did creating.

Warmest wishes,

Holly Flynn xx

DISCOVER THE ROSE QUEEN SERIES

FROM THE UK'S NO. 1 BESTSELLING WWII SAGA AUTHOR

Katie Flynn

LOVED BY
4 MILLION
READERS

DISCOVER THE LIVERPOOL SISTERS SERIES

  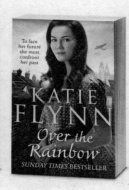

FROM THE UK'S NO. 1 BESTSELLING WWII SAGA AUTHOR

Katie Flynn

LOVED BY
4 MILLION
READERS

DISCOVER THE WHITE CHRISTMAS SERIES

  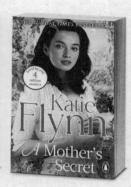

FROM THE UK'S NO. 1 BESTSELLING WWII SAGA AUTHOR

Katie Flynn

Katie Flynn

If you want to continue to hear from the
Flynn family, and to receive the latest news about
new Katie Flynn books and competitions,
sign up to the Katie Flynn newsletter.

Join today by visiting
www.penguin.co.uk/katieflynnnewsletter

Find Katie Flynn on Facebook
www.facebook.com/katieflynn458